# Chinese Box Mysteries

SHERLOCK HOLMES
Volume I

By
**Dan Kilcup**

# Copyright Notice...

Copyright © 1996. All rights reserved. Printed in the United States of America. No part of this book may be used or reproduced in any manner whatsoever without written permission except in the case of brief quotations embodied in critical articles or reviews. For information, address Allen Wayne Limited, 5404A Port Royal Road, Springfield, VA 22151.

**Library of Congress catalog card number 96-60634**
**ISBN 0-9652636-0-6**

## Special Thanks

Inspiration—Arthur Conan Doyle* et al**
Editorial Asst.—Susan Olson-Kilcup
Proofing—Virginia LaFrance
Original Art—Marie Kuhn Cheek
Accent Art—Lenore Sullivan
Typesetting and Printing—Allen Wayne Limited

## Special Notice...

Proceeds from the sale of this edition (40%) are donated to Washington Metropolitan area community service providers as listed at the internet Website—"Washington Needs You"
<http://www.allenwayne.com/washcares/>

---

*The characters of Sherlock Holmes, Dr. John H. Watson and Mycroft Holmes are based on the creations of Sir Arthur Conan Doyle. This book was not written by Sir Arthur Conan Doyle. Further, it has not been sponsored or authorized by the estate or heirs of Sir Arthur Conan Doyle or by any person or company licensed by them.

**Readers are advised to search the internet for Helen Keepler's list of authors who have continued to help keep the "real" Sherlock Holmes alive, which is posted in the Usenet Newsgroup, Alt.fan.holmes.

To Mike & Michelle

May you never "solve" each other's mystery.

Jan

# Chinese Box Mysteries
## SHERLOCK HOLMES
### Volume I

**By**
**Dan Kilcup**

## Introduction
Page v

## Time Study
Page 1

## The Devil To Pay
Page 83

## Mystery of the Chinese Box
Page 215

## One Last Case
Page 247

## A Final Word
Page 268

# Introduction

Before you begin this story some truths should be known, accept them or not. My name is Dan Kilcup and I was born in Coney Island Hospital in Brooklyn, New York on March 26, 1942. I won't bore you with my history after that date...no, that's not important. It's the events preceding it, or rather my grandmother's. You see her name was Martha Styffe, at least her married name was. Her maiden name had more prominence: Hampton.

Name doesn't ring a bell? No? Hmm, I thought not. When tracing your lineage (an act usually thought to be done late in life) some surprises may occur, oh, like a distant connection to some lord or duke, but this is not the case. No, this link to me had a different significance, one that I'm sure you will scoff at, but be that as it may I will offer it to you anyway. You see my grandmother was the niece of Mrs. Victoria Hampton, who in turn had succeeded Mrs. Hudson as housekeeper to Mr. Sherlock Holmes, not of 221B Baker Street but of Hudson Farm, Surrey, as it was named by its owner, the same Mr. Sherlock Holmes! At least that is how it was related in my grandmother's diary.

My grandmother, Martha, was the daughter of Mrs. Hampton's husband's brother Cyrus Hampton and his wife Sylvia. Complicated? Not really. Sylvia died of consumption at an early age (I couldn't

# INTRODUCTION

trace the date) and Martha was given many opportunities to come in contact with her aunt and stay at Hudson Farm. She evidently formed a close relationship with her aunt (again, reading from her diary), but as her age was quite young she had no social interaction with their famous host. It would also seem that Mrs. Hampton achieved a sort of bond with Mr. Holmes, at least by her writings, that would border on love, as the two people grew quite old together. Numerous treatises have been written about his incapacity for this emotion but, well, that will make another story.

To summarize, this diary and other papers contained references to numerous tracts and cases that the renowned detective had worked on during his retiring years, years that have never (to my knowledge) been documented. It was from these copious notes that I tried to recreate the case known as the Time Study et al. That's it in a nutshell except for one other incredible revelation. It seems the Official Secrets Act (British) had a major influence on many of the stories previously attributed to Sherlock Holmes, most written by Arthur Conan Doyle. There are several pages which are written in a more flowing manner, obviously by someone else, and since the tone is in the first person singular, that someone purports to be Sherlock Holmes. In these pages, he makes mention that the Act had made it necessary to fabricate many stories to create a smokescreen for the true ones—an idea that he lays at his brother Mycroft's door. It is also implied that Mr. Doyle was conscripted by the Queen, herself to be the main conspirator. His last statement was to the effect that only John H. Watson, his best and truest companion, ever knew the full truth during their collaboration and only revealed it to his son, John S. Watson. We can only assume the "S" stood for Sherlock. The complete story is revealed in "The Mystery of the Chinese Box."

No more. The game's afoot.

                                        Dan Kilcup  
                                        On an island off the  
                                        North Carolina coast

# Chinese Box Mysteries
## SHERLOCK HOLMES

# Time Study

### Editor's Comments

The notes of this case were found in an ornate Chinese Box and are believed to have been originally written by John S. Watson, the son of Dr. John H. Watson, MD.

There were no dates on the notes and I have made the reconstruction based on references either to the seasons or the weather.

Finally, dramatic license has been applied in an effort to assist the reader in following the action.

# TIME STUDY

# A Foul Deed

*April 12, —Mayfair, London*

The woman turned quickly, but it was too late. She froze as the candelabra, though held unwieldy, dealt the lethal blow. One moment, a radiant woman. Now as blood gushed over the bedclothes, a waste.

Life's clock measures out to each of us a different amount, and in the normal realm of things we are masters of our own fate. The killer changes the formula instantly.

*April 21, —Hudson Farm, Surrey*

The old man looked down at his hand. It still smarted, but he knew the sting was harmless. As for his dress, it was shabby considering his assets, and looked out of place in the Surrey countryside. He was city born and bred, and though he could afford to garb himself as a country squire, he did not. Rather, he still wore clothes that were out of style, and worse, beyond their normal life span. To this man, the clock of time had stood still 'lo these past seven years and, since he was not a man of passion, he accepted his dress as just a logical expression of his own choosing.

# A FOUL DEED

While in his reverie, he failed to notice the young man climbing the hill heading towards him. When the man's movement finally caught his eye, he raised his head and stared until he could fully focus. The old man's jaw gaped and he dropped his mesh net and work glove simultaneously as recognition dawned upon him.

"John," he gasped, "my God, John, I, I...."

"No, Mr. Holmes, I'm not my father. My name is John, but I am my father's son, John S. Watson. My father is dead, I'm sure you know that."

The pleasantries of spending a day in the country are well known to any who have been in Surrey. The smell of new mown hay, combined with the scent of wildflowers in the field, and the senses—once anesthetized by urban living—come alive. A longing to join, to align oneself with the very roots of the earth; a feeling that repeats itself whenever one sees the setting sun or hears the lowing of a cow as it heads for the barn. It was this ending of a perfect day that led to the awakening of other senses, senses that had become somewhat dulled.

The dishes were cleared by Mrs. Hampton. She was not as capable as her predecessor, whose name now adorned the property, but she knew her place and what was expected of her. Mr. Sherlock Holmes, as demanding a master as you can imagine, had lately fallen sanguine in his requests, and it was almost as if no assistance were needed at all. Mrs. Hudson would have been suspicious, if not appalled, with his conduct. But Mrs. Hampton, unaware of the proclivities of her employer, assumed nothing and gave nothing more in return.

The household was unremarkable in any way save for the unique sleeping habits of the solitary occupant. Mrs. Hampton never saw Mr. Holmes in a retiring state. At times she was known to remark, "Nary a nap or a drooping of his lids do I ever see." As far as she was concerned, the man never slept.

The guest for afternoon tea was a welcome break for her, and so it seemed, for Mr. Holmes.

"Quite remarkable your father was, quite remarkable. Oh, he may have embellished some of our escapades and made them seem extraordinary, but that was considered acceptable in those days. Actually, it was a lot duller than he made it all out to be, but of course he told

# A FOUL DEED

you all of that." Holmes grinned at that and poured himself another glass of claret.

"Actually, Mr. Holmes, father was quite reticent about his adventures with you. Oh, I implored him to give me details that the newspapers would not be privy to, but he was quite adamant in letting 'sleeping dogs lie.'"

"Oh? Do you think he wasn't proud of my, uh, our accomplishments, lad? Speak up man, your father knew full well. In fact, I always felt that with his ability to, shall we say, explain our involvement in certain affairs, that well, uh, his place in history would rest assured. I'm surprised to hear that Watson, my dearest, dearest friend, would feel embarrassment, nay, perhaps even remorse, over the encounters that my deductions had led us to."

Holmes slumped in his chair, his eyes misted, then suddenly revived. "No, no, not that at all. Of course, of course, his sense of proprietary. Oh, Watson, Watson, you old fool. The reputations we sought to protect readily undid themselves. You cannot save a man from himself." And with that, Holmes leaned back, took a long draught from his wine, and allowed himself to reminisce. Young Watson listened raptly as the magic of times gone by wafted away.

The afternoon sun sped away and when the shadows finally draped themselves over the window, young Watson stated his case.

"Mr. Holmes, Mr. Holmes." Holmes raised up and his eyes, though seemingly not entirely alert, focused on the young man who had addressed him.

"Mr. Holmes, my coming here today is not only to rekindle memories of my father, who we both respect, but to ask for help. My father told me that your uncanny abilities to fathom the real truth, when all others are willing to accept what may pass as the truth, is the main reason why you are revered throughout the world. Mr. Holmes, I wish to present to you a dilemma, a wrongdoing that will go unpunished unless you intervene. Please, Mr. Holmes, help me."

The claret had taken hold, not the young man's remarks. "Too long," remarked Holmes, "it's been too long. My faculties are at rest. The bees, though simplistic in their wanderings, elude me to decipher just what they are about. All of my energies have been spent. Can't

# A FOUL DEED

you see that? My housekeeper has even become insolent at times. I am not the man you seek. Sherlock Holmes is dead, just as your father is dead. Not even Moriarity or Colonel Moran himself will allow me to manipulate my synapses as in the past. Time and time alone is our master. And, even the great Sherlock Holmes must bow. Go, young Watson. If you seek the truth, try religion. If that does not satisfy, then perhaps Scotland Yard. The truth is at my door every day—and I do not wish to confront it." And with that, Sherlock Holmes drained his glass and, walking out the door, left his young guest.

*April 22, —Scotland Yard*

Inspector Delacroix looked up at the gentleman who was occupying all of his time this morning. Roman D'Angelo, an American insurance investigator representing the Allied Insurance Companies of North America, was just finishing, "…flimsy alibi or not, you have a motive. Now, do your job, Inspector."

"It's not that simple," Delacroix interrupted. "This man is a respected member of the community. No, more than that. He is a pillar with a perfectly clean record. Also, Springer and Duffey is not only a respected brokerage house, but quite profitable. Your premise that a man, a full partner in his business, murders his wife for £50,000 in insurance money is almost ludicrous in its assertion. And let's not forget that the man has an alibi." The words had hardly escaped Delacroix's lips when D'Angelo jumped on them.

"Alibi? You call Miss Melinor an alibi? For God's sake Inspector, this woman is Charles Springer's mistress. You want proof? Check out any employee at the firm, they'll tell you. Alibi, hah!" The dapper man, with a slick Italian suit combined with an equally slick, well-groomed mustache, paced the floor in front of the Inspector's desk.

Inspector Delacroix did not like D'Angelo. In fact, he had never liked anyone who fancied himself a detective without carrying the proper credentials to prove it. He himself had moved up the ranks the old-fashioned way, earning his keep every step; no way was he going to accept an outsider's interpretation of the facts. His mentor,

# A FOUL DEED

Inspector Lestrade, now retired, had a name for these types: "Hindsight and Luck, at your service." It was so easy to be glib when you're on the outside, but inside, at the Yard, answers had to be set in stone. Not mere speculation. You made an accusation towards someone who had position and you'd better be damned sure you're right. Or else. No, you couldn't afford hindsight and luck, you had to have damnable facts. One hundred percent.

He tried to dismiss D'Angelo with a wave of his hand, but he was not going to quit that easily.

"Inspector," D'Angelo continued, "we have all of the ingredients that any jury requires, even in His Majesty's Court." Delacroix winced at the slur.

"Motive: the man does not love his wife, he loves another, and of course the £50,000 payable by my firm. Which, incidentally, was a policy only instituted a scant two months ago at the insistence of Mr. Charles Springer, personally. Now who is this other woman? Why, no other than Miss Clarissa Melinor, who just happens to turn out to be Mr. Springer's alibi on that particular night, which answers the question of time. Is this not an obvious fait accompli? Inspector, you don't have to be a Sherlock Holmes to see the obvious. Springer is a businessman. A shrewd businessman. He wants out of his marriage. Does he press for a legal solution? No! He sees opportunity. Opportunity to have his cake and eat it too. Damn it, the man is a killer, as ruthless in his feelings towards people as he is in business. Now what are you going to do about it?" With that, D'Angelo finally sat down, his face still slightly burnished from emanating his emotions.

"Proof, Mr. D'Angelo, proof. You bring conjecture. If I operated the way you do, my case books would all be closed. My detectives start with conjecture or what may be obvious to you, but an arrest must always be proceeded with undeniable proof. Bring me proof, D'Angelo, and quit harassing Mr. Duffey—or perhaps charges may be brought against you. Now get out of here. I have real work to do."

# A FOUL DEED

*April 22, —Hudson Farm, Surrey*

"Mr. Holmes, you must come back to London with me."

Sherlock Holmes stood in the doorway to his kitchen, one hand resting on the doorjamb, the other in his nightdress pocket. His demeanor changed little with the morning sun and he showed no amazement that the boy was still under his roof. Obviously Mrs. Hampton had invited him to stay when the hour drew late.

"I shall not let you occupy my thoughts this morning, young Watson. A new theory of mine is to be tested. Perhaps, though your brain is not quite formed as yet, you would perchance care to join me. The results that I wish to obtain may not astound you, but someday you may reflect back and realize that genius—nay, logic—can define even the complexities of Mother Nature. Come, the bees are awing."

The morning was spent in pure observation. Bees, specially colored with a light dye made of crushed leaves so as not to affect their mating habits, were released three kilometers from their hive.

"Mr. Holmes, I'm sure the bees will find their way back to their hives, the homing instinct has been proven in many species before." Holmes' eyebrows creased themselves and slightly crinkled in what was not quite a frown.

"Back to their hives, young Watson? No, that's not the point. It's not where, it's when. How long will it take? Time, Watson! Time dictates to all things. And when a creature moves by instinct alone, time is everything." The great man paused, and then, "You don't find this interesting, do you? No, wait, I know your answer. Tell me what I don't know. Why must I go to London?"

# The Inquest

*April 23, —Scotland Yard*

They were all there. Some attempts were made at conversation, but mostly they kept to themselves. Though it was a somber occasion, one was heard to emit a shriek of laughter, the source of which was immediately traced to Miss Clarissa Melinor. Miss Melinor, dressed haughtily enough, seemed to be at the center of things. She was a very pretty woman, not quite beautiful, but an attractiveness that most men find quite irresistible. Her eyes, seemingly set too close, still managed to emote a hint of boudoir knowledge far beyond her years of twenty and two. There was no other woman present, which heightened the illusion that Clarissa was central to all who gathered there.

The men were as diverse a lot as could be possible, considering their number. The presiding magistrate, Sir Calvin Brewster, was old and tired-looking. His bouts with insomnia were tempered too often with extra nightcaps at night and they were taking their toll. Inspector Stephen Delacroix, on the other hand, was strong and robust. His twenty-two years of dedicated police work had earned him a solid reputation as a man who got the job done, and properly. Higher-ups at the Yard tended to think of Delacroix as a man who could be trusted and counted upon. The Loreli Springer murder was a case that dictated this sort of talent.

# THE INQUEST

Thomas Duffey, a distinguished gentlemen with muttonchops and debonair mustache, belied his age of fifty-three. To many observers he seemed to be a much younger man, perhaps in his thirties, and yet the success he had obtained would certainly have taken much time, since his family roots had provided no early start. His partner, Charles Springer, was a younger man, forty-six, but he had not kept himself fit and seemed to suffer from as many maladies as could affect a prosperous middle-aged businessman of the times. A bit of gout, lumbago, and a raspy cough were indicative of his overindulgence in pursuing life's pleasures. Whereas Duffey might play away an afternoon on a tennis court, Springer would wine and dine with a business associate. That they were partners in one of London's most successful brokerage houses could not be denied, but their methods and manners were totally at odds.

The only real witness, though not to the actual crime itself, was Alf Donnegal, Mr. Springer's gamekeeper. His testimony would bring some confusion to the proceedings, which would have to be addressed today. Roman D'Angelo would have liked to be the one doing the questioning, or at least to have been in the room, but Inspector Delacroix was firm in not allowing the insurance investigator to be present. He was waiting downstairs for the outcome and its effect upon his company.

There was one person missing. The inquest was to begin at 1 p.m. and the wall clock read three minutes after. Sir Brewster banged his gavel and bade the gathering to take their seats.

"Gentlemen, uh, and Madame, though Mr. Watson has not arrived as yet, his role in these proceedings is minor, and so I shall begin. Mr. Duffey, would you please come forward and...." Before he could finish, the door flew open and there stood young Watson, hat in hand, obviously quite distressed.

"Your Honor, I'm sorry. The 11:05 was late getting into Victoria, please excuse me." Watson entered the room followed by an elderly gentlemen who did not speak, nor make excuses for his presence. Inspector Delacroix, at first speechless, started towards the two and moved to establish order.

"Mr. Watson, this is a formal inquest and your conduct is out of order. Please remove yourself and your companion at once. When

# THE INQUEST

your presence is required, I will have the sergeant-at-arms escort you back." Delacroix placed his arm upon young Watson and, with a firm grip, maneuvered him towards the door from whence he came.

"Unhand the boy!" boomed the old man. "An inquest such as this one, where no charges have been brought, is quite informal, and any person who may have knowledge or involvement in the case should be allowed to speak before it."

"Oh, is that so?" Delacroix remarked. "Well, perhaps you may not be so well-informed. And by the way, since charges have not been forthcoming, there is no need for any person in this room to have retained legal counsel. Unless, of course, they feel a strong need for same. May I assume that you are representing young Watson here?"

"You must be Inspector Delacroix," the old man responded. "The Lestrade method of deduction has been passed on without losing any of its subtleties. Watson, fetch me a chair, lad."

Delacroix fairly fumed, "Who in blazes are you? Put that chair down, Watson. This has gone on long enough. You both must leave—and right now!"

"I think not, Inspector. Excuse me, Lord Brewster. Common courtesy has been detracted during this banter, but I beg your indulgence to allow a friend of the court to observe these proceedings. My young colleague felt it best that I be present, and perhaps, I may be able to be of some assistance in its deliberations. I remain, still, a humble servant of His Majesty's court and kingdom, and though I have been knighted at St. James, I still bear the simple salutation, Mr. Sherlock Holmes."

Lord Brewster half-rose from his chair, Inspector Delacroix fell back a step, and Thomas Duffey appeared visibly shaken. Gathering his wits about him, Lord Brewster spoke.

"Mr. Holmes, it is a great pleasure, yes, and an honor, to have you with us. Of course you may stay, and young Watson as well. Though I must say, the matter before us today is quite straightforward, the court certainly appreciates any help that its distinguished guest may provide."

"Sir Brewster," Delacroix implored, "this is highly irregular. May I have a word with you in private, Sir?"

# THE INQUEST

"That won't be necessary, Inspector. There is no need for secrecy nor for counsel. Please let us begin. Mr. Duffey, come forward, thank you."

And so, the inquest began.

# The Problem

*April 23, —Scotland Yard*

"Mr. Duffey, would you please repeat the statement that you gave to Constable Dollard when he first informed you of Mrs. Springer's death?" Lord Brewster leaned back and cocked his head for the answer.

"I was stunned. No, more than that. I just couldn't believe it. Here I had just hosted the most elegant, uh, important party, celebrating our firm's success and then to learn that, ah, my partner's wife had been bludgeoned to death. Why, it seemed impossible. No, incredible."

"Was your partner, Mr. Springer, at this party?" queried Delacroix.

"Why, of course he was. If this is part of those ridiculous accusations that insurance man, D'Angelo, is making, why it's quite ridiculous."

"I don't mean to interrupt, your Lordship," spoke Holmes, "but may I hear the official police report of the crime, especially as it concerns the known time factors involved?"

Delacroix spun around in his chair. "What the hell…oh, this is too much! Your Honor, we mustn't let these proceedings be interrupted. Everyone in this room is as informed as they need to be. If

# THE PROBLEM

this gentleman requires the most basic information, I suggest he retire to the Central Files and read it for himself, rather than taking our time to do so."

"Inspector Delacroix," Lord Brewster said, "perhaps you are unaware of this man's reputation. No, I am sure you are not—even Scotland Yard's best harbored some resentment towards his involvement. But now, out of respect, please read the police report."

Delacroix inwardly fumed. His face reddened, but he picked up the official form and began.

"Constable Dollard was summoned to a residence in Maryleborough, known as D'Orly House, at 1:40 a.m. on the morning of April 12. Upon arrival, he was met by the owner of the dwelling, a Mr. Charles Springer, who informed him that his wife, Mrs. Loreli Springer, had been killed. A statement was taken by Constable Dollard from Mr. Springer at 2:15 a.m., same date. The statement indicates that Mr. Springer, upon arrival home at approximately 1:15 a.m., found his wife bludgeoned to death. Mr. Springer had just come home from a party given by his partner, Mr. Duffey, and his deportment at the time suggested that he had more than his share of spirits." Delacroix looked up at Duffey and continued.

"Constable Dollard sealed the premises according to regulations and summoned the Yard."

"Time of death?" queried Holmes.

"We can't be precise," continued Delacroix, eyes darkened, "but it would seem at least several hours before Mr. Springer arrived, say between 10 p.m. and midnight. As further proof, the mantel clock in the bedroom where the murder took place was smashed and on the floor. The face read 10:46."

"Very interesting," said Holmes. "And of course, Mr. Springer had an alibi prior to this time. He was with Miss Melinor. Correct?"

"Damn it!" shouted Springer, rising from his chair. "This man is an agent of D'Angelo's. The ludicrous rumors that I would kill my wife for the insurance money is ridiculous to say the least. Fifty thousand pounds? Is that the amount? I'm not even sure, and if it is, that makes it even more preposterous. My safe deposit box at Lloyd's contains trice that amount." Springer started towards the door.

# THE PROBLEM

"Wait," implored Holmes. "Your assistant, young Watson, assures me of your innocence. That is why I am here. If my remarks seem caustic, remember that truth sometimes requires a cutting edge to obtain release. Bear with me, and if you have doubt of my abilities, stay them and allow me my digressions. Understand the suspicions that form the clouds above you. It has become well-known that you have taken a lover." Anger crossed Springer's face, but Holmes continued. "And she has given evidence which is favorable to you concerning this matter. It is highly suspect, can't you see?"

Springer slumped back in his chair. Finally he spoke. "Yes, I see. No one in their right mind would believe a fornicator. I have trespassed upon my marriage, why not on other commandments as well? But I swear, Mr. Holmes, I did not kill my wife. I did not."

Inspector Delacroix, after watching this exchange, rose up, looked down at Charles Springer, and said: "The motive was not robbery. Her jewels, and yes, even some money, were still on her person or within the room. A crime of a carnal nature was not performed either. What, then, would you have us believe? The only person who would gain by her demise was you, Mr. Springer. And yet you are correct when you say that the sum of £50,000 is not a motive for someone like yourself. But what about the motive of freedom? The freedom to pursue another. For instance, Miss Melinor."

Springer jumped to his feet and shouted, "For Clarissa! Inspector, men have always been fools for attractive women. And I the biggest fool of all. But for Clarissa?" Springer turned to her. "Sorry, Clarissa, you have been a wondrous dalliance, but that was it. Mere dalliance. If another woman is your motive, Inspector, then perchance you would like to question another dozen; nay, two dozen more, of the same ilk. I'm sorry, but I am not your man. Mr. Holmes, your presence here, and your statement that my innocence is not in doubt, is highly complimentary and...."

"Mr. Springer," Holmes interrupted, "it was Watson's assumption of your innocence, not mine, that brought me here. Your sense of morality is suspect, but I will not hold it against you. I seek the truth, and if you do not fear it, then it will come as a welcoming sight to you. Now answer me, man, account for your time on that fateful night

# THE PROBLEM

when your wife was murdered. You have no remorse in your heart for her, and I know that. But be faithful to the times and places, as it may be the most important chronicle that you may be called upon to deliver."

"Yes, yes, of course, you're right. I, I, let me think. The party was to begin at 7 p.m. sharp, and since several important clients would be in attendance, I made it my business to be there straight at the onset. Isn't that correct, Duffey?" he implored his partner.

"Certainly," Duffey remarked. "We had just completed the underwriting of a new company that would possibly treble in value and, naturally I took the opportunity to plan an occasion to celebrate. My partner, Mr. Springer, was quite instrumental in the undertaking and his presence throughout was required. Though I daresay, Charles...I do recall a period when I can't quite remember seeing you for a while. It seems it was about 9:30 or 10 p.m. Isn't that so?"

"You know exactly that it was so!" Springer replied sharply, and then, somewhat petulantly, "I'm sure you saw me leave with Clarissa, and I know you don't improve of my relationships with women, especially when they are employed with the firm. But, afterwards, I, I just lost track of time and didn't realize it was so late when I got back to the party."

"At what time was that, Mr. Springer?" Holmes interrupted.

"Why, uh, it was almost two hours later. Close to 11:30. Clarissa and I were in the greenhouse the entire time. I swear it. Please believe me, I did not go home until after I left the party, which was an hour later, uh, about 12:30 a.m. Then, when I got home, that's when I, I...." His voice trailed off.

"It's true, Mr. Holmes," a new voice said. A young, girlish-sounding voice, yet somewhat confident in its demeanor. "We did go to the greenhouse, and though Charles may have a somewhat laissez-faire attitude of our relationship, I must defend his position. We made love there. The greenhouse is a most romantic and charming place. Charles, though you may not notice it to look at him, has a way with words and is truly a man of action when it comes to women." At these words, Charles Springer's face turned crimson and a small, bashful smile spread across his mouth. After a slight pause, Clarissa

# THE PROBLEM

continued, "Of course his way with words and actions today take a decidedly new turn, as it were." And with that she rose and headed for the door.

"Wait, Miss Melinor!" Inspector Delacroix barked. "This inquest is not through with you yet." Clarissa paused with her hand on the door. She directed herself to the Inspector.

"I have been humiliated enough, Inspector. You have heard my testimony. I have nothing further to say." She opened the door.

"The sergeant-at-arms will place you under arrest and shackle you to that chair if you don't sit down. Do I make myself clear?" Delacroix, a big man, found himself at odds. Any type of fugitive he would have man-handled himself. But this woman, this snip of a woman, no doubt was testing him and he couldn't lose face. No matter what.

It seemed as if hours passed by, but it was just moments later when Clarissa Melinor closed the door and once more took her seat. A puzzled look appeared on her face as if she, too, felt she was being tested, and not understanding why, succumbed to this man's entreaties. It was not a normal state she found herself in, and hence her confusion.

The sound of the gavel interrupted all thoughts, and Sir Brewster spoke. "This crime, this death of a young woman, must have a solution. The evidence so far presented gives cause and fear—fear of the worst kind—that this deed was performed by a person who, having no apparent motive, killed indiscriminately. If this is so, then it will happen again. Gentlemen." He disregarded Clarissa. "We must get to the bottom of this."

Inspector Delacroix turned and faced Sir Brewster. "Your Honor, I do not believe in motiveless crimes and I think the perpetrator who caused the death of Mrs. Loreli Springer had a motive. Now, I have a witness who may or may not shed some light on these proceedings. I say 'may not' because I have some doubt as to his reliabili...."

"Wait, ho. I say, what are ya talkin' about?" Alf Donnegal jumped up and started towards Sir Brewster's desk. "This bloke's been harping on me doing my duty as if I was some kind of drunken fool." Sir Brewster started to bring down his gavel, then paused and said, "Mr. Donnegal, you will have an opportunity to speak. You must...."

## THE PROBLEM

Donnegal interrupted again, "I don't get paid to come here and I don't care what ya think. Look here, ya let murderers run loose 'cause they've got money all the time, but this one's different. Miss Loreli's a good woman, a real lady, not like his tramps."

Delacroix reached out and pulled Donnegal away from the desk. "You heard Sir Brewster, now step back."

"Sir Brewster," spoke Holmes, "allow the man to speak and allow him to speak in his own manner. It will make for a more expeditious telling, I am sure." Holmes glowered at Delacroix who made no move to release Donnegal.

"Yes, yes of course, Mr. Holmes," Sir Brewster remarked. "Let the man take this seat, Inspector. And, Mr. Donnegal, kindly tell us exactly what you know about these matters that concern us, and, take your time."

Donnegal eased away from Delacroix and slowly sat down. He ran a hand through his ruffled hair and in his mind the image of a pint of bitters took shape. He looked up at Sir Brewster. "He killed her, your Honor. He killed her." Donnegal lapsed into silence.

"Who killed her, Mr. Donnegal?" queried Sir Brewster. "Do you mean…Mr. Springer, the husband? Do you mean him?"

"Yes, yes," replied Donnegal, "of course! Who else? It had to be him."

Charles Springer, watching the proceedings, finally had enough. "This is preposterous. Do you know who this man is?" Without waiting for the answer, he continued. "He is my gamekeeper, and not a very good one. In fact, I had planned to have him replaced, and I think he knew that. The man is disgruntled and, oh my God, I almost forgot. Once I had caught him looking into my wife's bedroom. She was just getting ready to retire for the evening and I decided to take a walk about the grounds. I gave him a sound thrashing and he swore it had never happened before and would never happen again. You, you bastard. You killed her. She resisted your advances and you killed her." Springer leaped from his chair, but before he got halfway, Delacroix interceded.

"I think not, Mr. Springer. Return to your seat. There is something further Mr. Donnegal has to say. Donnegal, tell Sir Brewster what else you know about that night."

# THE PROBLEM

*"I plainly saw Mr. Springer on the road..."*

# THE PROBLEM

Springer, seated, fussed and fumed and turned to seek out Holmes' face. Finally their eyes met, but nothing could be revealed from the look that passed from the countenance of the famous consulting detective.

"Well, your Honor," Donnegal began, "I plainly saw Mr. Springer on the road leading to his house at ten o'clock or thereabouts. And I swear, that's the truth."

Charles Springer's mouth dropped open, Clarissa Melinor gasped and her hands went to her face, Thomas Duffey's eyes narrowed to a slit, and John S. Watson, son of the famous chronicler, tugged at Sherlock Holmes' sleeve and said, "You've got to do something, Mr. Holmes. Please."

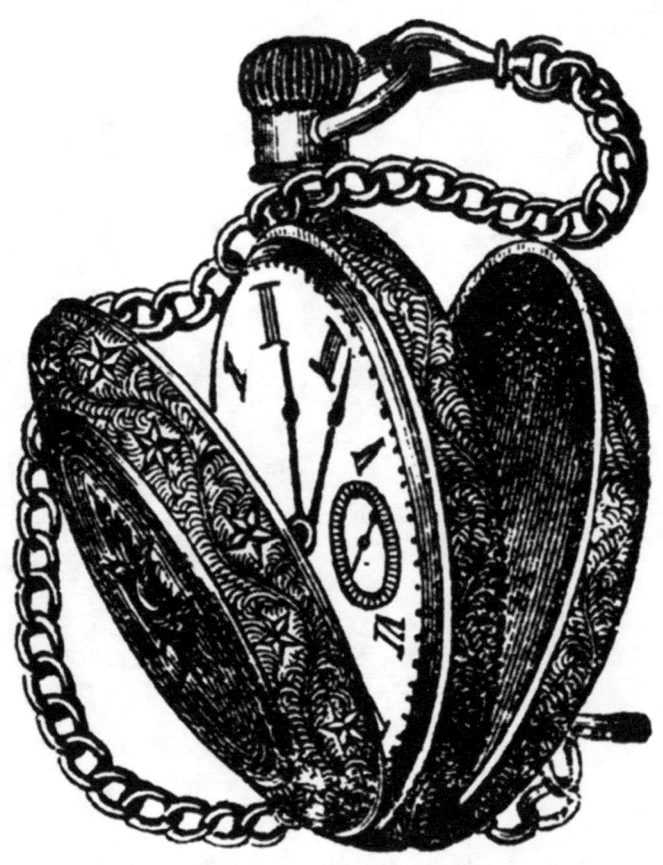

# New Surroundings

*April 23, —Later that day, The Russell Hotel, London.*

"Mr. Holmes, I hope you enjoy your stay. I, and the staff, are entirely at your disposal. If there is anything that we may do, please do not hesitate to call." With that final sentiment, the manager of the Russell Hotel, the newest in London, made his exit.

Holmes observed the room, or rather rooms, that had been reserved for him by young Watson. Ornate wall coverings did little to hide the fact that the place was entirely under-furnished to suit his taste. The cheery fire and comfort of 221B would not come easy in this establishment. The fact that there was no fireplace, nor a good-sized easy chair to recline into, made matters worse for the elderly detective. He could not begin to imagine what awaited him when he required "room service," as the Indian porter had called it, compared with the uncanny abilities of a Mrs. Hudson waiting in attendance. No, he would not like it here. Watson had told him that his old lodgings had been bought and made over into a sumptuous townhouse for some London aristocrat, a man who had made his fortune the old-fashioned way, inheriting it.

The only large chair in the room, somewhat awkward in its appearance, beckoned him to sit. He did so and at once rose up as he realized he had sat down on something that was hidden beneath its cushion. His hand found the slipper, and fondling it, a moist tear welled up in one eye. With practiced hand, he rolled back the sock-like top and revealed the cache of tobacco hidden within. It *was* his old Persian slipper, but it contained fresh Turkish tobacco. The tobacco fell to his lap as he rubbed it between his right fingers, and his left hand continued to search in vain under the cushion.

"Looking for this, Mr. Holmes?" Watson asked. There stood Dr. Watson's son with a wide grin on his face and Holmes' meerschaum held out at arm's length.

"Precisely, Watson. I suppose your father retained this after I had left. It is a habit I quit, just as I had quit the other. But now that you have managed to involve me in this particular matter, I shall have to be left alone for awhile, at least three pipes. Do you understand me, Watson?"

"Yes, Sir, I just wanted to please you with...."

"You have no need to please me Watson, nor I you. If you are looking for gratitude for having saved these things, let me remind you that it will be you that will be grateful for my having allowed you the opportunity. Now be off with you. Be back here for breakfast at 7 a.m., as we have some calls to make, but right now I must think."

Watson started to say something, but thought better of it. Instead he turned and left without saying goodbye.

Holmes filled the pipe and then, realizing there was no fireplace, and hence no matches, let out a gasp. The door reopened and there stood Watson. Without uttering one word he approached the world's greatest consulting detective and placed a container of wooden matchsticks on the small end table and turned for the door. He was more than halfway there when he turned again and said, "There is some sherry in the other room, on the desk."

"Watson," Holmes began, "I'm...." But Watson was already gone.

The problem ran through Holmes' mind like a dog chasing its tail. An immoral man kills his wife. Possible? Yes. A wealthy businessman with everything to lose, kills his wife. Possible? No. A motive of money? Enough? No. Not enough? Yes. But could there be other debts or money problems facing Springer to force his hand so terribly? Maybe. At last, a maybe. The woman, Clarissa Melinor, beautiful and charming enough to murder for? Yes, to some men. No, to Charles Springer. At least he says so. Or did he realize that a confession of love for Clarissa might also end up being a confession to murder? And what about time? He admits leaving the party at 9:30 and not returning until 11:30. Two hours unaccounted, except for Miss Melinor. She swears they are together. Are they? Or are they in it together? Maybe. Another maybe. Perhaps she is playing a role also and the truth is that they both love each other enough to commit murder. If Donnegal is not lying, then this would seem the case. Is Donnegal telling the truth? Maybe. Another damnable maybe. If he is not, then perhaps he did kill Mrs. Springer and sees this as an opportunity to pass guilt. Does Donnegal seem diabolical enough? No. Why did he come forward at all? As a gesture to Mrs. Springer? Delacroix tried to discredit him before he even spoke. Is Delacroix afraid of Springer? And finally, Thomas Duffey. He seems so aloof to the proceedings. There is more to him than meets the eye. He doesn't like his partner, no matter how successful the partnership has been, and this is quite obvious. Perhaps he is jealous of him. A motive for murder? Maybe. Why murder the wife? To implicate the husband, his partner, of course. Diabolical? Yes. Is Duffey capable of being so? Yes. And so it went round and round, suspect after suspect. It was not a three-pipe problem, it was more. It was fortunate for the hotel's guests that Holmes did not have possession of his famous violin.

*April 24, —The Russell Hotel, London*

"Watson, you're late!" chided Holmes. "I have already ordered up breakfast, so you will have to deal with the choices I have made. By the way, do you understand the term, 'no substitutions,' Watson. I only pass it on as it was made known to me by the surly porter this morning when I placed our order."

"Mr. Holmes, I'm sorry I'm late. As for breakfast, I am not very choosey so I am sure it will be fine. But the real reason I am late is very important. Mr. Holmes, Inspector Delacroix has placed Alf Donnegal under arrest. He has been charged with the murder."

"What! Incredible! There is suspicion, yes, but what brought him to this conclusion? Speak up lad, do you know?" Holmes literally leaped up and then quite sagged back into his chair.

"Well, Sir, it seems Mr. Donnegal had once assaulted a young girl many years ago, in Lancashire, where he worked as a stable hand. She brought charges against him and he served thirty days in a workhouse."

"Were these charges for assault or were they more, uh, how can I say this delicately, uh...." Holmes looked at Watson imploringly.

"No Sir, he did not attempt to have his way with her. He claims she was stealing from him and when he confronted her, she spat at him and, enraged, he thrashed her. At least that is his side of the story."

"So," Holmes said, "he, a stable hand, unkempt, is placed in a position of his word against hers, similarly in our case, against Charles Springer's"

"Yes, I suppose so," Watson remarked. "And they didn't believe him then and they won't believe him now."

"Watson, you told me you believed in Springer's innocence. In fact, you summoned me to find out the truth, which you felt would exonerate him. Why? Why do you believe he is innocent?"

"Mr. Holmes, I've worked for Mr. Springer for almost two years, not a lifetime perhaps, but still enough to get to know someone. That he was unfaithful to his wife seemed an unlikely event to me. But, his liaisons with Miss Melinor leave no doubt to that matter, and yet it seems out of character. Does that make sense?"

"Nothing has to make complete sense to be the truth, Watson. What about his candid remarks yesterday concerning other women he has been involved with? Did he make that up?"

"Yes, I'm sure of it. Our offices are not that large and the comings and goings of Mr. Springer, and Mr. Duffey as well, are common knowledge of the employees, including myself. Mr. Springer's time spent outside of the office is very business-oriented. He is basically the social side of Springer and Duffey and it is an important aspect of the type of business that they do. You really don't know, Mr. Holmes, how much entertaining...."

# NEW SURROUNDINGS

"Watson," Holmes interrupted. "How do you know that these meetings that Mr. Springer was attending did not entail female companionship as well?"

"Well, certainly I did not go with Mr. Springer. But as his personal assistant, I can assure you, the contacts he made at these gatherings, and the following up that I had to do subsequently, would require a lot of different people being involved in hiding Mr. Springer's assignations. It does not seem possible."

"I think you are quite right, Watson. Now, why did you think Springer would need my help?"

"I really was more concerned about your helping Mr. Springer after that insurance man, D'Angelo, came around and started making insinuating remarks...."

Holmes once again interrupted, "What remarks? Exactly what did this man say, Watson? Be as precise as you can remember."

"I can't remember exactly, Mr. Holmes. It was something about how suspicious it was that his firm had written a policy on the wife of a very important businessman, and now she was dead. D'Angelo likes to quote from the actuarial tables that were supplied by his company—the Allied Insurance Company of North America, I believe, is the name of the firm. He said the policy was just written in February during a brief trip abroad, and the odds were incredibly high for this to happen. If you meet him, Mr. Holmes, you won't like him. He's very slick and seems quite distrustful of any and everybody. I'm sure he is an unhappy man."

"Watson, good fellow," Holmes chuckled, "you have developed your father's trait of judging a book by its cover. Perhaps this man has reason to be suspicious. Or perhaps, it is just the nature of his work. Insurance fraud is a singularly criminal activity. It rarely involves professional thieves—except for that one case involving Professor Moriarity and some very famous jewels."

Holmes eyes took on a faraway look as he reflected upon a past glory.

"Mr. Holmes." Sherlock raised his eyes. "Mr. Holmes, I may not have your capacity to detect the culpability of someone, but in my heart, I know that Mr. Springer is innocent of Loreli's death. But now that Donnegal has been charged, I, I feel that he is innocent too. And yet one of them must be the guilty one. Rather than being elated at Donnegal's arrest, I feel morose. Why is that, Mr. Holmes?"

"Elementary, my dear Watson. Your understanding of Springer's character, that he is not truly the womanizer he appears to be, undeniably places further guilt upon the man. For now we have the added motive of love. Unrequited love, as the poets would say, or maybe not so unrequited, if we can believe Miss Melinor. His wife is the only thing standing in his way. The insurance policy, which he may even forgotten having purchased, comes as a piece of damning evidence against him, brought to the fore by this bulldog of an insurance investigator, this, due to the 'luck' of the matter as verified by the actuarial tables. Remember that actuarial tables are written by learned men who do not take coincidence as a factor in their calculations. And perhaps rightly so. Nevertheless, the act of murder in this instance would require a co-conspirator. An alibi. In this case, Miss Melinor. And that is where your true problem comes in, Watson. Tell me, how long have you been in love with her?"

"What! I, I...Mr. Holmes, how could you know? Clarissa is, she's very, I, she is afraid, so afraid. Mr. Springer and she, it's not what you think."

"Never mind what I think, Watson. Now, out with it. Just what is your relationship with this girl? And what happened that night? Please be truthful, a man's life is at stake. I know Alf Donnegal is innocent, and so do you. You have nothing to fear from the truth, for it is the only thing that can protect you. Now tell me!"

# Truth is Stranger

"I started at Springer and Duffey a little over two years ago," began Watson. "Although my position as an assistant to Mr. Springer did not pay very well, I felt it would prove very beneficial in learning the business. I'm quite ambitious, Mr. Holmes, and as such, was given many responsibilities which other young men of my age and schooling would not have been trusted with; and all because of Mr. Springer. You see, he recognized a kindred spirit in me, even though we were years apart, and he took me under his wing. I am sure if I had been Mr. Duffey's assistant, it would have been a different story."

"Pray tell," Holmes queried, "how so?"

"For one thing, Mr. Duffey maintains his own accounts and does not allow another individual access to his office files. Further, his comings and goings are a private affair, and he is meticulous about keeping it so. No, there would be no advancement under his tutelage. You cannot learn from a man who is afraid to reveal. I feel he may be very insecure in his real feelings and about his own abilities."

"Judging another book, Watson? Oh, never mind, continue."

"The work was tedious at times but still rewarding, at least to me, and then one day I discovered the problem."

"Problem?" Sherlock could hardly keep back his excitement. "What do you mean by *the* problem and not *a* problem? Something major was wrong, wasn't it?"

"Yes, oh yes, something major was wrong. You see, all along I believed that Springer and Duffey was a full partnership, but that wasn't so. I found a file containing the stock dispositions of the company and it was unbelievable. Mr. Springer held fifty-one percent of the stock and the remaining forty-nine percent was held by Mr. Duffey. This meant that Mr. Springer was really in control."

"This file," interrupted Holmes, "where did you find it? In Mr. Springer's office or Mr. Duffey's?"

"Oh, Mr. Springer's office, of course," replied Watson. "Mr. Duffey didn't allow anyone near his office—or his files, for that matter. I told you so. Anyway, I guess I forgot to put the file away after reading it, because Mr. Duffey came in and saw it opened on Mr. Springer's desk. He looked furious. He didn't say anything right then, but later I overheard him with Mr. Springer. It was a terrible row. Things changed at Springer and Duffey after that. Mr. Duffey was out quite a lot and Mr. Springer seemed quite preoccupied."

"And is that when Miss Melinor came to work there?" queried Holmes.

"Yes, precisely. At first I thought her just a twit. Oh, she was pretty enough, but the mental prowess required to handle the duties assigned her seemed beyond her abilities. And yet, she seemed to grow into the job."

"Just what was it she was required to do?" Holmes asked.

"Oh, sorry," said Watson, "she was made executive secretary of the firm. Not just a secretary, but *the* secretary. Strange, what? The firm always operated as a partnership and now to add this title. Perhaps they were planning to go limited, though I think not."

"Perhaps," interjected Holmes, "a slight tax advantage to the firm was in the offing. Could a new alliance change their tax status?"

"No, oh no, Mr. Holmes. I am not completely versed on the tax situations, but I don't think this new position was created to divert funds. In some way, though I can't put my finger on it, it did seem somewhat as an appeasement to Mr. Duffey. Somehow Clarissa added balance once again to the firm, but I don't know how."

"Did she work directly for Duffey?" inquired Holmes.

"No, nothing like that. She was equally shared by both partners."

"Indeed," said Holmes. "Perhaps your quaint way with words is more apt than you can imagine."

"Now, see here Holmes, I told you Clarissa is innocent of any wrongdoing and, as for this liaison with Mr. Springer, I'm sure she can explain that." Watson rose up and started pacing the floor. Holmes watched him for a moment and then said, "Watson, there is a diabolical game afoot and I am powerless to stop it. That is, unless you tell me exactly what happened the night of the party. Begin with your arrival at Mr. Duffey's residence."

"Gladly. But first you must tell me how you knew of my feelings for Clarissa. And don't tell me it's elementary. I can't see how you could read my emotions so easily. After all, if Springer is her lover, then wouldn't I be crazy to ask your help in defending him?"

"It may not seem elementary to you, my dear Watson, but think. A young girl, quite attractive, comes to work for a firm where there is an equally attractive young man. The fact is, they are the only young people employed there. Is that not a fact?"

"Well, yes, I suppose so," stammered Watson.

"Well then, as with the bees, who are guided by instinct alone, so are the young. It is only natural that you are attracted to each other. That her position is one of importance to the company is also easy to see. Her manner of dress, the expense of her jewelry and yes, even the style of her hair. Obviously she is a woman who commands attention and, in due respect, a healthy income. As for why you would wish to protect a man who purports to be her lover? Quite simple. If he is guilty, then she may be guilty also. Or at least be the motive of his guilt. You wish him innocent to prove her innocence. To you. Now, tell me what happened on that fateful night, and leave out no singular detail that may perhaps be useful in ending this nightmare for you." Holmes once more reclined in his chair and awaited a reply.

Watson appeared astonished and then, composing himself, responded.

"Very well, let me see. I arrived at Mr. Duffey's at about 7:15 p.m.; no, make that closer to 7:30. Practically all of the guests were there."

"How many guests?" queried Holmes.

"A dozen. Exactly twelve. It was not a large gathering. It was meant only for the key gentlemen who were involved in the new stock offering the firm was making. They were an awesome sight, I can tell you that."

"Why was that?" said Holmes.

"Oh, that's right, you don't know. Mr. Duffey is very proud of his parties and most always plans a theme around them. That night's theme was to be Japan. You see, the new stock issue was for a company that was planning to import fine art and curios from Japan. When I said they were an awesome sight, it was because they were all wearing hapi coats, a ceremonial type of robe, and they were so colorful, with dragons and what all stitched right into the material."

"Did you wear one of these robes?" Holmes asked.

"Why, yes. Everyone did. We donned them the moment we came in. Mr. Duffey and one of his household staff, I don't know which, I'm not that familiar with his home, also assisted. As I said, we wore these robes and went straight to the library for a cordial. It was quite a festive evening. Mr. Duffey, though he may be strait-laced in the office, proved to be a most hospitable host at this party."

"It must have been uncomfortable," Holmes remarked. "I mean, considering the warmth of your own coat, plus this robe over it, quite warm, I should think."

"Oh, no, Mr. Holmes, quite the contrary. We removed our waistcoats when we entered. In some respects we have some things to learn from the Japanese. I think we shall do an inordinate amount of business with them in the future."

"Really, Watson? Considering the quality of materials I have seen, if there is going to be any real trade with the Orient, it is with China that fortunes would be made. But now I digress. After you went into the library, what happened next?"

"As I said, cordials were served, as well as sake. Do you know what sake is, Mr. Holmes?" Holmes waved his hand to go on. "Well, it was the first time I had tasted it. Very sweet and quite nice. I don't know how long we spent in the library, but Mr. Duffey had more surprises in store. He bade us wait while he went out and prepared, and then a few moments later...."

"How much later?" Holmes asked. "It is very important Watson. Think! How long was Duffey gone?"

"Not long. Oh, less than ten minutes to be sure."

"You can't be certain, can you?" Holmes pressed.

"No, not really, but it was not long. Not long enough for him to go and kill Mrs. Springer, that's for sure. You're not suggesting...."

"No, no. It's alright Watson. What happened next, after Mr. Duffey returned?"

"Let me think. Oh yes, the doors were opened and we were led into a long dining hall—but there was no table. At least not at first. What I mean is, after we entered, we were formed into two lines facing each other, as if there was an actual dining table, and told to sit down. Right there, on the floor! You can imagine the confusion of these learned gentlemen being asked to sit on the floor. But, in good humor, one and all did just that. I was mildly surprised, and then the opposing doors opened up, and in came several servants. I can't remember how many, but at least four. They placed several small tables in front of us. Well, thinking that was all, some of the men started placing their glasses down, but Mr. Duffey, he said no, hold onto your drink. Next, the servants returned with what appeared to be a dining room table, shorn of its legs. They placed it on top of the small tables and the effect was our knees and backs were cheek and jowl with the table and the wall. Quite a sight, Mr. Holmes."

"Indeed, Watson, a picture starts to form. Obviously Mr. Duffey was trying to create the customary dining positions as practiced in the Japans. Naturally, none of the guests could move when once 'locked in,' so to speak, would you say?"

"Oh, quite right, Mr. Holmes. It was somewhat uncomfortable, but yet it was also an exhilarating experience. Have you ever dined that way, Sir?"

"Yes, at the request of the Japanese Ambassador. Perhaps your father told you about the case of the 'Missing Cloisonné Vase?'"

"No, he didn't. Was it quite famous?"

"Evidently not as famous as I thought. Well, back to your dinner."

"Dinner was several courses, and rather time consuming. Especially due to the amount of passing around that had to be done. It was enjoyable, but perhaps I felt a little disappointment since the spices seemed so bland and I truly expected something more."

"What time was dinner over?" Holmes interrupted.

"Oh, precisely 9:15 p.m." Watson replied.

"How can you be so sure, Watson?" Holmes queried.

"Mr. Duffey informed us all that there would be a show in the drawing room at exactly 9:30 and we had just fifteen minutes to wash up, if we needed, and to be there promptly."

"Show? What kind of show?" Holmes' brows furrowed slightly and he checked his own watch to see that it was already 8:15 a.m., and their breakfast had not arrived. Before Watson could answer, he jumped up.

"Watson, have you any idea what time it is?" Watson also checked his watch.

"Yes Sir. It's a quarter after eight. Is there something wrong, Sir?"

"Just our breakfast! Please excuse me lad, I have not been much of a host. Let us hold this inquisition until the matter of breakfast can be resolved. All this talk of dinner and I am famished. Now, what is the number for that porter?" Holmes stalked into the other room and Watson could hear murmuring going on as Holmes used the telephone. Fifteen minutes later, a boy appeared at the door with a tray. Holmes was furious and let the boy know it. The boy appeared indifferent and this incensed Holmes even further. After he left they ate in silence. When they were finished, Holmes poured a third cup of coffee and, sitting back, stared at Watson.

"You look nothing like your father, did you know that?" he remarked.

"Actually no, Mr. Holmes, I've been told I bear a strong resemblance to him."

"No, nothing at all. Ah, where were we? Oh yes, the show. Tell me about the show."

"The show was really a game. We gathered in the drawing room, as I told you, and Mr. Duffey had us memorize the layout of the room.

Details, he said, every corner, every niche, remember it well. Then he put out the lights."

"What! He put out the lights? What on earth for?" Holmes, now keen-eyed, moved forward on his seat.

"Well, as I said, it was a game. Each man in turn was to move from one assigned point to another. That is, he was handed a piece of paper with two places listed. Then the lights were turned off, and when they came on again, he would be judged on how well he was able to find that place. It can be rather disorienting, don't you think Mr. Holmes?"

"Yes, but more importantly, how long were the lights out each time?"

"Oh, I don't think long. Maybe five minutes, perhaps even less. Remember, not all of us were moving, only the one man."

"Did you notice if Mr. Duffey ever left the room during this time?" Holmes asked.

"No, I don't think so. He has rather a booming laugh and as each gentleman ran afoul of a piece of furniture or what, I can distinctly remember hearing that laughter. But I do remember one thing." Watson paused.

"Yes, yes, go on Watson, what is it?"

"Mr. Springer was gone. He was definitely not there. In fact, I don't remember seeing him after dinner at all. Oh, much later, yes, but not during the show, or rather, the game. He was not there."

"And where was Miss Melinor during all of this?" Holmes implored.

"Clarissa was not invited to this party, Mr. Holmes. Mr. Duffey, as you may be aware, is a lifelong confirmed bachelor and belongs to only the best English clubs. You know the type, where feminine guests are not only discouraged, but emphatically denied entrance."

"Yes, my brother Mycroft frequented those establishments when he sought human companionship," Holmes replied.

"And as to her whereabouts on that night? I was equally surprised when Mr. Springer said he was with her. Mr. Holmes, she will not talk to me about the matter, but I fear she may be in grave danger. If there is a diabolical plot, as you say, I am afraid that poor Clarissa is moving in the center of it."

"Quite possibly you are correct Watson. Perhaps she will divulge the answer to me, but right now, I have another question to pose to you. What time did this game end and when did Mr. Springer reappear at this party?"

"I'm not perfectly sure, but I think, no...I'm sure it was 11 p.m."

"What makes you certain of the time, Watson?" Holmes asked.

"The clock in the library. Oh, we adjourned to the library afterwards for a nightcap, and the chimes were sounding as we went in. I am certain it was for 11 p.m. Mr. Duffey, the ever-gracious host, had large balloons of brandy poured for everyone, and that's when he made the announcement."

"The announcement? What announcement?" Holmes stared incredulously. "No, don't tell me Watson—let me tell you." With that, a grin formed on his face.

"There is no way, Mr. Holmes, that you can guess what Mr. Duffey said that evening. It was not mentioned at the inquest, and I have not repeated it to a soul. Please don't tax yourself with mere speculation. Mr. Duffey just requested...."

"Not requested," interrupted Holmes, "he demanded. Or should I say, made it imperative that his guests, yes, and even his trusted employee, Mr. Watson, must spend the night. And, even as he spoke, rooms were being prepared for one and all, and he would not take 'no' for an answer. Correct, Watson?" Holmes actually beamed as he reclined into his seat. Watson, on the other hand, let out an audible gasp and stared at the master detective.

"How on earth could you know? It's not possible. I, I..." stammered the young Watson.

"Watson, this case grows stranger by the minute. Explanations are not necessary now, and if they are given may only serve to confuse you, and in turn, confuse myself. Just accept that there are some facts in life that become very obvious to a few observant individuals, like myself, and that time is a very important factor and we must make use of it. Was Mr. Springer in attendance when Mr. Duffey made his request?"

Watson, starting to compose himself, replied, "No Sir, he was not. He joined us at about 11:30 p.m., just as he, himself said. So it is true he was gone for two hours. As for the rest of us, we drank and conversed until about midnight and then I went straight to bed. I believe a few others may have stayed for a second nightcap."

"And Mr. Duffey? When did he turn in? And when was the last time you saw Mr. Springer?" Holmes seemed impatient for Watson to answer.

"When Mr. Springer got back, at 11:30 as I said, he and Mr. Duffey went straight to Mr. Duffey's den. Mr. Duffey bade good night to us but he did seem upset at Mr. Springer. I thought it was due to his condition; it was obvious that he had been imbibing while he was away. Now, of course, it has been alluded he was with Clarissa. Oh, I can't believe it. Anyway, when they left the library, at maybe 11:35, that was the last time that night I saw them."

"And in the morning? Obviously Mr. Springer had gone home. But Mr. Duffey and his guests, including yourself, do you remember what time breakfast was served?" Holmes, ever watchful, glared at Watson.

"Hmmm, let me think," Watson mused. "I believe it was around 7 a.m. Quite early, I thought, considering the long evening our host had put us through, but yes, it was 7 a.m. A good breakfast it was, too."

"Watson, you have been extremely helpful this morning, even though our breakfast was not so good. But now, let us be off. Oh, speaking of time, are you not employed today? It is only Wednesday."

Watson, taken back, replied, "No Sir, Mr. Springer has declared the rest of the week a holiday, in memory of his wife." Watson lowered his head.

"Perhaps the man has more feelings than he lets on, Watson. Then let us make haste. There is someone in danger who needs our help most of all."

"Clarissa, Mr. Holmes," Watson cried out.

"No, my poor misguided youth. Alf Donnegal, the man nobody trusts."

# Justice is Served

*April 24, —Scotland Yard*

Delacroix leaned back in his chair and was enjoying the moment of superiority as Sherlock Holmes stood before him waiting a reply. Holmes had requested permission to question the prisoner. Highly irregular, thought Delacroix. The man was charged with murder, no bail had been set and only his appointed attorney should be allowed admittance. Quite irregular. After an inordinate amount of time had passed, but not as long as Delacroix would have liked, he responded.

"Of course, Mr. Holmes. It is an exception to the rule, as I am sure you know, but I will make one in your case. Fair enough?"

"Thank you, Inspector. But one question, please. You were obviously prepared to say no, and I would like to know what changed your mind?" Holmes appeared discernably more relaxed and for some reason, this upset Delacroix more than the remark.

"Do a little mind-reading as well, Mr. Holmes? Or is that your methodology of deduction? Never mind, you may see the prisoner as I said, but on one condition. I, and I alone, shall accompany you. Not young Watson here, that won't do at all."

"Agreed," said Holmes readily. Too readily for Delacroix's comfort. "I'm certain your presence will not detract from Mr. Donnegal's answers to any pertinent questions I may put before him, and it will obviously help you to observe for a change."

"Now don't go pushing your luck, Holmes. The higher-ups may hold you in some regard, but we in the trenches don't enjoy amateurs playing at theatrics which may get them more publicity, but don't necessarily get the job done." Delacroix was starting to lose control. Holmes recognized this and softened his attack.

"Inspector, rest assured that the printed material that told the world of my deeds, did not come from my doing. I sincerely prefer to remain unheralded in this or any matter that I become involved with. As you may be aware, my chronicler, Dr. Watson—*the* Dr. Watson—has passed on. This young lad, though he bears the same name, has no wish to reforge this link with his ancestral past. Further, any information that I may happen to stumble upon will assuredly be turned over to you, the proper authority, to ensure that justice is done."

"Well," Delacroix said, visibly cooling down, "make sure that is so. I've got my eye on you. Lestrade admitted that you had some talent, but you must understand that interference, not matter how small, can muck up a good case faster than anything, understand?" The humbling look on Holmes' face brought relief to Delacroix's.

"Certainly, Inspector. Now, shall we see the prisoner?"

"Yes, wait here and I'll be right back." And with that, Delacroix left the room. Watson, positively chomping at the bit, stage-whispered to Holmes.

"Turn everything over to him? Mr. Holmes, what about your observations of the party? You won't tell me. Are you going to tell him?"

"In due time, Watson, in due time. Now, let's not mention anything I've said to you, is that clear?" Sherlock fairly chuckled at this.

A few minutes later, Delacroix returned and escorted Watson back to the anteroom. He led Sherlock Holmes to the detention cell on the third floor. There, in a nondescript room, sat Alf Donnegal. His expression was one of a man beaten, of failure, of rejection. He stood up when the men came in, but did not address them. It was as if he were waiting to be told what to do, and it was obvious imprisonment was taking its toll on him. The room, small by any

# JUSTICE IS SERVED

standards, held four chairs and a small table. Silently, the men sat down, one by one: first Inspector Delacroix, then Holmes and finally, Alf Donnegal.

"Alf, do you know who this man is?" asked Delacroix.

"No, I don't. He's not my lawyer. Who is he?" The voice, sullen and lifeless, registered defeat. Holmes looked at the man, his sharp eyes trying to detect a spark in the man, but there was none. Finally, he spoke.

"Mr. Donnegal," Holmes began, "I believe an injustice is being performed here. You are an innocent man." Holmes' words reached the man like fresh air and seemed to breathe life into him. Donnegal turned and looked at his salvation.

"You're, you're Sherlock Holmes, aren't ya? You're Sherlock Holmes. You were at the trial, I saw ya. Nobody believes I saw ya, but I did and here you are. Am I right?" His face brightened with each syllable. Even Delacroix could not fail to notice the change in the man's disposition.

"Quite right, Mr. Donnegal. And, I've come to help you. But first you must help me. Do you understand?" Donnegal did not speak. Holmes placed his hands on the table, showing them to be empty, and then placed them over the other man's hands.

"It's going to be alright, Alf. Now tell me, the first time you saw Loreli Springer get undressed, what happened?" His voice was so silky-smooth that the question came totally unanticipated. Delacroix was the first to react.

"What the…damn it, Holmes, we're not interested in those sordid details. This man killed a woman for God's sake, and her memory should rest in peace." Delacroix was beginning to heat up again. Donnegal's face turned ashen and he started to crawl back into the hole in his mind.

"Inspector," Holmes said in as authoritative a voice as he could manage without his anger coming through, "I know you believe this man to be guilty. You have to believe he's guilty. And I know why. If you don't believe I know, we can discuss it in front of Lord Brewster. But, if you value your badge, you'll let me continue, and then we can discuss it in private afterwards. Is that clear?"

## JUSTICE IS SERVED

Delacroix half-rose from his chair. His mind was racing. Holmes could see that. In his best of times, he could judge a man's reactions to a crisis, but he was old now, really too old to be here, doing this. Holmes was not bluffing, but it still required more bravado than he could muster to face this bull of a man. Delacroix made his decision.

"Fine, Mr. Holmes. I'll play it your way, continue." He slumped down into his chair. Holmes, breathing a sigh of relief, turned once more to Alf Donnegal.

"You see, Alf. The truth is better than lies. One cannot back down from the truth, no matter what. And, neither can you. Now, the first time you saw Loreli Springer undress, you weren't at her window were you? You were in her room, her bedroom, isn't that so?" Holmes waited.

"I, I didn't mean, I, she's a good woman, Mr. Holmes, really she is. Not like the others. I'm not a handsome man, anyone can tell that. But me, she thought I was handsome, she told me so. When she touched my face, it was, I don't know, love I guess. Ya, I was in love and I think she was too. Oh, she wouldn't say it. Naw, she was too much of a lady, what with being married and all. I've never done nothing like that, Mr. Holmes, ever. I know it's one of the commandments. I've never been married and a man gets lonely and I just didn't think a lady like that would, would ever, oh damn…." Alf Donnegal started to cry, and then bawled like a baby.

"There, there Alf, you were a Godsend to her. As you know she was very unhappy. Her husband treated her badly, didn't he?"

Composing himself, he looked up, "You know that, don't ya, Mr. Holmes? He beat her. Honestly, he actually took a whip to her. The man's no good, rotten. I don't care if he's rich and, and, well, he's no gentleman, no gentleman at all."

"Alf," Holmes continued, "when Mr. Springer caught you with his wife, what happened? Where were you at the time?"

"Oh, God forgive me, I was in the lady's bed with her. She was so good to me and then I noticed her face took so strange. I knew someone was behind me. I turned 'round and, oh my God, there he was, whip in his hand! And, and Jesus, Mr. Holmes, he thrashed

# JUSTICE IS SERVED

*"Alf Donnegal started to cry...."*

me right good, just like he said, but I wasn't at no window, I was right there in her bed, and he almost killed me that night. She begged him to stop and finally he did, but not before he made her promise, to promise, oh God, please, Mr. Holmes, it's hard for me to say it."

"I know Alf, the truth is hard, but you must say it. Go on, man, clear your conscience, your very life is at stake here, can't you see that?" Holmes closed his hands over the man's shoulders as he had been shaking. Moments passed and finally he spoke.

"She promised to do it again."

Delacroix jumped up. "WHAT THE HELL! Promised to do it again? Do what again? Are you trying to tell us that her husband, Charles Springer, an upstanding businessman, made his wife promise to go naked and fornicate with his gamekeeper?" Delacroix's eyes looked heavenward and almost retreated into his face.

"Yes Sir. That's exactly what he did." Donnegal started to shake again, but Holmes held tighter.

"And did you?" Holmes asked.

"Yes, oh God yes, many times." Donnegal started to cry again. Delacroix sat back down and stared at the man and then back at Holmes. He started murmuring to himself.

"Alf, Alf, just one more question," Holmes implored, "just one."

Donnegal pulled himself together and, realizing his terrible secret was no more, finally felt inner relief. His eyes were glistening from the tears and from his new-found freedom.

"Certainly, Mr. Holmes, what is it?"

"On that fateful night. The night Mrs. Springer was murdered. Did you see Charles Springer, or not?" Holmes held his breath while Donnegal turned around to answer.

"Yes, Mr. Holmes, I did. I surely did."

"And what time was that, Alf? Be sure now, no guesswork. What time was it?" Holmes tried to remain calm, but inwardly his stomach roiled and his brain burned for the answer.

"Just like I said at the trial, Mr. Holmes. Just after 10 p.m., I checked my watch, look here, they didn't take it away, it's a good'un. My old boss, who really ap'reciat'd me, gave it to me. I know it's a good'un."

## JUSTICE IS SERVED

Later, back in Inspector Delacroix's office, Holmes sat and the Inspector paced back and forth. They were in almost opposite positions from when Holmes had first come in.

"Do you still believe he's guilty, Inspector?" Holmes queried.

"No, no I don't." Delacroix replied. Now it was his turn to look like the beaten man. He continued, "You have to understand, the situation is not so easy for a man in my position."

"You mean, Inspector, when a man, a wealthy man in the district, is cuckolded by his gamekeeper, new rules apply."

"No, it's not like that. I had no idea that was going on, please believe me." Delacroix paced some more.

"Inspector, I don't believe you. What I believe is that Alf Donnegal came to you and told you he saw Charles Springer that night, but you didn't believe him. Then, what did you do? I'll tell you. You confronted Mr. Springer, who then told you that he was planning to fire Donnegal and that the man was a disgruntled employee, and you believed that. Or rather, you wanted to believe that. Isn't that more the truth?" Delacroix placed one hand over his face. Holmes continued. "You're the one who's guilty, guilty of accepting truths only when it comes from clean, unsoiled hands. Did you check out the story of the assault on the girl in Lancashire yourself, or did you just accept it, based on the hard evidence that the man emanates in his appearance? You have deep-rooted prejudices, Inspector, and they affect your judgment as sure as liquor or any other corruptness of the soul."

"But why can't Donnegal be guilty, Mr. Holmes, tell me that?" His voice, almost whiny, shrilled at Sherlock.

"Because he loved her. I saw that at the inquest. You saw a disheveled common laborer. You think him incapable of pure love and it's easy for you to think of him in the worst. You are not a judge and jury. In this country, it is still the law that a man is considered innocent until proven guilty. That is the law that you must uphold, and you don't."

"Oh, Mr. Holmes, what can I do? You're right. You're so right. I acted on blind faith, which was truly corrupt. What can I do?" The big man slumped into his chair with both hands covering his face, obviously in pain and in shame.

# JUSTICE IS SERVED

"Inspector!" Holmes' voice, sharper than ever, rang out. "Inspector, your path is clear. You must help right this wrong. Obtain the release of Alf Donnegal and as quickly as possible. Imprisonment is woefully wrong for this man and it is taking a relentless toll on him."

"Yes, yes, of course I will. But what then, Mr. Holmes? Shall I resign? Shall I spend the rest of my days in repent, to…." Before he could finish, Holmes was by his side, and as he had done with Alf Donnegal, he now did with Inspector Delacroix. He placed both of his bony hands upon the shoulders of the big man and squeezed reassuringly.

"What! No, man, for God's sake, no. You are obviously a better man for what has taken place. No, resignation is not your fate, nor mere repentance. You are a man of action and a man of action you shall always be. Remember well this day, and promise furthermore that you will always look for the doubt, for the impossible truth, in even the obvious. No, Inspector, you shall make no more mistakes. You have gone through the fire, now go uphold the law, do as good a job as you can do with renewed vigor and, more importantly, new knowledge of yourself."

When Holmes came out into the anteroom, Watson looked at him with surprise.

"You're grinning, Holmes, what happened in there?"

"Truth, Watson, plain and simple. It really is the only justice. Now, let us be off." Holmes darted for the door. Watson followed quickly behind.

"But, what about Donnegal? Can you leave him in Delacroix's hands?" asked Watson.

"The best, and the most capable hands, Watson." Sherlock responded.

"I don't understand," said Watson.

"Of course you don't. You're Watson. And, since when do you call me 'Holmes' and not 'Mr.?'" Before Watson could answer, the great sleuth was out the door and halfway down the street.

# Springer and Duffey

*April 24, —Afternoon*

The lunch crowd at Simpson's was dwindling in size as the clock neared the second hour of the afternoon. Sherlock Holmes and John Watson were seated near a window enjoying their repast, along with a spectacular London afternoon. The weather was exceedingly mild for late April and nary a cloud could be seen. Walkers passed by hurriedly, obviously on their way back to their usual working places or pressing on to some well-calibrated rendezvous. Working London, like any other great metropolis, moves essentially to the beat of the relentless machine known as the clock.

"One of life's unique pleasures, Watson." Holmes remarked.

"Yes Sir," Watson replied, "the varieties of restaurants that a city like London can provide is enormous."

"No, no, Watson. Nothing as mundane as food. I speak of the people. Watching people as they pass by a window, any window, brings forth an abundance of knowledge. What, ho, see that woman in the green velvet dress? Where do you think her destination is?" Holmes leaned back.

"Her? Oh, I suppose she is shopping for the afternoon. Probably on her way to Harrods. No, no, more likely one of the smaller, more exclusive shops in Kensington." Watson also leaned back, a smug look on his face.

Holmes barked a short laugh, "Oh, Watson, Watson, you're as bad as your father. I remark upon her dress and you take to dissect it immediately. Look at the obvious man, use your brain! Admittedly she is dressed more fashionably than Harrods, but her make-up is awry. The woman's countenance also betrays her emotions. The woman is upset, worried. I think perhaps her rendezvous is something more urgent than a dress shop…perhaps a hospital. Yes, that's it! See the purposefulness in her strides, she has no time to tarry."

"Oh, Holmes, when you say it, it fits so well. But in reality, I just don't know," Watson remarked back.

"Then quickly, lad, catch up with her and ask her if we can be of assistance and be ready to offer her a cab. I'm sure her cause of distress is not allowing her mind to function very well. Now be off with you."

Watson dashed up to the street and Holmes could see him exchanging a few words with her. Shortly, a hansom cab pulled over and the woman alighted, and Watson ambled back to Simpson's.

"Not a word, Watson." Holmes looked up at the young man, "Not a word." They finished their meal in silence.

Later, the duo appeared at the home of Thomas Duffey. The home, more palatial than Holmes had surmised, appeared somewhat unkempt. The servant who had shown them in moved hurriedly away when the master of the house approached.

"Mr. Holmes, what a pleasure!" Duffey remarked. "And, Mr. Watson. You're not choosing a new profession, eh, what?"

"Oh, no Sir," quickly replied Watson. "Mr. Holmes is a very close friend of the family and I have consented to show him around the city."

"Hmmm, can't imagine a man of Mr. Holmes' reputation requiring an escort," Duffey replied.

"And it is a pleasure meeting you, Sir," Holmes interjected. "Young Watson has told me numerous things about you and he's quite right, you are certainly a leader among men."

"Watson said that? Oh, yes, respect is very important as a man moves on in life, isn't that so, Mr. Holmes?" Duffey, feeling quite amiable after Holmes' remark, gestured with his hand to enter his inner sanctum, his den.

"Respect?" Holmes answered. "Yes, respect is certainly important. I have received a modicum of it in my day, but as you say, as one gets older somehow it appears to be harder to obtain. Youth reaches out for its own, as it were, and its unguided grasp may unknowingly hurt."

"Quite right, quite right. Now that we are comfortable, is there anything I can get for you? A cordial, tea…." His voice trailed off.

"No, nothing for me. Watson, what about you, lad?" Holmes looked at his young companion.

"No, Sir. Uh, we just had lunch at Simpson's and, no, no thank you."

"Well, then," Duffey continued, "I assume that you wish to ask some embarrassing questions of me, Mr. Holmes. That is the only way to get to the bottom of things, is it not?"

"Truth can only be considered embarrassing to those who wish to hide it, Mr. Duffey," Holmes coldly remarked.

"Ah, touché, Mr. Holmes, touché. No, I don't believe I have anything to hide, but if I may, Sir, I would expect a more discreet audience at this time." Duffey turned his head towards Watson.

"Certainly. That is quite acceptable," Holmes answered, and, also turning to Watson, "Watson, be a good lad and wait in the foyer. We shall only be a few moments. Thank you." Watson appeared confused; and then, as if in resignation, he shrugged, excused himself and left.

"I wish to speak to you about insurance," Holmes immediately began.

"Insurance? Oh, the policy that was placed for Loreli. Yes, tragic coincidence. It must appear quite unseemly for Charles to have bought such a policy at such an inopportune time. What I mean is, considering the circumstances that have occurred, it must be thought harsh."

"Mr. Springer," Holmes continued, "indicates that his finances were quite glowing. Is that also your interpretation of his affairs?"

"Glowing? Strange word to call assets. Yes, Charles' handling of his own financial affairs were impeccable, to say the least. He managed to accumulate quite a bit."

"His own financial affairs?" intoned Holmes. "What about the affairs of the firm, did he also manage them as well?" Holmes' eyes narrowed slightly.

"I see," said Duffey. "The questions can become a trifle uncomfortable. No, his forté was not management of the firm's assets. His purpose was to bring in the business, so to speak. Convincing men of extreme importance, and yes, of wealth, requires a certain amount of spending of capital to, how shall I put it? Uh," he paused, then added, "to entertain, socialize with our clients, to place ourselves on an even footing with them and gain their confidence, this was Charles' position."

"And this required enormous sums?" Holmes inquired.

"I thought so," answered Duffey.

"More than you thought so. Much more?" Holmes continued relentlessly.

"Yes, damn it! Charles had no head for simple arithmetic. A balanced sheet should always reflect a reasonable return on investment." Duffey glared back at Holmes.

"This must have had some effect on your partnership, Mr. Duffey. Did you implore him to curtail his spending at any point?"

"Yes," Duffey replied, "of course, I did. Now get to the point, Mr. Holmes. I know my partner has certain faults. Are you implying that he also had other financial difficulties which forced him to commit murder for a paltry £50,000?" Duffey's annoyance with Holmes was becoming more obvious.

"You seem protective of Mr. Springer. Does he need protection?" Holmes quietly asked.

"Yes, of course he does." Duffey calmed down a bit and then, "He's more the boy than man, can't you see? I look after him like an older brother. Always have. In some circles, Mr. Holmes, it is considered an honor, not a burden."

"And in this circle, Mr. Duffey?" pressed Holmes.

"By God, you can be impertinent. I have a mind to dismiss you and send you on your way!" Duffey started for the door, thought better of it and turned back, "Oh, Mr. Holmes, this, this death has been a tragic event and I only wish to get to the bottom of it. Please forgive me." He appeared genuinely repentant.

Holmes, more assured of himself, began again. "Mr. Duffey, can I take it you believe the man currently in custody, Alf Donnegal, did not murder your partner's wife?"

"Eh, him? No. No, I can't believe it. The poor fellow seemed quite disoriented at the inquest. And that Inspector, Delacroix? He has no tact and more than likely, no respect for the likes of a Donnegal. Unfortunately, the man will probably hang for Loreli's death and we shall never really know who did it." Duffey pulled a box of cigarettes out of a desk drawer, offered one to Holmes, who declined, and took one for himself.

"No, Mr. Duffey, Donnegal will not hang, that I'm sure of. But, as for the real killer, who do you suspect, if not Charles Springer?" Holmes leaned back in his chair to watch while the import of his remarks sank in.

"Won't hang? Is there new evidence? What reason would they have for letting the man go? I don't understand." Obviously, Duffey was shaken.

"No new evidence to speak of," Holmes remarked, "just a reawakening of the common senses at Scotland Yard. What about Springer, Mr. Duffey? Is he a killer? Or do you suspect someone else?"

Duffey recomposed himself, thought for a minute, and then said, "Charles Springer is a very complex man, Mr. Holmes, very complex. His personal life was not very pleasant to observe. He had habits that a God-fearing man would say are damnable. I have never been a married man, but it is hard to believe that this so-called blissful state could have reached such a plateau. He beat his wife, I assume you know that." He paused and Holmes nodded. Duffey went on, "She was a noble woman, and it was hard to believe that she would also take a lover." Duffey paused again and looked at Holmes.

"Alf Donnegal," the detective somberly added.

"No, oh no," Duffey fairly moaned. "But it fits, it truly fits. It was the only way this woman, this woman of such status and bearing, could get even. My God, it fits. Mr. Holmes, I truly did not want to admit it to myself, but Charles did kill his wife. Not for the money, though it may play a small part, but in reality because of her unfaithfulness. Unfaithfulness which assuredly had been caused by Charles himself. But, he would never see it that way. He would be distraught if the knowledge of her, her liaison got out. Oh, Mr. Holmes, I feel so sad. Poor Loreli, poor Charles. How can people mess up their lives so badly? They had it all, and now, nothing." Duffey stood up and walked to the window and stared out.

"Yes, it fits alright," said Holmes, "but for one thing." He paused for a long moment. "Charles Springer knew of his wife's indiscretion and then forced her to continue it. This is certainly not an act of a man afraid of exposure, it is more unsettling than that."

Duffey spun around at the words. "You can't mean that. Charles is a gentleman, and though his code of ethics may have been tarnished, he could not possibly have allowed another man access to his wife knowingly and wantonly, without seeking retribution. I cannot accept that, Mr. Holmes. It's beastly."

"And it is so. The man is made more dangerous when his mind is so deranged. But, is it dangerous enough to kill? Knowledge of his wife's indiscretions and acceptance of them certainly removes the 'heat of the moment' defense from his vocabulary. And what of Miss Melinor? Is she so in love with him to blindly defend him also? Why are so many people willing to come to the aid of this man when his shortcomings are so obvious?" Holmes now strode towards the door.

"Wait, wait Mr. Holmes! You're right. Charles is such a charming man when he wants to be. So charming, in fact, one does tend to overlook certain other things. And ability. He is a resourceful and able partner. He has single-handedly increased our business fourfold. You can understand why I hold him in such high esteem. As for his wife, I'm afraid I allowed his handling of his personal affairs, as long as they didn't interfere with business, to go their own deadly course. I have failed him, Mr. Holmes. Failed him at the time he needed me the most. I should have counseled him better." Duffey's face took on the look of a man who was at odds with himself.

"I have one further question, Mr. Duffey. Is there a large insurance policy on your life with Mr. Springer as the prime beneficiary?" Holmes asked.

A shadow passed over Duffey's face. He looked up. "Oh, my God, Mr. Holmes, £500,000. Purchased last year, I believe. Oh, my God...." Holmes closed the door silently behind him.

# Contemplation

*I*t was late afternoon when Holmes and Watson returned to the Russell Hotel. Watson thought they should order tea and scones sent to the room, but Holmes implored the young man to join him for a sherry in the hotel's bar.

After they had each poured from the glass decanter, Holmes spoke, "Ah, Watson, how sweet the grape can become. It is amazing what the art of wine-making has done for the civilized world as we know it. Perhaps you read my treatise on the complex subtleties that the various vintages offer when in the hands of different artisans?" Watson shrugged his shoulders. "No?" Holmes continued. "Pity. Knowledge is as rare these days as are the proper processes by which this product comes to market. Anyone can make wine, Watson, but only a few can create wine. There is a subtle difference. One, I hope, you'll understand someday."

"Holmes," Watson asked, "you have questioned Alf Donnegal and also Inspector Delacroix, and now we've just left Mr. Duffey. What have you learned? Why can't I be made privy to these conversations? I feel quite inadequate to comment on our adventures so far since you have failed to include me in your observations. Please don't patronize me, I wish to know the answer. Did Mr. Springer kill his wife, or didn't he?"

# CONTEMPLATION

Holmes looked at Watson and a slight mist formed over his eyes. "Ah, Watson, my old friend, I have been derelict in keeping you informed, have I not? I promise to make amends. And soon, but not right now. In a moment our guest shall be here, and I think clarity will become apparent, more apparent than the clarity in this glass of wine I hold in my hand. Oh, there she is now." Watson, unhappy with Holmes' remarks, craned his neck from the booth and shock registered on his face immediately.

"Clarissa? What is she doing here?" he gasped.

"Why I invited her," replied Holmes. "My dear Watson, you do ask the dumbest questions. Have you not learned anything at all? Oh well, take that ridiculous look off your face and go greet our guest and fetch her here." Watson stumbled getting out of the booth and, turning up the aisle, went to meet Clarissa Melinor.

"Miss Melinor, a pleasure," beamed Holmes. "I'm so glad you could come. Sherry? Perhaps you would prefer tea?"

"No, Mr. Holmes, Sherry would be nice. Do pour for me, John, you know how clumsy I can be. Thank you." And with that, Clarissa took her seat opposite Sherlock Holmes and next to John Watson.

She seemed in good spirits, and after exchanging pleasantries about the surroundings and the hotel, she remarked, "Mr. Holmes, I'm sure John has mentioned to you that we, uh, well, we have…." Her talkative state dissipated and she sought out Watson's support.

"Yes, Clarissa, Holmes knows that I am fond of you, and I believe you are fond of me also." Watson paused, allowing Holmes to respond.

"I'm sure that is the way it should be. After all, two young people engaged by the same firm, it is only natural you would gravitate towards each other. I think I made the same point only yesterday to Watson, uh, John here, isn't that so, John?" Holmes started grinning, almost to the point of smiling.

"Yes, quite right," Watson remarked.

"But that's not the reason you asked me here today, is it, Mr. Holmes?" queried Clarissa, "Or may I call you Sherlock?"

"No, not the reason," continued Holmes. "And you may call me whatever feels comfortable for you, my dear." The old man's eyes

## CONTEMPLATION

met the young girl's and a silent moment passed between them. Watson felt a tad uncomfortable.

Holmes went on, "Perhaps, just for the sake of understanding," Holmes implored gently, now allowing the eye contact to break, "you could explain why you lied about being with Mr. Springer that night." The bombshell dropped and Watson involuntarily flinched, but Clarissa held fast and, without missing a heartbeat, replied, "I did not lie, Mr. Holmes. Charles was with me, but not for the whole time."

"Eh? And what amount of time was he gone? Please be precise."

"Oh, no more than a half-hour. Let me see…we went to the greenhouse at about 9:30 and I think Charles left, oh, maybe it was 11 p.m.…but he came right back, I'm sure of that."

"Oh, Clarissa," Watson said, "please say it isn't so! Why were you with that man? Don't you know how this hurts me?" Watson turned his face away from her and faced the wall.

"Easy, Watson," Holmes assured, "the lady has a good reason, don't you?"

"It is not easy being a woman alone in London, Mr. Holmes." Holmes winced at the formal tone of her voice. An ally lost. "Men, all types of men, try to take advantage. Even John's intentions did not seem quite so honorable at first. I'm sorry, John, you must see it from my side. Mr. Springer did not truly make advances towards me, he was more fatherly. If I seemed to be defending him, it is because he needs defending. He *was* with me that night, Mr. Holmes, and John, don't look so shocked. We didn't make love like I said at the inquest. I said that because I was so angry that people did not want to believe that a young woman and an older gentleman could actually be innocent of any wrongdoing. Don't you believe me?"

Watson put his arms around Clarissa and pulled her into him. "Of course, I believe you," Watson continued. "Oh, you silly fool, why didn't you tell me there was nothing between you? I would have believed you."

"Would you?" Clarissa snapped back. "I doubt it. I'm sorry, John, but your look carried as much damnation as every other man's in that room. I expect complete faith in me from any man who wishes to be

# CONTEMPLATION

*"...but Delacroix grabbed her..."*

a suitor for my affections. I'm sorry, I'm still disappointed in you." She pulled herself from Watson's embrace and turned to Holmes.

"Is there anything else you wish to know, Mr. Holmes?" Again, the formal air, a little colder.

"No, but I believe there is something you should know." And with that Sherlock Holmes repeated the information he had learned from his interviews with Alf Donnegal and with Mr. Duffey. Clarissa's face turned from crimson to anger during the telling and when Holmes was through, both she and Watson, looking confused, tried to talk at once.

"Holmes, I can't believe it," Watson gasped.

"Oh, Mr. Holmes, I have been such a fool. How could I have been so taken in with the man. Oh, Charles, he, he's a beast. A murdering beast. He wasn't with me that night, Mr. Holmes. Not at all. I wasn't invited to that party and I never saw him that night. Oh, oh." And with that, she commenced to cry. Watson once again embraced her.

"There, there Clarissa, it's alright. I'm here, John is here."

"And so am I," boomed the strong voice from the adjoining booth. And there, much bigger than life, stood Inspector Stephen Delacroix. "It is a terrible thing you have done, Miss. The wrong man could have hanged because of your testimony, but now we must set the record straight. You will have to come along with me. And thank you, Mr. Holmes, the Yard owes you a debt of gratitude. Come along, Miss, I'll need your statement before an arrest can be made."

Clarissa, eyes still glistening, looked up in amazement at the huge figure before her. She looked back at Sherlock and then to John.

"You've tricked me!" she shouted. "Charles didn't do those things. You tricked me!" She turned to walk away, but Delacroix grabbed her and though he tried to be gentle, he had to assert more strength than he thought he needed.

"No, Miss Melinor," Holmes replied. "I told you the truth. Truth hurts when it comes unexpected. It has the razor's edge. But to the innocent, truth is also antiseptic when it cuts, and so it heals quite well. You'll see. Time will heal all."

Watson was still shaken after they had left. Shaken, but relieved.

"Oh, Mr. Holmes, I was also a fool. A fool to believe in Mr. Springer. He has deceived us all. How could I have been so stupid?"

# CONTEMPLATION

"Family trait?" Watson's face turned to hurt at Holmes' remark. "Oh, sorry, dear Watson, what I mean is that even your father was charmed by certain people, especially the ladies, and could never suspect them of wrongdoing. Charles Springer was quite an adversary to say the least. He is indeed a diabolical sort of man. He should be punished and he shall be. Yet, something still disturbs me, Watson. Something still does not quite fit."

"What is it, Holmes?" Watson, once again addressing him in the familiar, asked, "Please don't confuse me anymore. Mr. Springer killed his wife, and don't tell me that's not obvious. He's a menace, a beast, just as Clarissa said after realizing his, his evil doings."

"Yes, a beast. But murderous? And what about the times?"

Holmes stared out into space. "What about the times?"

Watson started to speak, thought better of it, and the two men sat in silence. Later, they would say their goodbyes, with Holmes begging off dinner by saying he was terribly tired, and returning to his room. Watson, still somewhat confused, took an early supper on the Strand, not at Simpson's, but at a small fish and chips shop that was boisterous and too warm for the night air. Watson didn't even notice, he just ate silently and wondered.

# Unwitting Accomplice

*April 25, —The Russell Hotel, London*

Friday morning the weather still held. So unseasonably warm for a London spring. Sherlock Holmes, who rarely slept late, had already been seated in the main dining room when the morning papers arrived. It was just 6:15 a.m.

"Over here, young man. I'll have a paper." Sherlock, his mood somewhat improved over last night's deliberations, cheerfully placed a full shilling in the boy's outstretched palm.

"Thank you Sir, THANK YOU!" the boy remarked when he saw the coin, and off he went to serve his other customers of the day. But, no others would reward him so lavishly for his efforts.

The sounds in the dining room were fairly, muted with only a handful of diners present at this hour. So it was appropriate that the serving staff would gasp as one when the lone gentlemen at the corner table jumped up with a shout, spilling coffee and utensils in every direction.

"Damn, damn, damn!" shouted the detective.

"Please Sir, the other guests..." implored the table captain.

"Damn the other guests," he went on, and with a scowl on his face, he stalked out of the restaurant and towards the lift, stopping at

# UNWITTING ACCOMPLICE

the front desk to bark some orders at the poor desk clerk, who was still on-duty from the night before.

It was within the hour that young Watson appeared in Holmes' suite. He looked a little disheveled and noticeably unshaven and his eyes were as large as they could possibly be at so early an hour.

"Watson, did you read this morning's paper?" Holmes queried.

"No Sir, I have not. Is there something wrong? What is it?" Watson stared incredulously at the old man, as if he thought he might be losing his mind.

"I quote, 'A Mr. Charles Springer of D'Orly House, Maryleborough, had been arrested early last evening for the slaying of his wife, Loreli Springer. Sometime during the evening of his imprisonment, Mr. Springer took his own life. Inspector Delacroix of Scotland Yard refused to release details, but said that circumstances leading to Mr. Springer's arrest were perhaps more sordid than known and the gentleman, unable to face the consequences, took a coward's way out. It has also become known that Mr. Sherlock Holmes, the consulting detective, is residing once more in London and connections, if any, have yet to be revealed.'" Holmes finished with a flourish and looked up at Watson.

"My God, Holmes," Watson stammered, "he, he couldn't...I, I guess justice will be served quicker than usual, this time."

"Oh, I don't know, Watson. I think this premature death may hamper the wheels of justice, not serve her. I told you I had a gnawing doubt about this case." Holmes mused some more and walked to the window.

Finally, Watson spoke, "But, surely we can take this at face value. The man is a murderer, and also some kind of deviant. His treatment of his wife, even before he killed her, is heinous to say the least. When he is confronted with all of this, and knows full well the implications of standing trial, he, he does the only noble thing he can think of. He kills himself."

"Really, Watson? Is it that simple? A man who has not demonstrated one shred of gentlemanly conduct now, all of a sudden, develops into a full-fledged nobleman? I hardly think so, it is out of character for him. Just, though I can't prove it yet, it was out of character for him to kill a wife that was bringing pleasure to him."

# UNWITTING ACCOMPLICE

"Pleasure, Holmes? My God, she was cuckolding him. And with his gamekeeper." Watson looked almost astonished.

"Think again, Watson. A man is not being outdone by a man who is being allowed access to his wife. No, Alf Donnegal did not cuckold Charles Springer. He was used by him. As was his wife. The man was diabolical, and in a sadistic way. But not with murder at heart, no, not murder, just pure unadulterated, misdirected lust. And, as for suicide—yes, I am sure he took his life; but not out of guilt, for he was innocent of murder. Nor out of shame; his degradations did not permit it. No! The real reason Charles Springer did away with himself was the pure and simple fact of being incarcerated. Prison wreaks havoc with a person's psyche. Remember my discussions with Donnegal, and the toll I felt prison was taking on him? Now multiply that ten times to imagine the effect on a man of Springer's intellect and breeding. Combine that with the knowledge that suddenly not one of his friends was on his side: Duffey, you, and of course, Clarissa Melinor, who he somewhat trusted. And last of all, imagine if you can how hopeless he must have felt when the one man who might have been able to untangle this web of deceit, this man, Sherlock Holmes, brings about his current state of affairs. For him, all hope is lost."

Watson did not respond and the two men sat silent for a long time. Holmes wished for a morning fire to bring warmth to his bones. He not only felt old this morning, but also very cold. Watson noticed the old detective's hands trembling and brought a blanket from the bedroom, placing it on Holmes' lap. The old man looked up, and the generation gap that was apparent when looking at them melted.

Finally, Holmes spoke, "Thank you, Watson, I, I do feel a little chilly. When one gets old, the warmth that courses through the body dies a little bit each year as well. It is hard for one to admit that death is clamoring at his door. I have not been very useful to you, have I?" Holmes raised his hand to halt a response and continued, "No, I haven't. You wished to protect Charles Springer and now he is dead, and Miss Melinor, Clarissa, even she feels used by me and apparently blames you for my deductions. Do you still harbor feelings for the woman, Watson?" Holmes turned his head to look at his companion.

"Yes, I suppose so. But not exactly as before. She, Clarissa, I guess, is more knowledgeable of the world than I am. I mean, she has an air of sophistication that I have yet to attain. Oh, damn it, I guess I mean that although our ages are close, she is years older than I. I have a lot of growing up to do, Mr. Holmes, don't I?" The innocence on young John Watson's face brought tears to Sherlock's eyes.

"True, young Watson. And the growth will hurt, just as truth hurts. It is a process of learning, and yes, unlearning. For nothing is constant but change…that…I remember…." But before Holmes could finish, the telephone rang. "Get that, would you Watson? I certainly would appreciate it." Watson went to the other room and answered the phone. Holmes, though his sight still held, had suffered a noticeable decline in his hearing abilities, and had to wait until Watson returned to receive the missive that had arrived.

"Mr. Holmes, you have a visitor. It's D'Angelo, the insurance investigator. I told him to come straight up. Is that alright?"

With a sigh, Holmes replied, "Certainly, Watson. If I am right, we are about to hear some startling news concerning Mr. Thomas Duffey. I began to realize it last night, but let a simple detail slip through my brain. You see, Watson, I had deduced that there was also a large insurance policy on Mr. Duffey, payable to Mr. Springer. Further damning evidence, which I didn't need. I believe Mr. D'Angelo is about to confirm that such a policy also exists on Mr. Springer, payable to Mr. Duffey. Ah, there's the bell…now we shall have our answer. Show him in Watson, and observe how when truth cuts, it sometimes uses a double-edged blade."

"That's right, Mr. Holmes. Payable to Mr. Duffey on the demise of Mr. Charles Springer, regardless of how he dies. Actually the policy is payable to the firm and, since Mr. Duffey is the major stockholder, he would be the one to collect. It is known in the trade as a 'key man' policy. It is meant to protect companies from the loss of their key individuals and the potential loss of revenue that they may be responsible for bringing into the firm." D'Angelo, slick as ever, slid back and forth on the chair he was in as if it were made of ice.

He continued, "It's really a nasty predicament for my company. You see, the policy payable to Mr. Springer on his wife will now, of course, become null and void. You see, you can't collect on insurance for someone you kill…." Watson shot a glance at Holmes, but Holmes ignored him and addressed D'Angelo.

"And if Mr. Springer didn't kill his wife?" Holmes asked.

D'Angelo, visibly shaken, said, "I don't see what you're driving at. But, let's say for the sake of argument that the police find out someone else killed her—like that Donnegal character—then the policy would be payable to Mr. Springer. But seeing as how he's dead, it would revert to his survivor, which would be his company—again, into the hands of Mr. Duffey. That would be pretty incredible, Mr. Holmes. A man collecting on two policies in one felt swoop. £550,000 is not a bad paycheck if I do say so myself."

"I agree, Mr. D'Angelo. Could you tell me when these policies were bought? I mean exact dates, if you don't mind." Holmes leaned back into his chair, trying to appear as nonchalant as possible.

"Well, it's actually against company policy, Mr. Holmes, but if you think it could be important, well, I could use all the help I can get. I don't mind telling you if any of these claims appear false, I get a percentage as a reward for my time. It's customary." D'Angelo shuffled some papers out of his bag. "Oh, here it is. You see, I was suspicious about Loreli Springer's death because of the actuarial tables. The policy was purchased on February 12, this year, and she died on April 12. Exactly two months, and not very smart planning if insurance is your motive. Now, the key man policies. Let's see, ah, here it is, January 19, also this year. You can understand how my firm questions this uncanny need for insurance."

Holmes digested this piece of information and then asked, "Who bought these additional policies, Mr. D'Angelo? Who paid the premiums?"

"Well, I've not dealt with Springer and Duffey before. I'm not a broker, and my job is on the other end. But from what I know of the transactions and of the firm, Mr. Duffey is the managing partner and Mr. Springer is the business partner. If I understand correctly, Mr. Duffey took care of all the paperwork and Mr. Springer was the real business-maker, if you get my drift."

"Then," said Holmes, "I take it Mr. Duffey took care of obtaining any necessary insurance that the business would buy? What about casualty insurance and such?"

"Not really my department. As I said, our salespeople may have tried to sell them everything we've got, but my money would ride on Duffey being the one to make the decision on this sort of purchase." D'Angelo placed his papers back in his bag and beginning to stand, asked, "Is there anything else, Mr. Holmes?"

"Yes, how is it possible for a man, even a partner in a business, to buy insurance on another man's wife?" Holmes' question dangled in the air as if it had a life of its own.

D'Angelo, at first taken back, replied, "Oh, quite easy. In many companies power of attorney can be put in place to expedite legal matters without delay, in case one of the principals is away. That's it, I'm sure of it. Mr. Duffey must have had power of attorney."

D'Angelo left and Holmes turned to the Persian slipper once more. Watson, noticing, remained silent. They sat that way for the better part of an hour. Then, suddenly, Holmes spoke. "Watson, I know how he did it." Holmes' eyes glistened, not with tears, but with inspiration.

Watson was duly entranced, but still questioned, "How, who did what?"

"How Thomas Duffey killed Loreli Springer, while attending a party at his own house, and still managed to steal time as well! Come, Watson, we have new allies: time and truth. Inseparable. And at last, I, Sherlock Holmes, will not turn my back on either of them, but accept them with open arms." And the master detective and his young assistant sped off in search of the truth.

# Time Study

*April 25, —Scotland Yard*

"Mr. Holmes, I certainly appreciate your coming here with your information, but it is purely speculative, is it not?" Inspector Delacroix stopped writing for the moment.

"Yes, unfortunately it would appear so. But let's review the timetable once more." Sherlock stepped to the blackboard, as Watson watched in awe.

"The guests," began Holmes, "arrived at 7 p.m.—quite early for a dinner party, but even that was part of the plan. Duffey meant to disorient his guests as much as possible. And what happened when they arrived? They removed their waistcoats and donned 'hapi' robes and were told they were part of the evening's theme as it were. Interesting, eh, what?"

"Now, Holmes," Watson said, "I was there. What is so disorienting about removing a garment, I don't understand."

"Elementary, my dear Watson," continued Holmes, "elementary. For what else is removed once you take a man's waistcoat away…?" Holmes let the implication hang. It was Delacroix who spoke.

"I'll be damned. The man's fob—his watch, of course. They wouldn't be able to tell time while they were gone." Delacroix's

# TIME STUDY

face showed mild astonishment, then perplexity, "But he couldn't keep them in the dark the whole night. What about the house clocks, the mantel ones or the ones in the hallways?"

"First things first, Inspector. Now, with watches left behind, Duffey bids his guests into a library, where he has them wait, with cordials in hand. Incidentally, the library does not contain any clocks. None at all. He leaves them there momentarily while he makes some simple preparations. For you see, gentlemen, as he guides his guests from room to room, preceding them by one step, he simply turns the clocks one hour ahead. Now think, Watson. Remember you told me your only method of measuring time was based on the room you were in at that moment? And were you not guided step-by-step, room-by-room, through this ceremonial party? The unique dining experience in one room, the 'show' or game in another. But at all times, the guests were moved, herd-like and isolated from outside sources, unable to verify the passage of time being laid out before them."

"But, the servants," said Delacroix, "what about them? Surely they knew what time it was."

"No, they didn't," Holmes decried. "For the same type of charade was being played on them. I must assume they were in full costume, though you didn't mention it, Watson, and, therefore, had no watches on their person as well."

"Why yes, that is correct," Watson gasped. "This is incredible. Then everything occurred one hour earlier than it was indicated?" Watson, his mind reeling with this information, tried sorting it out for himself.

"Precisely," said Holmes. "Now follow if you can the other time schedules. Springer did leave the party at 9:30 and was gone two hours, but it was, in reality, 8:30 to 10:30. And he was with Miss Melinor, I am sure of it. In fact, it was Duffey that suggested that they go to the greenhouse. I imagine he had allowed Springer to bring Clarissa and then, feigning second thoughts, told him to take her away for awhile. Springer did leave her for a few moments and that was when Alf Donnegal saw him. Donnegal said it was just after 10 p.m. But to Springer, it was already 11 p.m. The properties adjoin and the greenhouse sits almost exactly on the dividing line. Donnegal must

# TIME STUDY

have thought the drunken Springer was heading home, but actually he was heading back. When he arrives at the party again, it is 11:30 p.m., 'Duffey time,' shall we say. All of the guests are having nightcaps and probably feeling tired due to the lateness of the hour, when, in reality, it is only 10:30. Duffey and Springer go to the den, where Duffey entices Springer to lie down for awhile and take a nap. Consequently, the amount of spirits he has consumed, possibly at Duffey's urging, allows him to pass out. He lies there for *two* hours, not one, and when he awakes, it is truly 12:30 a.m. He heads home to disaster. During that two hours of restful napping by Mr. Springer, his partner, his friend, Mr. Duffey, goes to Loreli Springer and kills her. Time of death, approximately 11 p.m. To make sure the hour is known, he also stops the clock on the mantel by destroying it. There is no other apparent reason for this to have occurred as there is no evidence of any struggle. He returns back home and goes straight to bed just like his other guests, except for one other thing."

"Yes, yes, Mr. Holmes," Delacroix implored, "what is it? What else does he do?"

"Why, quite simply, he turns back all of the clocks in the house and all of the fobs in the waistcoats in the guest closet. All but one, that is!"

"But some of those guests might have left early, not stayed on. Wouldn't they be suspicious of the time change when they reached their destination?" Delacroix asked.

"No, Inspector," it was young Watson who answered, "Because everybody stayed. Mr. Duffey made certain of that, he would not take no for an answer."

The three men stared at each other as the wonderment of one man's diabolical plot to commit murder, not once, but in reality twice, unfolded.

"Holmes," Delacroix spoke, "you said there was one watch not advanced. Whose watch was that?"

Holmes reached into his pocket and pulled out the ornate gold watch, chain still intact, with a minute piece of clothing attached.

"Before Watson and I came over we stopped at Mr. Duffey's place," Holmes began.

# TIME STUDY

"...he turns back.....all of the fobs...."

"My God, you haven't confronted him already, have you?" Delacroix gasped.

"No, we approached the property from the far side. It was more of a reconnaissance on my part. I really wanted to judge the distances involved between the two properties. We did go into the greenhouse and that is where we found this." Holmes held the watch up once again. "The inscription, 'to Charles, love Loreli' leaves no doubt as to whose watch it is; it is only unfortunate that it was not found sooner. It's main spring has entirely run down and there is no way of knowing if it was advanced or not, but I am sure that it was. Pity it can't tell us more."

"Well, as I said in the beginning," Delacroix said, "I do believe you, though it will still appear somewhat theoretical in nature in a courtroom. How can we convince anyone that this really happened the way you said?"

"I think," replied Holmes, "that a thorough investigation of the household of Mr. Duffey is in order. As you have noted, perhaps he did not fool all of the servants. In fact, on my previous visit there, I noticed that there was a certain lack of care in maintaining such a large home. Perhaps certain servants have recently lost employment and their memory can be refreshed by a fellow of such persuasive powers as yourself."

"Well, I shall certainly take care of it. Thank you, Mr. Holmes. It is incredible how many details a man can go through in order to cheat his fellow man. I'll keep you posted on what my investigation brings to light. Good day, Sir."

Holmes and Watson arrived back at the Russell Hotel in time for afternoon tea. The tea was good, but the scones seemed quite dry and unfulfilling. Neither Holmes nor Watson commented on them as they seemed content to spend this little time together almost silently. Holmes appreciated Watson's awareness of when solitude was in order. His father had the same ability. Finally, Holmes spoke. "Well Watson, what do you think? Will Delacroix bring his hound to lair or well he let him slip through?"

"You know, Holmes, I was thinking the same thing. Now, I know you feel your involvement is at an end. You said on the way back that

## TIME STUDY

it is only the tedious which needs to be done now, and not anything that should require your skills as a consulting detective. But, you may be wrong."

"Oh, ho, Watson, you can't be serious. Listen, at my age, and even when I was younger, the knowledge of knowing who and why and how is quite sufficient. The actual capture and hanging stuff, I leave that to the courts. And, in some cases, even they can't get the job done. At some point I must leave matters alone, don't you think?" Holmes leaned back in his chair, a small smile playing on his lips, and for one quick moment he appeared many, many years younger.

Watson stared for a moment and then asked, "What now, Holmes? Back to the bees? I hope not, I have certainly enjoyed our adventure."

"I suppose so, Watson. The pace is a little too quick for me in London these days. I still wish to live a somewhat longer life. Yes, I shall return on tomorrow's train. Of course, I must pay my bill at this establishment, which I am sure will be my last unsettling matter to be taken care of."

"Mr. Holmes, oh, I'm sorry," Watson said, "your bill is, and has always been the responsibility of Springer and Duffey. I should have told you straight away."

"Really?" Surprised, Holmes said, "Now I must guess which one. Springer, I suppose."

"Wrong, for the first time, Holmes. Mr. Duffey. Remember, I thought Mr. Springer needed help. I mentioned your name to Mr. Duffey and he authorized it. He is the business partner."

Strange, thought Holmes, very strange.

# The Unmasking

*May 14, —Hudson Farm, Surrey*

The valley was completely overcast in clouds. A strong thunderstorm was on its way and the promised deluge would bring welcome relief to many of the local farmers. Sherlock Holmes looked out over the countryside and allowed his thoughts to gather. He looked back down at the telegram in his lap, and picking it up again, reread Watson's words.

"FOX CAUGHT STOP ANOTHER SUICIDE STOP THIS TIME AT HOME STOP DELACROIX UNHAPPY STOP FIRM CLOSING STOP STAYING AT MANCHESTER HOTEL STOP LEAVING SOON FOR EUROPE STOP SAY HELLO TO BEES STOP LOVE STOP YOUR WATSON"

Holmes slowly lowered the telegram and again looked out into space. His eyes, at first somewhat unfocused, began to clear. He jumped up and hurriedly moved back into the cottage.

"Mrs. Hampton! Mrs. Hampton, come quickly!" the old man hollered. Mrs. Hampton peered down from the top of the stairs.

"What do you want, Mr. Holmes? Are you hungry?" she replied.

"No, no woman, I'm not hungry. Get my overnight bag and be quick about it. I must get to London this evening! Oh, call the neighbor's lad—I'll need him to drive me to the station. I must make the

# THE UNMASKING

6:22. Now be off, woman, I'm in a hurry!" And with that, the small cottage moved into fast gear. In thirty-six minutes, Sherlock Holmes, the world's most famous consulting detective, was barreling along on the 6:22 to Victoria Station.

*May 14, —London*

After the hotel staff did its utmost to make Holmes comfortable, he still complained at their lack of speed in answering his needs. He arrived without notice, and although the Russell Hotel prided itself on service, they were never put to the test as much as this one singular guest did that evening. In addition to lodgings and a quick meal, warm, mind you, he also required several messages to be sent. The one to Inspector Delacroix came back with a mixed response. No, the Inspector was not in. Yes, he was due back. No, they did not know when. Yes, they would let him know it was urgent. As for Watson, he was also out on the town, as it were. The Manchester Hotel, not in the best part of London, still managed to sound standoffish in a snobby sort of way. Same sort of message was left. The third message brought better results. Mr. Alfred Garner was not in, but when his manservant, Clark, was informed of who was calling, he promised to get in touch with Mr. Garner and have him ring back promptly. It was this call that Mr. Holmes received in the hotel bar at 9:36 p.m.

"Mr. Holmes! Is that really you?" inquired Alfred Garner.

"Yes, Alfred. It is I. Do you require proof of my existence? I think if I hum a certain tune whose musical notes can be counted upon to open a particular safe, you would know it is me." Sherlock smiled into the mouthpiece at his little joke.

"Oh, Sherlock, this is fantastic. You must come and visit with me. You know there are still a great deal of people who owe you more than a customary 'thank you.' You should allow them to repay their debt."

"In a way, that's what this call is about. Alfred, it is not money that I am after, it is knowledge. And I think this knowledge should be close at hand to a fellow like yourself." Alfred Garner enjoyed being

## THE UNMASKING

referred to as a fellow, for in fact, he was at least 94 years of age and still quite active in his firm.

"Well, I'll see what I can do. Now what kind of information do you require?" The two old friends went over the details with the only stumbleblock being the lateness of the hour, but Garner said he would do his very best. And he did.

The fourth thing the hotel did for him really proved their mettle. The night manager, Carruthers, was not the same one they had previously, but was still quite bright. He approached the detective. "Mr. Holmes, you are in luck. One of our guests, Bill Danvers, is an American and he is with our operator now. It seems he is getting your message across quite clearly and, from the sound of it, I believe they are going to comply." He looked extremely pleased with himself.

"Excellent, Carruthers. I will make a note to contact your superiors and let them know what a remarkable job you are performing, not only for me, but in general as well." This final comment had Carruthers absolutely beaming. Dismissing the man, Holmes looked up to see Watson hurrying in the door.

"Watson! Watson, over here, over here, lad," Holmes boomed out. Several guests looked up from their readings to see this strange pair embrace in the center of the lobby.

"Holmes, I don't understand? What brings you to London?" Watson blurted out quickly. "I sent you a telegram. There is nothing more to be done. You didn't need to come see me off, I shall return in a fortnight and I surely am planning to come visit you when I get back."

"Watson, old friend," the sleuth shot back, "there is much to be done. For you see, I was wrong. Remember last time we were together? You said I was wrong. You were right. I was wrong. But tonight, we shall set the record straight. You and I. Oh, Watson, my juices are flowing, the old synapses are at work and everything is splendid. I bungled this from the start because I did not follow my own advice. But now everything is going to be alright, you'll see."

Watson stared at the man he thought he knew. But now a kernel of doubt crept in. Is it possible the man had turned senile? Will he never know rest until everybody is dead who was involved in this case? This is madness. The time study that revealed how Duffey was the true killer was an incredible piece of deduction and yet that should have finished it. Why wouldn't he let go? Was it my fault for bringing him out of retirement? Their eyes met, the old man's shining with inspiration, the young man's with doubt, and slowly each one's gaze turned away.

"You don't believe me, Watson, is that it? You think I'm just a cantankerous old fool?" Sherlock moved away.

"No, no, it's not that, it's just…well, think about it yourself. It's over, isn't it?" Watson implored Holmes.

"No!" said Holmes defiantly. "It is not over. And you will bear witness to that fact. Along with Delacroix, for if my eyes don't deceive me, that is his shape creating the shadows on the far wall." And sure enough, the Inspector came into the lobby and, after recognition, moved toward the two waiting men.

"Well, Mr. Holmes, I came as you asked, but for the life of me, I don't know why," Delacroix said. Watson remained silent.

"Inspector, when I used the term diabolical before, you automatically assumed that I was talking about the extreme measures that Thomas Duffey took in manipulating the people who surrounded him. But now I am going to rephrase that term and call this crime much more than diabolical. No, this reaches a level that only Moriarity, that blackest of blackguards, that demon from Hell, could appreciate."

Watson, fearing for Holmes' sanity, feared even more for it at the mention of the name Moriarity. He recalled his father telling him that Holmes had more than a preoccupation with the man's doings. Also, he felt that maybe he placed too many crimes or deeds at his doorstep to ever have the man be a reality. Could Holmes now be reinventing Moriarity for this crime as well?

"Go on, Holmes, what are you leading up to?" Delacroix implored.

"Manipulation is, and will always be, the most incredulous crime, and its implementation and success can only be achieved by the most infamous and ingenuous of minds. Mr. Duffey was no such genius. Oh, he was wily. And his methodology surely would have almost gone undetected if I had not intervened." Delacroix fairly winced at

## THE UNMASKING

the words. Holmes went on, "But, even he was being manipulated by an even greater master puppeteer."

"And who was that, Holmes?" Watson interrupted. "Professor Moriarity? No. Then perhaps Colonel Moran? I thought they were both dead. If so, then who is this evil force that we are to reckon with tonight?"

"It is doubtful that our fates will bring an encounter this evening, and even if it were so, I wish to be more prepared. Inspector, it is quite important that I get to see firsthand the scene where Mr. Thomas Duffey allegedly took his own life. Shall we go?"

"Mr. Holmes," Delacroix replied, "I also was disappointed that the events turned so black. But clearly, the man was distressed by our pursuit, even young Watson saw this was the case. In addition, he left a clearly worded note that confessed all. What else would you have me do?"

"Nothing else, Inspector. It must have appeared quite obvious to you, and to anyone else who perchance reviewed the facts. But the obvious is not always to be taken at face value. Especially when it concerns the devil that we are up against." Again, Watson inwardly groaned, fearful once more that Holmes was alluding to a nameless, faceless being that would haunt him evermore.

Holmes continued, "Now let us make haste, for if I am right, then time—which has always been calculated to the nth degree by our adversary—must at all costs be returned to the rightful side. The truthful side. Come gentlemen, the game is afoot." And with that, the three went out into the warm London evening, guided by genius or blind faith, not knowing which.

They spent several hours at Duffey's home. Sherlock seemed bent on scrutinizing every inch of the den where Duffey's body had been found. The placement of the note. The position of the gun after the fatal shot. Every detail was indelibly being registered into that incredible brain. At long last, he announced he was finished, but for one detail.

"Inspector," said Holmes, "The note, I must see the note. Is it still here or is it at the Yard?"

"Why, at the Yard, of course. Do we have to go over there now? It's getting late. I really hate to maneuver people into producing

# THE UNMASKING

evidence files at such an hour." Delacroix made sounds as if it would be a real imposition, but Holmes was insistent and off they went.

As the case had been closed and the date of the incident so recent, finding the file proved to be no great hardship for the night clerk. Within thirty-five minutes after leaving Duffey's residence, Holmes was reviewing the original note that was left behind. His examination seemed cursory at best, and within minutes he placed it back into the file and without any explanation, headed for the door.

"Well, Holmes," Watson implored. "Did you find out what you wanted?" A slight trace of scorn was in his voice. Doubt still lingered.

Holmes stopped as if struck, turned to Watson and said, "Obviously, Watson. It is exactly as I thought. This mission tonight was simply a reaffirmation of the facts. Nothing more. If there was a doubt to be had, it was erased by a transatlantic phone call earlier this evening. This time I have let no stone be unturned. You shall see." And again the great sleuth left with the other two, mouths agape, following obediently in his tracks.

They returned to the Russell Hotel where Holmes, more reticent than ever, refused to discuss the case. He announced there was one further foray he would have to make in the morning and that he would do alone. He also insisted that they should meet tomorrow night, promptly at 7 p.m. The Russell Hotel had arranged a meeting room for Holmes and his guests and, at that time, all would be explained. Watson and Delacroix watched Holmes mount the lobby stairs with puzzlement covering their faces.

*May 15, —The Russell Hotel, London*

The room was quite spacious, could easily have held fifty or more, but at the present, it held only three.

"I don't mind telling you, Mr. Holmes," Delacroix began. "I've been on pins and needles all day waiting for this. I hope you know what you're doing."

"Ha, ha, ha," laughed Holmes. "Oh, Inspector, ye of little faith. And after all we have been through. Well, I guess it is understandable

# THE UNMASKING

that you are a mite confused. I daresay, I myself have been somewhat amiss in this case, what else could you expect of yourself? But please be patient, the confusion shall come to an end. Ah, Watson, pour us some sherry, would you, lad? My throat becomes quite parched when the synapses of my elaborate brain are required to manipulate so loathsome and slow a thing as one's own tongue."

Before Watson could finish pouring there was a loud knock upon the door.

"Enter. Please," said Holmes in a much stronger and authoritative voice. Into the room came two tall thug-like characters, and in between them, sliding and shaking, was Roman D'Angelo.

"Ah, good evening Mr. D'Angelo, welcome, welcome." Holmes offered, "Please take a seat." Then, addressing the other two men, "Gentlemen, that will be all, you may take up your positions."

"WHAT THE," began Delacroix, "what in blazes is going on here Holmes, who were those men?"

"Friends, Inspector," replied Holmes. "Well, more to the point, friends of some friends. They owed me a favor and did me the service of bringing one of my principals here. Mr. D'Angelo, I have taken the liberty of having a bar set up, would you care for a cordial?" D'Angelo sneered at Holmes, but sullenly went to the bar. Shortly he returned with an aperitif and still no words came from his lips.

Watson, once in doubt, now seemed perplexed. "I say, Holmes, what does D'Angelo have to do with Springer and Duffey, other than bringing all of this to light?"

"That's exactly it, Watson. Yes, he was the one to start the ball rolling, wasn't he? You'll see in a moment. We have another guest who should be arriving shortly." The four men exchanged glances and it seemed as if only two knew full well what was going on. And one of them was not really prepared to talk. After a few minutes of silence, another entrance, this time without a knock preceding it.

The door opened and, if you strained, you could make out the shape of one of the big men who had brought D'Angelo into the room. The new arrival was petite. And pretty. And dressed exceeding well.

She stared at the gathering and smirked at Holmes. She stalked up to him. "You are a crazy old man, do you know that?" she shrieked.

# THE UNMASKING

"Good evening, Miss Melinor. When I told you that you could address me in any fashion that you felt comfortable with, I didn't mean 'crazy old man', but be that as it may, may I offer you a cordial?" Sherlock reached for a new glass.

Clarissa looked at the other attendees and latched onto Delacroix first. "Inspector, this man has had me kidnapped. Do you understand, I have been brought here against my will. Now do something about him. Arrest him!" She stamped her foot as she spoke.

Holmes looked back at her and before Delacroix could reply, interrupted, "Oh, not having a cordial? That's unfortunate. I truly wish this gathering could be more civil. Truth enjoys civility. You can understand that, can't you Clarissa? Now take your seat." Holmes' voice changed to one of authority.

"Now see here, Holmes." It was Delacroix who spoke. "If you really brought these people here against their own will, well, it's not just highly irregular, you could be jeopardizing yourself."

"I know exactly what you mean, Inspector," Holmes interrupted. "But understand that my life, yes and yours too, has been manipulated against our own free wills, and the few hours of time I rob from these two, well…consider it a form of payback, and a small one at that."

Before anyone could speak further, the door opened again. This time it was the night manager, Carruthers.

"Ah, here you are Mr. Holmes. First, here's the package you were expecting, and Mr. Danvers has your information for you as well, it's in this envelope." Holmes thanked him and he handed over the material with a perfunctory nod. Then, scanning the people in the room, he decided it was not a very happy gathering and made his exit.

"Now, let me see what we shall see." And Holmes sat down to read. Several minutes passed without anyone saying anything, save for the sounds Holmes made, or rather grunted, as he passed over the documents. Slowly he got up and moved to the head of the table.

"It is just as I thought. Oh, Clarissa, your father would have been so proud. Shall I tell them? Or, would you rather?"

# THE UNMASKING

*Article in the Morning Telegraph—June 9*

"Roman D'Angelo and Clarissa Melinor are to be hanged on June 23. The defense counsel, a Mr. Hayden, had sought clemency for the woman, but the star witness for the prosecution, Mr. Sherlock Holmes, made clear her involvement and clemency was declined."

*June 14, —The Russell Hotel, London*

Inspector Delacroix and John Watson were sipping their cordials while the master sleuth, stroking his meerschaum, enthralled them with how he had first tumbled to the plot that was sweeping through the dailies all over England, and also America.

"Elementary, my dear Watson, and my dear Inspector. You see, it was you, Watson, who gave me the real clue. If you recall, after the inquest you said it appeared that Clarissa seemed to be at the center of everything, and, of course, she was. And what a magnificent plot. Of course, after I received verification of her previous employment and also verification of D'Angelo's non-employment, it all fit. She is an incredible woman. Working at the law firm of Winston and Martone, she was privy to the financial records of many a successful firm. And also to the problems concerning these establishments. When she learned that Springer and Duffey, a partnership, was planning to go limited, that's when she saw her chance. She knew that old Mr. Martone was going to suggest holding three percent of the stock in escrow, as a method of achieving parity between the two diverse partners. Using her feminine wiles, and I must admit, brilliantly, she seduced the partner, Duffey, and became his mistress secretly. She then planted the idea with Duffey to name her as the so-called non-voting silent partner. At first this was rejected by Springer, but then he too fell under her charms. Yes, Watson, you were so right. 'Shared equally by the partners' is how you phrased it. Quite so, quite so. The only potential problem Clarissa could envision at this time was an objection by Mr. Martone, her former boss. But, even here she was forceful and magnificent. My meeting with him

## THE UNMASKING

revealed exactly what I had deduced. With veiled threats, she intimated she would have Springer and Duffey take their business elsewhere. Martone kept his objections to himself."

Holmes took to pacing the floor while warming to the subject. After a short pause he continued, "The second 'suicide' was really her undoing. I had played along with everything she had fed me up until that moment. For you see, as Mr. D'Angelo would have quoted: the actuarial tables would be hard-pressed to accept that coincidence. And neither did I. But, what a plan!"

"But, Holmes, she could not have known that Springer would kill himself. How did that fit in with her 'master plan' as you call it?" Watson remarked.

"Of course Springer's suicide sped up Clarissa's plans. It was really planned that the Crown would have done the job. But then she had D'Angelo, who we all now know, never worked for any insurance company, but was indeed the real paramour of Clarissa Melinor. He came to me and made sure that it was known that Duffey was the prime beneficiary of all these proceedings and I, unwittingly, set the wheels in motion to get him."

"Holmes, don't feel sorry for Duffey," Delacroix responded. "He was as weak to the flesh as his partner, and, though he may not have dealt the deadly blow, he was just as guilty of killing Loreli Springer, and indirectly, Charles Springer."

"True enough," said Holmes. "but it saddens me to see a man turned inside out over one petite, attractive woman. Perhaps he really did not know that Clarissa planned murder that night when they played their charade with time. Perhaps he thought she was just teasing him. We will never know. What I am certain of, though, is afterwards. After the murder was revealed, Thomas Duffey was too far enmeshed to let go. Too much an accomplice and worse, too much in love. A deadly web she had woven over this man. And to think, he didn't realize that she was not done yet. That when her arms embraced him next, she planned his demise."

"And that's where I came in" quipped Delacroix. "I hounded the man with the evidence we had. The serving girl who knew the trick that had been played with the clock, the insurance money as a motive.

# THE UNMASKING

And even the footprints he had left coming from his den to cross over to D'Orly House. Of course, they never reached there, but we used it to pressure him. How did those prints get there, Mr. Holmes?"

"Clarissa, of course. She simply wore his shoes. Not very incriminating, though. It was obvious the impressions were made by a much-lighter person. Not as obvious a mistake, as when she took Springer's watch in the greenhouse so he would not be able to reorient himself. She tore his waistcoat and the piece of cloth on the chain matched easily enough. I imagine she really did make love to him while there. Not as an act of love, but to delay him. Ah, the machinations that this woman was capable of." Holmes finally sat down in his chair.

"I really feel badly, Mr. Holmes," Delacroix said. "I, I know I was derelict in my duty when I failed to notice the color of ink that was supposedly used by Duffey when he committed so-called suicide. It was a terrible oversight on my part."

"Not really, Inspector," replied Holmes. "You were not privy to the fact, as I was, that Mr. Duffey was meticulous in his surroundings and that he took care of his own files, and more importantly, his own desk paraphernalia. Watson told me that, didn't you?"

"That's right. But I never saw the note, for if I had, I too would have noticed the wrong color ink. Even more important was your observation that Mr. Duffey's style of writing is quite unique. That note was not like anything of his I have ever read."

"Yes, my lad." Holmes smiled. "I'm sure you would have noticed. Inspector, are you sure you have no openings at present for an able-bodied assistant. My Watson would surely be an asset to the calling, say what?" And with that, all three men laughed long and loudly.

It was Watson who brought them soberly back. "She would have had it all, wouldn't she, Holmes? All of it?"

"Yes, Watson, and a tidy sum it would have been." Holmes gestured wildly with his hands, "One million pounds in insurance money, that is £500,000 per man, plus the bank holdings of the company, which under Clarissa was liquidated immediately. That amount was in excess of £850,000. Gentlemen, a return on investment, as the late Mr. Duffey would have said, of £1,850,000." Both Watson and Delacroix let a long, low whistle escape.

# THE UNMASKING

"Of course, the £50,000 for Loreli Springer's death was pure fabrication. Just the seed 'motive' to get the game going. A more complex and diabolical plot is hard for me to remember." Holmes started to muse, "but, if old Watson was here, I am sure he could…oh well."

*June 15, —The Russell Hotel, London*

"Well, Watson, what time is your train?" queried Holmes.

"Not for another hour. Are you sure you won't come with me, Holmes?" Watson implored. "I plan to spend some time in Belgium first. I understand there is a man who is making quite a stir as a consulting detective, like yourself."

"Really!" said Holmes. "Well, I am sure he is a much younger man. It takes youth to move freely about and to be able to act quickly when times warrant."

"No Sir, he is not a young man. And as far as youth is concerned, I can be your active partner, just like my dad was. He told me of the many times you sent him into danger, pistol in hand, while you, in the relative safety of 221B, calmly deduced things through."

"Ah, your father told you that, did he? Hmmm. Well, Watson, then it was so, your father was just that kind of man. Dedicated and trustworthy, I owed my life to him on more than one occasion."

"Yes," said Watson, "he told me that also."

"Hmmm, he told you quite a bit, didn't he? You'll have to tell me all about his stories when you get back. Be sure to come up to Hudson Farm as soon as you do, understand?"

"Of course, Mr. Holmes. Uh, Holmes, in case you need the information, I will be staying at the Blackbird Cafe Hotel in Brussels. They say it is quite an intriguing place. Well, I must be off. Do take care, and give my regards to your bees and to Mrs. Hampton." And with a last embrace, he was off.

# The Game is Afoot

*Later that same day—The Russell Hotel, London*

"Goodbye, Mr. Holmes. It has been a pleasure," Carruthers said. The bellhops gathered up the small satchel, really just an overnight case, and placed it into the hansom cab.

"Take Mr. Holmes to Victoria Station, cabby, the 7:12 for Surrey, and drive carefully," Carruthers intoned to the driver.

The horses clopped up the street when suddenly the passenger within shouted up, "Driver, what time is the next train for Brussels?"

"Why, that would be the 6:45 from Kensington Station," the driver shot back.

"Well, then, move on driver, we have no time to lose. There's an extra guinea in it if we make it in time."

"Yes Sir, governor. We'll make it." And with that, there was a cracking of the whip and a high-pitched whinny as the horse pulled 'round, creating a sight to behold: that of a hansom cab with a fiery steed with eyes raised to the back of its sockets, racing down Holborn Street for the Kensington Station. And its passenger, almost lost in the carriage, save for the shadow effect that only a flowing cape and a deer stalker cap can make.

## THE DEVIL TO PAY

# Chinese Box Mysteries
## SHERLOCK HOLMES

# The Devil To Pay

### Editor's Comments

This continues the adventures that were found in the Chinese Box.

Again there are no dates on the notes and I have made the reconstruction based on references either to the seasons or the weather.

As in "Time Study," dramatic license has been applied in an effort to assist the reader in following the action.

# Crystal Clear

*June 14th, Brussels, Belgium*
*Prefect dé Police Headquarters*

*I*nspector Monsieur Galen Maigret examined the remnants of the letter once more. It was obvious that the correspondence had been placed in the fireplace for the purpose of destroying it, and the perpetrator had almost succeeded. The remaining portion he once more held to the light, to see if the characters would become clearer. It was of no use. A few sentences, incomplete, was all that could be ascertained.

"...the past has become your future. Do not re.." he said out loud.

Again, he read, "distance is no measure for my reach, consider the deed..." and from the last fragment, "ay the tithe, or else!"

No, he thought, this is not enough, not nearly enough.

When he had been called in it was considered more than a clear-cut case of pilferage. A dozen cases of crystal goblets had been stolen from La Fleur dé Lis shippers. Their manifests had shown they had indeed arrived in Brussels from London, and yet the custom's house could not locate them the following morning. They were registered in Sir Gregory Almstead's name and were slated to be delivered to an auction house in Brugge. Valuable? Yes, extremely so. It appears also that they were not insured. An oversight which would cost Sir Gregory Almstead dearly. He, and other members of his family, were quite often mentioned in the society notices when they entertained their important business associates. Now, the Belgium government wished to ensure that no stone was unturned in assisting this most honored guest, and therefore M. Maigret was assigned. He was considered the best.

The inspection of the warehouse had revealed nothing. Immediately Maigret thought, "someone on the inside, someone with knowledge and, yes, keys obviously."

But the suspects proved elusive. Everyone connected at the warehouse was of sterling character, at least at first glance. This had led him to Sir Almstead's villa in Leige. The first interviews with the servants had shed no light on the problem at hand but did give some insight to the household and its inherent problems. It seems that Raymond Almstead, Sir Almstead's younger brother, was something of a black sheep in the family. Raymond had a reputation as a gambler and also a womanizer. He was not in Brussels at the moment, but there had been a terrible row over his actions in London, as it became known to Sir Gregory through other unknown channels. None of the servants knew where this information came from but it had become obvious to them that there was indeed bad blood between the two. The only other factor to come into play was the letter. The recollection of the butler, Geroux, was that it had been postmarked from France, that he was sure. No, he did not watch his master read the correspondence, nor saw if he had in fact placed it into the fireplace. That it had survived in its present state was only a matter of luck; it had been quite warm lately, and with nobody tending the fire, it had probably been allowed to go out on its own. The remnant, as it was, was salvaged by M. Maigret. He was, after all, considered Belgium's best, and he was going to turn every stone he could find. He was especially alert since Sir Almstead had denied him an immediate interview, with the absurd statement that the loss was his and it was an imposition to discuss the matter at this time. His superiors bade him to allow this dereliction and to bide his time the best he could.

## CRYSTAL CLEAR

Doing the best he could, and not trampling on important feet at the same time, was not the methodology that M. Maigret would be happy to employ, but he tried his best. As his inquiries led him to Raymond Almstead, who indeed could have a motive and, more importantly in this case, access to the necessary keys, he sent a telegram to the British authorities to ascertain his whereabouts and in particular, his movements in the last several days. Imagine his surprise when he found out by return telegram that Mr. Raymond Almstead, brother of Sir Gregory Almstead, had been shot dead in a gambling den in Limehouse four weeks ago.

# A FRIEND AT HAND

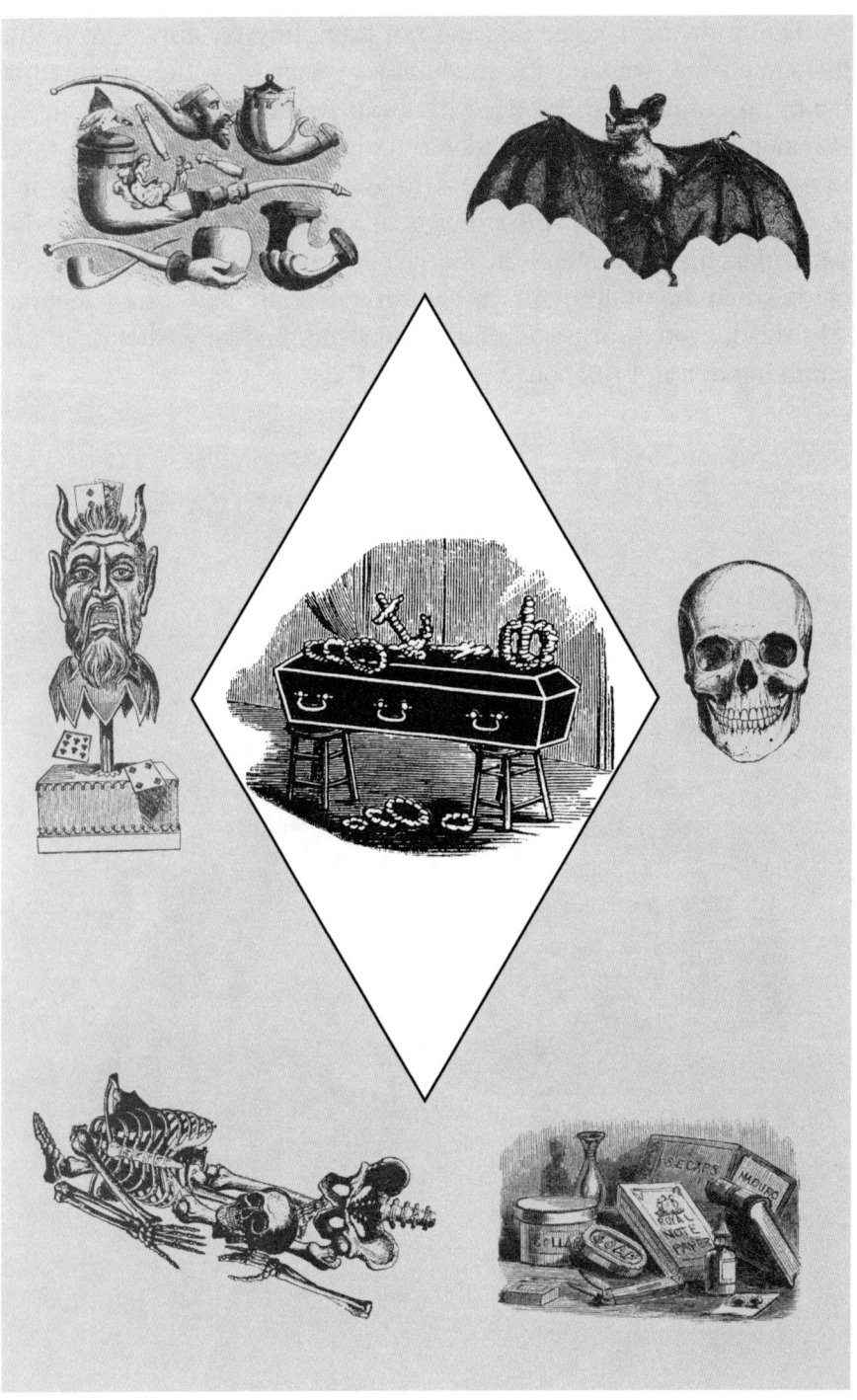

# A Friend at Hand

*June 17th, Brussels, Belgium, Blackbird Café Hotel*

"Monsieur Watson, you have a visitor in the bar, please go to him at once. He wished entrée to your rooms but I could not allow it," said the desk clerk, quite flustered, as he continued on.

"We had no idea when you were to return, and we told him of this fact, but he insisted that he was your guest. As you had made no mention we could not make this accommodation. I sincerely hope we have not erred as he has become quite mad" At this, the clerk rolled his eyes heavenward and turned on his heel and moved quickly back to his position behind the counter.

Watson, his thoughts racing, also spun around and headed in the opposite direction, towards the hotel bar. His first thoughts were of his interview this afternoon with Monsieur Dalmont and how badly it had gone. Perhaps he had a change of heart and an opening was possible after all.

As his eyes grew accustomed to the darkened interior he searched the few faces assembled and could find no physiology to match this afternoon's adversary. Only one face, deep in shadows, was not completely visible, and this individual was entirely too tall, and that nose, aquiline and...it couldn't be...no...but it was....

# A FRIEND AT HAND

"Holmes! It is you, isn't it? I can't believe my eyes. I, I, I...," Watson stumbled on.

"Oh, tut, Watson, of course it's me. Do you think you can galvanize me into action in London, and then let me disintegrate back into a catatonic state of immobility so quickly? It's unfair, man. Entirely impossible. You should have let sleeping dogs lie. My synapses have had their appetite reawakened and now they will not let me rest until they have been fed again. Though my physical prowess may be impaired, my brain is not. You, Watson must be my active part, my legs, my, my, oh...I'm tired, I must rest." And with that, the great man slumped back into the booth where his small overnight bag still rested.

"Holmes....Sir...have you not rested since I left London? Why, I've been here two days...and you...you're still wearing the clothes I last saw you in at the Russell Hotel..I...I,...where are you staying?" Watson stammered.

"Staying? Ahh..I thought with you, but that damn impertinent clerk, but never mind all that Watson, I am here. Help me to your rooms and I shall rest and, and, well, we shall see, we shall see," his voice trailed on.

Watson placed his arms tenderly around the old man's torso and gently guided him towards the small service elevator. His prior dour thoughts, completely replaced now, were inconsequential as he assisted the old man to his rooms.

*Later that evening....*

"It's so good to see your appetite has returned," Watson commented.

"Returned? Hmm, can anyone not have a taste for delicious Belgian delicacies such as this filet dé sole? Ahh, Continental cooking. You know, when your father and I travelled, his tastes were always somewhat academic and predictable, but I have always loved the nuances of gaelic touches. I once did a study on spices and their effects on the palate but it became too complex even for me to fully explain to a less informed public."

## A FRIEND AT HAND

It was amusing to watch the great detective's eyes as they obviously peered into a distant past and recaptured moments that the young John S. Watson could only imagine from his father's pastiches.

"And Watson, it is settled. The bank has finally transferred the necessary funds—so foolish of me to have left without making the necessary provisions—but alas, I was so used to having Mycroft, bless his soul, handle those bothersome details. Now, as I was saying, it is definitely in your best interests, as you are not presently engaged, and mine as well, to accompany me in my travels on the Continent. Though my arrangements with your father were never of the monetary type—after all he had his military retirement—with you, this is not the case. It is only fair that you receive some stipend for your endeavors on my behalf. Is that all clear?"

He leaned back and peered at Watson, and his eyes still had a sleepy look to them, though Watson knew this was not the case. The time they had spent back in London proved to him that Sherlock Holmes, though up in age, still noticed details with a remarkable clarity and perceptiveness that belied his physical characteristics.

"Mr. Holmes, I would be honored to act in whatever capacity you deem necessary to aid you in travelling the Continent. Do you have a particular itinerary in mind? Are there friends you wish to re-visit? And, well, when do we start?"

The boyish exuberance that Watson extolled was not lost on Sherlock Holmes. He knew that the boy would follow him to the ends of the earth, as he quite rightly surmised that the loyalty qualities that were inherent in John H. Watson, M.D., were also quite abundant in John S. Watson, his heir and son.

"Where we begin, Watson, will be determined by the package I have sent for from Mrs. Huds..uh, Mrs. Hampton. During my retirement there have been obviously quite a few missives from previous and recommended clients for my services. I was not receptive at the time to take any action on these particular problems yet, I still maintained a catalog of the most intriguing ones for later consumption. I guess, oh, how I hate that word, it's as if I had a premonition that something of this sort would come to pass. And now it has. Perhaps this compendium will prove beneficent and bring me the mental action that I now whole-heartedly crave." Holmes stood up at the conclusion of this statement and started pacing the floor of the small room that constituted Watson's sitting area. He moved like a caged animal, though no bars were in sight, it was still obvious he felt constrained. He did not speak for quite a while and Watson understood, as his father before him did, that this was not a slight towards him, but just the great man's way to compose his further thoughts. Finally he sat down again.

"I do recall one letter. It was probably over a year ago, nay, almost two. It comes to mind because of the import of the sender. The Duke...the Grand Duke of Luxembourg. The letter I can recall because of the distinct markings, the crest...but the contents, not a bit. As I said, my mind was not attuned to the undertakings that these correspondences might entail and so they passed through my hands as if I was just a post-master or, perhaps worst, a messenger. I'm sorry Watson," he intoned apologetically, "you'll just have to wait."

*June 18th, morning*

The package arrived the next morning. The two companions were seated at their breakfast table in the hotel dining room when the bellman called out, "Package for Monsieur Holmes, package for Monsieur Holmes."

Watson retrieved the package, tipping the bellman as he did, and returned to his seat.

"Well, Watson, I am as curious as you, but first, we must finish this delicious breakfast. Continental food, incredible, is it not?" And a merry twinkle came to the eye of the detective as he took another spoonful of omelette de jour.

Later, after the removal of the breakfast dishes, they studied the four piles of documents Holmes had assembled. The ledger that he had spoken of lay opened at the center of the table, and Holmes was deep in thought as he went over the copious notes he had made of each correspondence.

## A FRIEND AT HAND

"Watson, this first stack which I have obviously marked with the capital letter 'O', I have judged obvious or inconsequential to a man of my talents. I would appreciate it if you would send a short note as regards my involvement in superior cases, nay, better word that less condescending...you know what to say Watson, I'll leave it to you." Holmes didn't even look up as he moved his finger quickly down the list. Watson, in glancing at the letters, noticed that the dates were quite old and it was likely no written replies would be expected by the originators, but he held his counsel.

"Now, this next grouping, Watson, does hold some interest, but as you were so obviously intent on reading their dates you know they are quite old." At this, Holmes rose from the table and moved as if to leave the restaurant, but then suddenly turned and said, " I am afraid any potential clues or observations in these matters no longer exist. Scotland Yard has surely done its level best to muddy the waters. No, these won't do at all." He once more gained his chair and, reflecting further, added, "Of course, all of these have one further unique trait...that is, they have been reported solved by the authorities and therefore...well, it might be quite interesting to try to follow the conclusions reached by these august bodies....but no, I am afraid it would prove too time-consuming." Sherlock again paused, and once more his eyes raised up to face Watson's.

"Watson, I believe it will be necessary to send a reply to each of these. And...try to phrase our response so that if there is any doubt on the part of the recipient's mind as to the foregone conclusions, that they must resubmit their entreaties to me. I know this seems a waste of precious time, Watson, but if one of these cases, just one, has resulted in wrongful imprisonment, well, it is indeed a travesty of justice and I will hold myself personally to blame." The old man once more looked down at his ledger as a certain mistiness filled his eyes. His long fingers traced his notes belonging to the stack he had labeled with the letter "I" for inconclusive.

Watson used this moment to let his own eyes wander to the other two stacks. The third group was marked like the first two with a capital letter, the letter "M," which he now deciphered from looking at Holmes' ledger as 'mysterious.' The other, he quickly ascertained,

## A FRIEND AT HAND

was obviously from personages of some import. This was apparent due to the quality of stationary and the various seals displayed either at the top or on their envelopes. It disturbed him that he could not read the dates, nor any other parts of these letters, as Holmes had judiciously placed his napkin to obstruct his view. After wrapping the second stack carefully so as not to commingle with the first, Watson waited patiently for the great detective to continue his analysis.

"And these," Holmes said, a small, sly smile crossing his face, "these are to be our driving force for the next fortnight, I suspect. When you complete your correspondence on my behalf, Watson, I shall detail each and every one of these problems for your edification. That is, of course, the ones from my "M" stack. The others, well, they were intended for my eyes only...even your father was not to be allowed access...but....we shall see.....we shall see."

"Now, I have some minor errands to do myself," he concluded. Watson rose as if to join him.

"No, no Watson, I feel fine, I will require no more assistance this morning, nor this afternoon. I have taken the liberty of changing our quarters, the bellman has probably moved our things already. Let us meet in my..our rooms at 6 p.m., number 12, and we can make definitive plans as to our course of action. I assume that you will be finished with your assignment by then? Yes? Good. Then I am off." And with that the detective sailed out of the restaurant's swinging doors heading straight for the street, one hand raised as if waving goodbye without looking back.

# Case Histories

*First analysis....*

"These cases, Watson, have some redeeming value. All twelve of them display that one ingredient that makes them so precious to me: a crime yet unsolved. Yes, I checked today. That is one of the errands I told you about. Though all of these cases took place in London and, some as long as two years ago, a simple telegram to my friend Inspector Delacroix at Scotland Yard confirmed my ledger notations. Now, let us review my notes and the original missives which started these investigations." Sherlock stopped his pacing and sat down next to Watson on the small settee, facing a commodious table which he had ordered brought up to place the assorted papers upon.

"Case Number One," Holmes continued, "the oldest, by far, seems quite straightforward. A simple break-in at the home of Mr. George Calstrom, a financier with the firm of Calstrom & Mudges. He wrote me to indicate that he had received a blackmail attempt several months earlier and had scoffed at the man. This attempt came in the form of a somewhat dubious letter detailing some of his most confidential business dealings. His first suspicion was it came from someone who had suffered a loss due to this endeavor and was now trying to recoup through a more dastardly scenario. He expressed sorrow for the man's losses in his reply, which, by the way, Watson, was to an address in Paris. He also intimated that as his conscience was clear he would in no way make any reparations or payments no matter what the consequences. Then, what followed was the robbery, which as you have read in his second message to me, he places at the doorstep of this blackmailer. The items taken were not only of considerable monetary value but also of a personal nature, in the form of private correspondence, which further heightened the fears of Mr. Calstrom."

"So, Watson, what do you think?," Sherlock leaned back, turning his head in the direction of Watson, "Is this just a case of personal vendetta, as the Italians are wont to say?"

"I did read the last letter from Mr. Calstrom," Watson remarked. "He clearly states that the problem has resolved itself and he requests that you dismiss his prior communications. My immediate guess is the blackmailer's entreaties have succeeded and..."

"No, Watson, you're wrong." Holmes interrupted. "That would be the assumption to make, based on the facts as you currently know them, but I have investigated further. First, the robbery was reported as stated in the letter and has yet to be solved by Scotland Yard, except for one detail. A follow-up police investigation indicated that the so-called personal files were kept in a locked strong-box which was purloined along with the rest of the valuables. This box was found several days later in a deserted warehouse not far from Mr. Calstrom's townhouse. Though the lock was smashed and the contents strewn about, it was obvious that nothing else was taken. The papers, of which there were many, filled the box to capacity. The police felt that nothing had been kept by the thief or thieves and they, in their disappointment, just dumped the contents as they were found."

"Second, two days prior to my receiving his last note, the police were once again summoned to Mr. Calstrom's presence. This time it was to his office. Apparently, Mr. Mudges had committed suicide. He was found hanging from their upstairs cupola. A note left by the deceased was described as the ravings of a deranged mind. It seems it contained many quotations from the Bible, some even in Latin, all predicated on the same theme: begging forgiveness. This may seem typical, Watson, when a man faces death, but it caused quite a stir

# CASE HISTORIES

among Mr. Mudge's associates and even his wife, as he had always shown a disdain for any form of organized religion." Holmes moved to the mantel where he had left his slipper to retrieve some tobacco.

"So you think it was murder, Holmes?" Watson replied.

"Murder? Yes, in the most diabolical manner. The note may have confirmed suicide, but what about the rope? The rope, as described in the police report, was brand new—and there was no report of Mr. Mudge's having purchased one. Still, Scotland Yard closed this case based on the note and no further sign of foul play. No further sign....hmm...a strong, ruthless financier ends his life begging for salvation. No foul play? His business dealings made him many enemies, Watson, and no friends to mourn his passing. But I wonder....what drove this man to take his own life or...well, that sums up the first case until we get back to London. Then, I wish to have a meeting with Mr. Calstrom. Please send him a letter advising him of our return to London in two weeks time and my desire to meet with him.

The next four cases were obviously less interesting to the detective as he skimmed over the facts: initial letters requesting assistance, again hints of blackmail and then a final letter that the matter had been resolved. In all four of these cases the senders were prominent individuals, no robbery had been involved, and no suicide or murder. In two cases, again the blackmail letter was sent from Paris.

"Do you think there is a connection between all these cases and Mr. Calstrom's?," Watson asked.

"Yes, but it eludes me," Sherlock Holmes confided. "The victims, if we may call them that, travel in influential business circles. Two of them do belong to the same club, but it is hard to find a common link between them all. I am sure it exists. Without having the actual correspondence referred to by these cases, I cannot compare the writings to see if it is the same villain. My meagre investigations did glean some additional facts which may or may not have a bearing on their willingness to end my involvement. These facts—seemingly unrelated as I said—concern minor "accidents" which have occurred to household members of these four individuals. The most violent of these was the demise of a gamekeeper whose death was judged a hunting incidence, not at all uncommon in the Yorkshire heath. Now, all of these incidences may be coincidence, Watson. Or, dare I say it, part of a more heinous plot as evidenced by the capabilities expressed in the Calstrom case—and don't forget the Paris postmark. I wish to know your opinion, Watson, but before you reply, I must rest a while. And, I think dinner is also in order. Please contact room service for some refreshments, order what you like. For myself, a simple sandwich and some tea would be nice. I fear the rich foods of this country are taking their toll on this tired old body," the last he said with a small smile.

Watson busied himself with the task at hand, noting that his contribution to this evening's deliberations had been small, if not nonexistent. He wished to play a more active role and vowed that this would be the case when they sat down once again. In the meantime, while Sherlock rested, he reread the letters concerning the first five cases again. There was a definite pattern to them that even he could see. A thought crossed his mind that the most significant factor might be that all had decided to drop Sherlock Holmes' involvement. Was this tantamount to a "diabolical plot," as Sherlock would say? Or, was it the great detective's pride seeking a greater peril? No, he did say it might all be a coincidence, didn't he? And 'round and 'round these thoughts swirled while waiting for the light repast.

*Further analysis....*

"Holmes, I have made a discovery! There is another common thread relating to all these cases." Watson fairly beamed as he made this statement.

"Capital, Watson, capital," Holmes boomed. "Pray tell, what is this connection that you have obviously hit upon after reading the rest of the letters, but of course, not the ones from Royalty?"

"What..how did you know? Oh, never mind...I obviously did not put the letters back in the exact order you left them, correct?" Watson stammered.

"Not quite, Watson. You have an inquisitive mind. I could see that when I left you to lie down, your mind was racing over the possibilities. Naturally, you would wish to refresh your memory, and since the other letters were at hand, you took the opportunity to forge ahead. As to the letters from nobility; alas, no mystery. I knew you valued my trust, and for that, I thank you." A soft smile crossed the detective's face. Watson, sheepishly moved across the room, and once more, took his place on the settee next to Sherlock Holmes.

"Now Watson, out with it. What is this connection you speak of, I must know." The detective uncrossed his legs and leaned forward expectantly.

"Well, basically, I thought there might be a business project that would require their involvement in some way. I realize there is quite a diversity in their callings, but yet there might be something they would cooperate together in at some time. Then I read the other letters and realized the next five cases, chronologically speaking, were very different. Very different," he repeated.

"Different, Watson? Ahh...you mean because they occur on the Continent. One in Brussels, two in Paris, one in Amsterdam and the latest of these five in Luxembourg. And what conclusions do you draw from this knowledge, Watson?"

"Well, Sir, I realize your reputation is well known throughout Europe, and it might be, as you said before, a coincidence to these events, but there is one small link, one item all of these men might have in common. Mr. Holmes, I believe the connection might involve international commerce. Reading your ledger, I gathered that these gentlemen either bought, sold or exchanged articles of wealth—art, jewelry, antiques— and the link might entail their doings in this capacity." In finishing his summation, Watson poured himself a sherry, as if in congratulating himself.

"Well done, Watson. You may be right. This afternoon, after I sent my telegram to Inspector Delacroix, I stopped by the Prefect dé Police. As you said, my reputation is well known, and I was greeted cordially by one of the Inspectors, a Galen Maigret. We chatted amiably enough and he...oh, pass me the letter from Sir Gregory Almstead. Thank you, Watson. As I was saying, it turns out that this Maigret was the detective assigned to a robbery concerning our illustrious client, Sir Almstead. As you recall from his letter, Watson, he also intimated a threat or the hint of blackmail. Then this robbery. Here Watson, a copy of Maigret's police report. Study it well. I'll give you a moment and we'll discuss it." The detective rose and went to the Persian slipper for more of his tobacco and, as Watson read the report, sat back and smoked in silence.

"Shipment of crystal? That's another example of international trade. The brother's death does muddy up the waters, though," young Watson said.

"Yes, unless you put it into the light of Mudge's death. A close associate or relative. Hmm, now we have an opportunity, Watson. We must call on Sir Gregory Almstead, and perhaps shed a little more light on this matter. As you realize from reading the other four cases, we may have some heavy travelling ahead of us. Please make the necessary arrangements for our interview and I shall retire now. I am afraid I do tire easily, Watson. I will need your strength and your young, inquisitive mind in the coming days." The old man rose up, and with the aid of his assistant went to his bed chamber. After seeing to his welfare, Watson returned to the sitting room. He started to pour another sherry, thought better of it, and sat back staring at the remaining two letters. The first ten were now folded and placed back in their envelopes. These two, left to be explained, caused Watson's brow to curl. Were these men dead, he wondered, like Mudges? Such nonsensical ramblings, letters filled with hate...and what else? A warning. No other interpretation was possible. They were a warning. A warning about the devil. No, not a devil, THE devil....SATAN!

# The Investigation Begins

*June 19, Liége, Belgium, Sir Almstead's Country Home*

The interview with Sir Gregory Almstead was granted for 3 p.m. The fact that the official authorities had not yet been allowed to meet with Sir Almstead didn't faze Sherlock in the least. He had ascertained that his reputation of discretion was the major factor in this allowance. As they sped towards their destination, their discussions centered around the five cases mentioned before that had occurred on the Continent. The two cases in Paris definitely seemed related, especially considering the postmark of the previous events. The additional happenings in Amsterdam and Luxembourg gave fervor to Sherlock in his pronouncement that this was indeed an undertaking of major proportions. Watson could see excitement regained in Sherlock's eyes as he gave life to his theory of an operation so vast in scope. He told him that Moriarity had been an incredibly versatile adversary, as well as his number one lieutenant, Colonel Sebastian Moran. And, of course, he would never forget, nor perhaps forgive, his dealings with Miss Irene Adler. But...compared to them...this latest adventure promised more....much more. Yes, he had read the last two messages and their purported warnings about the nether world and their belief that their tormentor to be none other than Satan....Lucifer...and other mis-guided

# THE INVESTIGATION BEGINS

*"Holmes, Watson and Sir Almstead"*

## THE INVESTIGATION BEGINS

attempts to name the abomination that had confronted them. Sherlock had been very quick to dismiss these accounts based on one statement only, and simply said...."What on earth, Watson, would the devil need money for? Answer that, and I'll lend some credence to their story." Watson could not answer, and the conversation died on those terms.

"Sir Almstead will see you now. Please come this way." The butler led the way down on a long corridor off of the sitting room that had been the waiting area for Sherlock Holmes and young Watson. As they approached the inner sanctum of Sir Almstead, it was obvious that Sherlock was nettled by the amount of time he had been kept waiting— over twenty-five minutes. His jaws appeared tightened and his face grim as he entered through the vast double doors. Sir Almstead did not rise upon their entrance nor did he look up. He continued his attention to the documents at hand and seemed more statue-like as they approached.

"Ah, excuse me, Sir Almstead, Mr. Sherlock Holmes and his associate, Mr. John Watson," the butler intoned and continued, "ah, for their appointment per your instructions, Sir."

It was only a moment, but it seemed an eternity before Sir Almstead raised his craggy head. Here was a man used to protocol that allowed him his digressions. He was well over six feet tall but had an almost emaciated appearance when he rose, cadaverous in some respects. His face was thin and gaunt—not too unlike Sherlock's—except that his eyes would never display a twinkle or a playful smile. He was too serious. His voice, when he finally spoke, was deep and nasal, altogether too theatrical for description.

"Sherlock Holmes....THE Sherlock Holmes. Perhaps I have been amiss, but perchance what on earth can you possibly require from my expertise?" He finished his statement, and at the same time spoke with his hands, flailing the air to sit down, for God's sake, sit down.

"What on earth, indeed, Sir Almstead! Perhaps more to the point....something NOT of this earth," Sherlock paused for emphasis and noted the raised eyebrow from the nobleman. "May I remind you that you, yourself, wrote to me asking assistance, and now, I am here. As I have undertaken many a problem that to others may have seemed

## THE INVESTIGATION BEGINS

unsolvable, I may be your best and last resort. Do not take me lightly, I beg of you. Even in my weakened condition, as age has asserted itself upon my physical body. my mental faculties remain as sharp as ever. Trust yourself in me, Sir Almstead, and I will do my level best to right whatever wrong is threatening your household." Holmes turned to Watson at his conclusion and appeared to wink, or perhaps it was just a normal blink of the eye.

"SENT FOR YOU! Hmph. I didn't send for you. My assistant, more than likely." And then Sir Almstead's voice and manner softened, as he said, "Jamison has been with me quite a while. I realize he has my best interests at heart...ah...gentlemen, it is very difficult to explain....my position....my feelings....ah...he must think me transparent.....umm, perhaps I am. Let me detail the affair as I know it, and perhaps you would draw the same conclusions as Jamison did." Sir Almstead stood up and moved towards the fireplace. His steps didn't falter, but there appeared a hesitancy that could only be described as a mental disability to his movements. Upon gaining the hearth, he reached out and placed his right hand on a small statuette of Venus, which he obviously held in high regard as his fingers curled gently around its base. He paused before turning, and all parties present sensed that a revelation was forthcoming that would be painful in the telling. Silence pervaded the room, save the ticking of the small mantel clock, the only other object sharing the space with the Venus statue.

"Tragedy has struck my household, Mr. Holmes. Tragedy that has placed a pall on my normal discipline and demeanor. No, I don't mean that I was more outgoing or of a friendlier nature, that was not my usual disposition. I, I mean..," Sir Almstead groped for the words as Holmes rose from his chair.

"Love also changes a man, Sir Almstead. It has been known to blind men—yes, even stronger men than you—with its cloak of happiness." Holmes paused, waiting to see Sir Almstead's response.

"How, how did you know? I have taken great steps to ensure that my private life, well, remains private." Sir Almstead moved from the fireplace back towards his desk, weakly regaining his chair.

Holmes, still standing, reached into his coat pocket for his Meerschaum. Without asking for permission he proceeded to fill his

## THE INVESTIGATION BEGINS

pipe and began speaking in a gentle voice to the troubled man seated before him.

"It is well known, Sir Almstead, that your younger brother had an ineptness in handling his inheritance. It is no leap of the imagination to conjure the fact that he would also cross the boundaries as regards the fairer sex as well."

"Yes, that's true," Sir Almstead noted. "But who told you about Anne?"

"Anne? No, I didn't know her name, Sir Almstead. The truth of the matter was gleaned from simple observation. As I entered this room I noticed a photograph, sepia-toned and obviously hand-painted, hung in a frame that was not its original holder. That was easy to see by the fact that the image of the person, Anne, I may assume, was off-centered. Obviously it had been cut to remove a portion of the photo that had contained another image, another person. Since the surroundings depicted in the photo are definitely from the Yorkshire heath, which I believe, was where your brother resided, I deduced that this photo was of your brother and this woman, Anne. Further, by her dress and appearance, she is not a wealthy person but one who has some means of support. Perhaps a small bequest was in the offing and...this is why your brother had interest in her, was it not, Sir Almstead?" Holmes moved back from the desk, and in turning caught Watson's eye. One raised brow from the great detective gave Watson the initial thought that Holmes was testing the waters with his remarks, rather than stating them as pure facts as he was wont to do.

"You're quite right, Mr. Holmes. Anne was going to receive a small amount, oh, no more than 2,500 pounds, either upon her twenty-first birthday or her marriage, whichever came first. I knew Raymond had designs on her for this fact alone. He had asked, once more, for my help, and when I was in London on business, I went 'round to his flat. This time would be different, he said. Since he was to be married and this money would come to hand, he would be able to pay me back. He was a changed man. But I would have none of it. I knew him for what he was, a blackguard and a cheat. This affair, whatever it was to be, would be just another delaying tactic in his slow descendency. I begged him to leave the girl alone, not to drag her down with him. I

## THE INVESTIGATION BEGINS

told him I would go to her and bare all. Tell her the whole truth of his debaucherous ways and where they would lead. He told me she would not believe me. She loved him too much to be swayed by a dried up money-pincher like me. More angry words were exchanged and I left, not knowing then the chain of events that were to follow."

Sir Almstead paused and in his eyes a glint of a tear started to form. He recomposed himself and continued.

"He was right, of course. Initially. My entreaties to the girl were lost upon her. She was madly in love with him. The more I tried to convince her, the more she steadfastly defended him. I grew jealous of my brother's ability to win the affection of this beautiful young woman. Beautiful? Perhaps not in the fashionable sense of beauty, but a beauty that is much deeper. You can even sense it from her photo, can you not?" Holmes, and even Watson, murmured their agreement.

"It was on my second visit to her that I noticed a perceptible change in her demeanor. I believe it was the combination of my words and Raymond's deeds that began to change the tide. He, in his most cocksure manner, was treating her abominably. His less than chivalrous attitude caused her to remark that he was taking her for granted—that perhaps his brother was right and marrying him would not be the right thing to do. Raymond laughed at her outburst and told her to hold her tongue, that he was the best that she would ever do and was lucky that he was willing, nay, condescending, to marry her. With these comments, obviously spoken when he had imbibed more than his usual amount of brandy, Anne ran from the room crying. I was all at sea. I wished to go to her but I did not know then how my comforting would have been received. Raymond, for his part, took his leave without another word spoken. It was that night that he was caught cheating and took a bullet in the chest. In some ways, I feel guilty, and yet, deep down I know it was inevitable, and yet..." Again, tears formed in Sir Almstead's eyes, but this time they cascaded beyond their natural retainer.

Watson, being the youngest present, felt uncomfortable at this display of sorrow. Holmes took the opportunity to move around the desk and placed his hand on Sir Almstead's shoulder, and in a soft voice bade him to continue.

## THE INVESTIGATION BEGINS

"My brother's death shocked me, and yet I knew that the style and manner he had chosen to live would eventually cause him pain. I, I, thought prison was more apt to be his fate than a bullet." Sir Almstead gripped the side of the desk and rose, once more moving to the mantel. Turning, he faced his guests and a small, grimaced smile crossed his face. His hand started up, fell down to his side, and his eyes closed for a moment. Another moment passed and his eyes opened, clearer now. A swallow, visible from his throat, subsided, and he began again.

"Anne was more stoic than I. It was as if Raymond's death was a planned event and she had to continue going through the motions. She depended upon me and I on her, in a way. It was during this interlude that we became close. No, I did not make love to her—but the beginnings of a relationship that consumed my every waking moment was at hand. I tried to separate her necessity for me based on the situation that had been brought about by my brother's passing, but more and more it became apparent to me that her feelings for me were deeper. Weeks passed in this blissful state. I rationalized away the difference in our ages, our stations in life, and steeled myself to ask her hand in marriage. Was I mad, insane? I've lived a full life, I thought. And yet, in comparison with the days I spent with this woman, my life seemed to be cloistered. I had been a monk in every sense of the word until she came into my life. I know this sounds maudlin to you gentlemen, but it is true. As the poets described the meaning of love: glorious, pithy and full of contradictions, it was all true. I felt it. I lived it. I was in love, hopelessly as any man could ever be." The look on Sir Almstead's countenance conveyed a semblance of humbleness that rarely any of his constituency would ever see. The truth of the statement was evident, but sorrow pervaded nevertheless. Silence reigned supreme.

"How did she die, Sir Almstead?" Holmes's voice quietly broke the interlude.

"My God, how..yes, it's true, but..." Sir Almstead stammered.

"Taking at face value your scenario of the events after your brother's death, Anne had placed herself in your care. She was susceptible to your entreaties in this instance...I mean, your proposal of marriage. And, to put things delicately, since this has not taken

## THE INVESTIGATION BEGINS

place, the only possible explanation would be an illness. Now, since you are here, and not at the side of this woman who has captured your heart, I must also assume that she has perished. Is this not the case?" Holmes went to the fireplace and again, his hand rested on Sir Almstead's shoulder, their eyes meeting in understanding.

"Yes, Mr. Holmes. She did indeed accept my proposal of marriage, but understandably had mixed emotions as concerns my brother. She bade me to be patient and allow her to grieve. I pressed her as I would a business associate, much to my own chagrin. She fell ill with this turmoil surrounding her. Her doctor was summoned, yet to no avail. The human heart is not to be trifled with, gentlemen, and she succumbed. Again, I held myself to blame. My God, how stupid I was. Time was needed. Time. I couldn't give it to her. I needed her so much that I thought my desires would help her overcome any affliction. Doctor Forbes, her physician, was perplexed, but accepted the fact that her constitution was not strong. I was devastated. I returned to Belgium within forty-eight hours of her demise. London held nothing for me. I poured myself into my financial affairs as a solace to my state of mind. That's when the first letter arrived."

"And this is what caused your secretary, Jamison, to write to me?" Holmes inquired.

"No, not then. This letter, which I felt contained an undefined nebulous threat, made me burn in anger. I was stricken with remorse at the time and was not in a mood to entertain any aspersions towards my personal affairs. I didn't realize at the time that the contents of these notes were referring to my business dealings and not my filial relationship with my brother or his fiance. The written torment continued weekly, and then stopped. Jamison, bless his soul, as my confidant and secretary, felt that news must have spread about my involvement with Anne and my enemies, my competitors, were using this information to unnerve me, in hopes that I might falter, give them an advantage. I felt my old self returning. A new strength came into my mind, a new passion. I knew what business could do to a man, and I then and there resolved not to be taken unawares."

"These letters, Sir Almstead, do you still have them? Or, did you burn them all, as you did the first and last?" Holmes asked.

## THE INVESTIGATION BEGINS

"I burned them all. I am somewhat impetuous and placed no great credence on their currency. The last? Ahh, you have spoken with Inspector Maigret. Good, that brings you somewhat up to date. But there are facts you do not know, Mr. Holmes, facts that even I doubt can be, and yet, and yet...." Sir Almstead's voice trailed off. Holmes turned away, as if in doubt, and turning back, said,

"What frightens you, Sir Almstead? What has turned a man who has succeeded so obviously well in the international arena and now, does his utmost to quell any appearance at weakness but yet it shows? Do you believe that the devil, Satan, has actually come forth to possess your earthly soul?" A smirk travelled across Sherlock's face as he concluded.

"Yes. Yes, I do, may God have mercy on my soul, I do." Sir Almstead fairly shouted his response and, with nary another word, crumpled to the floor.

*The secretary reports....*

Sir Gregory Almstead's collapse had not been unforeseen by Chalmers, the butler, as he immediately arranged to have his lordship moved to his private quarters and the doctor sent for. As much as Holmes and Watson tried to intervene, they were treated by the other staff as superfluous and their protestations went unheeded as they were escorted back to the original sitting room where they first arrived. It was there that they had their encounter with Gordon Jamison, Sir Almstead's secretary.

"Mr. Holmes, I do appreciate your response to my entreaties and I do hope you accept my apologies as I am sure you felt that they had originated with my master, Sir Almstead." Jamison, hopping from one foot to the next, was comical in appearance. Nervousness was only one trait of Gordon Jamison, a confirmed bachelor of forty-six. He also had a tendency to repeat the last words spoken to him by others as if in affirmation of their truthfulness. In appearance he would be considered fastidious. He had a full mustache and sideburns that were clipped too close to the face which negated the possibility of style. It

## THE INVESTIGATION BEGINS

gave his face a severe look, almost Germanic, and yet, he was Irish through and through. This was revealed in the twinkle of his eyes as they darted to and fro. It was hard to imagine this man being the repository of deep and dark secrets to a man of Sir Almstead's stature. And yet, he maintained he was, upon questioning by Sherlock Holmes.

"Aye, Mr. Holmes. 'Tis true. We regarded the first letter as ravings of some jealous competitor trying to throw a scare at the master. But later, as they got more defined, it would seem they got the hang of it. What I mean is, they were privy to some very confidential doings and though they didn't right out say so, they were threatening in nature. And always the same old reprise. That is, pay the tithe, pay the tithe. A religious way of putting things, I would think. At first, my thought was of a blackmailer with a queer sense of humor. Then, after Miss Anne and all, well, it put us in a black state of mind, that's for sure."

Holmes noticed that Jamison tended to think of himself and Sir Almstead as one and the same. It lent a credence to the dedication that Sir Almstead had given to Jamison as a trustworthy servant. He tried in vain to have Jamison disclose further personal facts as related to the case, but to no avail. He insisted that we must wait for Sir Almstead to reveal any more, and at that juncture we made our farewell.

Later, on the early evening train back to Brussels, Holmes awoke from his quandary and addressed Watson.

"Interesting, eh, Watson? Is it a simple case of blackmail or something more devious? Whoever this Paris connection is, they seem to know a great deal of Sir Almstead's business dealings. Is the tragic misfortune of his brother's death, coupled with that of this unfortunate lady, part and parcel, or...just a coincidence? If not, we are definitely involved in a Machiavellian plot of the greatest magnitude." Holmes stretched his long lanky legs and leaned back into his seat. Watson, his own mind racing, tried to surmise exactly all of what they had learned since embarking upon this adventure. He thought over the analysis they had made of the previous cases which seemed to be directly linked to this one. Blackmail? That would be the obvious conclusion. But why make mention of the devil? As Holmes had said,

# THE INVESTIGATION BEGINS

"What does the devil need with money?" It didn't make sense. And if they were all connected, what mind could have thought out all of these machinations but a Machiavelli or...worse. Watson squirmed in his seat as the possibilities went 'round and 'round in his mind.

Back at the hotel, Holmes indicated his tiredness by his desire to retire immediately after a light supper. Before he went to bed he remarked, "Watson, I need you to send a telegram to Sir Almstead, it's quite urgent." He handed Watson a crumpled note upon which he had wrote a short sentence. Watson, for the life of him, couldn't remember when Sherlock had written it, but took it nevertheless. When the great man had gone to bed, he unfolded it and read, "Since you paid the tithe, why are you not at rest? S. Holmes." Watson didn't understand. Sir Almstead hadn't spoken of any agreement with the blackmailer, so why did Holmes think the payment had been made? Did he miss something? Watson tried to reenact the conversations of the afternoon, but prior to Sir Almstead's collapse nothing had transpired to indicate this was the case.

# Brussels to Paris

*June 20th, Brussels, Belgium, Blackbird Café Hotel*

The next morning Watson, having spent a somewhat restless night, pressed Sherlock Holmes as to why he felt Sir Almstead had indeed paid the mysterious correspondent in Paris.

"Watson, I thought it was obvious. The disappearance of the crystal. I am placed in a somewhat difficult situation as regards Inspector Maigret, but surely it is obvious that the crystal never landed in Brussels, regardless of what the shippers might think. The fact that they were uninsured was the first obvious clue. A man of Sir Almstead's business acumen would never have undertaken a valuable shipment without procuring the necessary insurance as a standard precaution. Therefore, what was shipped was simply empty containers. To his business associates he would appear remiss. But, it was more important for him to have this transaction fall upon his shoulders alone. He had paid the tithe. It was what was expected of him and he performed. That is why the question now is, why is he still afraid?" Holmes poured another cup of coffee and leaning back, his eyes met Watson's and fairly beamed.

"If that's the case, Holmes, wouldn't the shipper on the London end know the boxes were empty?" Watson asked.

"Perchance if it were the same shipper. But I am sure Sir Almstead took the liberty of sending the boxes through more than one company before this Fleur de Lis organization took hold of it. Remember, we are dealing with international shipping, and manifests are written and rewritten as articles are transported along." Holmes, somewhat smug in his reply, arose and started his typical pacing.

"Now, more importantly, what do we do next? I trust that we will not receive a reply for awhile from Sir Almstead based on his condition." Then, as if in answer to his own question, "Watson, please make arrangements for any messages to be forwarded on to our hotel in Paris, the Hotel du Louvre du Imperial[1]. We must leave immediately." The detective whirled about, in defiance of his age, and headed straight for the lobby desk. Watson, dumbfounded, reached in his pocket for the necessary currency to pay for their breakfast fare. He just managed to reach the concierge to make the arrangements when he caught a glimpse of Sherlock engaged in a heated conversation with the desk clerk.

"What on earth, Holmes, what was the matter?" Watson gasped when they were finished packing and waiting for the bellman.

"Matter? Eh, oh—my little tête-à-tête with the desk clerk. Well, Watson, I miss having Mycroft tend to all of the little details when I am so wrapped up in a case, and hotels, though they try their best, never seem to follow through like a trusted old friend. I had simply required a listing of all rail destinations and stations accessible from Brussels within a forty-eight hour travel time. You'd think I had asked for an original transcription of the Rosetta stone. They failed miserably. The meagre pamphlets they had on file were abominable and I told him so. He went on to say that this is the Continent and that each European nation is separate and all, as if I didn't realize that. He further stated that the information I requested did not exist. Well, Watson, what do you think? Imagine how easy it is for the criminal brain not to have to worry about crossing country lines and being pursued, since the pursuer would have no knowledge of rail movements once he

---

[1] Hotel du Louvre, Place André Malraux—inaugurated in 1855 by Napoléon III. It is still in operation today.

## BRUSSELS TO PARIS

crossed that border? Someday an organization[2] will have to be formed to answer these types of global problems. The criminal mind knows no boundaries, I can assure you of that." With that last statement, Sherlock Holmes went into a quiet reverie until they were aboard their train to the capital city of Paris, France. They would spend a pleasant night at the Hotel du Louvre, a favorite of Holmes.

---

[2]Interpol: The International Criminal Police Organization was established in 1923. Its headquarters are in Paris, France.

# A CASE OF WINE

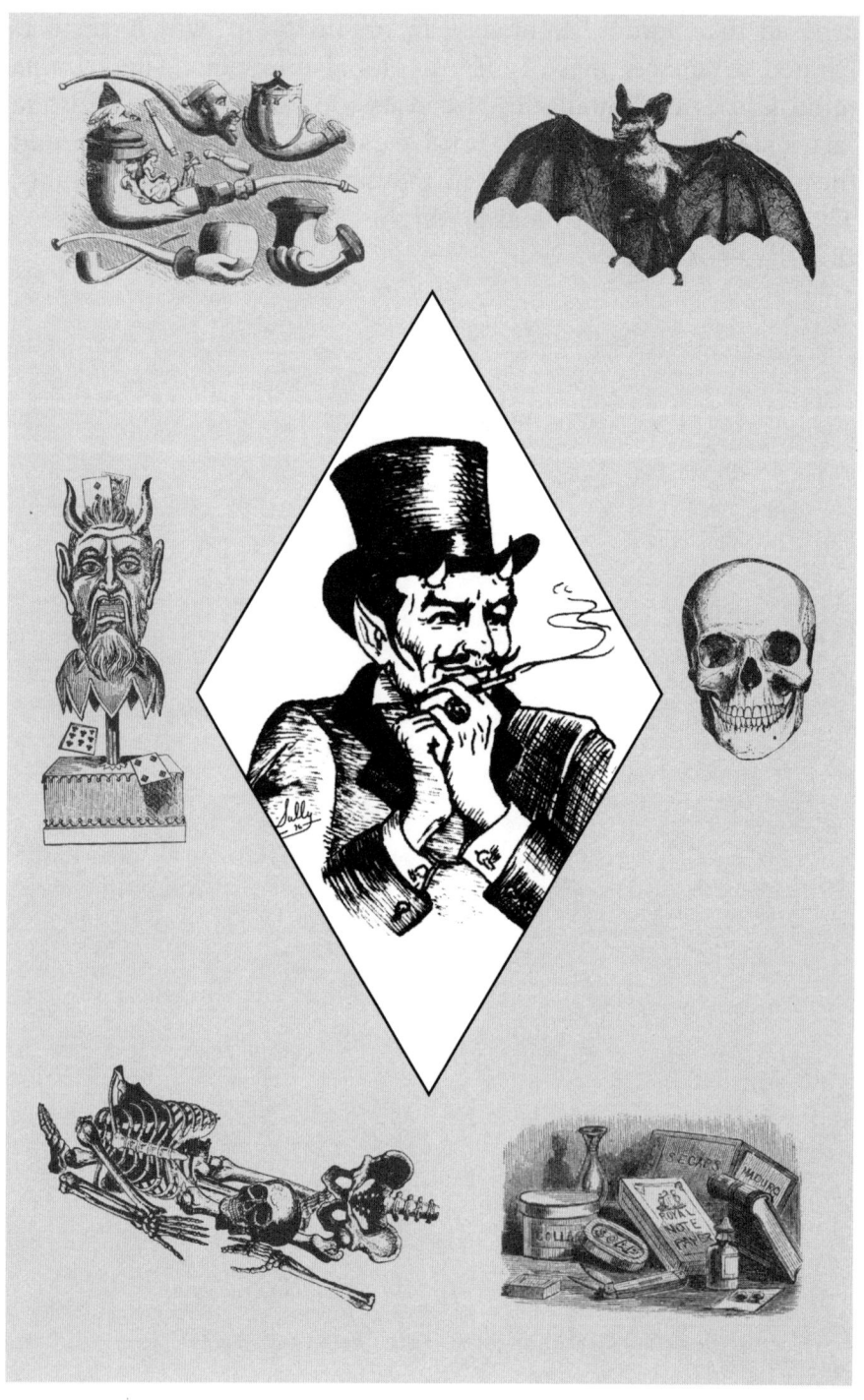

# A Case of Wine

*June 21st, Paris, France, Sureté Headquarters*

"My father is innocent. Please, please help us. He does drink, but he did not do this, please, believe me." The young lady continued her rant in the Sureté courtyard to anyone passing by. She had already been once removed from the booking desk by a gendarme who tried to be gentle but had to assert himself with greater force as she had not given way to his authority. The old man and his younger companion also received her pleadings with lesser impact, as French was noticeably not their primary language.

"Ah, M. Holmes and...M.....," the question hung in the air from Inspector Maurice Caleur.

"May I introduce John Watson. He is the son of my former collaborator bearing the same name," Holmes intoned as hands were shaken and and other pleasantries were accomplished, including a bottle of port being made available. When they were settled, Holmes stated his case.

"You are very mysterious, M. Holmes," the Inspector replied. "Cases of blackmail, if there were, could not be discussed publicly, no, and you, yourself say you cannot divulge any names. Ah, such a blind circle, such as what comes first, hmm, chicken or its egg?" the

## A CASE OF WINE

last was said with a slight laugh. "But, the other... thefts of great art or objects of some value, that I could discuss, mais oui. We have so much great art in France, n'est pais? So, theft is always a possibility. Recently, a painting, quite valuable, was removed from its frame at the Musée de Cluny[3] and is believed in the hands of a private collector whom we believe had not the funds to purchase such a piece and required just this one alone. The right ingredients you would say, for this type of crime, yes? And yet, a thorough search of his apartments has not revealed anything. But, we will watch him, oh yes, we will watch him forever if necessary. That is the way we French feel about art. Now, as to blackmail...It is as I said, you would have to reveal a little more, before I could reveal...how you say....tit for tit, M. Holmes?

"Tit for tat, Inspector Caleur, tit for tat." Holmes corrected. "May I assume that the painting that was removed from the museum was owned privately, or by the museum in trust?"

"Oh, both might be the right answer. It was on loan and had been for quite a while by a great benefactor of the museum. He is long dead, M. Holmes, and his heirs have never made any move towards regaining possession. The family is quite respected in all of France and I would not trouble them with any inquiries into the investigation of its theft. No, this was an outside operation, I am sure of it." Even as Inspector Caleur made known his thoughts the wailing of the woman in the courtyard, caught by the early afternoon breezes, again wafted through the open window and snatches of it interrupted the ongoing conversation. Watson, looking out at the window, gazed upon the young lady and was transfixed by the emotion emanating from her countenance. He turned to the Inspector.

"Sir, Inspector Caleur," Watson started, "that young lady...what is she crying about? She seems in great distress. Shouldn't someone assist her?"

"Ah...she has caught your fancy, eh, young man? She is a voluptuous woman, n'est pais? Her case, or rather that of her peré, father, was presented early this morning. It is quite straightforward. A little matter, not significant. But if you find her so attractive, why not go to

---

[3]Musée de Cluny, 6 Place Paul-Painlievé—a renowned repository of church art and castle crafts of the middle ages.

# A CASE OF WINE

her and see what you can do? It is out of my hands, eh?" A smile crossed his face and he winked at Holmes. Watson, not knowing what to do, hesitated until Holmes spoke.

"Go ahead, Watson. We are at liberty this afternoon since there are no major crimes that the Inspector wishes me to assist in...go, gather information from this damsel in distress and bring it to me at our hotel. I, for one am famished and would cordially invite the Inspector to have lunch with me, if he would do me the honor." The same type of smile that had appeared on Inspector Caleur's face now appeared on Holmes'. Watson turned to bid goodbye to the Inspector.

"I would be delighted, M. Holmes, if you would allow me to pick the establishment. It's quite near here, a short walk. I would love the opportunity to discuss with you some of your most famous cases." With that, the Frenchman placed his arm around Sherlock's shoulders in a comradery embrace and led him down the corridor, paying no attention to Watson and his outstretched hand.

*A case at last....*

When Watson arrived back at the hotel he found Holmes up in their room hunched over a ledger notebook. Spread before him were the two letters he had received from Paris asking his help. He was so deep in thought it appeared he had not heard Watson enter the room, until he spoke without looking up.

"Watson, the similarities are astounding. This one, from M. Lapelé, is couched in the same wording, if one translates the French literally, as the one that was sent in the Calstrom case. The other, obviously from not as educated a mind, reeks of the same sort of problem. Of the two, it is this latter one that shows a more disturbed response. He is the one we should see next, Watson. Monsieur Donner." Holmes, hearing Watson give out a short yelp, turned quickly about.

"Donner? Monsieur Donner, you mean Geraud Donner?" Watson couldn't hold back his surprise. "He is exactly the man we must see!" shouted Watson.

## A CASE OF WINE

"Calm down, Watson, calm down. Yes, of course, we shall see him. Have you heard anything more about him than this letter I hold in my hand?" Holmes searched Watson's face for a clue and then, as realization crossed his mind, said, "Ah, but of course. That girl. The girl in the courtyard. Her father works for M. Donner, does he not? And he has been accused of a crime. Tell me all about it, Watson, leave no detail undone, tell it exactly as she told you. Now, sit down, pour yourself some sherry and tell all." The great man led his young protegé to a chair and commenced his ritual pacing. Watson, gulping down the sherry, paused to catch his breath once more and began.

"It's as you say, Holmes. Her father, M. Jean LaPorté, has worked for M. Donner for a long time. He is a sommelier, a wine steward, they call it. M. Donner is a very large wine merchant. It seems there was a case of wine that had been bought at auction, quite reasonable in price, but afterwards it was learned that the wine was worth substantially more. M. LaPorté was credited for making this acquisition for M. Donner. Subsequently, M. Donner announced the betrothal of his daughter Gabrielle to a young officer, Captain Michel Gaulen and, as a wedding present, promised this particular case of wine, ah, a Bordeaux, I forget the date, Holmes, but during the wedding reception it was discovered that the case was destroyed."

"Destroyed?" Holmes interrupted. "What do you mean, destroyed?"

"Smashed. Each and every bottle. Justine, that is, M. LaPorté's daughter, the girl in the courtyard, she says her father is responsible for the wine cellar and though it is true he does imbibe, he was asleep and for the life of him does not understand how they could have been broken. I believe her, Holmes, and in that light I guess I accept her father's story as well. And yet, if he does drink to excess isn't it possible..." Watson's eyes moved to the floor as his words drifted away.

"Watson, when did this happen?" Holmes barked.

"The wedding was Saturday, this is Monday. Just two days ago. Mr. Holmes, Justine told me her father has been told to make good on the wine or face prison. And even if he does make restitution his reputation is gone. He will never work as a sommelier again, that's for certain."

## A CASE OF WINE

But Sherlock Holmes was not listening to the finish of this pronouncement of sentence, for his mind was elsewhere.

"Take me to this Mlle. Justine. That is where we start. But don't expect miracles, Watson, as you said, when a man takes to drink, his sense of responsibility may have also taken a holiday."

They arrived at the back door of a very large inn called the Auberge de Crillon[4]. It was here that M. Donner hosted extravagant parties, including his daughter's wedding, and it was in the basement that his prized wine cellar was kept. Watson had hardly knocked when the young girl, Justine, opened the door, and with the international sign of a single finger to a lips to indicate silence, led them down a darkened corridor to a small door inset with a large brass ring in its center.

"Oh, M. Holmes, M. Watson said you would come. I have been told to leave the premises immediately and I am afraid if I am caught more punishment will fall upon my family, but he told me you would have to look at the cellar to get any idea at what happened." She was quite breathless in her speech and her eyes kept darting about the candlelit space they found themselves in when the door was opened.

Holmes led the way as if he had been there before. With no hesitation he went to the area where the mishap was to have taken place. Without regard for his clothing he kneeled to the floor, his aquiline nose almost rubbing its surface. His thin, long fingers snapped out and deftly picked up minute shards of glass that were still to be found in the remotest corners.

"It's a shame that everything has been cleaned up," he remarked.

"Yes," Justine said. "The master was quite adamant that he did not wish to set sight on the cellar again until it had been swept clean."

Holmes turned to Watson, but before he could speak another voice boomed out.

"Come up out of there or I'll shoot!" The two visitors and the girl turned as one towards the lone figure at the top of the stairs. It was hard to make out his face with the darkened shadows behind him, but Justine recognized the voice.

---

[4] Hotel de Crillon, 10 Place de la Concorde—a 200 year old establishment that might have been named Auberge at this time.

# A CASE OF WINE

"M. Donner, it is I, Justine. These men came at my request. They are great detectives who are going to prove my father innocent."

"If you don't leave right now, you'll be dead detectives. I mean it. GO!"

A shot rang out, striking one of the stanchions in the middle of the room. The bullet ricocheted with a whine as it reflected and imbedded itself in the floor. Watson instinctively grabbed the girl and dropped to the floor. Holmes stood his ground, his nose flaring, his eyes penetrating the darkness and seeking out the man at the top of the stairs. Their eyes locked.

"I am Sherlock Holmes, M. Donner," the detective's voice calmly, quietly spoke. "You sent for me. I am here to help. Now, put down that gun or I shall be forced to hurt you." Silence pervaded the wine cellar for almost a minute as M. Donner thought over his options. Then, slowly, the gun was lowered and placed back into the vest pocket from whence it came.


*A case resolved....*

The clock ticking on the mantel indicated half-past seven. At Holmes' direction Watson was escorting Justine LaPorté back home to her father. M. Geraud Donner and Sherlock Holmes were sitting in the private study atop Auberge de Crillon.

"Have you paid the tithe, M. Donner? Is this case of Bordeaux the tithe?" Sherlock questioned.

"M. Holmes, I don't know what you are talking about. The matter I was referred to you about has been cleared up. As to the Bordeaux, ah, unfortunately, regardless of what Justine may think, her father has been remiss in his duties. As a marchand de vins, a wine merchant and a connoisseur, M. Holmes, I appreciate people who enjoy my produce but not to excess. Do I make myself clear?"

M. Donner was a small man, not just in stature, but in all bodily aspects as well, having a small head, hands, limbs, etc. The way he carried himself, one would say he had a Napoleonic type of psyche. He could be dangerous, as he was just a moment ago in the wine

## A CASE OF WINE

cellar. His wife, Annette, lived in fear of him, but not his daughter. Gabrielle, high strung and spoiled, ruled the roost when she was present. At the moment she was with her new husband, Captain Gaulen, in Marseilles, courtesy of her father. Holmes gathered these facts from looking over the items displayed in this man's personal habitat. The certain way photos were displayed, the keepsakes from Gabrielle's spoiled childhood, the receipt from a luxury hotel in Marseille. All pretty mundane except for one item: the bars that had been recently installed on the window looking out.

"Clear, M. Donner? Oh, yes, some things are patently clear. Let's start with the Bordeaux, shall we? One, it was not THE bordeaux that was destroyed. No, this was a much simpler version, less complex in bouquet and in substance. My nose tells me an '93 or '94. As for the smashed bottles. Again a mistake. Those bottles were broken elsewhere and brought to the wine cellar. Do you wish proof? Actually, you know that's true, don't you, M. Donner?"

"This is insane. Are you a wine expert? They cleaned that cellar, not a drop on the floor remained. Proof, yes, damn it I want proof. Go ahead, tell me, tell me and get out!" Donner's face turned reddish purple at this outburst and it was obvious he was reaching another breaking point.

"A wine expert? No...but I have done a small treatise on the wine process, and as you know the type of cask can make quite a difference in the final bouquet of a bordeaux. The wine I sniffed did not have the appropriate woody aroma that is characteristic of a fine old bordeaux, but that of a young one. The earthen floor also allows any wine spilt to seep into it, and though other spills have surely permeated its surface none have done so as recently as this one. Secondly, this same earthen floor contained no fragments of glass that would have been embedded in it, as surely as your bullet this afternoon, if a bottle had been dashed to it in such a way as to fragment it. No, these bottles were smashed elsewhere, that I am sure. But why? The simple conclusion is to hide the disappearance of this rare and valuable case. In the hands of the Sureté they might believe it was because you had second thoughts of giving so valuable a present to your daughter, after discovering its true worth....but we know the real reason, M.

Donner, don't we? You have paid your tithe." Sherlock Holmes rose as if to leave, then moving past Geraud Donner, he paused at the recently barred windows.

"These will do no good, Sir. Not if you truly believe what you face is the nameless one. You paid him out of fear, I understand that. Do you believe it's over? I think not. For now, you must right this wrong done to M. LaPorté and his daughter. Do that and I shall do all in my power to help you. Otherwise, may God have mercy on your soul."

Sherlock Holmes turned and walked out the door.

# A Client Once Again

*June 22nd, Paris, France, Hotel du Louvre*

T he following morning found Sherlock Holmes and his young companion in a most agreeable mood. The breakfast fare at the Hotel du Louvre was more than ample and the coffee exceedingly delicious. It wasn't until the third cup of this brew that Sherlock smilingly allowed himself to be goaded into replying to the mail that had agitated Watson to no end.

"Hmm, so he will drop all charges....good....good," Sherlock remarked.

"Yes, and what's more he will continue to retain M. LaPorté at his regular salary and position," Watson answered and then continued, "But, he is making no apologies to the circumstances that preceded these events, nor does he want any public statement to be made, either. It seems there still might be a shadow placed on M. LaPorté's reputation after all."

"Watson, oh Watson. This is all they will get from this man, M. Geraud Donner. He is hardened and somewhat heartless, but nevertheless, he will try his utmost to procure my services in the very near future. In fact, I do believe that second unopened letter from the gentleman will be asking just that. Go ahead, Watson,

## A CLIENT ONCE AGAIN

satisfy my ego." Sherlock fairly beamed as Watson fumbled open the elongated envelope.

"Holmes, you're right. He asks 'permission,' his word Sir, to come to the hotel at noon today. As a further inducement he has enclosed a check for one thousand francs, and also...." an audible gasp escaped from Watson's lips. "Holmes, there's an actual letter from the phantom that has been chasing these men across Continents, here....look!"

Holmes reached out for the missive. Carefully holding it up to the light, his lips moved in a semblance of reading out loud without actually doing so. His eyes darted over the surface and then his hands caressed the paper, smoothing it out from its folded state. He finally placed it on the table squarely in front of him.

"Frankly, I am a little surprised. The paper, yes, definitely quite old. I believe you will find it to be handmade. A parchment...I think.....Bavaria...yeess, Bavarian in style...the same with the ink." A wistful look appeared on the detective's face as he thought of other missives he had received from Bavaria. He continued on, "Look, Watson, see how the surface of the paper appears to have depth....yes....handmade....expensive...very rare. And that ink....ink normally lightens as it spreads away from the nib of a pen, but not here....no...the pen, undoubtedly a quill...yet the ink maintains its color throughout....very interesting....very interesting. You know Watson, what that means?" Holmes looked up at his young friend.

"No Sir. I can't imagine. How can someone write with such evenness as to not allow the ink to spread, as you say?" Watson, a quizzical look on his countenance, continued to stare at the document.

"Because this pen has been fed a continuous supply of ink throughout the writing stage. And yet the fine point it makes during certain forming of letters tends to make me still believe it a quill. Hmm...someone went through great lengths to either disguise their handwriting or....well, that's enough about this production. Now, the meaning of these words, Watson. Read it out loud to me, with emphasis and intonation.... the way you feel the writer is trying to make it sound." Holmes passed the letter to Watson.

## A CLIENT ONCE AGAIN

"First, the date is given in roman numerals, fairly archaic, but in keeping with the hoax, I guess," Watson started. "I'm not sure exactly what date it is, but...," he continued.

"No!" Holmes fairly shouted, rising from his chair. "It is a detail, one that may make a difference, but I agree, it is given more for window dressing than for necessity. Proceed, Watson." Holmes moved to regain his seat.

"Greetings, if I remember my Latin, a salutation with an imperative tense." Watson said.

"No, no, Watson, do not include your personal observations. We're going about this all wrong. Please read it silently to yourself and then, as dramatically as possible, re-read it out loud, the way you believe it would be interpreted after studying it for a while. Take your time." Holmes once again began pacing the room, waving his hands to indicate that Watson should take his seat. Watson did and several minutes went by in silence as he read the note from their adversary. His face, as a mask, revealed nothing, then, as if on cue, it winced noticeably. Holmes almost moved to his side to stare at the words that caused his consternation, but checked himself and turned, facing the mirror to once more observe his young companion.

Watson sighed and placed the note on the table. His eyes, looking up, appeared to seek out his mentor. As they made contact Holmes could see the effect that the words had had on his young friend. He appeared shaken, almost frightened and it took the detective's words to allay his fears.

"They are just words, Watson, just words. They were written to intimidate, to make believers out of non-believers. But they are just words all the same. Throughout the ages, priests, rabbis, mystics, whatever, employed such words for what they believed to be the common good. Is it not so far-fetched to imagine that the forces allied against them were also as artful in their chosen professions. I do not imply that these words come from the forces of darkness, just as it may be said that many a man of the cloth does not mouth the exact words of God himself, though they may think so. Interpretation is the key. And, in this instance, I wish to hear yours. Be theatrical, be dramatic, but do not embellish. As you have studied this missive make it

## A CLIENT ONCE AGAIN

known to me the way you feel it sounds to you. Do I make myself clear, Watson? It is very important that you understand what I am asking of you. Do you?" Holmes stood over the young man, their eyes once more locked, unblinking. Watson shook his head in comprehension, letting saliva water his mouth, and, rising up from his chair, exchanged places with Sherlock Holmes as he began his oration.

"Greetings! Thy existence shall be no more. Thy soul, immortal to end, is no more. Agreement? No more. Tithes are no sanctuary. Thy will is done. End. No more. As agreed...fulfillment is no more....time, no more. Salt, fire, pain, no end. Redemption no more. Sand is thy enemy. Thou has reaped no more. Time is enemy but not for you alone.....the fruit of your loins shall suffer ignobly for your trespasses....at the sign of eight. Eight. Our pact is done." Watson paused, looked down at Holmes. "That's it Holmes, no signature, no address."

"Hmm," mused the detective, "not quite fire and brimstone, but as the last in a series of threats, it must have made quite an impact as it did on your impressionable mind. As to me, I find it lacking in substance, except for the part about fruit of his loins, which is an obvious threat to the daughter." Holmes rose up and started pacing, continuing his analysis.

"So, even though the tithe had been paid, the cases of wine in this instance, it must have come too late, or didn't quite meet the terms of their so-called agreement. Now the question that comes to mind first is...what did M. Donner receive for his end of this bargain? It certainly reeks of a scene from Danté's inferno, but no, I won't accept that, and neither shall you, Watson. Our meeting this noon with M. Donner is our only hope of drawing any other meaning from this incredibly cryptic missive. Time is an enemy, eh? Then we must make the most of it while we have it. Watson, fetch me the ledger detailing our cases to date. I must recheck the dates, and also check with the hotel clerk, the manager even, and see if you can obtain the most recent rail schedules between Paris, Amsterdam, Brussels, London, and, oh yes, let's not forget Luxembourg."

# A CLIENT ONCE AGAIN

*The Director involved....*

"Ah, it seems that M. Donner has taken his problem a little more seriously since we last met." These words were spoken by Sherlock Holmes, as he peered out the window at the approaching gentleman—surrounded on both sides by two other gentlemen.

"Oh, I see," said Watson. "Inspector Caleur is with him. But who is the other gentleman?"

"Gentleman, indeed, Watson. A most inestimable gentleman. You are in for a real treat." Holmes watched as a quizzical look spread over Watson's countenance.

"Ah, you are not familiar with that gentleman, the one with the apparent limp to his walk. We shall not spoil Inspector Caleur's introductions, but you, Watson, are about to meet the driving force behind the Sureté, M. Francois V. Robuchon." As Watson still made no indication of apprehension, Holmes resumed.

"Many years ago, Watson, a close relative of this gentleman, one Eugene Francois Vidocq[5], was once considered the most resourceful of thieves until his capture—or should I say surrender for the French police were helpless in their pursuit of this master criminal. He convinced the French government to not only pardon his acts as a master criminal but also to award him a post, a special post, newly created, that would engage his previously criminal mind in much better pursuits. And that is how the Sureté was formed. An incredibly intelligent police force within a police force, guided by a former master criminal. The ultimate act of contrition blended with the formidable scenario based on that ubiquitous old bromide, 'to catch a thief'....etc., etc. Clever, eh? Now along comes this man, with the same potential, but he also had gone astray. It was during my hiatus after the incident at Reichenbach falls that his name first came to my attention. As you may recall, Watson, after Moriarity perished, his first lieutenant, Colonel Sebastian Moran, was operating openly on the Continent and it was

---

[5]Eugene Francois Vidocq (1775-1857)—though established as a professional criminal at an early age he reformed and reorganized the Criminal Department of the Paris Police. In 1811 he became Chef de la Sureté. Surprisingly he left and formed his own private consulting detective agency at the age of fifty! There are some who believe he was an inspiration to Sherlock Holmes to become his own consulting detective.

## A CLIENT ONCE AGAIN

quite worrisome to me that the twain should meet, and that's when Mycroft became involved. The details are not important, but suffice it to say he, Mycroft, convinced the young man to change his allegiance as his uncle had once done. We can only wonder what would have happened if Moran and he had become allies. I shudder at the thought. But, that did not come to pass. What did happen was a stroke of genius, Mycroft's genius. Holmes fairly laughed out loud when he finished, and turning 'round with the crinkly grin still upon his face, he bade his companion to go downstairs where they could meet their illustrious guest and pay homage over a glass of sherry or port.

As they waited for the lift, Watson, in his own thoughts, recalled his father's writings and his own experience, and couldn't remember a member of any police force receiving such accolades from Sherlock Holmes.

*First interview....*

The introductions were made, the drinks poured, and the four men were seated in a private salon off of the main dining room with the two beveled-glass French doors closed and inspected to ensure their privacy. Though it was obvious to Watson that Sherlock Holmes would rather have engaged M. Robuchon in discussions of his past life, he quickly brought the conversation to the topic at hand, the torture of M. Donner and the blatant threat to his daughter, Gabrielle.

"I assume, Inspector Caleur," Holmes remarked, "that you have alerted the Marseilles authorities of the potential danger to M. Donner's daughter?"

"Of course," the Inspector shot back. "The note, though expressed in such, how do you say, devilish ravings, still contained an obvious threat. I took it seriously, and based on M. Donner's statement," the Inspector turned to face the wine merchant, "that other misfortunes have occurred, decided we should not take this threat lightly."

"Other misfortunes?" Holmes seemed surprised. "Pray tell, M. Donner, and try to be as explicit as possible." The detective noted that Director Robuchon maintained his silence.

## A CLIENT ONCE AGAIN

"I, I...thought it just a coincidence....I had been receiving these malicious letters for about a month, one a week...when...the threats...they were not as specific as this one....just general, hateful....I....I would never have....oh my God..." his hands swiftly went up to cover his face, which had lost all composure as he relived the events of the last few months. No one moved to comfort or aid him, and eventually he came round and once more continued.

"My wife, she is good to me, yes...but I have taken a lover. A young lady of no consequence to these proceedings, believe me. The evening that haunts me to this day...I was coming home from a rendezvous with my paramour when I heard this awful scream. It froze my blood, it seemed to take forever to open the latch to my front door. When I entered, I found my wife lying at the bottom of the stairs, she had fallen. There was no one else about. The staff, the maid, all were gone for the night, she was alone and she fell. Her injuries were not insubstantial but she survived. Naturally, I felt guilt, not just from my absences, which I felt helped bring about this...this accident, but....ah...you see, my wife was quite drunk...a state she was bringing herself to, to placate my absences. Rationally I knew it must be just my guilt, and yet...and yet.." his voice trailed off.

"And yet you feel other forces were at work here." Holmes flatly stated. The wine merchant just nodded his agreement.

"Even though, as you stated, her abilities were impaired, you felt that your inaction to respond to the demands of your tormentor caused this accident." Holmes had risen and moved behind M. Donner's chair as he spoke, his eyes making contact with Director Robuchon's opposite him. "May I also assume," he continued on, "that you didn't examine the staircase, nor test the wine she had drank, nor investigate any other possibilities besides your guilt and this veiled threat as the possible cause?" He paused as M. Donner's head slumped forward. "No, I thought not." A small smile appeared on Holmes and the Director's face simultaneously as a conspiratorial moment passed between them.

Inspector Caleur, feeling somewhat displaced by his superior and the renowned detective, tried to reassert himself.

"That occurrence could be the act of a diabolical criminal mind," he interrupted. "Yes, the wine could have been tainted, the

## A CLIENT ONCE AGAIN

stairs also, and yet it is too late to examine the cause and effect at this late date. A simple answer might in fact be just the guilt felt by a wayward husband. But, there is one other incident, is there not, M. Donner?" Inspector Caleur's voice had risen as he spoke, unsettling the vintner, who now raised his head, looked around the table at what he hoped would be his salvation, and, willing himself to speak, stood up.

"It is no use, I am lost. I have bargained with the devil and now he has come for his due. I am lost." His voice cracked, and trailed off once again as he slumped down, his hands covering his head as he openly began sobbing on the table. It seemed forever as the wretched cries of a soul in torment filled the now stale and closed room. It was almost airless and even the young Watson moved to open his shirt collar.

"I recommend we adjourn to my suite, gentlemen," Sherlock intoned, "while the hotel doctor is called for and a mild sedative is administered to our indisposed friend. Watson, please take care of the details. The doctor may place him in a vacant room as my guest. This way, gentlemen." Holmes left no doubt as to who was in charge at this particular moment. They ambled out of the cloistered room and headed towards the hotel lift. Watson, looking back over his shoulder as he aided M. Donner towards the front desk, could not help but notice the scowl that had appeared on Director Robuchon's face. He wondered if this was due to Sherlock's behavior or to the gravity of the case at hand.

*The Inspector reports....*

"Now, Inspector Caleur," Holmes began, "you obviously have been informed of another incident, one that is more in keeping with the tone of these threats than the preamble we have just been through." Holmes, having seated his guests, moved to his slipper for tobacco, stopping to realize that though they had declined liquid refreshment he had no other source of tobacco, cigar or cigarette, to offer, and decided to forego his own desire.

"Enjoy your pipe, Mr. Holmes." It was Director Robuchon, his first words since the introduction. "It is well known how you enjoy tobacco when your mental faculties are engaged. It is also obvious that was your purpose in moving to the credenza with that box of matches in your right hand. So, go ahead and enjoy. I myself do not partake of that particular vice. It seems when I made my conversion, shall we say, all vices appeared too indicative of the past and have become persona non grata to me. But I understand other's cravings. As for the Inspector, he is a cigar man and I know he has several fine panatellas within his easy reach at any time. So, you, also, Inspector, have your cigar, put yourself at ease. It will make the telling of your story a little less formidable if we are in a more relaxed frame of mind. As for me, you will take note that I will close my eyes during, it helps me concentrate. I believe your biographer, no, that's not quite the right word, ah, Dr. Watson, ...that's his son with you, is it not? I thought so. As I was saying, Dr. Watson made mention in his writings that you too had the habitual of turning off extraneous senses to aid in deliberations. It is my way also...see, I do have a vice. Now, continue Inspector, tell us what we don't know." With that, the Director eased his spare frame back into the chair, crossing his obviously lame leg over the good one with the aid of his hands. He then clasped them behind his head and, as he had said, closed his eyes and appeared to be in a deep sleep in seconds.

Holmes, pipe in hand, regained his seat and almost assumed the same posture except for keeping his pipe in full operation with the necessary lighting and relighting the dark, coarse shag required. Inspector Maurice Caleur looked from one personage to the next, wondering if he was indeed supposed to begin speaking. He felt like a school teacher about to begin a fairy tale for his young charges, who at the moment were just beginning their mid-morning nap. A quick smile crossed his lips, but quickly disappeared as the realization of the seriousness of the situation and who these men were. Small beads of sweat were forming on his brow and he removed his handkerchief to wipe them away. It was obvious that his audience was in no great hurry and were biding their time until he was good and ready. He realized he was thirsty and went to the sideboard for a glass of water. It was warm, not especially thirst-quenching, but it performed its purpose. He was ready. The room was silent save for the ticking clock, the occasional scratch of a match

## A CLIENT ONCE AGAIN

and the sound that only a pipe can make when air is forced through its chamber. It appeared the Director was capable of holding his breath, or ceased breathing in the interim.

"Insanity was the word that came to mind when M. Donner first came to my attention. I shouldn't say came to me, for that is not the fact. Rather, the gendarmes had taken him into custody, this was about three weeks ago. It was not a case for the Sureté but the general city police. They had been contacted by a woman, a prostitute who was afraid that her mark was going to kill himself, or perhaps worse, her. They had found him in a cheap garrote, near the Seine but in an unfashionable part of town. Its exact location is unimportant, as the gentleman himself did not know how he arrived there, but the officers guessed it was a room for conducting the lady's business. Suffice it to say, he was rambling incoherently and the officers thought him either mad or under the influence of some stimulant. They could not interrogate him in his condition and were going to bring him to the holding pen, the one in the rear of the central train station. As they descended the narrow set of stairs he broke free of their hold and ran pellmell into the streets. They searched the area for over an hour with no trace of him, and then returned to the garrote and his companion. The woman, a hag, as she was described, seemed somewhat mad herself. The gendarmes, I can give you their names if you require," he paused, and, as no response was forthcoming, he continued.

"They pressed her for more information about this mark and she, probably out of fear, for it was obvious the man was of a higher station, told them she knew his name, he was M. Donner, the wine-merchant. They took her statement that she had picked him up at the pont de Sully as he was crossing. He took a fancy to her, she said. She was exactly what he needed, he also told her. What's more, he wanted her for a mistress, his exact words, she said. The officers took little stock in this, as just one look at her confirmed that no sane man would make these types of entreaties. Still, she had the name right."

"She also had his purse." This intoned flatly by Director Robuchon.

"Obviously," agreed Sherlock, "else how would she know his name? Her faculties were addled, no doubt, and the only way she could remember his name was seeing it printed on what she had purloined from his debilitated state. Unless this charade goes further, and he handed her a calling card on a silver salver." Holmes fairly chortled at this, and so did the Director. It was at this junction that Watson rejoined his companions.

"He's sleeping well, gentlemen. The doctor will check on him in the morning as well." Watson spoke up when all eyes addressed him as he entered the room.

"Capital, Watson." Holmes assured his friend, "The Inspector was just beginning to tell us of his encounter with M. Donner on a more rarified occasion. Please repeat your story from the beginning, Inspector, my young friend's impressions might not be as confident as ours."

Inspector Caleur repeated the story as foretold with the conclusion of the name gleaned from the purse of the deranged M. Donner.

"The gendarmes made their report and as the name of M. Donner was well known in higher circles, the case was turned over to the Sureté, not because it was our type of case, but because of a desire to maintain discretion, n'est pais?" Now in his element, Inspector Caleur assumed a more commanding tone.

"I took the tact of phoning M. Donner and arranging for an interview on the pretext that I was planning a very large social affair for key members of Parliament, and would have his advice and assistance if he would be so kind. Naturally, he was more than happy to accommodate me. We met, I believe it was a Thursday, at 2 p.m., at the Auberge de Crillon. If he was a deranged man it was not shown to me in our initial meeting. He was the epitome of the gracious host. I continued this masquerade for only a short while. Though I may be gracious myself," a small smile escaped the Inspector, "my time is valuable and I wish to conclude what I thought would be a simple matter of too much spirits, too much libido, eh? So, I interrupted my host while he was espousing about the wonderful harvest of grapes this season has brought and made him aware I knew of his activities three nights before. His face grew ashen, no worse, almost corpselike, so drained of color. Like tonight, he slumped and cried, like a

## A CLIENT ONCE AGAIN

baby. I tried to make sense of his ramblings, but they were just utterings, until I did what I thought we should have done earlier tonight: I slapped him. Hard. It revived him, I thought, but only for a minute. His eyes focussed on me, but I could see fear gripping the man as real as if fear had a life of its own and it was standing over him, towering over him, commanding him to cower and beg for mercy. I have never seen a man so possessed. I realized that the man was indeed insane or close to it. If I pressed him further he would disappear inside himself, never to surface. His wife, she had not had her 'accident' yet, came to him and begged me to leave, which I did. And that concludes my interview with M. Donner, except for one other detail."

"A detail that unnerves you, Inspector?" It was Holmes speaking.

"Yes. The girl he mentioned before, the one he says is inconsequential to these proceedings. She is..."

"Dead." Director Robuchon declared.

"True. She is dead." Inspector Caleur resumed. "Her name is Chantal Meurer. Their affair lasted less than two months, but her death, accidental, affected M. Donner obviously a great deal."

"How did she die?" Holmes asked.

"Drowned. It was two nights prior to M. Donner's appearance in the garret. That report I checked. They had gone boating together, just the two of them, and she, according to his report, stood up in the boat in a moment of gaiety, causing it to turn over. She was not a good swimmer and as the night was dark, she perished before he could find her. That report, and then the incident with the old hag, did arouse my curiosity, and yes, my suspicions, but I do not believe he caused Mlle. Meurer's death. And, just like the incident with his wife, guilt is driving this man insane."

"Plausible, Inspector," the Director responded, "but then there are the letters and those threats. What are we to make of that?"

"The letters I am just now aware of. Perhaps the girl, Mlle. Meurer, has another lover or relatives who wish to avenge her death. I will have my staff check on this when I return." The Inspector reached methodically for one of his Panatellas, and proceeded to light up.

# A CLIENT ONCE AGAIN

"There is, of course, one very important fact we are overlooking, isn't there?" Sherlock, again rising from his seat, started pacing the floor in that familiar pattern that Watson had seen.

"You're quite right, M. Holmes." the Director said. "Quite right. And I am surprised that the Inspector hasn't mentioned it."

"Mentioned what?" Caleur gasped.

"Why, if his paramour, Mlle. Meurer, has been drowned," Sherlock paused, "then who is the woman he was with the night his wife took her stumble on the staircase? You do recall he said he felt guilt because he was with his mistress? Who could that be?"

"Ah, mais oui, but, of course. There must be another woman. This man, he has success with women, eh? Perhaps too much success. I will question him once more, in the morning. Now I will go back and dispatch my men to see if Mlle. Meurer did have any other lovers, relatives, what have you, that might shed light on this matter. With your permission, Director?" Inspector Caleur smartly saluted and clicked his heels.

"Of course," the Director responded, "check it out and by all means conduct your interview first thing in the morning. I'll expect a written report by tomorrow afternoon or, if necessary, the following morning. Send another telegram to the préfect in Marseilles under my name directing them not to take the threats against this young woman lightly. Goodnight, Inspector." With that the Director turned his back, not in a callous manner, but as to hasten the Inspector's departure. It was obvious he wished a moment of Sherlock Holmes' attention before retiring as well.

Watson once again found himself poised, arm half-raised in anticipation of shaking, but received no response on the part of Inspector Caleur as he saluted Holmes and made his departure.

"An interesting case, eh, Watson?" Holmes remarked to Watson, obviously trying to make him part of the assembly.

"Yes Sir, very similar to Sir Almstead's ca.." Watson started

"Right," Holmes interrupted, "but that was years ago and the tribal customs in South America add such a different perspective," and turning to the Director, "don't you think?"

## A CLIENT ONCE AGAIN

Watson caught the stern look in Holmes' eyes and kept his counsel.

"Hmm, one of your past adventures, eh, Sherlock? By the look on Watson's face I don't imagine he has any real recall of it. Now his father, I am sure, had first-hand knowledge and would add a certain zest to our dialogue as his style was more verbose. Tell me, Sherlock, what have you been up to lately? I thought you were retired and then I heard you were involved recently in a case in London, stockbrokerage or some such. Come, let us repair to the bar, and if you're up to it, I'll tell you a story about a gang of safecrackers, yeggs you call them, that will raise your admiration of the lower set. Come, you too, Watson, what good is reminiscing if we don't have anyone to enthrall but ourselves?" He fairly laughed at that, and they proceeded to the door.

Watson realized Holmes wanted him to keep quiet about their current investigations and he would do so. He also noticed how Holmes winced whenever the Sureté Director used his given name. Perhaps his admiration for the Director was wearing a little thin.

# Strange Interviews

*June 23rd, Paris, France, Hotel du Louvre*

When Watson awoke he saw that Holmes was already dressed and had ordered up breakfast for both of them. The strange fact of the matter was that Watson was still feeling the aftermath of their late night bout with one too many glasses of gin and tonic, but Holmes appeared nimble and alert.

"Come, come, Watson. Inspector Caleur is due here any minute and I want to be certain the appropriate questions are gleaned from our worrisome friend, M. Donner. He alone, it seems, can shed light on this creature who is causing quite a stir, not just here, but it appears all over the Continent."

"It's amazing," Holmes continued as Watson began his ablutions. "This spectre has sent out his tentacles quite far afield and yet, up 'til now he has left nary a trace, except these boorish references to fire and brimstone he labels threats. You'll notice I have given our adversary a sex...male, to be precise. My powers of observation may not be as keen as they once were, but I would bet any of the ransoms, for that is what these tithes represent, on the fact that this is no supernatural creature from the nether world. No, he is real alright, and though his reach may seem extraordinary, it doesn't take much effort to employ modern mail delivery service to cover the territory that he has so aptly done to date. Yes, the mail, carried by trains from Europe's most central city, Paris, leaves no doubt as to his methods of operation. Naturally, I verified mail and train schedules against the known dates we have so far and the formula fits tolerably. What do you think, Watson?" Holmes appeared quite satisfied with himself and eased into the sofa in an unorthodox manner, allowing his long legs to hang over one arm.

"Well, Sir," Watson said, finishing off a piece of toast, "I follow your logic as to these horrible notes our clients have been receiving, but how do you know it can't be a woman? I mean, a woman can write and mail letters equally as well as a man. I just don't see how you can fathom that, since we don't have any physical evidence of this person."

"Physical evidence? Why, Watson, I am surprised. What do you call the letter that our poor M. Donner gave unto our hands just yesterday? That is physical evidence of the first order. A woman? Hmm, time is short, we must go downstairs, but let me just say, it is not a woman. The writing is definitely that of a man, not only a man, but one who was educated in the eastern parts of Europe, Bavaria or Austria possibly. He is more engineer than scientist, more practical than romantic, and his demeanor would appear harsh to his inferiors, though he would demur to his superiors. The man undoubtedly would have facial hair, a mustache at least, and be fastidious in his dress. More, Watson?" Sherlock Holmes had risen from the couch, and, opening the door, led the young Watson towards the hotel lift.

"But Holmes, the wording on that letter couldn't have told you all that."

"Of course not. But they did tell me the type of individual we were dealing with, an engineer, not a scientist. As for the rest, reexamine that paper. If you recall it was of the highest quality. Further, it contained a watermark, small, just barely visible. The paper is handmade, Watson and not readily available. In fact my investigations revealed only one source: not Bavarian, as I originally suspected, but Prussian. Quite expensive. The type employed by aristocrats and also a certain university in Heidelberg that is renowned for its advanced degrees in mechanical engineering. Further analysis of the ink confirmed its source as also used by this university. Rare. And finally, the flow of ink, remember? Consistent throughout from stroke to stroke. The nib was definitely quillish, but not an ordinary quill, no, this quill was mechanically fed its supply of ink. It would appear that our adversary is either lazy or was involved in too many reproductions to handwrite each missive. Finally, what woman do you think is pursuing an engineering career? No, Watson, our fiend is definitely a man, cunning, yes, but just a man. Ah, the lobby, let us see what our M. Donner has to say."

"A mechanical letter-writer? Holmes, why not use a printing press?" Watson stammered.

"Hah! Watson, I am ashamed. To have any effect these threats must contain one essential ingredient....the PERSONAL TOUCH!" It was on this note that the desk clerk on the lobby level looked up and glared at the two Englishmen who had raised such a ruckus during their short stay at the Hotel du Louvre.

*The Inspector calls...*

Holmes and Watson, after learning the room number where M. Donner had been placed, headed once more to the lift but were interrupted before the metal gate had shut.

"M. Holmes, wait! Stop, you must wait for me, the Director insists!" Inspector Caleur, somewhat out of breath, raced to the lift, his briefcase carelessly catching itself and remaining in the hotel's revolving door.

"Of course, Inspector." Holmes calmly said. "But shouldn't you bring along your case? Hotels are notorious places for pickpockets and other type thieves. It wouldn't bear well with the Director if you were relieved of his copious notes in such a haphazard manner." Holmes broke into a most becoming smile, which was interpreted by the Inspector as not condescending but in good cheer, and he returned it with alacrity. Watson pushed back the gate, obviously holding it in place for Caleur's return.

## STRANGE INTERVIEWS

"M. Holmes, thank you. I hope you understand. I was told specifically to include you in the interrogation but not to allow you, how you say, first crack, at our witness, eh?" For a moment, Caleur seemed nonplussed as he rearranged the case in his arms and steadied himself against the lift's wall.

"You mentioned the Director's notes, n'est pais?" the Inspector said. "How did you know he had supplied me with any notes? I met with him very early this morning, did he call you in the meantime?" The Inspector was quite agitated at the possibility that his superior was bypassing his services in favor of this outsider who may have a very creditable reputation but was, after all, a foreigner.

"No, Inspector, he didn't call me. I would think it quite obvious based on my discussions with M. Robuchon last night that he was intending to do further analysis on the evidence—the letter sent to M. Donner by our phantom. And, since I also realize your Director is a man of action, he would act quickly and pass on his findings to his most reliable and pervasive detective which, of course, is yourself." Inspector Caleur fairly beamed at this laudatory comment by Sherlock Holmes. Holmes waited for this rapture to subside and continued. "Of course, the fact that a briefcase is basically used for only one purpose, that is, to carry documents, and further, it is monogrammed with the Director's initials, there, centered over the brass lock, can result in only one conclusion. Unless of course, you have turned rogue and have purloined the case for ulterior motives." Holmes burst out laughing at this and the Inspector, at first somewhat chagrined, did the same. Watson thought about adding to the levity by repeating Holmes' theories concerning the letter, but thought better of it.

*A second interview*

"He is awake and lucid." the doctor said. "He has had his breakfast and his signs are normal. But please, gentlemen, try not to excite him too much. He is obviously still in a weakened condition. Thank you." The doctor tipped his hat, picked up his medical bag and made his exit. The two detectives moved at once to the connecting room,

## STRANGE INTERVIEWS

and realizing only one could fit through the door at a time, Holmes allowed Inspector Caleur to proceed him.

"Good morning, M. Donner. It is good to see you looking so well." Inspector Caleur began. Holmes quickly took a seat so as to not appear threatening to the bedridden gentleman.

"Yes, good morning Inspector, M. Holmes. I do feel better. The breakfast was wonderful, thank you for your hospitality." The man looked from one to the other, not knowing who his benefactor was.

"Ah, you can thank M. Holmes. He was quite concerned for your condition. As I am, I can assure you, M. Donner." the Inspector said. Holmes acknowledged the gratitude with a small smile and casually drew out his pipe, then, thinking better of it, leaned back in his chair and waited for the interrogation to begin.

"Now," Inspector Caleur began, "we are on your side, Monsieur, but to really do anything we must have your cooperation, understand?"

"I'm quite tired of the whole thing." He paused, then, "But rather than asking me any questions which may not help at all, may I just complete my statement from yesterday? I think I can get through it if I address it in my own words and sequence."

"But of course, mais oui, by all means. Wait one moment, I will just get out pen and paper, then you may proceed, yes, at your own pace. Merci."

"Several months ago, I started receiving these threats, as you know. I didn't take them seriously, not at first. Then they got more specific and implied a definite knowledge about some of my business activities. Gentlemen, I, I, I can't defend myself, I know that I have not always been fair in my....yes, I may have cheated some of my rivals, but..."

It was obviously becoming uncomfortable for him to continue. The Inspector, first looking at Holmes, turned to M. Donner and remarked, "M. Donner, my Director, M. Robuchon, has assured me that information concerning your finances, etc. are not subject to investigation. No, in fact he made it clear that if you were to discuss problems of that sort they were for my ears alone and not to be repeated. I am sure M. Holmes can give you the same assurances." Again, Caleur snubbed Watson by not mentioning or looking in his direction.

"Certainly," Holmes said. "My obligation is to my clients, M. Donner. And they, like you, have been victimized by this trickster, for that is what he is. My only goal is to bring him to heel. Your prior machinations have no interest to me, save for their possible connection to finding this fiend. You have my word, and that of my associate, John Watson as well." Watson murmured his agreement audibly, and mentally thanked Holmes for acknowledging his presence.

"I'm glad to hear that, and I understand. I'll tell all. As I said, there are some things I am ashamed to admit were not sound business practices. It became obvious to me that this, this devil knew everything. At first, I thought he was someone I had wronged, someone seeking revenge. The list of suspects was quite large, I'm afraid, and it drove me crazy trying to imagine which one could be the sender of these notes. Finally, my memory brought back to me one deal that could possibly be the connection…but it seemed so remote." He stopped as the recollection formed once more in his brain.

"Remote, but memorable, M. Donner." Holmes remarked as his eyes, before hooded, opened and narrowed to a sharper stare.

"Yes, quite memorable and in keeping with the tone of the letters. You see, this man, Sar Olderman, came to me with a most incredible proposal. A gypsy if I ever saw one. Quite old, so scraggly, full bearded, very bohemian, even wearing an earring. He carried a staff but was not Alpinish, but more, more…"

"Prussian, M. Donner?" Holmes said quite suddenly, casting an eye towards Watson.

"Yes, precisely, Prussian. He puzzled me immensely. Though he appeared quite crude, his mannerisms, as I said, like a gypsy, lots of hand waving and all, but yet there was something of an educated way about him….I can't put it into words. Regardless, this offer he made seemed very simplistic. He had in his possession a bottle of wine whose bouquet was quite incredible. The container was some kind of flask, an animal's skin, perhaps goat, I don't know. He bade me to taste this concoction. I was somewhat skeptical and I guess also afraid. After all, I still had those threats on my mind. He, by example, poured some into one of my finest tasting cups and proceeded to sample the wine like the finest sommelier. This also put me on my guard, but when he finished he poured another and handed it to me. There was something hypnotic about his eyes. Did I mention that one eye appeared blind? No, I thought not. It was all milky and yet the orb was quite visible and seemed to be staring straight ahead at all times. I couldn't get my eyes off of it. Well, I did take that sip, and more so. It was delicious. Not a Bordeaux of course, but a Sauterne....but what a Sauterne...sweet yet not cloyingly sweet. It was dry, as a great wine should be, but flavorful. Drinking that wine transposed me to a cool forest in my mind, a babbling brook, soft shaded trees, ah, I digress. Gentlemen, as you know, wine is my business. And this wine, this wine meant success. I knew it. And what do you think he wanted for his blend, gentlemen?"

"Your immortal soul?" asked the Inspector, much to Holmes' obvious displeasure.

"No," Donner laughed, "Not my soul. At least I thought not. His offer was simple. He knew where these grapes grew and the process used to bring them to fermentation. In short he promised the ability to reproduce in prodigious quantities the elixir, his word, I had just drunk. And I was drunk, not from the small amount of wine, but from the thought of being the producer of such a pungent, tantalizing wine. I was ready to do anything, sign anything and he knew it, oh yes, he knew it. But he wasn't after riches, nor my soul, all he wanted was...was....oh, oh gentlemen, may God have mercy on me...ah...ah.."

"Easy monsieur, take some water." Inspector Caleur poured from the basin and held the glass to his lips, and, lifting the glass skyward, gently allowed the liquid to flow down his throat.

"Thank you," he said, as his one free hand, the other obviously under the heavy blankets, dabbed at his mouth, drying the overflow from his lips and cheeks.

"I am so ashamed. You remember I told you I had taken a mistress, Mlle. Meurer? Yes, good. She was an incredible woman, rather a young girl. Too young for me, eh?" A small smile played on his lips.

"And perhaps that, coupled with Sar Olderman's request, makes my story so..so macabre. His bill for services rendered, again his words, was that I would give my seed, my future life to...to that hag....that woman the gendarmes found me with. Yes, I had lain with her....and my

God, I did it...I have sown and now I shall reap." Muffled sobs wracked the body of M. Donner as tears cascaded from his eyes. He became silent and the small electric light cast a foreboding shadow over the room. The three other men exchanged glances that revealed their revulsion of the secret just now given by the wretched man lying before them. The silence was broken by Sherlock Holmes.

"I require data, M. Donner. Not of your physical involvement with this woman, you are past that abomination. Let us concentrate on details. Since this was your 'contract' with this man, was it put in writing, and if so, do you have the document? I would also like a more detailed description of your paramour, Mlle. Meurer and, as untasteful as it may seem now, also of the old woman chosen for this charade." Holmes reached into his inner pocket for his shag and pipe and thought no more of offending sensibilities.

"Yes, you're quite right, M. Holmes." the sick man replied. "I must try to put it in your perspective and remain aloof from the past. As to the contract, yes, there was a document, but he would not allow a copy to be made. It is in his possession. I didn't sign it in blood, or anything, nothing that ridiculous. The fact of the matter is, I really believed I was taking advantage of him. Of course, at that time I hadn't imagined who was to be the recipient of my, my...you understand...anyway, my mind rationalized it that the poor man was probably concerned about in-breeding among his tribe. That's somewhat understandable gentlemen, if the scientific reports have any validity to them. As I said before, he seemed somewhat educated." He drank a little more water, this time unaided, and continued.

"The young lady, Mlle. Meurer, Chantal. So sweet, her hair, soft, not long, but incredibly silky....her face, not beautiful, but clean and wholesome. An angel." As he paused, Inspector Caleur interrupted.

"Do you not have a photograph of her, monsieur?"

"I did, but naturally, because of my wife it had to remain hidden. After her death—she drowned, you know that, Inspector—I destroyed everything. It wasn't that I didn't want a memento of her, but since my wife's accident, my remorse...I, I..."

"It is understandable. Perhaps you can supply some details about her personal life, where she lived, worked perhaps..." Holmes intervened.

"That's another sad or strange part. I really didn't know that much about her....she just came into my life one day. I was at a grape auction and she was there. She was curious about wines, and I very cavalierly tried to explain the complexities concerning the varieties of grapes. She was so naive and I am afraid I took advantage of her like a competitor in the marketplace. I lied about my domestic arrangements and seeing as she was a stranger to Paris...yes, she was obviously from the country...maybe the south, the coast...her coloring was warm, I, I loved her. I admit it, she captured me totally and I, her, I believe." Again a pause was necessary as other memories invaded the mind of M. Donner. Then a shadow passed over his face and he began anew.

"The old woman. She was hideous, ugly, a true witch. Olderman had pointed her out and told me if I didn't lay with her within three days the deal was off. I was at wit's end. I wanted that wine, that was for sure. I did the only thing I could think of. I went to my daughter's fiancé, Capt. Gaulen, and asked him to bring me some cocaine, the drug used by the Chinese. I thought its properties would alleviate any revulsion in performing my deed."

"There are other factors involved in using cocaine, M. Donner." Holmes said. "And other side effects as well." This, spoken from experience, as Watson knew from his father's writings.

"Yes, of course," Donner went on. "There was some fear on my part as to that, but I wanted that wine. I would do anything and I obviously did." He paused once again and looking back at his inquisitors said, "You really don't understand how an object or a person could consume someone so much. It is my French blood." He then realized Inspector Caleur was looking harshly at him.

"You understand, don't you, Inspector?" he asked.

"Yes...and no, after all I am on the side of the law," he responded imperiously.

"True...you are right. My morals have not allowed me to curb any of my appetites...to my own regret." This was spoken as an obvious apology.

As it seemed he was not going to volunteer any further information, Sherlock Holmes, looking first at Watson, then at Inspector

*"The Hag"*

# STRANGE INTERVIEWS

Caleur, rose up from his chair, and in a firm but gentle voice asked the question that all were waiting to be asked.

"A sad tale. Your life, quite complicated....threats from an unknown enemy.....a new mistress comes into your life....your wife neglected.....then this wondrous wine to compensate your coffers even more.....but a bargain that requires a certain amount of madness on your part to complete....cocaine, and obviously an overdose based on the gendarmes' report...and still...a wedding to be accomplished, which you made all the arrangements for, correct?"

Donner nodded, and Holmes continued, "Still threats keep coming....you even have time to send a request for assistance to me, Sherlock Holmes....which you later decide was not wise to do since I may uncover some of your more, shall we say, nefarious activities in my investigations. Then your lover meets an untimely death, drowning, most unfortunate. I assume the body was never found? Yes, I knew that. Then the night of your wife's accident. A fall down a flight of stairs, almost simultaneous with your arrival at home, was it not?" Again a nod of assent.

"But...M. Donner, you told us you felt guilt over your wife's injury. Guilt, because you were with your mistress. But she was dead. Who were you with, not the hag again?"

"No...God, no....not her.....I...I was with Chantal......she, .....she came back....she....came back to, ....to say goodbye....she told me so.....Sar...Olderman...he brought her back....I...I...." but before more words could be spoken, his eyes rolled upwards into his head and he collapsed into his pillow.

"M. Donner, M. Donner," Inspector Caleur implored. "He is passed out..no, it's all right, he's breathing...please M. Watson, send for the doctor.

Watson was galvanized into action the moment the Inspector said his name, even though his mind doubted the words came from him. Holmes moved closer to the distressed man, silently observing the twitches reflected in his face and even in his limbs.

"The man is suffering from his delusions, reinforced by his body's now craving need for cocaine. Tell the doctor when he gets here to administer no more than a seven percent solution or he will....that's all." Holmes moved to the door, took one more look back and was gone.

# STRANGE INTERVIEWS

*The Director returns....*

"Your diagnosis was quite right, M. Holmes." Inspector Caleur said. "The doctor regrets he was not aware that M. Donner was using cocaine. That, coupled with the depressants he was prescribing, could have been a lethal combination."

Holmes, obviously deep in thought about something else, waved his hand to acknowledge the remark and Watson, sensing an opportunity, volunteered, "My father often told me that if war didn't kill the solders, then the combination of their self-administering pain killers and field doctors could certainly turn the trick."

Holmes looked up at Watson and smiled. They were back in their suite and were waiting for Director Robuchon to arrive. He had been sent for almost immediately after M. Donner's collapse. Their wait was at an end as a soft knock was heard upon the door.

"Come in, Director, please come in." Holmes bellowed. A small smirk crossed his face as the Director gently opened the door and made his entrance.

"Well, well, Sherlock," again the use of the given name. "I know of your skills but I am curious as to how you knew it was me. Yes, I know I was expected, but after all, this is a hotel. The doctor, the bellman, desk clerk, what have you...you are not familiar with my knock." Director Robuchon moved as quickly as a cat to the furthest seat and once ensconced, looked inquiringly at the master detective.

"We have a major puzzle on our hands, Director, that requires more data to be solved. That is our priority. As for your knock, no, I am not familiar with it, nor do I need to be. As you said, you were expected but others could have come before you, as you so listed. But none of them, I daresay, would employ the cat burglar's approach, an acknowledged expertise of yours." Robuchon was visibly shaken by the remark. "Also none of them have reason to listen at the door surreptitiously before knocking, as you did. No, do not look surprised, it's simplicity itself. As I recall, the electric lamp is located on the opposite hall wall and is quite bright, and I caught the distinct shapings of a biped creature standing at our door for several minutes now. You are a thin man, Director, but you still cast a shadow, not through the door but under the door. Enough?"

# STRANGE INTERVIEWS

"Yes, quite nice, Sherlock, quite nice. Now, Inspector Caleur has presented the facts to me about this morning's interview that, combined with my own research, indicates we are travelling in very murky waters. I need your help, Sherlock, and if you are willing I am going to take you into my confidence and reveal what our investigations have uncovered so far. Inspector, my briefcase, please." The Director made great pains to empty the contents of his briefcase on the table in an orderly fashion, squaring the edges of the documents in a most meticulous manner. Sherlock Holmes made no move towards the table except with his eyes, which glanced hither and yon as if he were at a tennis match. Satisfied with his observations, he went to the sideboard, obtained his tobacco and pipe, and without turning to address anyone in particular, he said:

"He's made a mistake. Quite possibly because the threats posed by his letter campaign were not bearing fruit quick enough. His methodical mind has invented an alter ego, this Sar Olderman. They are not one and the same, that I am sure of. Wait, let me finish." Sherlock had turned around and, sensing that the Director and the Inspector were ready to interrupt, he raised his hand.

"Our original protagonist is from Austria or Bavaria. He has attended or graduated from the University at Heidelberg, an engineering student. The paper, and the ink bear witness to this fact. He is not operating entirely alone, there is a woman also. This woman, attractive, but not glamorous, he has employed with M. Donner to seduce him and push him further over the edge. I am also quite certain that she was employed once before."

This time the Director could not be quieted. "You mean with Sir Gregory Almstead, M. Holmes?" He looked at Watson while he spoke, and took Holmes' acknowledged wave of a hand and continued, "Of course I didn't believe your concoction of South American Indians. How could I? Sir Almstead is well known on the Continent and the troubles concerning him, though they are unknown to me, are troubles affecting many businessmen, including our M. Donner."

"Aha, just as I suspected!" Holmes shouted. "This plot is Machiavellian in its purpose."

"And," the Director shot back, "as you said, Bavaria seems to be the source, which is consistent with our own reports from that quarter. Our government is very anxious and concerned. Even as we speak there is unrest in your own country, Sherlock. The Irish issue, talks of general industry strikes, but still it is believed that something terrible is brewing throughout Europe."

"But there is a pattern to the blackmail." It was Watson who spoke.

"Pattern?" the Director asked.

"Yes, wine, art, crystal, each unique and special, but not for money alone. There is something more to this than meets the eye, I think..." but before he could finish Holmes interrupted. "That train of thought will leave us nowhere." Watson appeared crushed. "Now that our foe has shown himself, or at least an accomplice, we must try to draw him out. Gentlemen, let us order food to be brought up. After we dine, if I may, I will outline for you a plan of attack."

The Director winced at this show of authority by Sherlock Holmes and cast a glance towards his Inspector, who, in a typical gaelic reaction, shrugged his shoulders. Watson, still smarting from Holmes' remark, brooded silently.

*Another appointment....*

"It was as I thought," exclaimed Holmes, "M. Lapelle, you remember him, Watson, the other victim in Paris who has intimated that our services are no longer required?"

"Of course, Holmes." Watson rejoined, doubly glad to be addressed as an equal and especially after hearing the word 'our' used by Sherlock Holmes.

Sherlock continued, "I've taken the liberty to contact M. Lapelle and he has agreed to meet with us this evening. My conversation was short but I believe his interview will have some surprises in store for you gentlemen. In fact, it puts an incredibly new slant on the proceedings, thus far."

The Director and the Inspector exchanged glances laden with doubt. Director Robuchon realized he had let M. Holmes lead these inquiries, perhaps too far, but was somewhat afraid to change course at this late date as he was under strict orders not to interfere with Holmes' investigations, but to draw him out at every opportunity he was given. Thus, he kept his counsel. The Inspector, not quite understanding this change in command, also kept quiet, allowing that it was his superior's place to be the one to upstage this foreigner, not his. The air seemed filled with intrigue and this young man, Watson, seemed very agitated at the very least. Perhaps he knew more than he was allowing, or was allowed to tell. This was the theory Director Robuchon had espoused to Inspector Caleur. The men waited in silence, lingering over coffee and sweet liquors, for the arrival of M. Lapelle. Finally, the moment arrived as the bellman at the door announced a visitor who was waiting in the hotel lobby. He further stated that the gentleman preferred meeting in public space rather than the intimate confines of M. Holmes' suite. Holmes gave the boy several coins and when he had left, addressed his companions.

"Well, it seems our M. Lapelle is not as brave as my previous exchange would have him be, or something has happened to change his disposition. Quickly, let us make his acquaintance before he rethinks his position once more and is gone, just as our phantom friend does so ably on occasion."

The four men hastily moved to the lift, where Watson volunteered to take the stairs as a quicker method of obtaining the ground floor. Holmes most heartily agreed and Inspector Caleur went with Watson at a hastened pace. Once alone in the slow moving lift, the Director turned to Holmes, a small smile forming on his lips.

"Your young friend is dedicated to you. That is an admirable trait to cultivate in a person. In my own case, Inspector Caleur may respect me but I believe it is more from fear than my abilities. Pray tell, how did you obtain such allegiance? You don't seem to treat him as an equal, which in any case, you shouldn't, and yet, I can tell by the way he looks at you, he would follow you to the ends of the earth." The Director turned his gaze away as the lift reached the lobby level and the gate started forward.

"He has the same inherent qualities that his father had, I can assure you. The 'why,' ah, I am afraid is something I could never

# STRANGE INTERVIEWS

fathom before, and now, let us just say, chemistry is the answer. Our energies and life forces are a complement to each other and not in opposition. That is the only explanation I could ever devise as regards his father as well. It is not a case of superior and inferior but of plus and minus, no more. I leave it at that."

As they exited the lift, Sherlock Holmes went first, followed by the Director, whose voice, tinged with laughter, roared out, "Well then, let's see what your minus has accomplished in the interim, ha, ha, ha, shall we?" Holmes would not turn around and show the Inspector the nettled look his face now held.

*Another strange interview....*

M. André Lapelle was an obese man, quite fat. His face included numerous chins, which were quite evident on his freshly shaved countenance. He also had the misfortune of being extremely short, which gave him a most jolly appearance. His clothes aided in his rotundness as he wore a vest containing a most obnoxious pattern of splotches of greens and browns, which repeated themselves incessantly on his corpulent body. The suit, of expensive mohair, was bluish to purplish in color and contrasted terribly with the vest. A more comical appearance you would be hard pressed to find, that is, until one heard his voice. It was this aspect which changed his entire appearance to one of a more commanding posture, as it literally boomed authority.

"Yes, gentlemen. I understand your position thoroughly. Now, let me declare mine. These notes I have been receiving are ludicrous. That the Sureté and the notable Mr. Sherlock Holmes are giving them this much credence gives me pause. Pardon my addressing you as Mr. rather than M., Mr. Holmes, I do not share the French way of thinking that everyone should follow our appelations. Now as I did, in fact, write to you, Mr. Holmes, you are certainly due an explanation. It is simply this: the letters have stopped. I repeat, stopped. When I first received them they were threatening in nature, as you say. I didn't take them seriously, but as they did tend to implicate some misdoings on my part I thought it best to contact a private agency to dispel them on the spot. It was entirely unnecessary. No, I did not pay the tithe as required by these missives. As you may know, I am the premier manufacturer of clothing in all of Paris and my goods are not to be bartered for less than the going rate, I assure you. In summation, gentlemen, I scorned these entreaties and they gave up, period." M. Lapelle, after finishing his oration, snapped his fingers for the waiter to bring more port, which the large man had managed to drink during his speech in one quick gulp, without a pause, it seemed.

Holmes rose from his chair, starting to pace, then stopped, looking directly at M. Lapelle, and said, "If you are as fearless as you would have us believe, why, then, have us meet in this public salon and not in my private suite?" Before the man could reply, Holmes raised his hand and continued. "Further, why the necessity of carrying a concealed derringer[6], which you have had little acquaintance with, not to mention the Italian knife shield under your vest? And, finally, the armed guard lurking just outside this very room. Answer those questions M. Lapelle and perhaps, we can truly be of some service to you, after all." Holmes, a sly smile on his face, turned away towards Watson and gave again that quick wink that Watson knew so well.

"I'm, I'm astounded." said M. Lapelle, somewhat shaken but still sounding authoritative. "How on earth did you know? I mean, about the gun and all." He paused, awaiting Holmes' response, and seeing that he was not going to concede anything further until he did, Holmes responded.

"Elementary, M. Lapelle, quite elementary. The derringer has a very unique shape to it and its presence in your very accessible vest pocket, though hidden within, and to put it delicately, because of your shape, it has left its impression upon the outer part of the pocket. See for yourself." M. Lapelle's gaze, as well as that of others present, moved to the vest pocket.

"As to your experience with this same gun, that is also quite simple. The derringer has a small aperture where one would employ the

---

[6]The Derringer, a short-barreled pistol, invented by the American, Henry Deringer, first appeared in 1853.

## STRANGE INTERVIEWS

*"Interview with M. Lapelle"*

trigger. If you had practiced much it would have, again, because of your particular size, left callouses, or at least some indenture on your trigger finger. A quick look on your right hand revealed no such mark. Yes, it is obvious also that you are right-handed. All of your movements reveal that. Now, the Italian vest, which was developed due to the inordinate amount of knife fighting in that land of such heated passion, also is obvious. You may be in the clothing manufacturing business, but you are not in the tailoring end. No, that vest may be quite stylish in more southern climes, but here, in Paris, is a different story. Finally, can anything be more obvious than the stolen glances you have made with that gentlemen in the anteroom just outside? He paces the floor like the pugilist he is. His name is not known to me, but I am sure he has spent the better part of his life in the ring. One look at his face, especially the condition of his ears, would complete that picture. His days of professional fighting are long over and now, he seeks the only employment he is best suited for, bodyguard, and, in this instance, your bodyguard. Satisfied?"

"Quite. Very simple, as you said. Your observations are correct." The man beckoned once more to the waiter, continuing his response. "The letters, though threatening in nature, meant nothing to me, as I said. There is a saying, something about sticks and stones, etc., and I believe that. As a child, because of my condition of weighing more than others, I have been the recipient of many words aimed to hurt me. I have grown inured to such insults. It is physical danger that gets my attention. I have a very low tolerance for pain. Perhaps it is because of my size, I don't know, but I do. Therefore, whenever threatened, I do take the necessary precautions. In this instance, it is not the letters, as they have truly stopped. No, my fears now are based on substance. Let me refresh my glass and I will tell all, please be patient." The man rose up from his seat with extreme agility, considering his weight, and, moving to the table, poured himself another glass, this time sherry. The waiter was nowhere to be seen.

"Two weeks ago I received a letter concerning a business proposition which appeared quite favorably to me. I shan't discuss the details, as they were just a ruse, I'm sure. Gentlemen, my business acumen has rewarded me substantially over the years and yet, when a bargain is in the offing I am still tempted to cover my bets. I have many competitors, not just here in Paris, but all over the Continent, even in London. The world is becoming a smaller place, that is certain. The rail system is allowing foreign companies to bring their inferior...I digress, excuse me. In short, gentlemen, I agreed to meet this gentlemen just outside of Paris at an inn of some dubious reputation. I am sure the Inspector is familiar with Auberge du Voltaire[7], a misnamed establishment if ever there was one." Inspector Caleur demurred his assent and let the manufacturer continue his story.

"I remember there was a light rain falling and it made my dress even more haphazard with a cape added to the mix. No, I was not wearing this vest, for my fears were not aroused at this time. When I arrived I bade my driver to wait while I went inside. The place was quite large, with nooks and crannies to hold all kinds of nefarious activities, I am sure. It took me the better part of an hour to make my way through all those corridors, and when I was through it was evident that my appointee had failed to show, or so I thought. Upon leaving the establishment I once more entered my carriage, and to my surprise I was not alone. My first reaction was that this was a robbery, and that my purse was this foul fellow's objective, but he held no weapon nor was there any in sight. And then he spoke, he said, 'M. Lapelle, we meet at last. My entreaties have had no effect, eh? But, the opportunity to make riches, that has a more desirous effect, yes?' I was dumbstruck to say the least. This ruffian, for indeed that was his appearance, spoke on a much higher plane, that is, with a more educated tone than his dress, or for that matter, his own face would imply. That face, a gypsy if I ever saw one." Holmes and Watson exchanged a rapid glance in understanding and M. Lapelle continued, "My dealings with that type are limited of course, but the earring, the unkempt facial hair, even the one glass eye assured me of whom I was dealing with. I thought about escaping but the coach was too small a space to allow me egress from my unholy companion. And then the next thing I knew, he tapped the top of the box and we were rolling away into

---

[7]Hotel du Quai Voltaire, 19 Rue Voltaire, Paris—The hotel is located in the 13th arrondisement, which would be considered outside Paris at the time of this story. It once played host to Charles Baudelaire, Richard Wagner and Oscar Wilde, if this is the same establishment referenced.

the countryside. Can you imagine, gentlemen, my further surprise, in thinking that my driver, a servant who is in my service, would be taking his direction from this miscreant." He looked about him to see the effect his words were having, and as no one interrupted, he continued his story of abduction.

"We had set off at a fast pace, too unnerving for my constitution, but in a short while we slowed to a more tolerable speed and my abductor continued his diatribe towards me. In effect, he chastened me for disobeying his instructions to pay the tithe and reminded me of our pact. I told him I knew of no such contract, that he had mistaken me for someone else. He demanded silence and continued in this same irrational religious tone. I was terrified. The man was obviously insane. He finished his sermon, his way of putting it, with one more last threat. He said it was unfortunate that I was without family or any close friend as it was his way to bring obedience through example. Therefore he had no choice but to bring pain, excruciating pain, to my own person. Further, this pain would come at the sign of eight. And that was it. Without any movement on his part the coach stopped, he alighted and much to my further surprise, mounted this enormous black stallion, a great beast with the most excited and flashing eyes, no saddle on his hindquarters, he went bareback, and rode extremely fast away, with the most hideous laugh permeating the night air being my last memory of him. I sat in the coach for quite a few minutes trying to compose myself. I was even afraid to step out and face my servant. I called to him, softly at first, then louder as he did not reply. I really do not know how long I sat in this condition until I could steel myself to peer out. Finally I did. My servant was nowhere to be seen. The box was empty. I was alone on a country road with my coach and two and nobody else. I fairly swooned. Every night sound sent chills up my spine, I was terrified. Realizing at last that I had no choice, I made the steep climb up to the coach box, with some difficulty, I must say. I'm surprised the horses were not spooked due to my endeavors. The good animals they are, they patiently awaited my climb. Upon settling in, I noted that the reins were easily accessible as they had been tied to the foot rung before me. Even so, it took a while in that small space that constitutes the driver's seat to shift my body and reach down to the reins. For a moment I thought I would be stuck in that position, it was most unsettling. When I was finally ensconced in the appropriate position, reins in hand, seated firmly, my brain railed at the thought that I had never to date actually driven a coach. I must admit a small laugh escaped my lips at this thought, and I realized it was now time to learn. I tried to remember the commands my servant had used when I was in my usual place, on the satin seats just meters away. I won't bore you further, gentlemen, except to say, the weather is much more injurious to one's physical well-being from this vantage point than inside a warm coach with the ability to pull a warm coverlet in addition to closing the shades to the night air." As it appeared he was finished, the Director took center stage, rising as he did.

"The driver, your servant, has never been found. Correct?"

"Quite so, M. Director." he responded.

"Then, this gypsy, this madman or whatever, has not only reached a stage of desperation in his activities, as M. Holmes has intimated before, but has also resorted to the crime of murder to a person known. His prior deeds may be judged malicious parlor games, but now he has gone too far. Inspector, notify all authorities, including the border guards, giving as complete a description of this monster as we know it. In addition, I will have the King's guards sent to every gypsy camp and have every rogue of them imprisoned for cause. We will find this man, I will stake my reputation on it." As he finished he looked towards Sherlock Holmes, not to obtain his blessing, but to indicate his authority. The expression on Holmes' face was more Cheshire-like and as unrevealing as Watson had ever seen.


*Deliberations....*

Inspector Caleur had gone to do the Director's bidding. Holmes, once more pacing in his room, waited for the Director to reassert himself as he had downstairs. He didn't have to wait long.

"A most interesting problem, Sherlock," he started. "I will also state that the disappearance of the driver is not the first malicious act by our adversary. No, nor the last, I am sure. I have set certain wheels in motion which I am confident will bring this Sar Olderman his due. As for your statement that he and the originator of the letters are not one and the same, how do you draw that conclusion? And, if so, what plan of action did you intend to employ before this latest development came to pass?" The Director was obviously referring to the interview just completed with M. Lapelle.

"In absolute candor, Director," Holmes began, "certain facts have come into my possession which make this Sar Olderman just another player in this convoluted plot to extort, maim and destroy."

"Such harsh words, Sherlock. These facts you will now share with me, correct? I am not your adversary but your ally. We must work together if we are to bring this matter to a close." The Director, a hurt look on his face, his voice low, cajoling, made it evident he was trying to elicit more information from his illustrious companion. Once more, Watson was relegated to a role of witness to these two giants of deduction.

Sherlock looked at the Director but also acknowledged, much to Watson's relief, his young friend and, walking to the dresser, removed an envelope and handed it to Watson to read.

"Read it aloud, Watson." Sherlock said.

Watson unfolded the paper and stated, "It's from Jamison."

"Who?" asked the Director.

"Gordon Jamison, Sir Almstead's secretary." replied Watson and continued.

"Sir Almstead has somewhat recovered, he says. Though his health is still suspect, and his doctor forbade any travel, he is making plans to go to London. I fear he is suffering great remorse over his brother's death, and of course that of the young lady, Miss Anne. I am doing my level best to keep him in Brussels but he is being insistent, and when he is ambulatory he will go and that is final. The doctor is concerned that he is being precipitous in his endeavors and is noticeably worried that in treating Sir Almstead he is also aiding in his downfall. Mr. Holmes, I fear he has also become delusional as well as irrational. Lately he has espoused the thought that Miss Anne is still alive. What can I do? Your faithful servant, Gordon Jamison. P.S. His excited state has caused a relapse and the doctor feels that it should be at least two more weeks before he will be able to travel, though again he reiterates his dire warning of his lordship's doing so. Enclosed, also as you requested, the photo of Miss Anne. I thank God Sir Almstead has not noticed the facsimile in its place, at your suggestion."

"Ah, so you verified that the young lady in London is the same as M. Donner's paramour?" the Director stated.

"Naturally." Holmes replied. "I had my suspicions, and they were immediately verified by Mlle. LaPorté. Her position in the household notwithstanding, it is amazing what facts are available to the staff of a man who thinks he is deluding his wife." Sherlock fairly beamed at this statement and, turning to Watson, said: "I am sorry to have kept you in the dark, my friend. As I said, I do not like to state theories as fact until I can prove them. I also had another ulterior motive and that was simply to take advantage of your natural inquisitiveness and let you have your lead, as it were. Your observations concerning the types of payments required by our demon from Hell are quite astute, and I am sure will play an important role when this has reached its successful conclusion. I do have a theory as regards this, and as before, I hesitate to bring it to the fore at this stage."

Watson's face lit up as the accolades cascaded down around him. He could even catch a glimpse of respect from the Director as he shifted in his chair in a most nonchalant manner.

After enjoying the effect of his words, he continued to address him. "Watson, notify Jamison that we will be in London in less than five days. We will try to contact him in Brussels immediately upon arrival. Under no circumstances should he allow Sir Almstead to make this journey alone or let him out of his sight at any time. If he should arrive before we do, ensure that they stay at the Russell Hotel. Send that immediately, Watson." Watson, his instructions in mind, raced from the room down to the front desk.

"Well, well. Secrecy may be best at times, and it does avoid embarrassment if you are wrong in your predictions. But I must insist, Sherlock," the Director intoned, "I still don't see how this Sar Olderman can't be our main quarry? And you still haven't solidified any plan beyond the one that I have placed in action. What say you?"

# STRANGE INTERVIEWS

A smirk first crossed the Director's face, then slowly changed to a warm smile in an effort not to annoy his supposed ally.

"I'm surprised, Director. Very surprised. You did not grasp the modus operandi of our cunning friend. The letters, obviously, the letters." Sherlock smiled back, but his quickly turned to a smirk of the first order.

"Letters, damn the letters," shot back Robuchon. "Are you saying this Olderman is in Brussels and has visited Sir Almstead with his ghoulish news of his sweetheart's rise from the grave? Ridiculous! How can you surmise that from that short note of the secretary's? Hmph!" In obvious disdain the Director stood up, grabbed for his hat and was obviously making his exit.

"Secretary Jamison is quite efficient." Holmes said, in a calm and gentle voice. "Quite efficient. In fact, all correspondence, in and out, passes through this affable employee. So when he stipulates that Sir Gregory has received knowledge of Miss Anne's apparent resurrection, then suffice it to say, the messenger was Sar Olderman. In fact, Director, if you are sincere in apprehending him on French soil, I could suggest you study this photograph and look for her as well." Holmes paused as he reached into his vest pocket for the sepia-toned photograph the bellman had returned from his trip to Mlle. LaPorté's.

"The photo bears some likeness, but you will find some major changes in her appearance. Her hair is naturally black, darker than the woman in this photo. Her face will be more haughty, her cheekbones higher, a very imposing woman, imperious and with a smile that will melt your heart if it isn't a leer. She's Hungarian by birth but her alliances are much more suspect." Sherlock displayed a quick smile.

"She is as much a chameleon as this other fellow," said the Director.

"Maybe more so," Sherlock replied. "But I am afraid they are no longer in France. I also believe that M. Lapelle's precautions are also unnecessary at this time. But time will bear witness, I am sure. And you, Director Robuchon, will do what you will do, as I will do what I must do. Good day, Sir." Holmes' voice moved from calm to icy cold as he held the door for the departing officer, while Watson, now returned, open-mouthed, stared at Director Robuchon's back as he passed him and said, "Oh, My…"

# STRANGE INTERVIEWS

*On our own....*

"We are on our own, Watson, perhaps that is best. And yet," doubt seemed to creep into the detective's voice. "Well, we will proceed, but more cautiously. I am afraid these proceedings are taking a definitely dangerous turn. At this juncture I would insist that your father bring his old revolver, but I assume you are not trained in that discipline."

"No, Holmes, but I have had pretty extensive experience in the manly arts, boxing, though you might not know it."

"I have noticed your muscles have a more defined characteristic than laboring at a desk would suggest. But I am afraid your activities of late have allowed them to decline in their abilities. No, fisticuffs will not do. Though not my first choice, I will recommend you do as our client, M. Lapelle has done, and obtain a small derringer. It is the easiest of small arms to master, though only for very close quarters. I hope we will not have the need of it, but we must be prepared."

"What about you, Sir? Shall I obtain a second for your use, as well?"

"Oh, Watson, I have always relied on your father's abilities in that department. My weapon of choice is my brain. It has never failed me before, but of late it is probably a little rusty and may need a thorough cleaning before I fire these old synapses in perfect aim. I am concerned about putting you in harm's way based on the skimpy knowledge that I have so far gleaned. It has been a baffling case, one that I truly believe has more than one solution, unfortunately."

"More than one solution? Oh, Holmes, the man has been cunning, that's for sure. But you yourself said he has made a mistake. He has shape now, form. He is no devil or Satan, but a man, only a man. You will bring him down, I am sure of it." The look of admiration on Watson's face brought moist tears to Holmes' eyes.

"Such faith, Watson. I sincerely hope I can live up to your expectations. We must get some rest. Tomorrow is a big day, Watson. I've also placed some wheels in motion, as the Director said. Let us hope they move things further along than they have.

# The Game is Afoot

*June 25th, Paris, France, Hotel du Louvre*

Again, Watson awoke to find the great detective not only up and dressed, but gone. He moved as quickly as he could to ready himself and was just about to dash through the door when Sherlock Holmes made his reappearance.

"Watson, you're awake, wonderful. Unfortunately, you will have no time for breakfast, here take this." Holmes handed him the silver-handled derringer.

"Don't point it at me, for God's sake," Holmes laughed. "It is loaded. And remember it's range is quite short, no more than 8-10 meters at best. You don't recognize it but it belongs to M. Lapelle. Don't worry, he's safely ensconced in the room below. Ah, I forgot, you are still in the dark, my friend. Let me explain. After my initial discussion with M. Lapelle, you recall I spoke to him before he came over for his interview, well, he did offer that same bluster about there being no danger. That being the case, I took the liberty of placing an advertisement, in his name, in the Paris paper. My French is not bad, considering my ancestry[8], but he sounded a little dismayed last night

---
[8] This seems surprising since it is thought that Sherlock Holmes was related or descended from the French artist, Vernet.

when he found out, and at my insistence, he is safely established in suite 12A under the name of M. Chevalier. Further, the room clerk has changed the listings for our suite to the name of, why Watson, don't look so bewildered. If our adversary can play charades, so can we. And so, we are listed as..." Here, the great detective paused, looking quizzically at his friend.

"M. Lapelle!" Watson exclaimed.

"Bravo, Bravo, Watson! Quite right. Today, we are the quarry and like the fox we await the sound of dogs. Now, I am certain we will not fool our friend with this ridiculous change of names, but I only hope to draw him out. Therefore, I wish you to wait at the end of the hall, pistol in hand if necessary, and watch carefully, very carefully, for anyone who approaches our door. You will find a most convenient hiding place in the maid's storage area just around the corner from the lift. Pay strict attention to the lift as well, Watson, for he may be as bold as sin, if I may use his choice of words, and waltz straight up to the door."

Watson, full of questions, blurted out, "Holmes, where will you be? Surely not here, unarmed? And that posting in the paper, what did it say?" He could hardly catch his breath.

"I, I will be in the lobby, of course. There's no need to be physically in the room. No, let him gain entrance and have a good look. I've prepared a little surprise for him. I will also have a taxi waiting for my command to follow our bird of prey when he makes his exit. Therefore I will depend on you to follow him down. Your quickness on the stairs will come in quite handy, I am sure. Now, there's no time Watson, quickly, take your place." As he said this Holmes made for the door.

"But Holmes, what did the posting say?" Watson's entreaties fell flat as Holmes disappeared out the door. Realizing the full seriousness of the moment, he grabbed up the derringer, cocked its trigger as Holmes had instructed last night, and headed for the maid's storage area, almost forgetting to close the door behind him. Once in place, his mind raced back to yesterday and to the conversation that Holmes recounted between him and Director Robuchon. Didn't he say that Sar Olderman was in Brussels, or was it Liege? And if so, who were we waiting for now? Watson could make no sense of it, no sense of it at all. A sudden foreboding feeling coursed through his body, accentuated by the draft flowing through the cold, marble hallway. There are no devils, he thought. Only a very bad man or men. That's why it was possible to be in two places at once. He couldn't explain why at the moment, but that was a comforting thought, nevertheless.

*At the ready....*

 Meanwhile, Sherlock Holmes had seated himself in the lobby area with the latest edition of the newspaper opened full in front of him. As a hiding place it was not quite sufficient but he felt it would do for his purposes. Across from him was another part of his plan—the night bellman, specifically hired for today, to point out any morning visitors that made straight for the lift without checking at the hotel desk. Holmes knew that the hotel would be quite busy in the morning with new arrivals and visitors and he direly needed someone who would be able to sort out which was which at the hour at hand. The advertisement, which he now reread, was pretty succinct: I will pay the tithe at 10 a.m., Hotel du Louvre, M. Lapelle, suite 14A. Holmes felt a pang of guilt at not alerting Watson to his plan, or to the fact that he had already obtained from M. Lapelle the definitive method of contact that Sar Olderman had been given prior to his maniacal departure on that ghostly steed. He further wondered what avenues of pursuit Director Robuchon was following at this moment. He glanced at his watch, 8:27 a.m. It was early, but Holmes felt his man would at least do a reconnaissance before making his move. He was counting on it.

 Another half-hour went by and nothing. The old man had to move several times, as his body felt cramped when seated too long in one spot. Upstairs, Watson, finding the enclosed space somewhat warm, had removed his waistcoat and was allowing his eyes to wander from their appointed rounds–the lift and their door.

 At seven minutes after ten, Holmes made the decision to give up the game, but as he started to rise he saw an excited look on the bellman's face. As a clandestine operative he was almost comical as he bounced from foot to foot, with one hand, not quite so surreptitiously, pointing at the gentleman waiting for the lift, his mouth moving noiselessly but vehemently as if to say, 'it's him, it's him!'

Holmes made slight hand movements to stop the bellman but it was no use. If the man had seen him, it would be all over, but fortunately he appeared to not give notice and moved normally into the lift before he could turn around to face the lobby again. Holmes engaged the bellman in desisting his accusatory motions. The gate closed and Holmes relaxed his grip on the young man.

As the gate closed, Sherlock Holmes finished his appraisal of the stranger out of the corner of his eye. It was only a few seconds but it was enough.

"Damn, damn, damn." the detective said under his breath. "I should have realized Robuchon would not leave well enough alone."

Holmes, releasing the bellman, placed a ten franc note in his grateful, open hand and turned, moving to the lift to rejoin his companion.

When he arrived at his level, the gate opened and the stranger was standing directly in front of him. Holmes spoke first.

"Well, detective, did you enjoy your foray into my domain? I at least hope that Director Robuchon has had the good sense to not muck about too much on the premises or are there more of you about outside as well? Sherlock fairly bristled at the man.

"Oh, Sir, of course, Sir," he flustered back. "We've got four men at every corner of the building, watching to make sure he doesn't escape. Uh, how did you know I work for the Sureté? I've been specifically warned about my appearance and to act as natural as I can. We haven't met before, have we, Mr. Holmes? I mean, I know you because the Inspector described you in complete detail, but how did you know me?" Confusion reigned supreme on the officer's face.

"Act naturally? Enter a hotel you have no business in, and act naturally? A young bellman spotted you immediately. As for your being with the Sureté, that is also obvious. Our quarry is a foreigner, you've been informed of that, I am sure. You are traditionally dressed in the French style, though somewhat citified. As to your being an officer of the Sureté, look no further than your shield. No, of course you're not wearing it now, but the slight pin holes it has left on the vest of your suit are still quite evident. Who else is required to wear a shield in such a spot? The gendarmes are uniformed and have precise dress codes, while the Sureté, though more casual, still must have appropriate credentials for identification." Holmes finished his explanation and walked quickly away, heading straight for the maid's storage area.

"Watson, I am sorry..." Holmes began but soon realized the words fell on an empty space.

The Sureté officer, Cpl. Liaseté, moved quickly to Holmes' side when he saw the detective leaning forward, crumpling towards the wall.

"Sir, are you all right?" he asked.

"Watson's gone. My God, if anything has happened to him, I will hold myself personally to blame. And Director Robuchon as well, mark my words."

The Corporal confirmed that he had entered the room, as directed by his superiors, and, finding nothing but a small package addressed to the suspect, Sar Olderman, had left quickly and was heading back to the lobby when Holmes arrived. He had seen no one. The disappearance of Watson was a complete mystery.

Holmes, after being eased into a chair in his room, revived and uttered one word, 'roof.' The Corporal, comprehension crossing his face, and making sure that the detective needed no further assistance, bounded up the stairs three at a time and made for the rooftop door. It was several minutes before he returned.

"Not a sign, M. Holmes. Are you sure he didn't go out while you were in the lobby?" A simple question from a very simple man.

Holmes did not bother to answer the question but waved his hand as to direct the man to leave, and started towards the stairs leading to the roof himself, slowly but purposely. The Corporal, feeling slighted since it seemed the old man did not believe him, decided to go back downstairs and make his report. He was sure that this Watson was probably also down in the lobby, looking for this relic, more than likely. He had actually reached the lift once again when he heard an exclamation.

# THE GAME IS AFOOT

"Good boy, Watson, you've left a trail!" Sherlock boomed out.

The Corporal could hardly believe his ears and started to move towards the detective when the lift door opened and there in the flesh stood Director Robuchon and Inspector Caleur. Corporal Liaseté smartly saluted and made his report, as it was. Moments later, the trio followed Sherlock Holmes, as he made his way to the roof top.

"My man says your friend, Watson, has left a trail." the Director said. "Perhaps we can help. I've got a half-dozen good men waiting below to continue the chase, if you will show us the signs."

Sherlock Holmes, on one bended knee, a small magnifying glass gripped tightly in his hand, turned his examination on his followers and, after an obvious glare, turned back to his ministrations.

"M. Holmes, please. We have had petty differences, we must work together. Please, let us help." The humble words from Director Robuchon made their emotions known and Sherlock turned, this time a more chastened look on his countenance, and said, "You're quite right, quite right. It's just that I feel ashamed to have led this immature young man into a game that may have taken a terrible turn. I, I thought that blackmail was the object and blackmailers rarely use violence in their devious plans, and, if I am mistaken, then I must take the blame and it is wearing heavily on me, very heavily." The detective's voice trailed away and his eyes reflected a mistiness about them.

"Come, come M. Holmes, you must pull yourself together. This is the time for clear thought and clearer actions. Show us your so-called trail and we will follow it and hope to God we are not too late. But quickly, time may not be on our side." The Director, feeling more authoritative every minute, reached down to help the old man up.

"The trail is quite evident," Holmes said, rising without assistance since he had waved the helping hands away, "Your man dashed upon and down these stairs doing his level best to destroy what marks there were, but fortunately he jumped over many steps in doing so and didn't obliterate everything. Look here, Robuchon, do you see that chalk mark?"

The Director, noticing that Holmes had dropped his formal title, took no offense. He eased his spare frame down and looked at the

# THE GAME IS AFOOT

marks, quite visible without using a magnifying glass, and exclaimed, "Yes, quite simple enough, two lines making the letter 'x' it would appear, and then one of the points has two other shorter lines at forty-five degree angles. Is this some kind of code you employ, Sherlock?"

"Not a code of my devising, I assure you. No, this was Watson's own invention. There are more further along that clarify the meaning. You see, Director, the 'x,' as you call it, is simply the four points on the compass, and the angled lines on one point are to signify an arrow, the direction. It does appear chalkish at this point, but that will change on the roof where the surface is a different material than this marble. Oh, Watson, I do hope you are careful dragging that derringer's sight knob, for that is what he is using to break the surface, I am sure."

The Director looked at his Corporal, who began to shrug again in that Gaelic way, but stopped immediately upon seeing the look in the Director's eye.

The four men quickly moved up the remaining stairs onto the roof's surface where, just as Sherlock had said, there were more marks indicating direction. They moved to the edge of the building and looked down from the precipice.

"No way anyone went this way, Sir." said the Corporal.

The Director, realizing his man had made at least one mistake today, not counting his being recognized, didn't even look at him, but turned to Sherlock and asked, "How did he make it to the other building?" He obviously was asking in seriousness, no flippancy was detected at all. The Corporal and the Inspector could hardly believe the respect the Director was giving to Sherlock Holmes.

"Our demon does not have wings. Quite simply he lowered himself to that narrow ledge, there below us. It's not visible if you look straight down, the overhang prevents you from seeing it. I noticed that particular architectural trait when we first arrived. Observe, if a man is careful and swings his body inward, he should reach it with ease. It then would be a simple matter of grabbing the iron balustrades that are supporting the cornices. You see these smudges along the overhang, they are faint, as the wind does the housekeeping on the dust up here, but still there is residue that has been disturbed. It appears he has worked himself around to the electrical supply pole; my vision is not quite as good as yours, Inspector," Holmes turned and addressed Caleur. "Is that not the same 'x' mark on the pole pointing downward?"

"Yees, yes, it is. Of course, he used the pole to reach the street, but my men were stationed on every corner, they would have seen him make his departure or at least your friend on his trail. This is not the case, I assure you. I took their report before joining the Director and they are still posted, you can see for yourself. There, that one, the one with the umbrella under his arm. He is one of my very best. They could not reach the street from there."

"I am sure you are correct, Inspector." Holmes replied dryly. "But still, I would be more assured if the young Corporal here would follow the trail and see if any other marks have been left for us to follow."

There was no argument on anyone's part. The Corporal bravely dangled his legs over the precipice, his Inspector keeping a hold on his arms as an added precaution. No sooner was he over the side than his feet reached the ledge and his hand shot out and held fast to the iron balustrade.

"It is not a problem, it's easy," he said. He continued his move over towards the pole. Upon reaching the spot he saw the gap between the building and the pole was quite manageable also. In fact, if he had fallen he would probably have hit several of the spikes placed for workers who maintain the lines.

He was no more than ten meters away when he exclaimed, "Sacre bleu, another one, it is aimed at this window. They have reentered the building, mon dieu!"

Holmes, though the older of the group, led the charge down the stairs. "Of course," he shouted, "of course, suite 12A, M. Lapelle's room, quickly, quickly!"

Moments later they burst into the manufacturer's room. There he lay, trussed up like a pig, including the requisite apple in his mouth, held fast by a piece of tape.

"Hmm,...hmmm. hrmph.." he gurgled as they undid his bindings.

# THE GAME IS AFOOT

*Another interview with M. Lapelle*

"He must have followed me, gentlemen." His voice, now in a commanding tone, had regained itself from his earlier embarrassing predicament.

"No sooner than you left me, Mr. Holmes, he entered my room. My God, I think he had a key. He caught me entirely unawares. He tied me almost immediately in that ridiculous position. You can't imagine the deprecations I have had to endure all night. He knew about the posting, Mr. Holmes, that's for sure. I had to do my best to convince him it was not my idea, nor did I really know anything about it. He did seem convinced at last and said that it was time to teach you a lesson."

"Please describe him again, M. Lapelle." This time it was Inspector Caleur speaking. "It was obviously not the Sar Olderman that you had encountered before, n'est pais? So, this is a new entity, one we believe is the brains behind this endeavor, so please, be as descriptive as you can remember."

"Certainly, of course. Let's see, he was tall, quite tall, as tall as you, Mr. Holmes. His face was sharp, hawk-like if I may be so colorful. And mustache, very well cut, a dashing style with pomade. He was not close enough for me to tell if it was aromatic but I am sure it must have been. I know about clothing, of course, and his, very stylish, but not Parisian, no, more of the eastern design. I might say Austrian, no, perhaps, no, ah, the piping, yes I remember the piping on his jacket, that is definitely Alpinish, perhaps the Black Forest region, but I may be mistaken, I can't be more specific. I strongly believe in the French supremacy in fashion and style and other apparel is disdainful to me." He paused a moment, once more reached for the sherry, and, helping himself, continued his description of the assailant.

"His hair, very black, like the proverbial cat. It was cut too strict for my tastes and I thought his collar must hurt, it was so tight about his neck."

"Would you say he had a military bearing, then?" from Director Robuchon.

# THE GAME IS AFOOT

"Oh no, not military, but just the same, the way he addressed me was more like to a pupil than a cadet. I would say he was more like a headmaster than a soldier, if that makes any sense." Again he paused, then said, "I was very surprised to see your friend, Watson, that's his name, isn't it? Yes, as I said, I was surprised to see him also return through the window right after my tormentor. I was quite miffed that he did not stay to undo my bindings but kept straight after him right away. And you say no one knows where they have gone? Oh, that is a problem. I am not safe here as you said, Mr. Holmes and I must insist you return my pistol."

"You are correct in noting that we have a problem." replied Sherlock Holmes. "But as to the pistol, hopefully it is still in the possession of my companion, John Watson. I am truly sorry for the treatment you have had to endure, but it is a positive thing that no real harm has happened to your person other than your dignity." A sea of murmurs greeted this, and though M. Lapelle had felt very pained at the night he had just spent, he also had to agree it was a reasonable conclusion and yet, doubt lingered in his mind as to the outcome if his abductor had not been in the act of being pursued by young Watson.

*Later in the lobby salon*

"We have looked everywhere on M. Lapelle's floor. Definitely no more 'x' marks. The man who was guarding the other stairs, well, he was on the alert for two different types; Sar Olderman, the phantom from Bavaria, and possibly the girl, but not for young Watson. For all we know he might have just passed unharmed and went on a wild goose chase at this time and will be back shortly." Inspector Caleur finished his report, which he had addressed to Director Robuchon while Sherlock Holmes listened intently.

"Either this man," Director Robuchon began, "is of the spirit world and can disappear in thin air, or he's a chameleon, an actor perhaps, able to transform his appearance to suit the situation, I choose the latter, that's my diagnosis. In fact, I recall a group of jewel smugglers that used a laundry service as their main form of transport. It

# THE GAME IS AFOOT

worked for years, because they did damn good laundry." The Director laughed out loud, Inspector Caleur joining in with him. But Sherlock Holmes was not laughing. His attention was transfixed to the clock on the mantel which had just chimed the hour of 3 p.m. An hour not late for the day, but late as regards the time that Watson had been missing, since seven minutes after ten, this morning, just about five hours!

*A worried detective....*

Sherlock Holmes received no rest that night. He paced the floor, completely frustrated, powerless. His only choice was to remain where Watson knew him to be. All of his deductive powers were useless. Several times he went to the box containing the letters, notes concerning the cases and what they had discovered. It was all conjecture, all so many loose threads. At a time like this he would have been enjoying his pipe, or perhaps playing his old violin, something to help him concentrate his efforts. Deep down he knew this brooding was not the answer, but he couldn't help himself. He tried to recall the instances when Watson, senior, had been placed in danger...what then was his modus operandi? And then he remembered quite well. It would nettle him, yes, and worry him, but instead of deterring him, as it was now, he would forge ahead, knowing that success was the only salvation and hope. Why couldn't he see that now? Wouldn't it be wonderful if he could uncover the identity of this monster and therefore move the forces of good towards his lair with the hopes that young Watson could be saved.

Finally, his intellect broke through; the torpor was removed and with renewed vigor, papers went flying, stacks were formed, pipe lit, a bellow to the chambermaid to bring coffee, now! The game was afoot.

*Almost midnight....*

"M. Lapelle's coachman, you say?" Inspector Caleur looked at the flushed face of Sherlock Holmes and repeated the question, "What about the coachman?"

"We need a description, that's mandatory. I realize he was a 'trusted' employee, but it makes no difference, not to our devil. His machinations have been going on for quite a while, quite a while." Holmes, though haggard in appearance (he had not slept), still had vitality in his voice.

"Well, it's almost midnight. Can't this wait? I know the Director has given you carte blanche but really, M. Holmes, I myself have yet to go to bed and it is not wise to make pursuit without fresh horses."

"Go to your bed, Inspector, I shall not go to mine. But please, have the Corporal or one of your other 'best' men go to M. Lapelle and obtain that information and the other, of course."

The sarcastic use of 'best' man was not wasted on the Inspector as he recalled the incident on the stairs.

"All right, M. Holmes, we will once again have the interview with M. Lapelle. He is so scared out of his wits I am sure he will enjoy the company of an officer of the Sureté, but I will have to be there as well, I'm sure you understand. Any information obtained would have to be available to the Director as well, and in this instance, I am, how you say, the conduit." A small smile finally appeared on Inspector Caleur's face and Holmes, relaxing a little, followed him to the dispatch room to begin their trip.

In the coach, Inspector Caleur thought about this Sherlock Holmes and his reputation. He tried to recall that there was some link between the Director and the detective's brother but couldn't quite bring it to life. Coming 'round to the problem at hand he thought about the latest requests. Was he thinking that M. Lapelle was playing a part and was really involved in this plot? Did he tie himself up? Did he also invent the story of this Sar Olderman and his missing coachman? And what of the other request, one that M. Lapelle would surely resent, if not outright deny? After all, the personal banking records of a prominent businessman are, well, they are personal, and even the elite Sureté would not press this request.

The interview over, they rode back in silence except for the sound of a pen writing quickly. When they reached the station, Inspector Caleur alighted from the coach and Sherlock, still seated, handed him a piece of paper.

## THE GAME IS AFOOT

"If you will be so kind to employ your resources," Sherlock said, " I believe we will be able to move more knowledgeably in this affair. I also have some telegrams to send and would appreciate it if your driver could deliver me to my hotel."

Without waiting for confirmation, Holmes closed the door and settled back into the dark interior of the coach. The Inspector, about to speak, stopped, let out a little air from his lips, turned and walked into the station.

# BAD NEWS

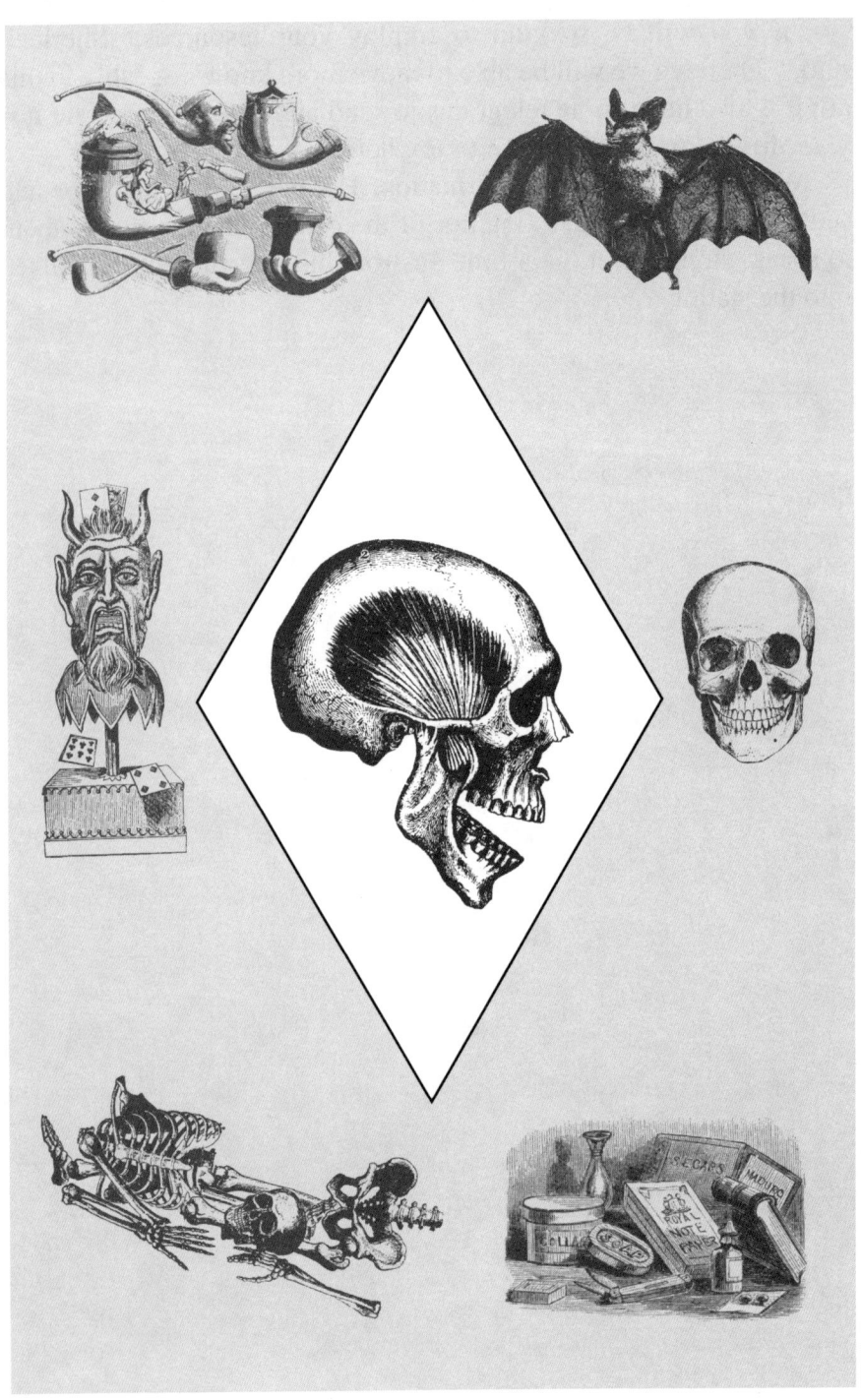

# Bad News

*June 26th, Paris, France, Hotel du Louvre*

"Y ou are to come immediately, Sir, those are my orders!" The Corporal, a different one, had just finished arousing Sherlock Holmes from a very deep sleep. It took a few moments for him to focus his eyes and realize he was not still dreaming.

"Watson, he's been found! Is he all right? Tell me man, I must know!" Though just awakened, the detective's mind went straight to his most pressing problem.

"I can't answer that Sir, my only instructions are to bring you tout suite." The Corporal, a smile on his face, indicated to Holmes that he truly did not know anything other than what he was told. Holmes quickly dressed, gulped a cup of black coffee that the Corporal had graciously brought with him, and followed the young fellow out to his vehicle.

Holmes, not wishing to make conjectures about why he was summoned, instead reflected on last night's deliberations. Of course, it would all be meaningless until he received his answers. Answers concerning the coachman and answers concerning his telegrams. Though he was still tired, and he had only a few hours' sleep, his mind was refreshed with the thought that he had taken action and if his deductions were correct, Watson would soon be safely back.

But that was not to be.

# BAD NEWS

*The sad news....*

"Good morning, M. Holmes. I am Inspector Galent, Inspector Caleur, as you know Sir, is having a well-deserved rest." Inspector Galent rose up to shake Sherlock Holmes' hand and, waving him to a seat, reseated himself. " I have been placed in charge of our particular problem and M. Director will be with us momentarily. But first, I have news about..." here, he shuffled some papers, much to Holmes' annoyance, and looking up said, "ah, M. John Watson, he's...uh.."

Holmes leapt to his feet and, fairly grabbing the bulky and obviously very strong Inspector by the throat, pulled him closer and demanded, "What has happened? Is he all right? I must see him, I must see him now!"

Inspector Galent, though quite strong, refrained from using brute force back, as he was quite familiar with situations like this when bad news was being delivered. After all, this is why Inspector Caleur had chosen him. Now, in a very calm voice, he spoke.

"M. Holmes, calm yourself, please. The situation is grim, but not hopeless."

Upon hearing the words 'not hopeless' Sherlock Holmes released his grip on the man and settled back into his chair, somewhat chagrined. "Please continue, Inspector. He is going to be all right, then, yes?"

"Well, they will do the best they can, that I can assure you. Let me tell you the worst and then the best, you know....ah....good news, bad news...no, no..the bad news first...all right?" Holmes assented, his eyes becoming quite hooded as he listened, reminding himself that this man was not a friend, just a messenger and he must deliver his message in the only way he knows. Therefore, he waited patiently for the man to explain.

"M. Watson had gone into a very, very bad part of Paris, oui? You have the same in London, I am sure. He, uh, was involved in a fight amongst these vagrants, and, uh, well, I am sure he would have given a very good showing of himself but he was so very out-numbered. It was unfair, they were a mob, uh, a gang, and they beat him pretty badly, I think. It would have been much worse, much worse, but fortunately he had a firearm with him, yes? Well, he managed to use this, uh, derringer and in doing so, he fortunately killed one of his attackers, and quite a mean one at that. This man, who we believe is a leader of one of these gangs, ah, his name is Roquefort, or at least his nom de guerre, as it were, well, with his dispatch the others lost heart, cowards that they truly are, and took flight. They obviously were not aware of the limitations of this particular type of firearm, eh? And so, the gendarmes were summoned. Thankfully, there was a gentleman nearby, and he had attracted their attention. It is most fortunate, for I am sure he would have perished if he had not received immediate medical care. Our hospitals are first rate, n'est pais? Yes, very, very good. He is there now and is having the best care, best care. I am told it would not be wise to have visitors at this time, but tomorrow, yes? Yes, tomorrow will be fine. I will have a driver take you there from your hotel at your discretion."

Holmes, tears welling in his eyes, thanked the Inspector for all of his considerations and was led from the room to where Director Robuchon was waiting.

*Regrets....*

"I am very sorry, Sherlock." That was all the Director said as the two men faced each other once again, this time any thoughts of adversarial positions completely erased. When Holmes had taken his seat, the Director did not, not to maintain any kind of command position, but merely to be able to place a consoling hand on Sherlock Holmes' shoulder as he spoke.

"He will survive, as my Inspector told you. I am also told that all vital organs are intact, but he will experience some pain in walking. One leg is shattered." Upon seeing Holmes wince, he softened, "The doctors assure me he will walk again, but there will always be seizures of pain. I think his father suffered somewhat the same, except from a war wound, shrapnel, I suppose, eh?" Since Sherlock made no acknowledgement, he continued. "I am afraid he will also bear some scars from knife wounds, really just scrapes fortunately. He must have put up an incredible fight. The cuts will heal but some will scar;

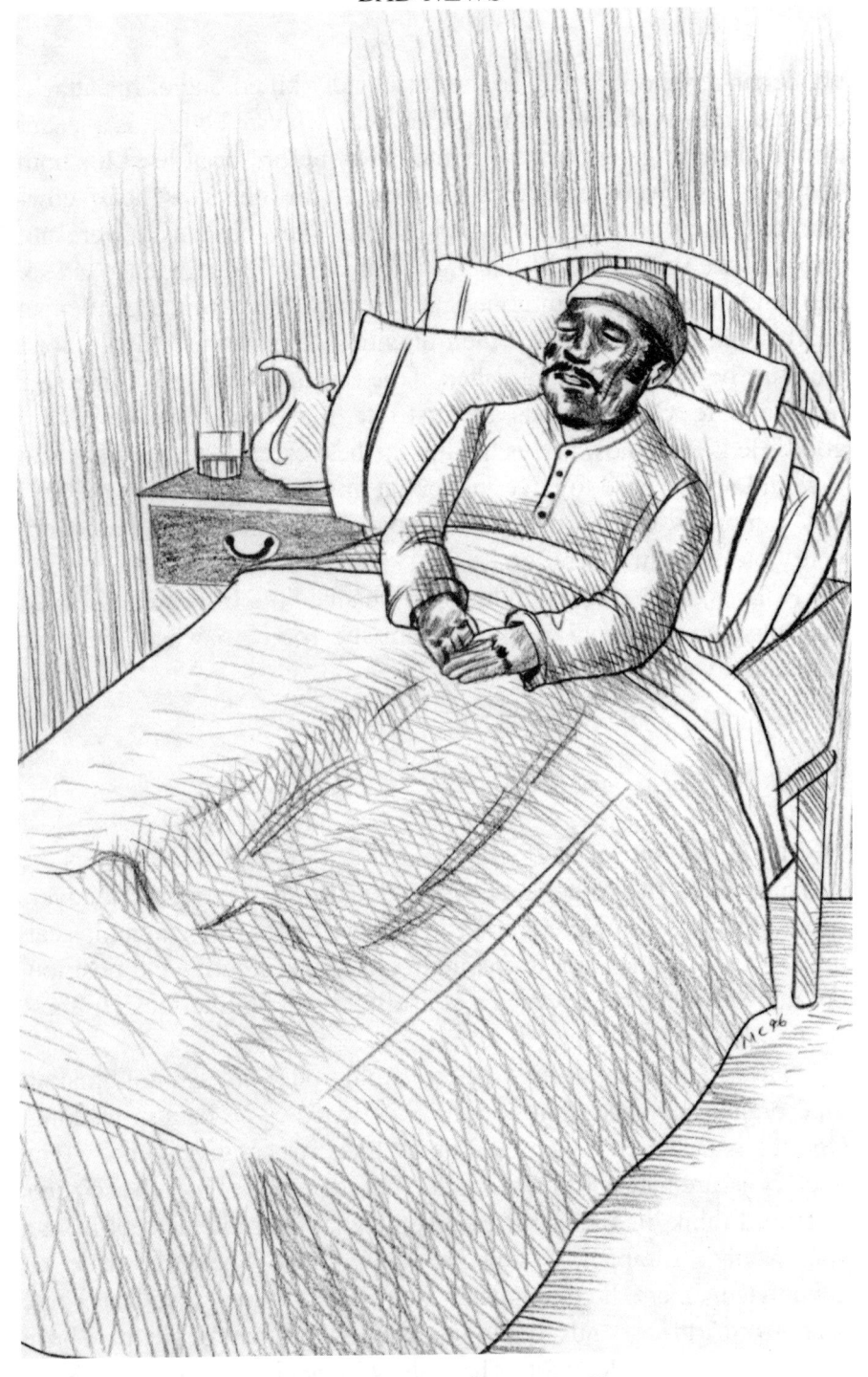

*"John S. Watson, incapacitated"*

## BAD NEWS

unfortunately, one is on his left cheek. He was..uh..is a handsome lad; on the Continent some women find it attractive in a man, I mean a scar."

Holmes, realizing that the Director was trying to be sympathetic and kind, raised his head and answered.

"Yes, he is a handsome lad. And as you said, he will survive. For the moment, M. Robuchon, I wonder if I will."

The dejected look upon Sherlock's face caused the Director to almost do an unmanly thing and reach down and hug the man, then he recalled that the British feel quite differently about these emotions and, recomposing himself, said, "I have some news about your questions you left with Inspector Caleur."

Holmes, his reverie broken, looked up, still with a mist in his eyes, and asked "Yes, I am right, am I not?"

"Yes, you are right. Very right. The coachman has been picked up at his sister's house and has told all. At first, he tried, as you said he would, to pass it off as a mere bagatelle, a spur of the moment thing to have riches in his fingers. Of course we searched everywhere and no large sum of money could be found. We pressed him as you suggested, and though we would not really transport him to English soil, he capitulated and confessed."

"Now I wonder, MR. Sherlock Holmes," though formal in the use of "Mr.", it was obvious it was meant in a friendly fashion, the Director continued, "What is the import of the banking information? Inspector Caleur told you that M. Lapelle would never reveal that, and yet, he told him. How did you know about his personal business? It amazes me. I am truly in awe. My reputation is not without some, what you call, feathers in the cap, eh? But your resources must be quite vast, quite vast. So, do you also suspect M. Lapelle? If so, say the word and I will have him by his heels within the hour."

"No, he is in the clear. Of course I cannot vouch for his business transactions. That has never been my objective. But the rest, yes, the rest is coming into focus. I shall have all my answers shortly." He paused, as if thinking of something very deep and dark.

"You know, Director, I think we got off on the wrong foot, and I know I must carry some blame, but I also believe this case is also part of something bigger that caused you to be, shall we say, apprehensive

# BAD NEWS

in working together. But, be that as it may, I promise, if any credit is due, your name shall be known as being instrumental in bringing about a successful conclusion to this heinous affair."

As Holmes rose up to take his leave, the Director did what he had previously forestalled. Holmes, held in a bear-hug, exhibited at first a surprised, wide-open look on his face, which slowly changed to a warm smile, and his own long arms reached out and hugged his new friend back. It took a double "hrmph" from Inspector Galent to bring the emotional scene to a climax. As Holmes started to take his leave, the Inspector addressed him once more.

"Sir, a driver is waiting out front for you. He'll take you to your hotel. If you'll tell him what time, he'll be back in the morning to take you to the hospital."

"That's fine, Inspector. But I won't be going to the hospital tomorrow."

"No?" asked the Director. "But, Sherlock,..."

"No, M. Director. Tomorrow I am off to Luxembourg. I have a previous engagement with the Grand Duke, and as you know, royalty should not be kept waiting." Holmes grinned as a quizzical look filled the Director's face, as well as the Inspector's. Holmes turned and headed out with a wave of his hand as if to let his audience know they were dismissed. The Director turned to the Inspector and almost simultaneously they gave that traditional Gaelic shrug. To their surprise, Sherlock Holmes returned to their presence and said:

"As for Watson, gentlemen, I am in full agreement. He is in most capable hands. And I am also quite sure, now that the game is more than afoot, he would want to me to continue the hunt. Good day, gentlemen. I will be in touch."

And he was gone.


*Back at the hotel....*

"Yes, M. Holmes. You have quite a few telegrams. Shall I send them to your room or would you prefer an aperitif in the salon?" The efficient desk clerk turned without waiting for a reply as

# BAD NEWS

Holmes had rushed towards the lift, one hand raised skyward, obviously indicating his room.

The telegrams, some on the floor, others strewn haphazardly around the desk, had all been read and Mr. Sherlock Holmes, formerly of 221B Baker Street, sat quietly smoking his pipe. The pieces were falling into place. There was still more to do, of course—tomorrow's trip to Luxembourg, and then on to London. It would conclude there and Watson would not be about. It was sad, but inevitable. He vowed to return to the Continent and take a vacation with his young protegé as soon as he was able. His medical expenses had all been arranged by the Director out of Sureté funds, or was it other government funds? Some questions would never be answered, Holmes knew. Perhaps Mycroft would have been better suited to the task at hand. He was more experienced in many ways. He missed the old fellow. He missed Watson, both Watsons. The young lad hadn't really replaced his old friend, but he was a great ally all the same. He dragged Holmes out of retirement with that puzzle in London and now despite the bad turn, somehow Sherlock Holmes felt the man would have wanted to be here nevertheless, regardless of the personal pain and suffering. It was that comforting thought that helped Sherlock Holmes retire for a much needed afternoon nap. This evening's exertions would be extremely light—unless one counts the sauce á l'orange as a heavy encounter.

# Paris to Luxembourg

*June 27th, Paris, France, Hotel du Louvre*

The next morning saw Sherlock Holmes up bright and early to handle the myriad of details that transcontinental travel required. Purchase of train tickets and requisite seat assignments, necessary communiques to hotels, baggage handling, and naturally, local transportation requirements as well. It all started with checking out of the Hotel du Louvre, and it was apt to continue unabated until this case was through. The very thought of it was exhausting the famous detective to his marrow. These were the sort of details others had so dutifully performed for him, except on those rare occasions when he had found it necessary to operate alone. This was one of those occasions, he ruefully but regrettably thought.

His arrival in Luxembourg was uneventful, save for the fact that the Grand Duke had seen fit to send a detachment of Royal Guards to escort Holmes to the Palace. Sherlock Holmes was a modest man in many ways–except, of course, when he was demonstrating his deductive powers. A phalanx of over-dressed soldiers was exactly the kind of thing he would most want to avoid, but accepted nonetheless in order to please his host. After all, obtaining information from a royal personage is not an easy task under any circumstances, and could prove far more difficult when one has offended them. Sherlock realized his reservations at the Boar's Head Inn would have to be cancelled, as it was obvious his resting place tonight would be one very large royal suite in the Duchal palace.

"Sir Sherlock Holmes, British Subject to his Royal Majesty, King Edward, your Highness." The colorful court servant quickly made his announcement and left unceremoniously, leaving Sherlock Holmes in a grand foyer extending well over sixty meters. At the end of this long corridor-like room sat the Grand Duke. Sherlock remembered him as a boy when he had done a special favor for another Royal, the King of Bavaria. The boy, of course, would not remember him, only that a good deed had been done. Its history was a permanent part of this kingdom's archives and required reading for those who had great expectations.

"Sir Holmes," the young Grand Duke said. "Come, come, sit by me, let us talk." The Grand Duke, twenty and seven, clean-shaven and wiry like his father, rose up and moved to greet his guest halfway. He moved even quicker when he realized how old the man appeared to be. At last, hands clasped, chairs were brought to the spot they were standing at, and they sat down. The light was fading in the afternoon and long shadows filled the far reaches of the room. The Grand Duke ordered gas lamps to be brought and it was somewhat clumsily accomplished, due to the drafts in the center of the room.

"'Tis a problem living in a castle, don't you think? Drafty, cold, thick walls may make a fortress but they make a damn cold one, ha, ha, ha!" the Grand Duke laughed. They exchanged further pleasantries and a light repast was ordered. Holmes wondered if there wasn't a room more suited for this type of entertainment, but held his counsel. You didn't remonstrate to a host, especially a royal one, at any rate. Civilities over, the detective reached in his coat and withdrew an envelope.

"Your Highness wrote to me requesting my assistance on a matter that cannot be discussed but in person. Your letter also contained a few hidden clues, which I am sure you knew I would comprehend. For instance, a slight aside concerning the value of the Dutch guilder and the British pound, how they are so different but alike in so many ways. A few other financial references and a thorough reading of the international papers in London brought me to the obvious conclusion that you are concerned about the new banking firm that just opened in your domain. I, of course, refer to the Banque du Classiqué."

"You are, Sir Holmes, the genuine article. You are quite right, quite right. This firm has in fact sought and received our protection as a reliable, international concern. I don't need to emphasize the fact that the assets that were brought to the monarchy were quite substantial, quite. Our local council has conducted extensive audits of their procedures and found them to be well within the charters of such an establishment and yet....there is something...." As the Grand Duke seemed quite lost for words, Holmes spoke up.

"I don't wish to seem rude, your Highness, but could you offer a description of the principals involved in this bank, such as their names, but also their backgrounds, as much as you may know?" Holmes longed for his pipe and also regretted the high back chair, which was offering no real support for his aging bones.

"Sir Holmes, I have a dossier that might answer your questions easier. There were, naturally, certain legalities required to transact business within our confines and it is within these documents you will find what you seek. I will have them brought to your chambers when you retire, and, as I see the seating arrangement is doing nothing for your comfort, I suggest we do so now." And with that said, the Grand Duke rose up, a smile on his face, waited for the servants to move the chairs back and then proceeded back through the main doors with his guest, arm in arm. Sherlock turned to the Grand Duke as they went through the door and spoke.

"Your Highness, I would much prefer that you address me as Mr. Holmes or Sherlock, if you prefer. And as to your observations of my comfort, it gives me greater comfort to see someone employing deductive powers and, in this example, for a very good reason." The Grand Duke laughed long and loudly, as did his guest. And all was well that night.

# PARIS TO LUXEMBOURG

*June 28th, Luxembourg Duchal Palace*

The next morning found Holmes seated in the lap of luxury. A most sumptuous breakfast had appeared without bidding and left no delicacy unthought of. Holmes, relaxed and thoughtful, reread the telegram from Director Robuchon advising him that Watson was doing wonderfully, and although he would require a wheelchair, it would be for just a short time. His mind once more reassured, he plunged once again into the documents the Grand Duke had brought for his perusal.

His mind and hands raced through the dossiers of the principals involved in this massive international undertaking. One moment, deep in thought, insight reflected on his brow as he exclaimed aloudly, 'Aha, just as I thought,' and proceeded through the files. Later he would ask the Grand Duke for permission to have certain photographs reproduced. Permission was granted, but not until he had promised to join the Grand Duke and his guests, the Duke of Asbury, visiting from England and Count Wilhelm Canard of Hesse-Cassal. It was, Holmes thought, an amusement arranged by the Grand Duke, as the Count was a key Director for the newly formed Banque du Classiqué. Holmes knew this dinner was a planned event and relished the thought of meeting the Count, for more reasons than one.

*A royal dinner....*

The dinner was not a lavish affair. In fact, it was quite ordinary. Holmes had made his concerns known that as his clothes, though serviceable for travelling, were not meant for royal dining, and the Grand Duke, rather than to try to add any puffery to Holmes' wardrobe, changed the dining to an al fresco setting requiring more casual sporting attire. Upon setting eyes for the first time on the Count, Holmes realized this was a coup on his part. The Count, coarse and severe in appearance, as his photo had indicated, was also somewhat of a stylish dresser. He had just made the trip from Paris and had not planned on attending to any sport, therefore he unfortunately was considerably over-dressed for the event. One snide servant was heard to remark that 'the Count should be serving dressed like that, or pouring the wine.' The Count was obviously uncomfortable, and when the repast was finished, he begged leave from the Grand Duke as the day's trip had completely tired him. The Grand Duke would have none of it and commanded his guest to retire to his private den, where he and Sir Holmes might become better acquainted over a cordial and some cigars. He dismissed both gentlemen and continued to hold court with the rest of his guests, thus ensuring that the two adversaries would have their time.

Sherlock, realizing that the Count was not going to begin any conversation, spoke first.

"It is quite amazing how easy it is to travel to Paris, or even to Brussels, from Luxembourg these days. The connections have improved tremendously, haven't they?" Holmes stared openly at the Count.

"Easy? Yes, and that is why Luxembourg makes a very good location for a bank. I thought you might be wondering why the bank has chosen this particular location. Am I right?" The Count, finally finding a cigar to his liking from the rack, proceeded to cut the end.

Holmes moved closer and reached for the long stemmed matches on the sideboard and striking one, brought it closer to the Count's face. Their eyes met, both hardened, both sets of pupils reflecting the flare of the flame as it seared the end of the cigar.

"The Board of Directors, Count. How are they chosen?" Holmes asked the question just as the Count had made his first deep inhalation. It produced the desirous effect since he fought back a choking sound as the smoke travelled indiscriminately to his nostrils.

Clearing his throat, the Count replied, "None of your business, Sir Holmes, simply none of your business. I am well aware of your business endeavors and I believe you are out of your elements in this instance."

"I have been asked to make some inquiries," Holmes said. You must also know that the person who seeks this information is becoming quite suspicious."

"You are very direct," the Count said. "I appreciate that. But again, if you are employed by the Grand Duke, I do not wish to become informed of any of his peccadilloes. I have enough of my own," this said with a small smile.

"I repeat, he is becoming suspicious," Holmes paused. "Suspicious of you." The words hung in the air for a moment. The Count, raised his head and looked once again directly at Sherlock Holmes.

"Of me? That is what you said, hmm? Of me? Hah, I have brought prosperity to this, this picayune monarchy. It holds no real place in history. It has not paid the price for freedom that others have paid. Bah! I am the one who should be suspicious, and I am."

Holmes, having seated himself away from the door, achieved his second coup, as the noble eyes of the Grand Duke peered through the half-opened door, listening to the Count's tirades. The Count, not realizing the Grand Duke's presence, continued his defense.

"You may continue your investigations, Sir Holmes. I have no doubt that you will. But beware," the Count continued, "You are involving yourself in an inevitable failure." Holmes started to rise up.

"Ah, I see those words have meaning to you. Good. Mark them well," the Count said.

Holmes, still rising, raised up his hand and fairly shouted, "Don't, you fool!"

The Count, believing this outburst was aimed at him, hurled his glass at Sherlock Holmes. The Grand Duke, ascertaining that Holmes' remark was meant for him, quietly closed the door once again.

Holmes, wiping the syrupy liquid from his coat, paid no attention to the Count for a moment, and then spoke.

"Perhaps this glass may constitute 'sticks and stones,' he remarked.

"What on earth are you talking about? You're an imbecilic old man. You better fear more than sticks and stones, and fire for that matter." A mischievous appearance overcame the Count.

"Yes, fire. Fire like the world has never seen. Ha, ha, ha, ha," the laughter bellowed out of the Count, as Holmes moved to the door.

"Nothing to say, Sir Sherlock Holmes, no threats or words of wisdom to hurl my way?"

Sherlock Holmes did not answer but moved swiftly away from the Count, down the long hall, cascades of laughter dogging his every step.

And all was not well that night.

# Confrontation with a Devil

*June 29th, London, England, Russell Hotel*

The Russell Hotel was more hospitable than Holmes remembered. The staff had even managed to bring a semblance of order to his somewhat unorthodox demands, and his room was equipped with all the necessary accoutrements he had previously ordered while abroad. Matches were plentiful, as well as a very good brand of sherry on the sideboard with extra glasses for entertaining his guests. The shag tobacco he had requested, though not ordinarily available at the nearest tobacconist, was in ample supply. They had indeed exceeded themselves. Even the room service was provided with an alacrity that other guests did not enjoy, especially considering the somewhat rude manners of their illustrious guest. The management, having had previous experience, had learned its lesson well.

"Yes, Mr. Holmes, Sir Almstead and party are scheduled to arrive this evening. Shall I leave a message for you, Sir?," the desk clerk said.

"That won't be necessary. Sir Almstead's secretary, Jamison, is aware of my presence. I am sure he will contact me upon arrival. In the meantime, if you would be so kind, I would have the latest editions of all the international newspapers available brought to my room as soon as possible." Holmes placed a ten franc note on the counter top and turned and walked away without waiting a reply. The clerk, feeling somewhat snubbed, realized at least the detective had said, 'would you be so kind.' Well, that would have to do for niceties. He had been warned, after all, and he was a true professional. After leaving a short reminder to himself in the register next to Sir Almstead's name, he looked up and, sighting the nearest bellboy, said, "Boy, here. I have an errand for you to run. Quickly, now, that's the way." The rest of his conversation was muted and was not overheard by the man sitting in the lobby, newspaper wide open in front of his face, similar to Sherlock Holmes' method in another time and place.

The knock on Holmes' door was soft but distinct. "Come in, Jamison, I've left the door unlocked. Please come in," the lone occupant remarked.

"Mr. Holmes, how nice to see you again. I, but how did you know it was I? Our arrival was not scheduled until this evening. It's only five p.m. now and I am somewhat early. I am afraid Sir Almstead is still in a doctor's care, and it was decided to travel separately as I was not needed during the crossing." Jamison seemed somewhat flustered as he moved to the chair indicated by Holmes' raised hand.

"Quite simple, my dear Jamison. Sir Almstead, as you say, is not expected until later this evening, yet the necessary arrangements have already been made for his arrival. I could tell that simply by noting a few comments made on the hotel register by the desk clerk. I am afraid I am guilty of taking liberties with the hotel's nonchalant attitude. These preparations were obviously made in person since even a telegram would have not arrived that quickly. Yes, the desk clerk time stamps every entry."

"Mr. Holmes, I could have telephoned those requirements, surely." The secretary responded. "After all, we are living in a modern age, are we not?"

"Yes, you could have, but you didn't. Why would you? The time indicated was quite recent and your physical presence in the lobby negates the expense of employing that medium, I assure you. No, you did this in person, and, upon seeing me approach, removed yourself to a settee where you engaged in a fruitless appearance of reading a newspaper."

## CONFRONTATION WITH A DEVIL

"Ha, ha, oh, Mr. Holmes, there's no fooling you, that I can see. Yes, it's true. Nothing clandestine about it, I just wanted to avoid any company at that moment. I had a lot on my mind, what with Sir Almstead's illness and all."

"Yes, I'm sure you have....and all. It's the 'all' I wish to discuss with you, if I might." The great detective moved to the sideboard, where a slight tilt of his head indicated the sherry container, and an approving nod by the secretary affirmed his wishes. Holmes poured two aperitifs.

"And, oh, by the way, the next time you hide behind a newspaper, be sure it's possible to be actually reading it. It does help to have the type right-side up, don't you think?" Holmes let a small laugh escape his lips before handing the drink to his guest.

"Now, as to these other matters," he continued, "I assume you have been contacted by this Sar Olderman with his entreaties to reintroduce Sir Almstead to his lady friend, Miss Anne." Holmes leaned back in his chair and stared intently at the secretary, awaiting his response.

"Yes Sir, it is as you say. We were contacted before, as you know, I sent word in my last message. This time though, he was more specific. He said we were to go to the museum side of Russell Square and a coach would be waiting. We should board, close the shades and await further instructions when the driver stops. It is all quite mysterious, Mr. Holmes, quite mysterious. I don't know what to make of it."

"Mysterious?," the detective replied. "Of course it would be mysterious. It is in keeping with his modus operandi. What time is this assignation to take place, Jamison?"

"Midnight, Sir. I thought that would be obvious." The secretary allowed a small smirk to cross his face.

"There hasn't been an obvious fact since I began this case, I'm afraid. But, be that as it may, certain details are beginning to come into focus quite clearly, quite clearly."

Sherlock let the secretary wonder at his remark and bade him to continue his duties and, at the appointed time, he would join them when they embarked upon this dire journey. The secretary voiced his opinion that Sir Almstead, in his great desire to see this woman once more, might in fact deny Sherlock the opportunity to be of service. The detective smiled at this and, with a simple 'tut tut,' let Jamison

## CONFRONTATION WITH A DEVIL

know that he would cross that bridge exactly when he crossed it, not a moment before. Jamison shrugged, finished his aperitif in one gulp, and quickly made his exit, a worried look upon his face.

Sherlock, upon seeing the man enter the lift and the gate close, remarked to himself, "The game may be afoot, but not for long. This devil will have a little difficulty with one cloven hoof in a trap, that is for sure."

*The encounter....*

"Sir Almstead, let me introduce you to Dr. Hardy, a most notable physician from Harley Street. I am sure you are aware of his reputation. This other gentleman is Inspector Delacroix of Scotland Yard. Gentlemen, Sir Gregory Almstead and his secretary, Gordon Jamison." Holmes watched the wild look in Jamison's eyes as he made his protestations.

"Mr. Holmes, this is highly irregular. We have sought your assistance in a very personal manner and did not wish to alarm nor involve the authorities. What is the meaning of this?" His anger was quite evident as he moved closer to Sir Almstead, as if to hold tighter on to his employer, either to protect him or to shield himself. The craggy peer, barely able to stand without assistance, uttered not a word as he collapsed back into his wheelchair.

"True," Holmes responded. "I rarely involve the official police in personal matters unless I feel my client needs that assurance. This case is different, and the danger is very real. Our villain has perpetrated a great harm on an individual who is very dear to me and I cannot at this stage rely on my own powers to protect Sir Almstead. No, I'm afraid it won't do. My plan is thus: Sir Gregory will stay here in the good hands of Dr. Hardy, it's obvious he is in no condition to travel, especially in this cold night air. Jamison, you and I will board that coach from Hell and make its journey our own. Don't look so worried, Inspector Delacroix here will be right behind us with some of his crack policemen, I can assure you. Now, is all at the ready, Inspector?"

## CONFRONTATION WITH A DEVIL

"Quite so, Mr. Holmes. My men have sighted that coach already and I'll make sure that we keep it in sight at all times. Good luck to you Sir, may God speed." Delacroix drew one hand across his mustache in a theatrical gesture and made his leave. Holmes, turning to Jamison, said "Ready?"

Jamison, appearing a little weak, allowed himself to be led across the square, looking back once over his shoulder at his employer, Sir Almstead, and the man who now held him in hand, Dr. Hardy.

"Mr. Holmes, I'm sure you think this is best, but I can't stop myself from worrying about Sir Almstead. He's been through a lot and though he made no protestations on his own behalf, I am sure he disapproves. Can't we go back and ensure his wishes are being met?"

But Sherlock moved straight ahead, as if he had not heard the voice resonating so close to him. It was if the coach waiting curbside, just dead ahead, held all of life's meaning to him. The coach, black, with no ornamentation, no outside lights at this late hour, was quite forlorn in its appearance. The passenger door was open but not inviting, just open. The driver was the only visible sign of life. He was not your typical cabbie, ruddy and rotund. No, he was gaunt and cadaverous, while his face held a luminescence that shone brighter than the moon–except that this was a moonless night. The sheen to his face might be attributed to sweat if he had been making any exertions, but as he sat perfectly still, eyes straight ahead, this could not be the cause of this effect. He was a most singular looking apparition on a very dark and misty night. Yes, even the fog was lending its aid to make this a most uninviting scene for the uninitiated planning to make a journey to the bowels of Hell.

Once aboard, Holmes did as the instructions dictated, he closed the shades. Scarcely a second went by and the coach was off at a gallop, a most startling speed. The fear on Jamison's face was evident even as he did his best to maintain his balance in the swiftly moving carriage. Holmes, on the other hand, endeavored a small smile through a very clenched jaw and showed no signs of lost balance. His was a most determined look. They proceeded for well over an hour in this same stance, nary a word spoken between them. Finally, the coach slowed to a normal gait but still showed no sign of stopping. It was then that Sherlock Holmes played his first card.

## CONFRONTATION WITH A DEVIL

"Jamison, it's no use, it's over," the great detective flatly said.

"Whaa, what are you talking about? You're mad. I want to go back. Please let us go back." The agitation felt by the man spilled out in a whiny voice that keened in the night.

"It's over, I said. Over. Shall I explain? I will anyway. The joke is over. That's your analysis, isn't it? A great joke. Let's see. We send threatening letters to dozens, nay, hundreds of businessmen. Businessmen who might have something to hide. But that didn't matter, did it? Of course not. It was expected that some of them would tell you to go to Hell. Apropos, eh what? Then, what next? Simply take advantage of every accident or catastrophe that came their way and call it your own doing. That was a stroke of genius. That was the part that really fooled me. After all, how can one plan on coincidence as an ally? You couldn't, of course, therefore you only pressed your terrible design when tragedy occurred. But even that was not enough. No, for the most valued customers you employed a more devious snare. That's where Sar Olderman and the woman came in, or should I say Hans Gunther and his sister, Elena. No, we are not on our way to meet them, they are safely in a Paris cell at this very moment." Sherlock's stare had not changed, but the look on Jamison went from terror to anger as the situation became clearer in his mind.

"I have no idea of what you're talking about," he shouted. "Every action I do is at Sir Almstead's bidding. It is he you should be talking to, not me!"

"No, that won't do, Jamison. You've made too many mistakes. For instance, sending me that photo is a prime example. Now, you must have known I would realize it's not the same one. By God, if I may use the term in your presence, it *was* a picture of a girl and it was sepia-toned and offcentered like the first, but the landscape was the forest area near Verviers[9], I assume, not the Yorkshire heaths where the first picture was taken. Now why would you send me an obvious fake? No need to answer, I know. Next, I sent you a telegram as I did many others, requesting the name of Sir Almstead's bank. Again, you replied with the wrong answer."

---

[9]Forest region, east of Liége, Belgium

## CONFRONTATION WITH A DEVIL

"This is ridiculous. I told you the name of the bank." Sweat gleamed from his face as he spoke. "I swear it's correct. How could you think otherwise."

"You would be surprised how easy it is to obtain that type of information from other sources. But really, Jamison, don't you remember a rather large crystal order from a Dutch company, in particular, a one Herr Henrik Gotlieb? I'm surprised. After all, Herr Gotlieb was a recipient of your initial campaign. Of course he did not comply, honest man as he is, and he was most willing to assist in bringing you down. I can assure you that I was not surprised when I found out where he was to send his funds to consummate this purchase."

Holmes paused as he watched these facts take root in Jamison's brain. Upon seeing a look that might portend salvation to the man, he thrust his last sword.

"Prior to coming here I had a most enlightening trip to Luxembourg. Have you ever been there? It's quite charming and amazing what this tiny municipality has accomplished since its forming[10], don't you think? There are many who believe it will become a major banking centre and a very important player on the world's stage." As Holmes words struck home he could see that his trap had closed and it was time to bring it to a halt. The secretary, slumping in his seat, his options limited as he thought of the Scotland Yard police that were just outside, wondered if it would be worth it to kill this old man, and thinking better of it, recomposed himself and played his very last card.

"Enough, Mr. Holmes. enough! If I am guilty, so be it. But guilty of what? Sending threatening letters......Yes, I did it. Causing physical harm and pain? No, I am innocent. As you said, accidents happened and I took credit. But they were just coincidences. I won't hang for that and you know it. So bring your proof. Let Sir Almstead know all. I will lose my job, that's all. He won't press charges, and why not? Ha! He has done worse, much worse, I can assure you. As for the others, the same will apply I am sure. If they paid the tithe, it

---

[10]The Duchy of Luxembourg became independent in 1890.

was because they did have something to hide. True? Then, who are my victims? Only those who had made victims of others before me. Now let us return. I am prepared to take my punishment." The look on Jamison was of a man gloating, his voice expressing no contrition to his deeds.

Sherlock Holmes, as if in expectation of this response, reached in his pocket and pulled out a small package of papers. He pulled one from the sheath and hurled it out the window, much to Jamison's surprise. At the same time the coach came to a halt. The only sound was the horse's acknowledgement which emanated as a forceful shrug to the whole affair. Jamison took heart at the look on Sherlock Holmes' face, which appeared very sad.

"These, I believe," the detective quietly said, "belong to you."

As Jamison took the packet in hand, the detective leaped from the cab and was gone, the night fog enveloping him and thus aiding his disappearance.

Jamison, with no light to see by, could not make out the writings upon the papers left behind. He sat there for a moment contemplating his next move. The detective was gone, that was for sure. The echoing footsteps were definitely receding far away. Now, he couldn't hear them at all. The driver, who hadn't said anything and obviously wasn't going to, must be sitting in his box waiting for direction. Where were those Scotland Yard police? Obviously waiting for Holmes to make his signal. Well, he's gone, thought Jamison. He might as well do the same.

After all of this contemplation Jamison indeed made his move. First, he exited the coach the same way Holmes did, and as he did so he looked up into the coachman's box. No one was there, no one. A small shiver went down Jamison's spine as he contemplated the driverless coach. Then, just as suddenly, he realized this was just Sherlock Holmes' way of letting him suffer the same foreboding feeling that M. Lapelle had suffered. He was not afraid. This was his game. And if anybody knew about suffering, he did. He walked slowly towards the street lamp that was casting the only light about this part of town. It was an electric lamp but with the fog its light was no better than gas. His memories returned as they always did when alone. Yes, he had suffered also. He would never forgive the British, never.

When he reached the lamp he recalled the packet of papers and brought them closer to his eyes. Though the light was weak he was now able to make out the words, and as acknowledgement creeped in and expressed itself on his countenance, he heard another familiar sound.

*July 1st, Scotland Yard*

"I hope everything worked out to your satisfaction, Mr. Holmes." The voice belonged to Inspector Delacroix, and though he meant what he said, a certain reticence could be heard in his voice. Holmes, a broad smile on his face, performed the duties of host and poured another libation for his guest.

"Satisfaction may not quite be the word, Inspector; if you had said revenge, it might be more in keeping with my objectives." Holmes noticed the change in Inspector Delacroix's demeanor and explained further.

"The world is changing; and not for the better. Hatred for our fellow man because of his beliefs, religious or political, seem to be the order of the day. As an island nation we have been pretty inured to these global problems, but I am afraid it's too late to keep our head in the sands of time." Inspector Delacroix, trying to keep pace with the conversation, shook his craggy head in agreement.

"You're quite right, Mr. Holmes. I know there are problems in the world that are beyond my understanding, but this situation with the provinces is getting mighty intolerable, there's no telling where it might lead. As an example, last night a body was found in Limehouse that was a horrible sight. Now, I know we have problems with our Irish cousins, but there was no call for what was done to this individual." Delacroix lowered his voice as he spoke, as if in reverence. "Why, we wouldn't have known exactly why it was done, except he had those malicious tracts pinned to his body. The blokes that did this were purely incensed, that's for sure. Why, this poor creature picked this particular neighborhood to push his wares I can hardly know."

And you never shall, thought Holmes, you never shall.

# The Devil To Pay

*July 3rd, Paris, France, Champs-Elysées*

The weather in Paris was delightful and summer was evident everywhere. The outdoor cafes were doing an extraordinary business. At a small bistro just off the Champs Elysées, Sherlock Holmes, Director Robuchon, Inspector Caluer, and an obviously disabled young man, John S. Watson were sitting, enjoying the balmy weather and a fabulous repast for their lunch.

"Jamison? Not the butler, eh?" said Inspector Caleur.

As the laughs subsided, Holmes took his rightful place, center stage. "It wasn't elementary, that's for certain. Such a convoluted way to extort funds. But his relationship with the bank....I did mention he was a Director, yes? I didn't know that for fact. My trip to Luxembourg brought that home to roost. It was most fortunate that the Banque du Classiqué had to file such detailed records on their principals. From there it was easy to find out that our Gordon Jamison was also a well-known agitator in the Irish provinces known as Gerald James. Not very imaginative for a name change. Unfortunately, this past was not a drawback in the international arena as one would think, if one was thinking provincially. That gave me his raison, n'est pas?" This said with a slight bow to Inspector Caleur.

## THE DEVIL TO PAY

"I understand," said Inspector Caleur. "Though it was most unfortunate to have that infernal letter writing machine destroyed."

"Quite right, Inspector," Holmes replied. "Sir Almstead, when he recovered, was completely informed of the facts of the matter. As I understand it he personally undertook a thorough search of Jamison's lodgings. Obviously, he was distraught, and well, his actions speak for themselves."

"But Sherlock," the Director intervened, "What led you to Hans Gunther as being this gypsy, Sar Olderman? I mean.....the description of this miscreant was so different....I am baffled."

"That is indeed elementary! Sorry, M. Director. Think! If M. Lapelle's story is correct, and it is, what do we have as fact? He arrives at an inn that is located some distance from town. He spends some time searching inside. Upon his return, he doesn't look at his driver because he is angry, disappointed, in point of fact: distracted. He enters his coach and another is ensconced, whom we know makes his demands known. It does seem impossible that the coach, driverless, makes its journey to the spot, where this apparition, whom we now know was Hans Gunther, makes his exit in a most dramatic style. Supernatural? I think not. In fact, I know not. Remember the turmoil that M. Lapelle went through to regain the coachman's box? His anxiety when he found the reins, though located just at his feet, almost unobtainable? But what else about this scene strikes home? Ah.....his comment about the horses, remember? They were so tame. They awaited his command. A real calamity would have occurred if they had bolted, as most horses would have done during this travail. But no, they were obedient, well trained. And who had done this training? Of course! Their master and M. Lapelle's faithful servant, Hans Gunther. Imagine then, if you will, how easy it was to design a signal to these same faithful equines to start and stop upon their true master's command? Quite simple. And quite diabolical. This same master horseman, whom we also know, based on his career in the Serbian circus as a rider extraordinaire, had another, equally trained animal, waiting for his command, to make his most sinister departure. Make no mistake, gentlemen, a true trainer does not require verbal commands of his charges. No, and neither did Hans Gunther. He had talent.

Unfortunately his political bent was not aligned with ours. As to his sister's part, I am more sanguine with her performance as paramour to both of our known clients and possibly more. After all, we may never know the full extent of this operation. Well, let us just say, she was consummate in her performance at such a tender age, and in a more legitimate endeavor, accolades would surely be her reward."

"Sherlock, you've painted the picture quite clearly, from my perspective," Director Robuchon intervened at this appropriate pause. "But really, our dealings with Jamison were nonexistent and yet, even with the evidence provided in Luxembourg and his pitiful attempts to mislead you with that picture and the bank records, your actions in London, if I am to believe Inspector Delacroix, show more venom than his participation would entail. I mean, after all, the real culprit..."

Holmes, not waiting for Robuchon to finish, rose up, spilling his wine in his anger, and said, "Jamison's efforts resulted in Watson's injuries! That was enough for me."

"Ah, your passion I understand," the Director replied. "But this Inspector Delacroix, he represents the authorities, how could he play a part in your charade, eh?"

"The Inspector owed me a favor," Sherlock said flatly. "And though I am sure he suspects, he has not made his suspicions known. The whole episode was simply put down as a practical joke," the last said in a stern tone without laughter.

Watson, seeing Holmes so obviously distressed and angered, remarked, "But Holmes, it was Jamison who called for the gendarmes. I was foolish to enter that area, dressed as a gentleman. I remember distinctly the sergeant that found me repeating over and over what a fool I was to be in that despicable place, and how lucky I was that a gentleman, noticing my entering that quarter, had called for the gendarmes."

"Oh Watson, Watson, my immature young friend. You were lured there, not necessarily to be harmed, that I can't be sure of, but....ah, this I know. If providence or coincidence led to your demise, then it was all right with your guiding angel, this angel of death we now call Gordon Jamison. Recall also, Watson, the suicide of Mr. Mudges. I am certain that the rope supplied to him came by way of Sar Olderman. Jamison may not have tied that particular knot but he certainly was instrumental in moving him over the edge. Have no sympathy for him, Watson, none. Is that clear?" Holmes stared intently at Watson until he could see the comprehension slowly taking place and concluding with a gentle nodding of his head.

The Director, seeing as how the conversation was taking a morbid tone, tried to turn it back to the professional.

"Any other salient thoughts that helped you pinpoint this man as our messenger from Hell?"

Holmes, regaining his composure, glanced at Inspector Caleur and then back to the Director, noticeably avoiding Watson's eyes.

"Description is everything, is it not? Jamison's description fit the profile I had first offered, almost. He was identified by the gendarme after Watson's beating." He didn't look at Watson as he spoke. "His physical description fit the member identified as Sir James Collander, Board of Directors, Banque du Classiqué. The dossier at Scotland Yard on Irish sympathizers, likewise. It's funny in a way. The man, politically bent, felt he was just in his cause. His actions to blackmail were aimed at what he thought were legitimate targets, men who cheated or stole in business. Of course not all were guilty, but that was the genius of the idea." Holmes paused, turned to Inspector Caleur. "Inspector, this is the name of the family that owned that most valuable painting removed from the Musée de Cluny, is it not?"

"Sacre Bleu! It is, but how, oh never mind, never mind." The Inspector smiled and then broke out in a small laugh. Watson couldn't help notice the portion of stationery he had once seen in a hotel in Luxembourg when this adventure had just begun. The Royal Seal was not visible from this angle but it was obviously one from that illustrious stack.

Holmes continued his explanation. "The innocent would scoff at these threats, but the guilty would bite. It was they who made it lucrative to pursue. This modus did not come clear to me until I had received confirmation from many of the recipients who treated these threats as much 'poppycock' and more colorful terms as the Continent affords." Holmes made a small bow to his French friends. "And he did hold true to the blackmailer's credo to avoid real harm, except for poor Watson here, which was another of those most unfortunate coincidental incidents."

"Which, as I believe," Director Robuchon declared, "was unforgivable in your eyes, eh, Sherlock?"

Watson realized that the man he had chased that day, leading him into an appointment with possible death, though not planned on his part, was now languishing in a martyr's grave in Ireland. It was justice of a sort, poetic justice.

The Director, seeing that Sherlock was not going to respond to his question, pressed further, "This Jamison, though he has paid his due, perhaps more substantially than he would have others, is not the only participant in this game, Sherlock. No, you've unearthed another for our troubles, haven't you?"

The light was starting to fade from the sky, night was once again reclaiming its domain. There would be longer days ahead, much longer. Even the wind dropped its pace, to signal a warmth in the air. Four men sat at a round table meant for two, cordials in hand. The mood should have been celebratory, laughter should have been the last course. Watson, the youngest, tried to grasp the meaning of the Director's question as it hung in the air, as if it had a life of its own. Inspector Caluer, equally uninformed but not maimed by the events, took it more lightly. His face bore a satisfied air that was brought on by the conclusion of the case, the meal and of course, the stimulus of the Panatella he had in his jaw. Sherlock had none of these accoutrements at hand. The meal, though quite exotic, was tasteless to the detective. Even his pipe was not in evidence. The Director, looking quite tired, also had a forlorn look about his countenance. It was several moments before Sherlock Holmes would make his response, and by the look on his own face, none dared interrupt him in his reverie before.

"The devil to pay. The Devil. I wonder, gentlemen. When I faced Moriarity, I thought I recognized evil. His plans, and that of his cronies, Colonel Moran et. al, they now seem so, so predictable, well thought out, but yet, predictable. Is that clear? I hope so."

Holmes paused and poured a glass of water, a rarity for the detective, and sipping, returned to the upturned faces once more.

# THE DEVIL TO PAY

"Watson was right, of course," his wan smile reached his wounded companion. "I should have realized it from the start. The link, that is. Art, jewelry, fine wine, crystals; what are they? Commodities for the rich? Yes, but something more, as Watson divined. International currency. It was not the object but what they represented. The link between all of our clients was just that: International currency, and that, gentlemen, leads to a bank. Pardon me, not just a bank, an international bank. A bank that would have financial, and therefore, very crucial personal information on each and every one of our clients. Since I had already received doubts about one in particular, this Banque du Classiqué, it was naturally my first choice. It proved precipitous, as you now know. Unfortunately, it does not end with this one member of their board, this Jamison. He was easy to be duped, since he had already declared his loyalties. No, the key player here is known as Count Wilhelm Canard. This is our real devil, our Satan incarnate. Based on my discussions with you, M. Director, and with a telegram I received from a person I am not at liberty to name, suffice it to say someone who was close to my brother, Mycroft[11], this person, this harbinger of hate, has been linked to plans to wreck havoc all over the Continent." Holmes paused, and before he could continue, the Director interrupted to voice his own opinion.

"And because of you, M. Sherlock Holmes, the necessary steps by my government, and yes, even the governments of Belgium and the Netherlands are being taken to remove these scoundrels from their positions of malice." Watson was noticeably awed by the respect and tone of the Director's response. The Director continued, "Such measures taken by those two countries[12] and ours working together gives me great hope. This bogus Count, yes, he is bogus, that we have checked, and as a Prussian he is once again trying to be a thorn in the side of France[13], eh?"

---

[11] Editor Note: This may have been a catalyst for the events depicted in the "Mystery of the Chinese Box."

[12] Luxembourg joined Belgium in an economic union in 1922. It was called Benelux after the addition of the Netherlands in 1944.

[13] In 1870, the Franco-Prussian War established a strong Prussian nation and ended the rule of Napoléon III in France. Wilhelm II was Emperor of Prussia, which later became Germany.

# THE DEVIL TO PAY

Voices started to rise, but Sherlock held command with his own raised hand. "No, gentlemen, hear me out! Fortunately, the Grand Duke, after hearing some rather caustic comments made about his kingdom, and as a result of further discussions I had with him, has made it quite clear that this particular devil must vacate. I must admit, though," Sherlock said, a small laugh escaping his lips, "I had the deuce of a time convincing the Grand Duke that I didn't believe him a fool."

While smiles made their rounds on each and every face, the great detective brought them up short. With his face like a mask, one hand raised, he continued his lament.

"Gentlemen, the seeds planted by this conspiracy run deep, for even on this glorious day, as countries as diverse as America and France prepare to celebrate their freedom[14], there is a plague unleashed at this very moment. A plague that goes by the name of hate. Its strategy may be unstoppable because it breeds on man's basic fears: the fear of difference. Difference in philosophies; political differences; religious canons; even the color of one's skin. And worse, much worse, gentlemen: its seed grows stronger in a field of *indifference*, and that is the crux of the matter." The great man paused, a tear welled in his eye, and once again age took its toll as he collapsed in his seat.

"Holmes, Holmes! Are you all right?" It was Watson who spoke. Watson who rose, painfully from his wooden wheel chair and reached as well as he could to the old man sitting next to him.

"I am powerless." Sherlock Holmes responded.

---

[14] July 4th, America's Independence Day; July 14th, France's Bastille Day.

# EPILOGUE

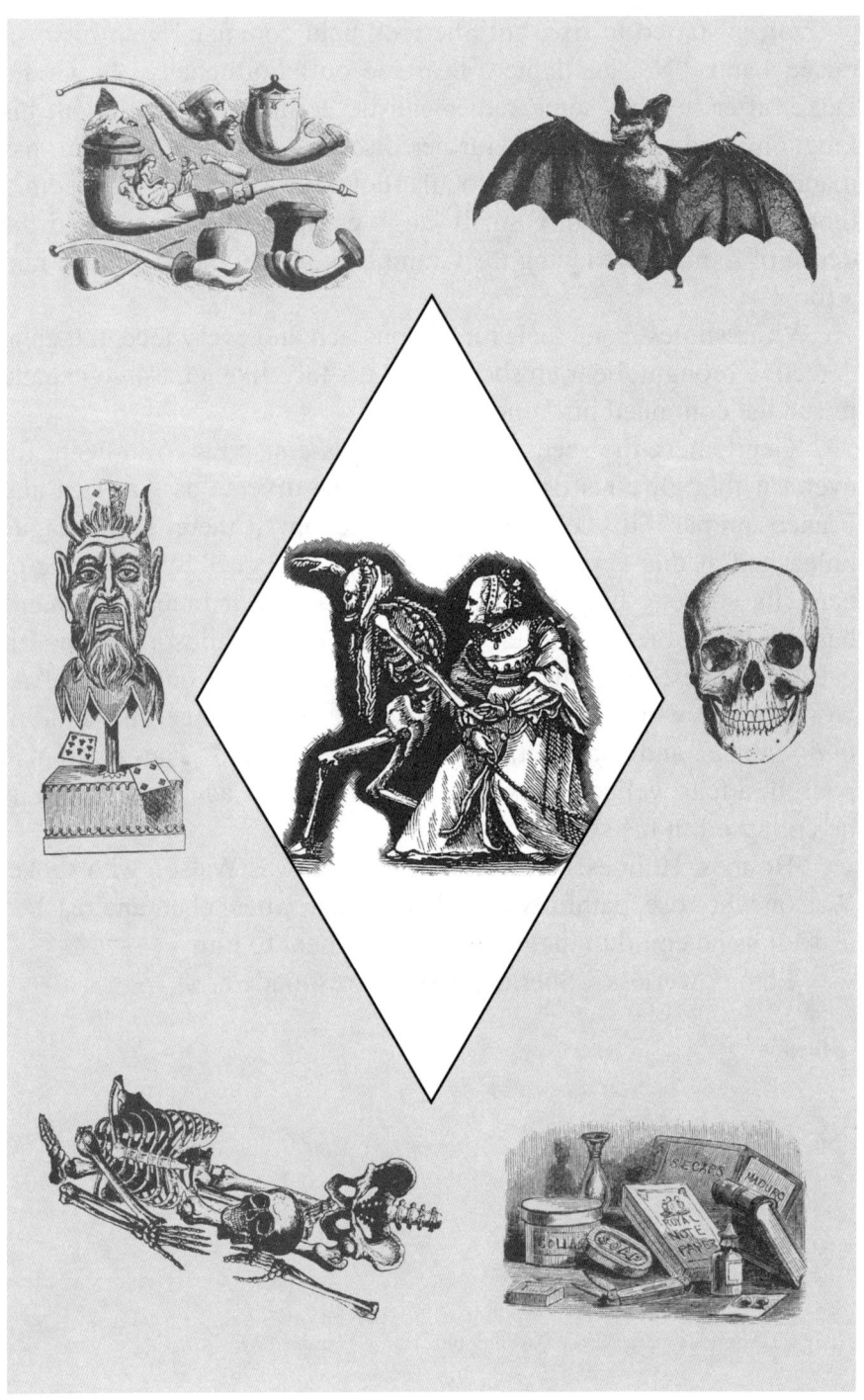

# Epilogue:

*I*t is believed that this story took place in the early 1900's. Actual dates have probably been removed due to the Official Secrets Act (British Government). It should also be noted that prior to this period, in 1870, the Franco-Prussian War established a strong Prussian nation and ended the rule of Napoléon IIII in France. Wilhelm II was Emperor of Prussia. In 1912, the Balkan states went to war to capture territory formerly part of the Ottoman (Turkey) Empire. Serbia also began entreaties through propaganda for annexing Bosnia and Herzegovina, which culminated in the assassination of Francis Ferdinand, Austria's crown prince, in Sarajevo on June 28, 1914. During this same period England suffered massive workingmen's strikes and unrest in the Irish provinces.

World War I began on August 1, 1914.

Wilhelm Canaris, a noted spy during World War I, later became head of military intelligence for Adolf Hitler.

The Devil had been paid.

# LAST THOUGHT

# Last thought....

The reader may find that Sherlock Holmes had acted badly in holding back vital information from the Sureté Director, Francois V. Robuchon. Please note though that it has always been his *modus operandi* to conceal data until it has become established fact. This may also be coupled with the notion that in his declining years he may have become more protective of his reputation or more cynical of the established authorities. We will never know, that's for sure.

# LAST THOUGHT

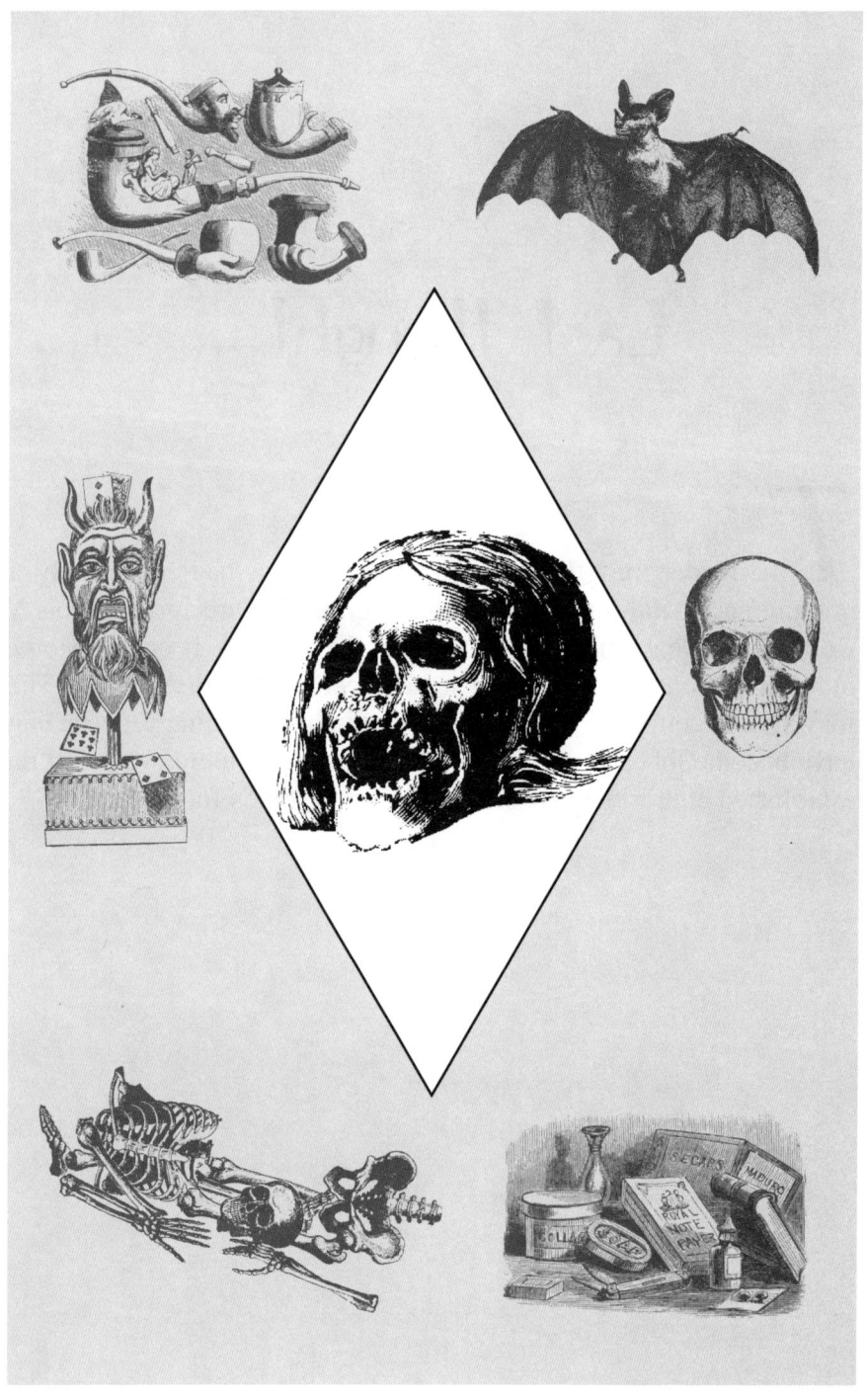

## Chinese Box Mysteries
### SHERLOCK HOLMES

# The Mystery of the Chinese Box

**Editor's Comments**

**Basically, how the preceding stories came into existence and... the stories to come.**

# The Mystery of the Chinese Box

by John S. Watson[15]

*An urgent call...*

In my previous dealings with Sherlock Holmes I had been the instigator[16] in bringing him out of retirement. I sincerely hoped that the urgent message I received from Mrs. Hampton, his trustworthy housekeeper at Hudson Farms, was another opportunity to collaborate with the great man, but I was sadly mistaken. His note had been cryptic but to the point, "Come immediately...bring all of your notes as regards our activities...tell no one. S. Holmes."

Naturally, I did as he bade—even to the extent of travelling somewhat circuitously in my travels to the Surrey countryside. It delayed my arrival only a few hours but there was still sufficient sunlight when I arrived at the quaint split-rail gate once more. The lowering afternoon sun cast a magical light over the main house and the outlying buildings, while the trees, swaying in the gentle breeze, created a danse fantastique on the windows from their shadows. The day was just perfect and

---
[15]Readers will recognize John S. Watson as the son of Sherlock Holmes' famous biographer, John H. Watson, M.D.
[16]See "Time Study" from The Chinese Box Mysteries

I heartily looked forward to seeing my friend once more. I couldn't imagine the scenario that awaited within.

Mrs. Hampton, her eyes reddened, dashed open the front door before I could knock. I was completely taken aback by her appearance. Her mouth was opening and closing, as if in speech, but no words escaped her quivering lips.

"Mrs. Hampton, what's wrong? Mr. Holmes, he…, is he all right? Please tell me, what is it?" I moved to her side, embracing her arms, preparing to shake the answers from her. Evidently my appearance and the firm but gentle grip of my arms did the trick, and she came to her senses.

"Oh, Sir, it's bad, real bad. The doctor has just left and he, he doesn't think Mr. Holmes will survive the night. What am I to do? I can't help him!" And with these words she fainted dead away in my arms.

I was dumbstruck by her words but realized the day had to finally come. When we had returned from Paris he had been somewhat weakened and I knew the exertions of our adventure had taken quite a toll on the man. Now the inevitable was at hand. Placing her gently down on the settee, I moved to the kitchen to get some smelling salts and water. When I returned, she had revived and was fixing her hair in the hallway mirror, humming absent-mindedly to herself. I realized it was her way of dealing with the problem at hand. It was common knowledge that she was more than just a housekeeper to Mr. Holmes. No, I don't mean they had a connubial relationship, but the unique happenstance that can take place between two elderly people when they are able to deal pragmatically and logically (especially as regards a man of Sherlock Holmes' mind) with life's necessities.

"I'll go and make some tea, Sir. He's resting now but he did want you to go up and.." Before she could finish, there was an incessant sounding of a bell coming from the kitchen area.

"Oh, he's awake. You must go straight up, Sir. He thought it was you when the doctor came and he gave the doctor the worst tongue-lashing I ever heard the man do, and in his weakened condition too." Her eyes met mine and for just a moment a small laugh escaped both our lips at the same time. Then, more composed, I dashed up the stairs while she went to make the tea.

The bedroom was dark, not entirely devoid of light, but enough to make it quite difficult to see the occupant within. Later, I realized that was purposeful. The room was a shambles, drawers pulled out, books on the floor, literally pulled from their places on the shelves. Even the closet door was opened, revealing a tangle of clothes strewn within on the floor.

"Close the door, Watson, quickly, it is bringing in light from the damned hall." Holmes' voice was not quavering as I thought it should be, but was strong and forceful as ever.

"Holmes," I said, "let me help you. I'll straighten up and.." but he interrupted me as I knelt to pick up a book.

"Leave it be. It's of no consequence, no consequence at all. The blackguards! They are as stupid as they are blind. Come here, Watson, come here. Sit on the bed, come close. There's not much time." His voice, now not so authoritive, lowered as I came close. By his comment, it was obvious he was aware of the doctor's pronouncement. Then, as if he were reading my mind, he spoke:

"Yes, I know. All of my dabbling in biology and your father's own talents had to give me some background in medical knowledge. At least I am glad that my brain is not the first thing to go, eh, Watson?" I could detect a slight sneer on his face, even in the darkened room.

"Holmes, Sir, let me turn on a lamp. It's difficult to see you under these conditions."

"No, not yet, Watson. First things, first. You've brought your papers with you?" I nodded. "Good. Very good. Get them quickly, along with the Chinese box."

"Chines...," I started to say.

"Victoria will know. It belongs to the young girl—her niece, Martha. It's in her room. Get it quickly. Go now, Watson, go!" The last was spoken with extreme urgency. I fled the room, realizing that Holmes had just used Mrs. Hampton's given name for the first time in my presence. A smile crossed my face as I dashed down the stairs, but it quickly disappeared. He said it obviously in endearment, but coming from his lips publicly at this time portended an urgency of a grave nature, knowing his disposition as regards the fairer sex.

When I reached Mrs. Hampton, she was just sitting in the small country kitchen. The tea had been made, and she was allowing me as much privacy with him as possible. I could tell her heart was breaking and she was doing her level best to contain the sobs that were threatening to wrack her body uncontrollably. I once again enfolded her in my arms, offering comfort and a gentle voice, allowing her needs to delay my directed quest.

"There, there, Mrs. Hampton. He does not seem to be in any pain and is.." but before I could finish, a cacophony of sound erupted. First, the call bell from Holmes' room began clanging incessantly. Then Mrs. Hampton began to howl, "No pain! Of course he feels no pain. And I helped him, God forgive me! Those ghastly needles and whatnot. It's an unholy solution, even he called it that."

My mind brought back my father's thoughts on the use of that dreaded seven percent solution that Holmes had experimented with whenever he was in a melancholy mood, as when there was no problem at hand to tax his tremendous brain. Was this one of those moments? It must be. Before I could delve further along these lines, the bell suddenly stopped, which, at this moment, seemed more disquieting to me than when it was ringing.

"Mrs. Hampton, the box, the Chinese box? Where is it? I must bring it to him." She looked at me as if I, too, was on some kind of mind-altering drug, but then clarification came to her and she whirled from my presence down the back hall. I followed as quickly as I could. She entered a small room at the end of the hall which may have been employed previously as some sort of storage or canning room, but was now obviously a nursery of sorts for a young girl. This must be Martha's room, Mrs. Hampton's niece, I thought. Why is she living here and where on earth is she? The small bed was made and the room had an unoccupied look to it, save for the small assortment of toys scattered on the floor. Among these was an ornate box, fairly large for the child, I thought, but quite light as Mrs. Hampton lifted it up in one fell swoop without any obvious exertion on her part. She handed it to me and I was amazed at the lightness of it. It must be completely hollow.

"It is," she said. Now, it was her turn to read my mind, I thought. Perhaps it is true what they say about people who live together. Maybe she was getting as observant as her host. Seeing that look in my eye she continued, "open it and see for yourself." I did, and all I could see was the red velvet insides of the large box. Quite empty. I imagined that the ornate wood design was made from that incredible balsa wood I had once read about it. I began to say more, but she made a hurrying sign with her hands and I turned and sped back toward my companion.

"Watson," he fairly bellowed. "What is the matter with you, man? Wasn't I explicit about the urgency of the matter?" Seeing my crestfallen countenance he softened his tone and continued, "It's all right. Hand me the box, that's a good fellow." It was almost like a complete mood swing. Was this my friend or the effects of the cocaine he had been administering? I wanted to question him about this but he silenced me with one raised hand, as I understood he had done to my father before me. I watched, fascinated, as he moved his long, tapered fingers over the ornate box. The light in the room was almost completely gone and I realized it was no use moving to the lamp. Fortunately, my eyes were now accustomed to the darkness, and I could just barely make out the movements of Holmes' hands. Suddenly, the box swung open and Holmes, like a magician, produced a stack of foolscap several inches thick. I was amazed. I was certain there was nothing within that box when I brought it up. Holmes reached out with his free hand and said, "Your notes, Watson, quickly, your notes." I reached within my pocket and pulled out the assorted cards and pieces of paper that had contained my copious notes as regards our only two adventures together, and handed it to the great man. He took a quick look at them and then, with additional moves of the elaborate wood carvings, they disappeared within the box. I distinctly heard a clicking sound, possibly a whirring noise also, but that could have been the wind. He then placed the original stack of paper within the box—which he again manipulated, and with a flair that I have seen often, threw up his hands in exaltation and shouted, "It is done!" Next, much to my surprise, he handed the box to me.

## MYSTERY OF THE CHINESE BOX

"Take a look, Watson, see what is inside."

I did as he bade and almost dropped the contraption as I peered deep within: I could see neither my notes nor the manuscript. Rather than reach inside, I held the box upside down to allow its contents to empty on the bed. Nothing was forthcoming. It was empty!

"My God, Holmes! Where are they? What happened?"

"In due time, Watson. In due time. First, see that this box is placed back in the good hands of Mrs. Hampton and returned to her niece's room. Quickly now, I mean it. Do not delay for any reason." I rose up instantly, and as I headed out of the room my eyes managed to gain his. I can only surmise that this is what my father must have meant, when he reported there was a merriment or a chuckle showing in his countenance that only he and my father understood—without a word being spoken between them.

Mrs. Hampton took the box from me, also without saying a word, and headed straight for that little room at the end of the hall. I turned away and headed back to Holmes' room, now more than ever anxious for my interview.

When I arrived at his door, a soft lamp was glowing. It was evidently permissible to let light permeate the darkness once more. I went in and started to speak, but saw that his eyes were closed and, as his breathing seemed calm, I tiptoed back to the hall and slowly made my way back down the stairs.

In the kitchen, Mrs. Hampton poured me a cup of tea. As I took my first sip, she spoke and her words almost made me spill every last drop.

"You can't spend the night, I'm afraid, Sir. It is his..." she paused, "and my wish that we have this time alone. I will go to him and stay. But you, you must leave now. Tomorrow, you will receive a special message. It is hoped that you will know what to do when it comes. I can say no more. Please, go Sir."

I, of course, was crestfallen, but at that moment I understood. At least I thought then I did. It was the last time I ever saw Sherlock Holmes.

# MYSTERY OF THE CHINESE BOX

*An arresting moment....*

My trip back to London was uneventful, and upon entering my rooms I was surprised to find myself feeling quite fatigued. I skipped my usual ablutions and went straight to bed.

I arose quite early, attended to my toilet, and had just settled on my choice of apparel when a knock came upon my door. Believing it to be my landlady and not wanting to embarrass her, I moved to don my dressing gown. Before I could engage the second arm, my door was forced open with a bang, as two maliferous gentlemen made their entrance. I use the term 'gentlemen' based on their dress, not their demeanor. I turned to them in outraged indignation.

"What in tarnation is the meaning of this!" I fairly shouted.

"Mr. Watson? John Watson?" As I gave no answer, they continued.

"You are ordered to accompany us for questioning under the Official Secrets Act as regards violations or potential violations. Do I make myself clear?" The Dragoon, for that is what I thought of him, was really quite imposing. He was a few inches taller than I—and I stand almost six feet. Everything about him seemed oversized including his hat. The other man, more normal in appearance—if somebody breaking into your room can appear normal—was obviously second-in-command and turned smartly to allow his superior to leave, assuming I would be right in tow.

"Hold it right there," I said. "I have no idea what you are talking about. None, whatsoever. I am not leaving this room and certainly not while I am undressed." I thought I had taken a strong position on the matter but much to my surprise, the shorter of the two grabbed my exposed elbow and hauled me straight out the door in one quick movement. Before I could respond, my other arm was also caught in a vise-like grip and I was ushered down the stairs in a highly expeditious manner. Even my efforts to lash out at the banister with my unshod foot met with little resistance to my captors. They simply lifted me higher and swung me in a most dangerous manner, and now I feared for my life as well as my dignity. Other occupants of the house, fortunately, caught no notice of me, as I was whisked out of the front door and into a waiting vehicle before they could even unlatch their doors. There was that consolation, anyway. In the vehicle my captors spoke nary a word but allowed me to prattle on about the consequences they would receive for this treatment of a loyal subject. They paid absolutely no attention, keeping their heads and eyes straight ahead. The trip took some time and we were obviously heading out of the city, so my thoughts took a decidedly darker turn as the familiar sights of London town became distant to my eyes. It was a full three hours, I believe, before we came to a halt. I now had become quite silent and tried to be as stoic as my father would want me to be if he were in this situation. I recalled from his stories the 'moments of truth' he had suffered while awaiting Holmes to either rescue him or bring reinforcements. I also thought about last night and came to the full realization that rescue from that quarter was completely out of the question.

When we alighted I was in front of a small roadside inn whose name was curiously covered over with a small tarp. It was of the type that had normally been a home and refuge for many a traveler before me, but I felt no warmth on this particular morning, even though the sun was shining brightly. The door opened from within as we approached and I went in, my arms suddenly released.

The room was bright and cheery. A fire was lit, though the day would be warm enough. The thick walls and beams normally would cheer my heart and have me looking forward to a good and hearty English breakfast. There was no one else within the room save myself. The chamber contained the usual assorted, rough hewn furnishings, table, chairs, etc. As I said, under any other circumstances, I would be quite content to breakfast there or even partake a later meal with some strong ale.

"Please sit down, Mr. Watson. Your breakfast will be forthcoming. I've taken the liberty of ordering for you. I am sure you understand." The disembodied voice—for surely that is what it was—seemed to be coming from everywhere and nowhere. I looked around, and seeing nobody, moved to the service counter and peered over.

"No, no," the voice laughed. "I'm sorry. I'm up here, look up, Watson, to your left."

I did so, and finally my eyes caught sight of the man. And then I wondered how I could have missed him. He truly was a large man, rotund, with an incredible girth. He must have weighed over 20 stone. The next thought almost brought a laugh to my throat: How in the hell did he get up there? My situation didn't allow me to be humorous, so I belayed that thought. His other features were equally impressive. Enormous mutton-chop whiskers, a mass of graying and curling hair that seemed more like a nest upon his head than normal growth. His nose, though, seemed too small for his face, and had that appearance which comes from consuming too much brandy or whiskey. But the eyes were the most amazing feature. They appeared gentle, intelligent, and in some inexplicable way, familiar. I couldn't quite understand why that was then, but it was so. Seeing that I was staring intently at him, he moved, as if I made him uncomfortable, and disappeared for a moment. In a few minutes he was by my side. I had not seen the stairs that had aided his descent, and I think that I was not being allowed that privilege for a reason. He walked with a limp and I could see that even though the room was quite small, and he only took a few steps, it was obviously with some difficulty. Either the weight or the leg, one or the other, caused him discomfort. He didn't sit when he came in, and I believe it was because there wasn't a chair in the room that could hold him. But he gestured me to a seat, which I took, and simultaneously the smaller of the two who had spirited me away came in with a tray laden with breakfast items. Boiled eggs, a rasher of bacon, more toast than was right for one, an oversized jar of marmalade, butter, good strong hot coffee and surprisingly, an ornate silver bowl filled with warm milk for my coffee. Strange as it may seem, my hunger became stronger than my fear and I attacked the morsels with a vim that my host seemed to enjoy—though he stood and took nary a bite.

    I finished my meal in almost complete silence. I say "almost" complete because my two original captors had been carrying on a spirited conversation in what I assume was the kitchen off to my right. I couldn't make out a word, just the sound of voices. My host, the large gentleman, whiled his time away smoking an extremely large cheroot. I am not opposed to cigars, but the gentleman was decent enough to exhale his smoke in a direction away from my olfactories. I could have told him that it did no good, as the stench still managed to permeate all within that room, and by the latter part of my meal it finally did affect my appetite. But, I was sufficiently sated and said nothing, as I wished to keep as harmonious a relationship as I could. Perhaps I was more afraid than I wanted to admit.

    "Let us get down to business, shall we?" he said, as I finished off the last of my coffee.

"Business? I'm afraid you have me all at sea, Sir," I said.

"Yes, well, be that as it may, Watson, I know all about you, and your dealings with one, Sherlock Holmes, eh?"

He said this to shock me, I am sure. I could tell by the way he raised his eyebrow. Again, that familiar feeling stole over me. Where had I seen that face before? My mind raced but to no avail.

"Sherlock Holmes? Yes, I've had the pleasure. I am sure it is no great leap of the imagination to understand that my father, who I am also sure you know, was a great collaborator of his. As his son...," but here I was cut off.

"Enough of this twaddle!" he shouted. "Yes, of course, I know all that....and more. Much more. It is not ancient history I wish to cover. No. It's more recent times. You went abroad with Mr. Holmes. That will do for starters. Tell me about that, why don't you?" His voice grew a little more conciliatory, more gentle. Again, that quizzical look in the eyes, and again a familiarity.

"Abroad?," my mind raced as I thought of the consequences of my words. "Yes, I went abroad. I was seeking employment in Brussels. You can't imagine my surprise when Mr. Holmes elected to join me. Why, I was flabbergasted. He evidently wished to relive some of his adventures on the Continent, don't you think?" I smiled as I said this, perhaps too smugly.

"Relive his adventures? Bah! New adventures, you mean! I know all about it. Do you believe the authorities in Brussels, Amsterdam, Paris, yes, and even the Dukedom of Luxembourg are beyond my reach? I know all about it, young Watson, Now, you had better be truthful with me or you will pay a very severe penalty." At these words, the man pulled himself up to his full size and, moving slightly closer, leered down at me in a most intimidating manner. As his eyes met mine, a realization swept over me and the mystery was solved. Holmes had said I was going to receive a message and I would know what to do. This was the message, or, at the very least, the messenger. I knew what to do.

"My dear Mycroft," I said confidently. "The report of your demise was obviously in error, for here you are." The big man reeled away from me, as if in horror. "And, as for that trip abroad. Well, from your own mouth, you obviously know all about it, so what can I say? Simply, I can only confirm whatever you know or believe.  So, that's the end of it. I would appreciate being returned to my room." I rose up and headed for the door, my host avoiding my eyes as he leaned on the service board.

"May I assume that a good and proper excuse for my absence from work has been take care of and I will have no trouble from that quarter?" The big man made no answer, just a simple confirming wave of his hand. I continued my way out the door with what I thought was a very cocky walk, when I was hit broadside with an object which felt like a wet bag of sand. Darkness surrounded me as I slumped to the floor.

To my surprise I awoke in my own rooms once again. My head felt terrible and there was obvious swelling from the villain who had done this devious deed. It was also obviously one of my captors, and as I was returned home, it was quite plain that it was meant as a warning. To further this scenario, my room had been thoroughly ransacked and had the appearance that Holmes' own boudoir had taken on. Was it my notes? Was that their objective? I was more than certain of it, after my conversation with Mycroft Holmes. I reeled at the thought that he could have faked his death and kept his brother in the dark. Then, I wondered if that were really true. Perhaps Holmes knew about the ruse and was only playing a part as well. After all, he was definitely capable of it. My father was brought through the same situation with Holmes after that infamous battle at Reichenbach falls. Could this be another example of that from the Holmes brothers, Mycroft and Sherlock? I knew I didn't have the answers but I thought I knew where to go. Perhaps his last night on earth was also part charade. But why? To make me report, as my father did, of his demise? And why this sudden reappearance of Mycroft? It was all so confusing. I finished cleaning myself up and dressed. I was not hungry and decided to head straight for Hudson Farm to see if I could possibly shed some light on this incredible mystery. Upon opening my door a note fluttered down and, my reflexes being quite good, I caught it before it hit the ground. I opened it hesitantly, fearing the worst from Mrs. Hampton. But the note was not from that fine lady; no, it was from Mr. Ransom, my boss at Clampton and Company. He was so sorry to hear about the death of my aunt, and understood that as she was instrumental in my upbringing it was quite appropriate for me to have the next week off as well. My aunt? Week off? Mycroft! Well, at least that's one loose end. Now to Hudson Farm and whatever that road leads to.

# MYSTERY OF THE CHINESE BOX

*Return to Surrey...*

The man was quite uncouth yet seemed appropriate for the place. The place I speak of is that same gate I was at just two nights ago, at the entrance to Hudson Farm. He appeared somewhat emaciated, though lanky might be a better word. He seemed to be paying me no attention as I strode up to the gate, but effectively barred my way. His bedraggled whiskers and floppy soiled hat further added to his appearance of an uneducated character.

"Pardon me," I said, as I engaged the gate, and just as quickly his foot tangled within it to prevent its moving any further.

"Whoa, hey, hold on there, young fella, where's the rush? We ain't receiving today, don'cha know?"

"Now, look here," I continued. "I've got business with Mr. Sherlock Holmes. I'm a very close friend of his. Let me by." The man seemed to appreciate my words and moved back to let me pass.

"Sherlock Holmes, eh? Well, I never. I knew he must've been somebody, what with all those wagons and carryings on. Sure, you go on down. It's not my idea. These fellas down there have got a mean way about 'em and if you want to join 'em, well, go on ahead." He smiled then, what would have been a toothy smile if not for the many missing teeth. I proceeded to head down towards the farm, then stopped, looked at the man once more, and said, "You don't like those fellows down there, do you?"

"S'pose not. They seem pretty uppity to me, I mean, considering a man's dying and all."

"Dying? Oh my Good God! Oh, Holmes, I'm too late. Too late."

I raced as quickly down the hill as I could. The door once again opened at my arrival but it was not Mrs. Hampton coming out to greet me. It was the short one again, my old friend. His eyes met mine and for a second I could see the humanity within, and he moved to the side and allowed me to pass unharmed. I bounded the stairs, two and three at a time and almost collided with another gentleman coming out of Holmes' room. He didn't even look at me as his eyes were focussed down the stairs, where the short man was nodding his approval. This latest unknown stepped aside as well and I went in.

# MYSTERY OF THE CHINESE BOX

The room was as I remembered it except for the strewn objects, which were all removed. The walls were bare. Not a book, not a knick-knack did they hold. A glance at the open closet revealed the same. None of the famous detective's clothes were in evidence. I sat down upon the bed and then realized that even the coverings had been removed. I had sat upon a bare mattress. I arose as if in shame and moved quickly away. I went into his washroom and the same scene of bareness greeted my eyes. Every personal effect had been removed. I edged out of the room and back down the hall towards the stairs. Mycroft's agents were evidently in the parlor, and their voices carried quite easily as they made a row in the kitchen below. My thoughts and heart went out to Mrs. Hampton in this, her hour of grief, but I was brought up short by the appearance of Mycroft Holmes coming through the front door.

"Ah, Mr. Watson. Good, very good. Now we can settle this once and for all. Come with me and have a seat in the parlor. This won't take long."

His immense Corporal presence and his manner of speech waylaid me from my purpose, which was of course to see to Mrs. Hampton's comfort and ease. He obviously saw my distress, for he continued his condescending manner and said, "Now don't worry about the lady, she is in good hands. All that can be done has been done. Except of course, for our little tête à tête, hmm?"

His look and his outstretched hand left no doubt upon my brain that any other course of action was out of the question. Further, the presence of the large fellow who had manhandled me before and now entered the foyer almost stealthily made my decision absolute. I entered the parlor and took the first chair I came to, which, as I recall, was one that my father normally occupied when it had been placed, lo those many years ago, before the hearth at 221B Baker Street. It gave me no respite from the chill in the air nor comfort for my tense body as I tried in vain to recline within its domain. Mycroft, as before, remained standing, as if the very thought of sitting would give his adversary an undue advantage, one that he would never accede. The clock on the mantel—still there, I noted with surprise—continued its relentless ticking in the subdued atmosphere of the room as I waited for the interview to begin.

## MYSTERY OF THE CHINESE BOX

"Young man...young man. why are you such an enigma to me? Can you answer that? For the life of me, I can not imagine a more unlikely villain in this affair."

"Villain!," I shouted. "What do you mean, villain? It's preposterous. I have aided and assisted your brother to the best of my abilities. No, more than that. I took a severe beating[17] during our last adventure together. Were you aware of that, Sir?" My voice was cracking as my emotions took their toll, not only because of the duress I was enduring but because of the full realization that my dear friend, Sherlock Holmes, was lost to me forever. The full brunt of this was finally sinking in when Mycroft responded.

"Yes, I know about your troubles while in Paris, but what you don't realize is that you and Sherlock were involved in something that you should never have undertaken. I warned him once before but he would not take heed."

"Warned him?" I asked. "How is that possible? He thought you were dead." I sincerely hoped that my voice was not registering sufficient doubt but he waved it away in the same manner as his brother did and continued.

"My warnings came sufficiently before my 'demise.' It was at the time of Sherlock's retirement when I paid my respects for his endeavors on my behalf, and, yes, for the government's as well. I cautioned him that he must continue to abide by the Official Secrets Act and never reveal certain, shall we say, details that could prove embarrassing. Your father, as well, was thoroughly briefed, but unfortunately it seems he had managed to conceal certain papers, further 'adventures' as he called them. Your father thought he was cunning and left a trail concerning a tin box, or some such thing, that was supposed to be stored in a bank deposit box. Naturally, that lead proved false. I, in fact, never believed it for a minute. And that brings me to you. Simply stated, young man, I know the papers exist. And I believe you know where they are." His stare was relentless but I managed to turn away before I spoke my denial.

"Ridiculous! My father told me that his readers wanted more, but there was no more to tell." I spoke calmly, I thought, but I couldn't stop

---

[17] See "The Devil To Pay" from The Chinese Box Mysteries

## MYSTERY OF THE CHINESE BOX

thinking about the Chinese Box and Sherlock's last actions. Of course, I remembered the gossip about those missing stories and the possibility that my father, did, in fact, deposit them for safekeeping. But I never before yesterday had any real knowledge of their existence, and I was hoping my face appeared guileless. Mycroft moved closer, a menacing grin forming around his mouth.

"My dear young man, you are in very deep waters here. Very deep. Your father also once proved uncooperative, and, if it wasn't for my brilliant concept of employing another author, why, well...." his voice trailed off, and then, "He did live a full life, didn't he?"

I sat stunned at the realization of that statement. My father had hinted at the immense powers available to this man and here was his insinuation that my father was permitted to live out his life only because he had found a way to conceal the actions of my father's writings. That, too, my father had hinted at but never elaborated upon. Was he too afraid for his life, or...for mine?"

"Ah, I can see you understand. Good. Then let us finish up this business. Quickly now, where are those papers?" Mycroft extended his hand as if I had them readily at hand and could just materialize them for his benefit. I rose up, somewhat shaken, ready to continue my denial.

"I must insist that you let me.." but before I could finish we were interrupted by the appearance at the door of Mrs. Hampton and a young girl who I assumed must be her niece, Martha.

"Mr. Holmes," she addressed Mycroft. "Would it be too much of a bother to ask one of your strong men here to help me with my niece's things? I asked them myself, but they seem to pay me no mind." She had a hurt yet contemptuous look on her face. Mycroft gazed steadfastly at her and appeared to give the matter great thought. Finally, he spoke.

"Certainly, Victoria. Tell Templeton what it is you wish to be done. He'll see to it." He dismissed her with a wave of his hand, again so like his brother, and turned once more to me.

"There is no sense in making denials, Watson. As my brother used to say, when you eliminate all possibilities, whatever remains, etc. etc." There seemed to be a distant look to his eyes, as if in recalling his brother's theory a nerve had been struck.

"As much as you would like for me to have these papers—if they even exist—I do not," I said. I would have said more, but again we were interrupted, this time by a bumping sound coming from the outside hallway. In a moment we could see Mycroft's henchmen carrying some heavy boxes across the threshold heading towards the front door.

"One moment," cried Mycroft quickly, turning and heading towards his men. "Let me see exactly what you are taking." His voice registered distrust and I did my level best to peer around his hulk from my poor advantage point.

"I've checked it thoroughly," said Templeton. "It's the little girl's clothes, kid things, you know, a toy box. That kind of stuff." He tried to assume an air of casualness that did not bode well with Mycroft Holmes.

"Yes, I understand. But let me see that toy box anyway. I know you did well, Templeton, but we still haven't found what we are looking for, have we?" The sarcasm was not lost on Templeton, and he slowly shrank away as his partner lifted the box from the large steamer. It wasn't the Chinese box. I breathed a sigh of relief inwardly and tried to keep my composure while Mycroft examined the child's gaily painted toy box. It was filled with small wooden toys and an assortment of dolls, but no Chinese box. I, too was becoming mystified at how it could have disappeared. When Mycroft was sufficiently satisfied, he directed his men to continue their task. I knew I was again on his inspection list, and, without hesitation, he turned back to me.

"Now, no more stalling. Where are those papers?" His patience evidently was at an end, but mine was as well.

"Mr. Holmes, I really don't care what you think or what you are planning to do. I really (and this was the truth) don't know the whereabouts of these mysterious papers you are seeking, and I frankly, don't give a damn!" With as much braggadocio as I could muster, I rose up and headed for the door.

"Stop, stop him!" Mycroft shouted. And the next thing I knew I was raised off the ground by the same industrious thugs as before. My head bumped on the door jamb and I screamed out in pain. As they lowered me back down I could see over their shoulders, and to my amazement, there was Mrs. Hampton. I watched as she quickly raised the trunk lid, while her niece, Martha, placed the Chinese box within. I realized that neither

# MYSTERY OF THE CHINESE BOX

Mycroft nor his men could see what I was envisioning as his two men were amply blocking the view. A small smile crept across my face as a single finger went to her lips. Then she was gone and I was once more ensconced in the living room chair, my father's very own.

"Very well, Watson. It seems that the spirit of uncooperation is inheritable. It is quite unfortunate for you for I have no more clever solutions at hand. Take him to the basement and apply a little lubricant to his tongue." The look that crossed Mycroft's face was more than harsh—it was malevolent. Fear struck my heart and I made to resist but failed. The two blackguards held me fast, and in the stupor caused from hitting my head, they had added a thin but strong wire around my wrists. My struggles only brought me pain as they manhandled me down the steps towards that black basement. They heaved me to the floor and I heard them ascend the steps and hoped that I might be free of them for a while, but to no avail. Moments later they returned and while one lifted me, the other forced some fiery liquid down my throat. I passed out.

*A prisoner...*

When I awoke, I had no concept of the amount of time that had passed. A single bare candle had been lit but I had no idea when. Its light flickered on the dank, dark walls, revealing nothing. I found myself on a primitive wooden table, tied in such a way that I couldn't turn my head or my body. I tried pulling my legs towards me but they were held secure with that awful biting wire. My hands, though tied in front, were also secured to that end. It wasn't painful if I didn't move, and so I didn't. That is, until....

Please, I must beg my reader's indulgence, for what I am about to reveal is so horrific, so incredibly evil I could not imagine one's fellow man performing such an act of terror on another. In short, in my incarcerated position, I heard the distinct scratching sound of that most nauseating of God's creatures, the rat. There is no mistaking the skittering, scratching patter of those hard-nailed feet. It wasn't on the table yet. I was certain of that, for my tactile senses were screaming from every pore. Sweat started down my brow and clouded my eye, but I couldn't do anything about it. The candle, providing little light, began to flicker as a small draft of air pulsed through the room. The door had opened. Now the sounds of footsteps—heavy ones, Mycroft's no doubt—came to my ear. And then he was there.

"Well, comfortable Watson? No, no, don't get up." He was obviously enjoying his humorous remarks as a flinty grin spread across his countenance. "I've brought you a guest, a roommate, if you will. As Sherlock was a roommate to your father, this will be yours." He held a nasty, vicious-looking rat by its long, pink gnarled tail. It was trying in vain to bite him but he kept swinging it in such a way that it could not gain purchase. Around the rat's neck was a silver chain which acted as a sort of leash. It was by this method Mycroft had managed to snare the creature.

"Now," he continued, "it doesn't make sense for you to be endure this kind of suffering, does it? After all, those papers can only bring harm to the very country you owe your allegiance to. Be wise, Watson. Give me the papers and I will see that no harm comes to you, otherwise..." as his voice died away, his eyes moved from me towards the struggling animal.

Thoughts raced quickly through my mind: the adventures I had experienced with Sherlock Holmes, watching him stash the papers into the Chinese box; Mrs. Hampton, her loyalty in removing that same box; and now, me, the lone standard bearer. I had not fought in any wars as my father had. I had never experienced the life or death decision-making that a soldier or any other lover of country had done. Mycroft represented the government, my government. Shouldn't I do what he asked? Or is that the coward's voice answering neatly for me? But if Mycroft is the government, then do I really want to support that government? His government has me tied to this table. Suddenly the answer became crystal clear.

"Go to hell! You are not my country's prayers, hopes and dreams. No Sir! You are its nightmare. I am for a government of daylight and humanity. Not for a dark basement and your inhumanity. If you fear words, words that are written on paper, for God's sake, you are as puny as the creature you hold by the tail. No, I'm wrong to compare you with the rat, it does the rat a disservice, Sir! The rat does by instinct, not by reasoning. You have a choice." In mouthing my words, my throat had run dry and the bindings tore at my flesh as my whole body tried to speak with me.

# MYSTERY OF THE CHINESE BOX

"Yes, John S. Watson, I do have a choice," Mycroft said, "and so do you. Obviously, you have made it. Now, my little friend here will make his. I will attach his chain to a small hook that is centrally located right between your thighs. He will have free roam of this table but he will not be able to get off. Oh, I see my remarks are having an effect. Yes, the fear is showing wonderfully in your eyes. Relax, Watson. He has been recently fed. He won't be hungry, oh, perhaps for at least an hour. Hmm, it's a wonder my able brother did not do a monograph on the feeding habits of vermin. Oh well, I'll leave you now with one last hope. When you begin to scream, and you will, I or one of my men will return. You will then have one last opportunity to speak. If not, well....we won't dwell on that, will we? Goodbye, Watson."

He was gone. The quietness coupled with the darkness seemed to bring a sort of tranquility to me. I must be going crazy, I thought. The rat was also very quiet, probably taking time to assimilate its new role in this hideous nightmare. I was grateful for the time to think and I found my mind wandering over the short few months that Sherlock Holmes had been in my life. My life. Am I a true martyr? I guess I must be. I had gone in harm's way in Paris, though really I was acting—or should I say reacting—to the situation there. The beating I had taken left indelible marks upon my psyche, as well as my body, but seemed amply rewarded at the time by Holmes' show of deep concern. I laughed inwardly at his method of obtaining revenge against Jamison[18]. Deep waters, Mycroft had said. Yes, they were. Even Sherlock was visibly upset by the outcome, which resulted in a solution but also revealed the madness that was gripping Europe day by day. And the Chinese box? Manuscripts of my father's that could still wreak havoc today? What on earth can those stories reveal? I shall never know. I was saddened further by this thought. And then I heard that scratching sound.....the rat.

*Rescued...*

How can I put the words down to explain my salvation? I thought I was lost, completely. One moment I was tied helplessly to this table

---

[18] See "The Devil To Pay" from the Chinese Box Mysteries.

with my fate in the hands of a creature no larger than a small cat. Then the next moment I found my wrists released in an instant, after the swishing sound of a well-placed blade had cut them free. In a trice, my eyes opened and were bathed by the warm light of a candle held close—a light almost superceded by the glint reflecting off of a silver stiletto...Mrs. Hampton. In a repeat of her earlier performance she held a single finger to her lips and stilled my inquisitive tongue. Silently, she at once went to work on my bindings until I was free. I gingerly rose up, my limbs seemingly at odds with my purpose. As my eyes grew accustomed to the dimly lit space I could just make out the still form lying at my feet....the rat. I shuddered coldly. Without speaking, she beckoned me to follow, which I most assuredly did. We passed quickly into another chamber, smaller than the previous one. The room was completely empty and obviously swept clean. The walls appeared to be closing in on me, that's how claustrophobic I had become. Then I realized one wall was really closing in, or rather moving in towards me. A secret passage. I felt a strong hand on my back and almost screamed out before I realized it was Mrs. Hampton guiding me through. It led into an extremely narrow passageway, where, guided by the one single candle, we made our way along slowly. The dirt floor appeared to be angling upward as we walked, with no relief from the ceiling until gradually I found myself stooping to make progress. In less than a minute the tunnel halted and I could see no egress. Mrs. Hampton, silent until that time, finally spoke.

"Step back, John, the trapdoor is quite heavy and it won't stop for nothing once it starts opening."

I was startled by the use of my given name, and then again by the rush of air and light that assaulted my senses as the heavy door swung quickly around. I was fortunate to have gotten out of its way, for it was at least four inches thick. My hand rose automatically to shade my eyes as the broad light of day filled our shaft. I started to ascend the short distance but was held fast by a firm hand on my shoulder.

"Wait, John," she said. "Peer out first to make sure the other one is not about. Mycroft is back in London and Miller, the tall one, is taking an unplanned nap, but Templeton is surely somewhere about."

## MYSTERY OF THE CHINESE BOX

I peered hesitantly over the edge and saw that we were in a small copse of trees no more than thirty yards from the house. I could make out the top of the house but not the lower portion, as the position of the opening was set in a small berm and limited my view. I raised myself further, my eyes now accustomed to the beautiful light of day, and almost gasped as I caught sight of Templeton. He was sauntering along with a casual air, a slight whistle escaping from his lips as he walked. He appeared as a man without a care in the world, and I hated him all the more for it. I thought how easy it would be to grab a rock or branch and smash that complacent face of his, especially as his back was towards me as he headed back to the house where I was no longer a captive. Mrs. Hampton was by my side, and I watched in awe as her face went from serenity to panic.

"Gawd, Mr. Watson! You must get away, quickly. Here, take this envelope. Read the letter Sherlock, Mr. Holmes, has left for you, and mine as well. He was a great man, John, a great man, and we must ensure that his memory is not sullied by these rascals. I've also enclosed 50 pounds for your use. Now, quickly, don't go home, they will go straight there. Choose your hiding place well. I will delay them for as long as I can." With that, she moved me aside as if I were straw and headed straight for the house...the house one of our adversaries had just entered. I was dumbstruck for a moment, then gathering my wits about me, ran for the open road as fast as I could. My limbs felt cramped from the torturous treatment they had received, but I still made fairly good time.

It took me more than two hours to reach the train station, but as luck would have it, a local was just coming in and I boarded her just in time.

As I rode along, my mind raced back to that house in Surrey, and I tried to imagine what Mrs. Hampton was saying or doing to delay those blackguards. But I couldn't concentrate. I saw my hands were shaking and knew I was fortunate to have escaped alive. The envelope she gave me was still within my coat pocket. I began to retrieve it then thought it better to wait. Suddenly, I realized I hadn't a clue as to where I was going. What is my destination to be? I couldn't go home, that was obvious. Where shall I go? All at once it came to me: The Russell Hotel. Holmes had made some deprecatory remarks about it when comparing it to his Baker Street abode. Would Mycroft know of our stay there? He knew everything, didn't he? But Sherlock always said the most devious place to hide was usually the most obvious. Hide in plain sight. Yes, the Russell. That's the place for me.

*Back in London...*

The desk clerk didn't recognize me or bat an eye when I gave my name as Charles Carruthers, but quickly and efficiently had a bellman show me to my rooms. I took a suite, further embellishing my 'open' visibility. I also took advantage of the hospitable room service of the Russell and ordered a prodigious meal. My long hours of captivity coupled with my normal appetite made me quite ravenous. For some reason, unknown even to me at that time, I held off opening the sealed envelope addressed to me from Sherlock Holmes. Perhaps I wished the reading of this last correspondence to be as ceremonious as I could make it. I even took the time to have a long bath and went as far as ordering an expensive cigar and even more expensive brandy.

Finally, with snifter and stogie in hand, I reclined on the settee and opened the envelope. Several sheets of foolscap spilled out, along with a few newspaper clippings. I went to the clippings first, my eyes scanning the headlines.

'Lord Latimore, first Earl of Greydon, passed away after a short illness.' Reading further, the copy read, 'The esteemed gentleman, held in high regard by his peers and his constituency, was scheduled to make an argument concerning the official ruling as regards the employment of His Majesty's Navy in foreign waters. His untimely death could delay the proceedings, but the opposition leader, Sir Gerald Matthews, will surely press for a conclusion to the matter. Representing New Scotland Yard, Inspector Lawson agreed with the official coroner's report as to cause of death and no additional actions were to be taken.' The article had been torn at this point and one word had been scrawled on its surface, 'Accomplice?'

The second article was of the same ilk. Here the report of death was described in detail as an unfortunate accident involving one of the new electrical installations at the Claridge Hotel. The deceased, one Lawrence

## MYSTERY OF THE CHINESE BOX

'Larry' Cavendish, was a well known Labor instigator and was recently involved in organizing the dock hands on the East End. Here Holmes had scrawled 'Revenge?'

It was all a mystery to me and I hoped the letter would explain exactly what these cryptic messages meant, but it still was unclear. To my readers, I write exactly what Sherlock Holmes wrote, as I believe this to be his very last communication.

'My Dear John,' it began. 'I am terribly sorry to have involved you in what has become a most tragic circumstance. In many ways I feel like the cat that chases its tail. Eliminate all possibilities and what is left, regardless of its impossibility, will be the answer. I said that, didn't I? Perhaps unwisely. John, the forces of evil are strong, very strong. With your father by my side we fought, what I thought, was the greatest criminal mind of all time, Moriarity. I was wrong. There is one better. My own brother, Mycroft, has superceded my old nemesis to the nth degree. How could this be? How could a man who on the surface purports to have this country's best interests at heart become so corrupt? The answer is so ridiculously easy, I grimace at the solution. Shakespeare said it best, "Absolute power corrupts absolutely." Isn't that simple, John? We, Mycroft and I, have argued vehemently over this very same point. His position he made clear. Results, he said. The end does justify the means. Peruse these clippings, John, and you will see what ends he would go to and what, in God's name, is his justification?'

I gasped out loud at the realization of what these words meant. Mycroft, Sherlock's brother, was a madman, out of control, in pursuit of what he envisioned as the nobler cause. I, lying on that table, was just another cipher in his calculations. I read on.

'But these disclosures and others, I unfortunately made too late. Too many times I have been a pawn at his disposal. Perhaps I am being too harsh, and the earlier adventures that your father documented were indeed worthwhile pursuits. It was the later ones that gave me cause for concern. Your father—my dearest, dearest friend—carefully documented our last outings, and it is these I have placed within the Chinese box, and that you must see get safely away from Mycroft's grasp. Your own father's death, John, I suspect falls squarely on Mycroft's shoulders.' I was shocked. I fell back against the chair, my head reeling. The papers almost slipped from my hand. Does this make sense? Is it possible? Yes, I thought, again remembering my own torment. Composing myself, I continued to read.

'I can't prove it, and you know I hate to depend on suspicions, but it must be said. It's how I feel. Now, your safety is threatened. Mycroft came to me and tried to force the issue of the missing manuscripts once more. But this time he was not to be trifled with, I found. It was not enough that his agent, Victoria, had kept me under constant surveillance, no, he was sure I was planning to have those papers published.'

Victoria? Mrs. Hampton? An agent of Mycroft's? But why, how... all sorts of questions bruised my mind. It was incomprehensible. I traced the words again with my finger, re-reading them to make sure I had truly understood what he had written. It was so. Finding my place, I read on.

'No, Victoria didn't expose me, John. I actually exposed her, so to speak, in more ways than one! What, is that a surprise to you, John?'

I felt a hot flash cross my face at his words. Sherlock? My God, can it be? Was their relationship carnal? Quickly, I returned to the page.

'She is an admirable woman, and, quite clever in her own way. As an agent she was placed with me by Mycroft with the most incredible credentials. In fact, her testimonials were her undoing. It was so patently obvious to me, John, that in this era of unemployment, she, somewhat up in age, had no problems gaining same. And, her willingness to work for me at such a reduced wage was coupled with the fact that she didn't have the foggiest knowledge concerning imported teas. A few real weeks of employment at any elegant household would have given her that knowledge! What other conclusion could I draw? It was a most unsettling denouement. But, rather than let her go and have Mycroft try some other devious way into my household, we elected to continue the charade. Little did either of us know where that would lead. In short, my good friend, we fell in love. A more mature love, to be sure, but still a true love. You may make what you wish of it. But in our current situation, we could ill afford a traditional wedding ceremony. Even this bit of happiness was not meant to last, for Mycroft became even more suspicious with her menial reports concerning my activities. And when you came into my life, renewing my old activities, it became too much for him. Fortunately, we moved too quickly for him to take action, especially as he was in his escapist mode after his supposed death. I knew that for the ruse it was, but kept my counsel. After my return from Paris, he made his, what he thought, unexpected appearance, and renewed demands for your father's papers. I naturally rejected him out of hand. That, unfortunately, was my undoing. The poison, oh yes, his hand again has worked its damage. I am sure I too will be a natural death by all appearances. Victoria didn't know but she suspected. I was afraid to tell her the truth and place her life in danger as well. But then I realized that Mycroft really didn't move in mysterious ways and would be quite predictable. All players must part the stage, and you must as well, my young friend. The existence and unobtainability of the papers are all that keep you and her alive I am sure. If you are reading this it is because the game is more than afoot. Keep those papers away from Mycroft, at all costs. Your life depends on it. Sherlock Holmes.'

I had completely drained my glass and I reached to pour another when a cosmic thought interrupted my actions and forestalled me from addling my brain any further. My father's papers existed. I had seen them placed within that ornate box, the Chinese box. Mrs. Hampton had aided in its removal from Hudson Farm and now it must be with her niece, wherever that may be. I must go and find it—and then what, I thought? Perhaps I shall have the papers published or, at the very least, see that they reach the appropriate authorities. But who are those authorities? Who is on my side? Is this tangled skein a conspiracy that allows for no one to be trusted? What kind of government allows its subjects to experience such fear? Questions, so many questions, and no ready answers at hand. Oh, Holmes, I thought, how I wish you were here to make the right choice for me. I looked down at the pages and my eyes caught the edge of an additional sheet, one I hadn't read as yet. I turned the page.

'Dear John Watson,' I read. I looked to the bottom. It was from Mrs. Hampton.

'Sherlock has entrusted me with seeing that his precious box be sent as far from here as possible and I have accomplished this, as you rightly know. My niece, bless her heart, thinks we are playing a silly game with those nasty gentlemen friends of Mycroft's and to her, mum's the word. She is a dear, but of course the game won't end here, as you have been taken prisoner and will never be allowed to leave this house. I will do my best to help you if I can. But if I am successful, then it will be a further tragic turn of events, for surely Mycroft will suspect and turn his attentions to me, and to my family. In that event, I must insist that you do your part in this madness and go to my brother's house in Terlington and remove that infernal box to ensure their safety. May God be with you. Victoria Hampton.'

*A decision is made...*

In this short but concise note my direction was clear. I would take the very next train to Terlington and do precisely as Mrs. Hampton had suggested. I called the front desk and found that the next train was at 7:20 this evening, from Paddington station. I had just about one hour, plenty of time. I quickly dressed in my same garments, which were somewhat wretched from my terrible night but would have to do under the circumstances. I thought of applying some bootblack, which I could easily obtain from the hallboy, to give the appearance of some facial hair, such as a mustache, but dismissed it as an unnecessary precaution. Time was of the essence and my duty was clear. I went down the back stairs and came out on Russell Square, where a large crowd of passersby were hurrying home from work. I easily dissembled into the crowd, and made my way on foot to Paddington with only a few minutes to spare. Once onboard the train, I tried to set myself at ease. But the nightmarish thoughts kept creeping into my brain. After only two stops the full realization of what was happening literally shot me out of my seat—much to the chagrin of my fellow passengers—as my thoughts found voice and I fairly shouted, "They'll kill her, they'll kill her!" Embarrassed, I regained my seat, but not without having to face down numerous others who looked as if I had gone completely insane. I know I continued to move my lips silently as that one vicious thought kept its relentless hold on my soul. She had taken my place in that hellhold. I must try and help her. But, the box? What about the box? Do I see to its safety first? Oh, Holmes, what would you have me do? To assist in my decision I removed the letter from Holmes and Mrs. Hampton and reread them carefully once more. There was no doubt: Sherlock Holmes had lost his life to keep these papers from Mycroft, and he had contacted me in his hour of need to assist in this endeavor; Mrs. Hampton also had done her best to secure the box. So now, even though her life might possibly be in danger, there was no doubt as to my loyalty in the matter. I must see that my father's papers survived, no matter what. And, once that was accomplished, I would return to Hudson Farm and seek out Mrs. Hampton, and pray to God that I was not too late.

In the time I had remaining before reaching my destination, I began to write down the dialogue that you are now reading, to serve as a permanent record of what had occurred, and to assist others in case I failed.

When I reached Terlington it was an easy chore to locate the home of Cyrus Hampton, Mrs. Hampton's brother. It was there I learned that Sylvia, Cyrus's wife, had passed on and that is why he had turned to Victoria as a helpmate in raising Martha. I did my level best to control my agitation, as I really did not want to implicate this simple man in the Machiavellian plot that was unfolding as we spoke. Martha was shy and somewhat reluctant to let me see her new 'toy,' the Chinese box. Eventually though, I convinced her that it was Mrs. Hampton's suggestion that I help her hide it from those silly men at the farm. As if she was aware of my relation to the box, she left me alone for a while while she went to make some tea. It gave me the opportunity to try the combination that I had embedded on my brain, oh so few nights before, as I had watched the great detective open the box. At first, I made mistakes and nothing happened. Then, the combination clicked into place, and a small compartment opened up. Within it I saw my original notes from our two previous adventures. I almost leapt for joy, but the sounds of Martha returning brought me to my senses and I locked it once more.

Trying to appear as composed as possible, I drank my tea and was on the verge of intimating to Mr. Hampton that I thought it best the box be returned to Hudson Farm. Suddenly, there was a hard rapping sound on the front door. I spilled my tea as I quickly rose up, moving towards the girl's room. Then a husky voice bellowed out, "Cyrus, I've got a telegram for you. It's mighty important. It's from your sister. Open the door." I rushed back into the room, reaching out with both hands to stop Cyrus from opening the door, but he pulled away and looked back at me as if I were crazy. His hands on the latch, he turned back to me and spoke.

## MYSTERY OF THE CHINESE BOX

"Young fella, what in blazes is the matter with you? That's Nathan's boy from the telegraph office. He's a big 'un, not so bright, maybe, but harmless all the same." His voice was just above a whisper as he obviously didn't want Nathan's boy hearing him. Then he lifted the latch and opened the door. Panic was still registered on my face, I am sure.

He was a big strapping boy, whose voice belied his age. He shuffled mercilessly from one foot to the other as he handed the envelope to Cyrus Hampton.

"Thankee, Thomas... I'm much obliged." With that, he reached in and pulled out a small coin, handing it to the young man with the raspy voice. In an instant he was gone. Cyrus brought the envelope over to the kitchen table and proceeded to open it in the better light. Martha glided quietly to his side. I, feeling somewhat embarrassed, kept my counsel.

"Oh my God!" he stammered, then looking my way, "Do you know what in Hell this is all about?" He thrust the missive towards me. I took it gingerly and read as quickly as I could.

"CYRUS TAKE MARTHA AND FLEE IMMEDIATELY STOP YOU KNOW WHERE TO GO STOP TRUST ONLY JOHN WATSON STOP TAKE ALL IN COALBIN STOP  VICTORIA STOP"

I looked up at the now unquiet eyes of Cyrus Hampton. "She's in grave danger, Mr. Hampton, and I must go to her aid. You and Martha are also in danger and must do as she says. Do you have a place to go, as she mentions?" I lowered my eyes as I spoke and his voice, subdued, came back to me.

"Yes, she warned me that something like this might happen one day, but she never told me exactly what it was she was doing.  We had always made plans to go to Nova Scotia, a great fishing place, you know." I nodded and he continued.

"The coalbin is where she kept her money. Quite a bit of it, I think, more than I need, but evidently, she...." his voice started to quaver and his stocky body started to crumble as he eased himself into the kitchen chair. I moved to his side to comfort him but he waved me away.

"I guess there's nothing I can do now, is there, fella?"

I imagined his mind tormented by his love for his sister and his necessity of protecting Martha. I was moved by this nobility of thought and also angered that Mycroft could be causing this much pain without even setting foot under this roof. I dashed these thoughts from my mind and tried to take command of the situation.

"Cyrus... Mr. Hampton. It is imperative that you and Martha leave immediately, tonight. Is there anything I can do to help you reach, what was the place? Nova Scotia? How would you get there?" My questions hung in the air like dirty laundry, but Cyrus Hampton was a man of the sea and though we were not taking on water, he reacted as if we were.

"That's easy. We can hightail it up to Mallow Bay, and leave at first light on one of the fishing skiffs. I know a fella there who will take us to Portsmouth. From there, by midafternoon, we can board any number of packets that make the North Atlantic their home, mostly mail boats and such, but I'm sure I'll find one to make the long haul." He seemed more in control now, not as helpless as he seemed before. Martha came over and hugged him tightly, creating a very warm, familial scene. I smiled thinly and continued.

"That should work perfectly. There is one other favor I must ask of you, however." He looked at me, suspicion forming then disappearing from his eyes.

"You want me to take that box with me, don't ya?" I nodded appreciatively. He grimaced back. "I knew it was part and parcel the minute it came into the house. Victoria keeps many secrets and some, well, not as well." I smiled at that and Cyrus smiled back. "What about you, young man? How will I know what's happening with Vickie and..." his voice trailed off.

"Sir, when this ghastly nightmare is through, I hope to have Mrs. Hampton and myself join you in Nova Scotia. Is there someplace in particular I can contact you?" I tried to sound as hopeful as possible, but I knew he saw through my charade.

"Go to St. John's. Not the Newfoundland one, the Nova Scotia one. 'Tis a small town, I'm sure you will be able to track me down. I shan't hide once I'm there. I'm not turned out to be that way." He said it so plaintively that again I felt the anger well up within me towards Mycroft and his machinations, and a chill passed through my body. The moment passed, and I said, "Very good. I'll be there. You can count on me." Cyrus weakly nodded back his agreement.

## MYSTERY OF THE CHINESE BOX

As they gathered their meagre things for this hardship voyage, I again went to the Chinese box.

Alone, I worked the combination until the compartment was opened to me once more. I peered down at my own handwritten notes, and pulled my latest report from my pocket, applying my pen one last time to place these very words on the page. I will fold this up as well and place it also within that box of trickery, and hope that all will come out well. That Cyrus and Martha reach their destination. That Victoria, Mrs. Hampton, is proven safe or is made safe by my actions. And, at the very least, that these papers, now my own as well as my father's, reach a safe haven. I sign my name, John S. Watson.

# Chinese Box Mysteries
## SHERLOCK HOLMES

# One Last Case

**Editor's Comments**

**When all before is fiction...**

# ONE LAST CASE

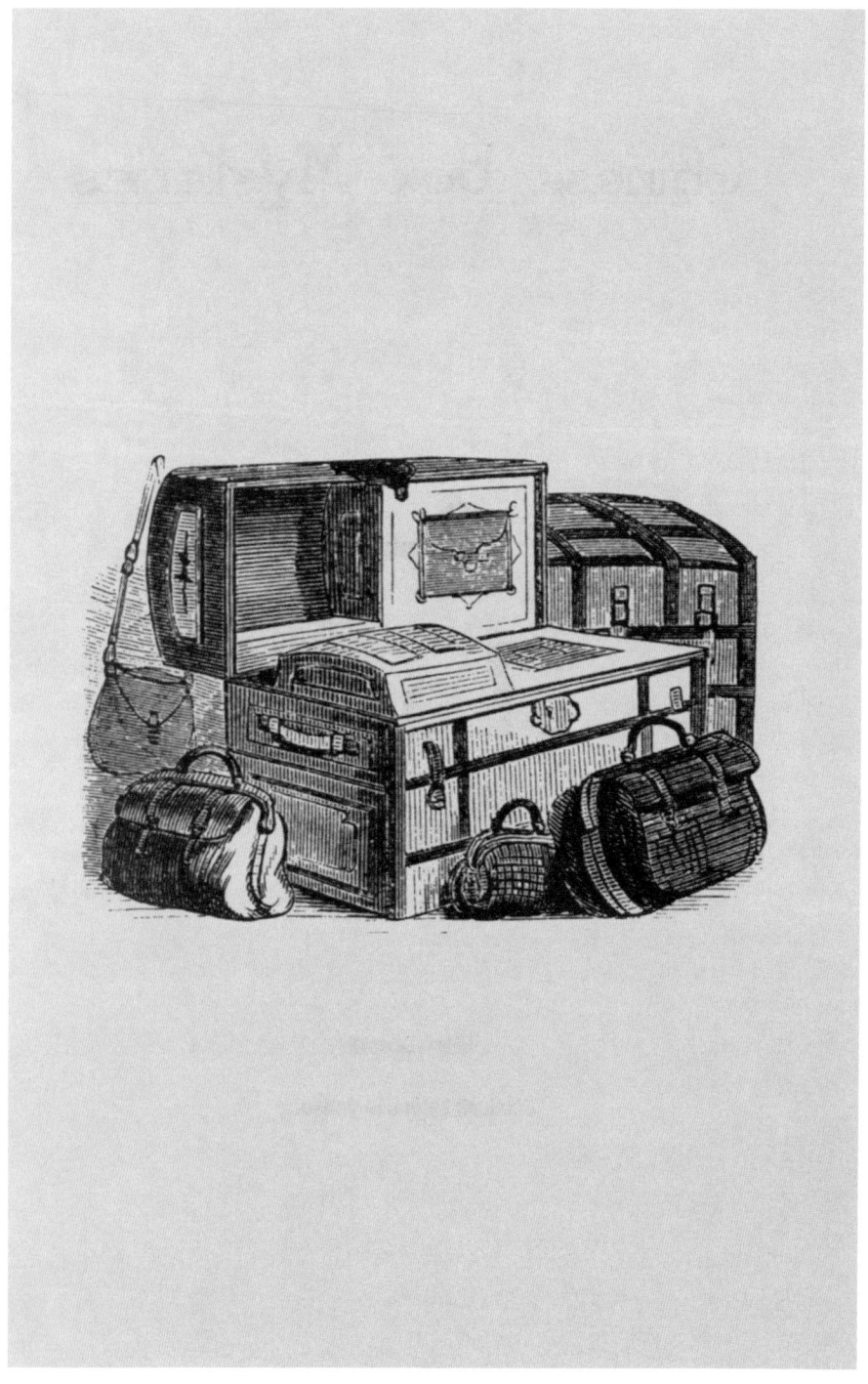

# One Last Case

Delta Flight 251 wasn't crowded but it felt it. Detective Sergeant Myron Goldfarb stretched uncomfortably in seat 36A, a window seat. It was obvious he regretted his decision fifteen minutes into the flight. He chided himself for not realizing that a flight leaving at 8:40 p.m. from Chicago's O'Hare to London's Heathrow would not afford much sightseeing while aloft, especially in November. The view had been spectacular at takeoff but had gone downhill pretty quickly as the 747 reached cruising altitude. Since he was going to ignore the advice of more experienced travelers and drink, he thought, he might as well go whole hog. He ordered two Dewars and sodas, smiled weakly at the stewardess, thinking that she might be glad he was saving her a trip, and, just as quickly, remembered that tipping is not an in-flight compensation. Once more he depressed the button which was supposed to allow his backrest to recline, only to discover he had already reached the maximum setting. A wry smile crossed his face as he remembered Seinfeld on TV letting out a short "ek" as he pantomimed reclining his seat and remarking, "Now, this is it. What a difference. I could sleep for hours!" and the audience howling in understanding. Detective Goldfarb understood also....now.

# ONE LAST CASE

The drink started to take hold better than the seating accommodations and relaxation came to his body. The scant sixteen inches of legroom no longer annoyed him, and since sleep was not an option, he gingerly pulled out his notebook to review once more the facts of the case.

Carolyn Masters, age 32, height, 5 feet 8 inches. Pretty tall, he thought. Weight, 112 pounds. Sounds like a model. A model victim for rape and murder? She was attractive and that is what apparently happened to her. There was a photo in his file as well but he didn't pull it out. He didn't want to upset the passenger on his right who seemed to be peering occasionally in Goldfarb's direction, and he was not looking out the window, which now was completely void of anything but black. Goldfarb shot him a glance and the man looked quickly away.

Guiding his mind back to the case, he traced his finger over the police report as the jumble of phrases reached out to embrace him. The victim had been raped and a condom was used, no trace of semen. How thoughtful, Goldfarb thought. She was also alone in a locked bedroom on the third floor. The door had not been forced, but was evidently locked after the perpetrator left. So, she must have known him. The cause of death was strangulation. The time of death was inconclusive, but considered to be about 10:30 p.m. based on an analysis of her stomach's contents. Goldfarb had investigated a lot of murders, some very grisly, but he still shuddered whenever he read a coroner's report. He did so now. He noted from the report that she didn't seem to put up much of a struggle, nor did the room show any signs of one. Again, it seemed as if she knew the perp. There was nothing stolen or reported missing, so robbery wasn't a motive. Her body was discovered by police after the housekeeper called in a panic after getting no answer to her knocks at the door. The housekeeper, Mrs. Simmons, a British citizen brought over by the husband, was sure that Mrs. Masters was in her bedroom as she, herself, had witnessed her return at 10 p.m. It had been a surprise, she added, and that was the crux of the matter. A surprise return. She was scheduled to attend this posh function at the St. Mark's Hotel but an argument had occurred with her husband, Stephan Masters, and she had returned

# ONE LAST CASE

home alone. This argument had been witnessed by several people in the hospitality suite taken by Mr. Master's company, Whitegate and Carruthers, Limited. Not quite a knock-down, drag-out type of fight but more of your typical spat. The pursed lips, tightened jaws type of thing, no real violence, and yet, it made an impression on several of the assembled guests. Probably more so in light of the outcome of the evening's events.

So the district attorney, Paul Callender, an up-and-comer, came out swinging. The pre-indictment papers were also in the file and it looked pretty bleak for Mr. Stephan Masters. First, he wouldn't disclose the argument he and his wife had, which tends to create a motive. That looked bad. Second, the locked bedroom and the lack of violence pointed to a known assailant. Who is more known to a woman than her husband? Third, the use of a condom is not normally a precaution taken by violent rapists. The more obvious scenario was trying to emulate a vicious rape while ensuring no DNA evidence. Fourth, his alibi was weak. Yes, he was at the St. Mark's Hotel, but during the presentation speeches nobody remembered seeing him. Thus, opportunity. St. Mark's was physically only a fifteen minute cab ride away. Coming and going and a little murder still allowed him ample time to rejoin his constituency in the hospitality suite at 11 p.m., when witnesses did vouch for him. It looked really bad. Fifth and finally, his company—or rather his branch of the company—was doing poorly. That was the rumor on the street. And that could spell a real motive. Mrs. Masters was insured for a cool million dollars, or its equivalent in British pounds. That really riled Callender and the fellow sitting in seat 36A. A childless couple? A million dollar policy on a non-working wife? Didn't fit. No way.

All of the above was evidence, no doubt about it. And then there was gut feeling. Detective Goldfarb's gut feeling. He did the interrogation of Stephan Masters, a grueling three hour oration with no lawyer present. Masters knew his rights but waived them. He explained that American jurisprudence was based on the British system, and since he knew that he was innocent, it would only hasten the capture of Carolyn's killer if he responded to our entreaties. This was all said very politely, even when he refused to discuss the quarrel that

# ONE LAST CASE

they had. He said it was very personal and had no bearing on the matter at hand. He was so terribly British and stiff upper-lipped, but Goldfarb could still see the man was trembling, not on the outside, but on the inside. It could have been plain remorse but he didn't think so. That gut feeling. Stephan and Carolyn Masters had only been in the United States a short time, less than a year. He had transferred to the States as a branch manager of an international architectural firm based in London, Whitegate and Carruthers, Limited. The insurance policy would have to be examined and those rumors concerning the office in Chicago as well. And that's why Detective Goldfarb was on flight 251.

Chief Inspector Latham Satterwhite leaned forward and rested his forearms on his desk, a stern look on his face as he conspicuously surveyed his counterpart from the States. Satterwhite, almost six and a half feet tall, weighing about 230 pounds, relished any chance to assert his presence and authority. The American, Goldfarb, was obviously distressed sitting in the small, uncomfortable sidechair Satterwhite had directed him to use. Goldfarb had just completed his request for warrants for Whitegate and Carruthers and for the insurance company, Royal Ascot Alliances. At 5 feet, 6 inches and less than 150 pounds, Goldfarb knew he would lose this Mexican standoff, so he took another tack.

"Look, Inspector," he said. "I know British companies have a right to privacy and I also know I have no jurisdiction, but this is a case of murder and it does involve a British citizen. Our D.A., uh, that is, the District Attorney, wants to prosecute this man, Masters, and I believe he is innocent. That's why I am here."

"You didn't contact Interpol." Satterwhite interrupted, now moving away from his desk, the wheels making an awful sound as they strained under the weight.

"I know, I know," apologized Goldfarb. "I didn't think it was necessary. I was just going to make some discrete inquiries. I didn't realize they'd get so bent out of shape. Now I know. I'm sorry. Now, will you help me?" The question hung in the air for a long time and again, Satterwhite let a look of annoyance cross his face.

"Where are you staying, Sergeant?" he asked.

# ONE LAST CASE

Goldfarb, realizing the little game Satterwhite was playing and enjoying, went along and replied, "the Russell, uh, on Russell Square."

"I know it! This is my city, remember?" The Inspector's eyes darkened. "Look, leave your papers with the Duty Sergeant and I'll call you if I can arrange something. That's all."

Dismissed, Goldfarb stood up, started to extend his hand, then realized the Chief Inspector wasn't even going to raise his eyes. He turned and walked out of the office.

As was his custom, he took the stairs and was deep in thought, thinking about how badly this had turned out, how stupid he was going to look to the D.A. and to his boss, Captain Scott, who had really gone to bat for him on this one. He was so deep in thought he didn't hear his name called out until the third repetition. He stopped and looked back up the stairs.

The figure coming down was in shadows, and the lighting was poor between landings. The man didn't say anything until he was almost nose to nose with Goldfarb.

"All right, now, no need to leave in a huff," he said.

"I wasn't leaving," Goldfarb replied.

"No? I'm surprised. Seems to me the Yard hasn't done its proper duty by you and if I was you, I wouldn't waste my time with these malingerers, I'd go where help is not only available, but amiable. Do you catch my drift, Governor?"

The man, somewhat grimy, appeared to be a street character—maybe even a chimney sweep—thought Goldfarb, as he recollected Mary Poppins. Yes, Burt, that was the name, played by Dick Van Dyke. That's exactly who he looked like.

"Say, who in the hell are you?" Goldfarb snapped.

"Me? Oh, why, Burt's the name." the man replied, and then seeing the look on Goldfarb's face, continued, "Nah, just having you on. Smiley, everyone calls me Smiley. I'm sort of a regular here, or rather an irregular, if you catch my drift?" A big grin flashed quickly across his face.

"Well Smiley, you're right about the help I've gotten here, but now I've got to go down and see the Desk Sergeant and make some

# ONE LAST CASE

arrangements." Goldfarb made to leave but Smiley moved quickly down the stairs and blocked his way.

"Well you're the boss, Guvnor, that's what I say. And I wouldn't do nuttin' to delay your rounds, that's for sure, but if I may be of assistance...." His hand held out a small white card, quite clean in comparison with the gloved hand that held it. Goldfarb took the card and glanced at the type upon it. It simply said, Consulting Detective.

"Well Smiley, if you're looking for a job, I'm afraid I'm not in a position to offer any. I'm from the States—Chicago—and I'm afraid I'm way out of my depths. Here, take your card. Give it to someone who might be able to use you."

"Ah Sir, you are a card, that you are, that you are! Might use me, yes, that's good, I like that." Smiley moved quickly past Goldfarb's outstretched hand and bounded back up the stairs, his voice trailing after him.

"Yes, you'll need me. You'll see, Detective Goldfarb, you'll see."

Goldfarb lowered his arm and turned around. The man had already disappeared into the dim recesses of the landing above. The amused look on Goldfarb's face changed to wonder as those last words echoed in his brain, 'you'll see, Detective Goldfarb, you'll see.' Now, how did he know my name? he thought.

The Russell Hotel was a wonderful old establishment that had kept many of its Victorian splendors but was modernized enough to attract business travelers from all around the world. A businessman's hotel it definitely was, and yet, it exuded a warmth that no Holiday Inn could ever hope to achieve. After the fruitless interview this afternoon and the humorless Desk Sergeant, the stay at the Russell was going to be Goldfarb's highlight of the trip. He had already completed his transatlantic calls, one to his wife and one to Captain Scott's voicemail, and he was done for the evening. He placed no great hope on the Chief Inspector's ability or desire to garner the resources necessary to get the information he needed. It was in this dour mood that he made his way to the small hotel bar for a late cocktail. As for dinner, he wasn't hungry. Detective Goldfarb was a bantam weight and it wasn't from working out but from the simple diet of voluntary fasting. It was a habit he picked up in college, going without food

# ONE LAST CASE

for several days at a clip. It worried his wife, not for his sake, but for hers. She was somewhat overweight, or pleasingly plump, as some might politely put it. She felt it patently unfair that his battles were never fought while she was at constant war. But life is never fair.

He was in the act of paying for his second martini—another habit of his, paying as he goes—when he discovered the card in his coat pocket. He read the card and read it once more, wiping his eyes in disbelief. He was sure when he first got the card it had said, 'Consulting Detective.' Now when he read it, it said '127 Marylborough Lane.' He turned the card over and it was blank. He repeated this action as if he could will the words to change. They didn't. It still said '127 Marylborough Lane.'

The bartender, seeing this mystified look on Goldfarb's face, brought a fresh glass of water and some chips in case the gentleman required some refreshment.

Goldfarb, brought out of his reverie by the tinkle of ice, looked up and addressed the bartender.

"Can you tell me where Marylborough Lane is located?"

"Marylborough Lane? You mean Marylborough Road, I think. Alf?" This last said to a waiter standing at the service bar area, who, upon hearing his name, walked over.

"This gentleman," the bartender continued, "is looking for Marylborough Lane. Could you get the street map from the concierge when you get a chance?"

Goldfarb, sensing a slight reluctance on Alf's face, rose up from the stool and said, "That's all right. I'll go to the front desk. Here, this is for you." He handed a five-pound note to the bartender.

"No Sir, that won't do."

"It's not enough?" Goldfarb asked.

"Not that, Sir. You've paid for your drink, remember? If it's a tip you're planning on leaving, I'd be obliged with the change on the bar. Here, Sir." He pointed to the coins that had been accumulating after each round in the glass ashtray which had gone unused. Another of Goldfarb's non-habits.

"Sure, sure, no problem." Goldfarb pocketed his bill and headed for the front desk, oblivious of the stares from the two hotel employees as he made his exit.

# ONE LAST CASE

"Let's see, Marylborough is right here, off of Waterloo, but that's Marylborough Road. Now sometimes a Lane intersects with a Road and that might be the case. Let me see." The concierge allowed his finger to travel the meandering thin line that represented Marylborough Road. "No, don't see it. Unless, of course, it's in this area. See Sir, this maze of streets down near the Thames." Goldfarb stretched his short frame over the deep marble counter to follow the concierge's eyes and fingers. "There's a lot of small alleys and byways there. An unsavory place, I might add. It wouldn't do to go down there at night, that's for sure." Goldfarb made a small mark with his state-issued ballpoint and thanked the man for the information. He left the desk and headed for his room, planning to take the concierge's advice and look for Marylborough Lane in the light of day.

He undressed and performed his nightly toilette, which included organizing everything from his pockets and placing them on the top of his dresser in the order in which he would put them back. It was a habit he developed after an unfortunate incident in which he had left a photo of his wife in his shirt pocket, back when they were dating, and it had come back from the laundry integrated with a gum wrapper that was in the same shirt pocket. Karen was not a Doublemint twin, but she sure looked like one then. His mind did not make the connection that today she weighed almost as much as both Doublemint twins. That was fortunate for Karen and probably for Myron also. She was acutely aware of her weight problem and he wasn't. It was that simple. Love was not just blind in this case, but blissful. Myron Goldfarb couldn't even imagine being married to anyone else. Karen would be a lot happier if she knew that or believed it when Myron told her. Life wasn't fair.

At 11:30 p.m. exactly the bedside phone rang. Goldfarb had put in a wakeup call and thought that this was it. Jet lag can do strange things to the mind. He answered before the second ring, ready to mouth the reciprocal 'thank you,' but rose half out of bed when he heard the voice.

"Good evenin', Guvnor. Aren't you supposed to be on your way? He don't keep regular hours now, you now. So, pip, pip, let's go. There'll be a cab waitin' downstairs as soon as you're ready. Oh, and

## ONE LAST CASE

by the way, don't take the first one nor the second. The third one's your man, you'll see, you'll see." And the line went dead.

Smiley, Goldfarb thought. The chimney sweep, or whatever. What the Hell is going on? Goldfarb was up, splashing water in his face, looking in the mirror. This must be some sort of joke of Satterwhite's. Of course. He wasn't satisfied with the cat and mouse routine. No, he wanted a little more fun. It had to be him. That Smiley character came along too quickly and he also knew my name, Goldfarb remembered. That should have been a sure sign he was well informed. Satterwhite must do this all the time as a running joke. That's how he is so prepared when strangers drop in, as he had done today. Did I notify Interpol? Yeah, Satterwhite, as if that mattered. So, what's next? A wild goose chase. Should I buy it?

Goldfarb started pacing his room while absent-mindedly beginning to dress, picking objects off of the dresser to insert back in the trousers he had already put on.

Yeah, I have to do it, he thought. Keep a cool head and let him make a fool of me. What do I care? I have a sense of humor. Besides, if this gets me the information on the Master's case, it's worth it. Okay, Buster, here I come.

With a determined look on his face, Detective Sergeant Myron Goldfarb swung open his door and stalked to the lifts. He would have taken the stairs but he hadn't orientated himself to the hotel as yet. Jet lag again.

It was a welcome surprise to find that the third cab was one of those unique large London black beauties, spacious and extremely comfortable. Goldfarb couldn't help notice the doorman's annoyance when he had turned down the first cab that came along. After all, the night had turned exceedingly cold, almost freezing, and a steady downpour made his request seem even crazier. Goldfarb tipped the man quite substantially, he thought, and dashed into the cab as soon as the door was open, ignoring the large umbrella the doorman had tried to employ. He was sure he was not enhancing America's image to this particular Englishman, nor did he care. He was completely set on playing out the string and letting Satterwhite have his laugh. The cab rolled off quite smoothly and with no hesitation, nor, Goldfarb thought, with any direction from him. He started to say something, then, thinking better of it, let the cabbie have his fun also. They drove on for almost three quarters of an hour this way. Finally, after making what seemed like a dozen turns in a row, the cab came to a stop.

"This is it, Guvnor," the driver said.

At the sound of the man's voice, Goldfarb strained forward to see if it was Smiley at the wheel. He had already deduced that this was not the case during the drive but now upon hearing the voice he felt unsure. The man bore no resemblance to the lithe, quickly moving, unkempt Smiley. No, this man was quite rotund and a bald pate that reflected every street light they passed. It might have been a great disguise, but Goldfarb didn't think so. Then he realized that a British accent was not routine to him and he was stereotyping too quickly. He reached for his billfold as the door opened, seemingly by itself, but was stopped short by the man's gruff response.

"No, no won't do, won't do, Guvnor. This here ride is on the house. But you'll sing for your supper yet, that I'm sure. Yes you will, yes you will. Take care now, and don't forget a spoonful of sugar, eh, hahaha."

Goldfarb had half turned around to respond when the door quickly shut with a thump and the cab rolled away silently down the damp street. He stood in amazement as he watched the red lights grow small, then appear to wink and disappear. Fortunately it had stopped raining and the air felt warmer somehow. He loosened his overcoat and took an appraisal of the street he was on. He wasn't at the corner, so no street signs were in evidence. Across the street was a warehouse-type building, boarded up and looking quite forlorn. Peering through the darkness he could make out some old faded lettering on the building, 'Boyce & Boyce Machine Works'; the rest was unreadable. The street was narrow and cobblestoned, Goldfarb knew that London had many old streets just like this, so it wasn't a total surprise. Looking down the street he couldn't see any traffic moving, though his vision was blocked by the twistings of the narrow road. This was definitely an old part of town, probably still had some bombed out buildings from the Blitzkrieg of World War II. History was not a strong suit with the detective but he did enjoy old buildings and their style of architecture in comparison with today's square, featureless structures. Turning to face the building he knew would be 127, he was mildly taken aback. The structure looked like a townhouse wedged between two factories. It was a complete aberration to the two, which were almost identical. Brick, reddish-brown, at least in this light, and no real design to speak of, unless all you have to work with are lego blocks. So how did this middle structure come about? Here was a townhouse that must have been quite elegant in its day. Lots of curlicue works, even some gargoyles, though quite friendly in appearance. The windows were huge with real green velvet drapes, which were drawn shut, letting no light out or in for that matter. Goldfarb advanced up the small set of stairs, handling the polished brass rail as he did. It was amazing, it was pristine. Upon reaching the large double-doors he took a moment to read the type below the numbers 127.

Charleton House
est. 1878
Architect: Archibald Hollinger
Builder: Montgomery Tharp
British Commemorative Society

Well, a plaqued home. Is this what Satterwhite wanted me to see? thought Goldfarb. A little late to take in a sight-seeing trip.

He reached up for the large, elephant head-shaped brass knocker, but found the door swung open as his hand fell short of the mark. It was obviously well oiled, for nary a sound escaped its hinges as it made its semi-circular arc to a full opening.

Goldfarb moved in to the dark interior and fearlessly reached along the wall searching for a light switch. Finding none, he waited in the doorway until his eyes grew accustomed to the dark, and with only the pale street lamp from outside he made out a small table with what appeared to be a hurricane lamp on it. He stepped closer and picked up one of the long wooden matches from a bowl and struck it on his heel. As the match flared, the door behind him swung completely shut. Not quite noiselessly, but with a low "whump"-like sound. He registered no surprise and quickly placed the flaring matchhead into the aperture on the lamp. It also made a "whump"-like sound as the oil licked at the open flame. Remembering his camping days, (which unfortunately were over, Karen did not like camping), he turned the small wheel to adjust the light until a warm glow filled the foyer where he was standing.

He surveyed the room, admiring the antiques, the tiny delicate crystal chandelier hanging above his head, the workmanship in the woodwork, and the exquisite French doors leading into the main part of the house, he assumed. The glass in the doors was leaded, but as no light came through from the other side, they appeared quite black at this distance. Upon coming closer, he noticed that the flicker from his lamp was reflecting a thousand times in the tiny panes and was quite mesmerizing to his eyes. He stopped suddenly when he realized that several of the panes remained quite black. He advanced once more, and upon closer inspection found that those panes were missing. His hand passed through effortlessly, but he pulled it back as it had felt quite cold in an instant. This startled Goldfarb for a moment, and made him reassess his thoughts that this was part of Satterwhite's plan. Upon further consideration he moved once more to the doors, this time turning one of the elongated handles. It was locked and didn't budge. Now he was perplexed. This room was intriguing but he was sure there was more to be seen, and it had to lie behind this door. Moving even closer, he lowered himself down on one knee and peered through the keyhole. He saw it was blocked and made the realization that the key must still be in it. He stepped back once more, surveying the distance from the door handle to the missing panes, and it appeared at first glance it might be too long a stretch for his arm to make the connection, that is, reach through and turn the key from the other side. Another possibility, of course, would be to simply break a pane nearer the key and gain entrance that way. This Goldfarb didn't approve of, and thus he decided to forgo this piece of the puzzle and make his way back to the Russell and lodge an official complaint with Satterwhite first thing in the morning. He was also starting to feel tired—jet lag was really setting in. He walked back to the table, set the lamp down, started to turn it off, but stopped. Hmm, he thought,

## ONE LAST CASE

no sense doing this in the dark. I'll open the door with the lamp in hand. Then I'll leave the door open, return the lamp to its place, turning it down, and hastily make my retreat. End of midnight madness. Satisfied with this plan, he retraced his steps to the door and pulled at the handle. Nothing. Locked. He jiggled it several ways, then tried the matching door. Still nothing. In desperation he thumped loudly three or four times on the heavy wooden surface. In the small foyer, the sounds reverberated and died, echoing away except for one sound: a creaking noise from a not-so-well-oiled hinge. Goldfarb spun around. He couldn't believe it. The French door was ajar—not quite open, just a hint but definitely out of its lock. He picked up the lamp and moved to the doors, pushing with one hand straight-armed in front. The door creaked and moaned as if in pain. It had been a terribly long time since it made this transition. Goldfarb followed his arm with another, this one holding the lamp at eye level as he went into the other room.

The scene here revealed a complete opposite to the foyer. Where before handsome antiques warmly filled the room, here gauzy spiderwebs lavishly covered furniture that had long since passed its usefulness. The velvet drapes were in tatters and dust-streaked, causing them to appear more grey than green. The room was much larger and also contained a chandelier, but this one was missing many of its icy ornaments and the dirt that coated it allowed no reflection from the lamp he held up to it. The air was cold, as his hand had indicated to him when he passed it through the pane. Deathly cold, unnaturally cold. He couldn't imagine that a building this old with thick walls shouldn't have provided some insulation from the night air, and, after all, it wasn't that cold out. Now he could see his breath escaping from between his lips. This was definitely going too far with a practical joke, and he moved to go back through the doors. Naturally they were shut. But that couldn't be, he thought. The front doors, I understand. They were well-oiled and moved without a sound. But these, these screeched when they opened. How could they be closed now and not have make a sound? It's impossible! Goldfarb reached down for the key but it was not in the keyhole. He kneeled as he had done from the other side and looked through, and almost fell completely prone as an eye made direct contact with his. He screamed and scrambled to his feet and bumped, hurting himself in the process, against a large rolltop desk which he hadn't realized was there due to the spiderwebs. Breathing heavily, his own breath forming a small cloud in front of his face, he tried to regain his composure. Minutes passed while he held this position. Finally, as sanity returned, he once more moved towards the French doors. They were still locked. But a change had taken place. Light was coming from that room, the one he had just occupied. It was streaming through the missing panes while the others remain dirty and opaque. Slowly, quietly, he moved to position himself in order to look through. His mind was racing at the possibilities and he had to steel himself to make those few little steps.

He was there. The bright light almost hurt his eyes. This was not candle-light. Not a small hurricane lamp. This was more modern lighting, for indeed, that's what it was. In amazement he realized he was looking at the bedroom of Stephan and Carolyn Masters. A bedroom that was back in Chicago. He wiped his eyes as if to make the image disappear, but it remained. He stared long and hard at the scene. There was nobody there. His eyes wandered over the bed, the scene of the murder. He didn't know if the room had been cleaned already or if he was looking into the past before the murder was committed. Since nothing was happening, he unbent his knee and turned to walk back to the desk, but slammed immediately into a tall, ugly lamp that had moved directly into his path. No, he didn't see it move, but it definitely was not there before. Panic started to overtake him once more. He backed away towards the open panes and felt a faint electrical shock hit his torso as he approached. His eyes, wide and wild, showed that his mind was reeling and he slumped to the floor.

When he awoke, he find himself still within distance of the open panes into the Masters' bedroom. The lamp was still blocking his path, but now he was seated in a comfortable but filthy chair. The scene in the bedroom was the same. For some reason he was unafraid. His mind rationalized that if whatever was happening to him was through some malevolent force, a force capable of locking him up, moving furniture, etc., it could also have easily killed him while he was lying prone on the floor just a few moments ago. He checked his watch and realized it was already past three in the morning. He also decided to stop giving credit to Satterwhite for his 'experience.' This was just too elaborate for that big hulk. At the thought of the Chief Inspector a wry smile crossed his face and once more he peered into the bedroom scene. Whatever forces had brought him here, they wanted him to take a good long look. And he did.

Two ultra-modern dressers, not to his taste. Opened jewelry box on dressing table; she was undressing, probably. Designer mirror over dressing table. Large wardrobe, both doors open, clothes on one side, his. Large walk-in closet, rows of clothes, shoes, hers. Modern-designed roll-top desk, his. A desk chair matching dressing table chair. End tables built onto platform bed. The bed where she was found. That's about it. He stared some more then gave it up. He started to rise but the chair pushed deeper into the back of his legs. He wasn't supposed to get up. He hadn't seen what he was supposed to see.

"What is it?" he spoke out loud. "Is this like Dickens, the ghost of murder past, or has it yet to happen? Damn it, what am I supposed to see?"

He was answered by a scratching sound, like a rat or a mouse skittering along a wooden floor. He searched the room for the source of the sound but found nothing. Then suddenly, he saw a face and almost jumped out of his skin. It was his own face, reflected on the filthy mirror over the fireplace, neither of which he had noticed. He rose up (the chair allowed him) and he moved to the mantel. He looked at his face and it seemed paler, more gaunt. His nose, typically Jewish, he supposed, appeared even more aquiline. He moved the lamp closer, and as he did so, the image appeared to get weaker instead of stronger. Strange, he thought. Then, just for a moment, the light caught the streaks of grime on the mirror and it appeared they formed a word. One word. Observe. His thoughts were interrupted by a sound coming from the chair he had just left. It was beckoning to him, rocking on its haunches. He moved back and resumed his position and looked through the panes once more. In disappointment the scene was actually the same, unchanged.

"How long must I look at this?" he said.

The lamp moved a bit closer and stopped.

# ONE LAST CASE

*How long must I look...*

# ONE LAST CASE

He returned to the bedroom scene and watched.

He examined, reexamined and analyzed every detail of that room. It took until five o'clock to make the discovery.

"Damn! Someone could have hidden in the tall wardrobe. It doesn't make sense for the clothes to be on just one side, right?" He looked around as if waiting for the lamp to doff its shade. It stood still.

"Okay, okay, that's for starters. The perp is hiding in the room when she gets home or probably went into hiding because she came home unexpectedly. Got it?" Without waiting for approval he continued, "That mirror over her dressing table doesn't give her any angle on that wardrobe. He could make a move and be on her like white on rice before she knew what happened. Bingo!" Excitement was in Goldfarb's voice.

"Now, what was he doing before she got up there. What was worth stealing? The jewelry was right in front of him. No TV in the room. What was his purpose? Was it just rape that went vicious?" As the questions reverberated in his brain he started to rise, but again felt the chair prodding the back of his legs.

"I've missed something, haven't I?" He smiled, patting the arms of the chair.

This time it took less than half an hour to find this particular needle in the haystack.

"The roll-top. Something in the roll-top."

It was locked from his view, and he tried to remember the police report. But that was a dead end since nothing was reported stolen, and though it was considered a desk, it contained no real drawers, no storage compartments except for its one hidden surface, so no papers, no documents. But then why have a hideaway top like a roll-top if there's nothing inside? Goldfarb stared at the desk once more. And then it dawned on him.

"Sonofabitch! A computer. A laptop probably for that small area. I can see the cord coming down the back and that square power pack near the wall must be a surge protector. That's what the guy was after. Something on that laptop." A small "yee-haw", western style, escaped from Goldfarb's mouth as he rose up and the chair politely moved back. The lamp was also back in its original

# ONE LAST CASE

place, no longer blocking his path. Even the room felt warmer, but that was probably his imagination.

"Hey, I don't know who you are, but thank you. Thank you." Goldfarb made a slight bow in the direction of the mirror. He couldn't help notice that the reflection didn't bend when he did and stayed in its cheshire-like pose, but the smile that appeared matched his own, from ear to ear.

The French door opened, not easily, for it was unoiled and out of practice, but open it did. He looked back over his shoulder and let another warm smile bathe the room before he left. The main door opened with ease, and as he prepared to step out into the dawning day, a crash was heard from the interior room. He raced back in and stopped short at the inner doors as he saw the plaque from the door lying at his feet shattered in two. He looked back at the beckoning front doors and saw that the plaque was gone. He picked it up, examining it as he did, and a laugh—loud and clear—bellowed from his lungs.

"Had to spoil my fun, didn't you? Didn't think I could figure it out without your help? Ha, ha, ha. Fantastic, just fantastic. If you're trying to teach me, this is a bit heavy-handed, don't you think?" The big smile beamed all the way into the cold recesses of the interior room. Goldfarb edged closer, not to enter, just to observe. And observe he did.

There on the mantel, a Persian slipper dangled precipitously on its edge. A meerschaum pipe, smoke curling from its oversized bowl, was also in view. The mirror no longer cast a reflection, but just one word formed from the grime: Elementary.

"Great work, Detective Goldfarb, fine job." It was Captain Scott addressing Goldfarb in front of District Attorney Callendar.

"This Clark Mathews' fingerprints" he continued, "were found on the wardrobe as you suspected, but more than that, the fact that he was duping Masters' firm, causing cost overruns on every project the man did, was a fantastic find. How did you tumble in to that? Even Masters himself was unaware, since he had no real knowledge of American methods. That firm, Whitegate and Carruthers, did make a mistake picking him, but evidently he was also ripe for the picking, heh?"

# ONE LAST CASE

Everyone laughed in that political way of laughing when a superior is in the room.

"And the keys," Collander enjoined. "Remarkable. Masters designed his own home, as an example, they said, for clients, then, this rascal is the builder. Naturally he had keys."

"Yes, he had the keys," the Captain said. " But he also made the mistake of allowing Stephan Masters a copy of his spreadsheets. That's what he needed to get that night, or to make changes to them. I really don't understand all that financial mumbo-jumbo. But it was important enough to kill for, evidently."

"Well," the district attorney responded, "he says he panicked, and I'm sure he'll have a complex defense, but by God, we've got him. An incredible job, Detective. You've saved my bacon, I can tell you that. By the way, that insurance policy on the wife? Well, it turns out she came from quite a wealthy family, and it was they who made that little purchase. It did make it look bad for Masters though, didn't it? Ha ha!"

Detective Myron Goldfarb was in a brand new office. New desk, new chair, new view. He even had a plaque on his wall, though it was broken.

Charleton House<br>
est. 1878<br>
Architect: Archibald Hollinger<br>
/\/\/\/\/\/\/\/\/\/\/\/\/\/\/\/\/\/\/\/\/\/\/\/\/\<br>
Builder: Montgomery Tharp<br>
British Commemorative Society

# A Final Word

As a publishing venture, this book was created to serve two masters: one, my urge to create; and two, my desire to make a contribution to non-profit, local (Washington, D.C.) community providers who, especially in these times, need every bit of help they can get. To this end, my company, Allen Wayne Limited has produced a website called, "Washington Needs You"*: a place where individuals can become acquainted with the organizations who are trying to better the lives of the less fortunate, and, where they may also sign up as volunteers.

As you are also aware, if you purchased this book from our website or one of our authorized resellers, my company has donated the proceeds (40%) to the charity you selected when you made your purchase. I thank you, and these organizations thank you.

Now, for you dedicated Sherlock Holmes fans, take heart! The Chinese box that has wended its way into my home** and heart just happens to contain eight more short stories or adventures. They will be forthcoming this fall in the Chinese Box Mysteries, Volume II—"The Missing 8." I sincerely hope you will be pleased.

                Dan Kilcup
                Still on that island off the coast of
                North Carolina

---

*Website address—http://www.allenwayne.com/washcares/
**See the "Mystery of the Chinese Box"—Chinese Box Mysteries, Vol. 1